T0349160

MAGELIGHT

BAEN BOOKS by KACEY EZELL

Magelight

THE ROMANOV REIGN
(WITH TOM KRATMAN AND JUSTIN WATSON)

The Romanov Rescue: Turning Point, 1918
1919: The Romanov Rising

NOIR ANTHOLOGIES
(EDITED WITH LARRY CORREIA)

Noir Fatale
No Game for Knights
Down These Mean Streets

MAGELIGHT

KACEY EZELL

A Baen Books Original

Baen Publishing Enterprises
P.O. Box 1403
Riverdale, NY 10471
www.baen.com

ISBN: 978-1-6680-7261-5

Cover art by Sam R. Kennedy
Map by Rhys Davies

First printing, May 2025

Distributed by Simon & Schuster
1230 Avenue of the Americas
New York, NY 10020

Library of Congress Control Number: 2024059702

Printed in the United States of America

10   9   8   7   6   5   4   3   2   1

For everyone who's ever been told
"you are not enough"...
They lied.

And in memory of Howard Andrew Jones;
inspiration, mentor, and friend.
May we meet again when this adventure is done.

Acknowledgements

The author would like to express her deepest gratitude
to the following individuals for one thing or another.
(You miscreants know what you've done!)
Marisa Wolf, Melissa Olthoff, H.Y. Gregor, Shady,
Nick Steverson, LeEllen McCartney, Leah Brandtner,
Joy Freeman, Toni Weisskopf, Sam Kennedy, Rhys Davies,
Sarra Cannon, Sharon Shinn, Larry Correia, and Jason Cordova.

And, as always, love and thanks to EZ, Corie, Ace, and Atlas.
Without you, there is no me.

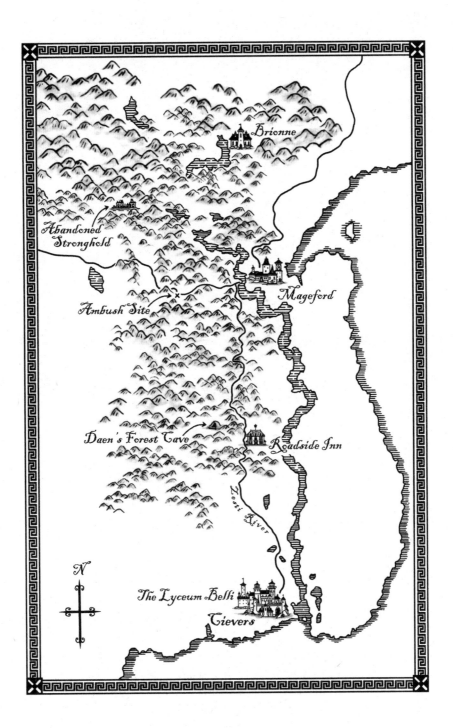

Brionne

Abandoned
Stronghold

Ambush Site

Mageford

Daen's Forest Cave

Roadside Inn

Zesti River

N

The Lyceum Belli

Tievers

CHAPTER ONE

FIRE STREAMED TOWARD AELYS OF BRIONNE'S FACE, CRISPING THE ends of her hair.

"Shield!"

In her mind, she envisioned a powerful, impenetrable barrier in front of her. The Sanvar's flames impacted the wall of air, flowed around, and created an uncomfortably warm sphere with her at the center of it. It shouldn't, strictly speaking, have been necessary for her to articulate the thought, but as she didn't say the word loudly, Sanvar Gilbain probably wouldn't hear it and dock her points. He could never hear her questions in class, after all, and her hastily erected energetic shield *did* work.

Breathe, she reminded herself as sweat beaded on her forehead. Her hands shook, so she curled them into fists and pulled harder on her pathetically thin flow of energy. Slowly, inexorably, the sphere of fire tightened around her. Dark spots swam before her eyes. She swallowed hard and pulled on her energy once more as the room began to tilt and spin.

Aelys's legs buckled, collapsing beneath her weight and she hit the floor hard on her hands and knees. The encircling flames winked out of existence. She sucked in a breath of cooler air and blinked rapidly, trying to dispel the darkness that crowded in around the edge of her vision.

"I know you typically spend your time on hands and knees scrubbing floors throughout this Lyceum, Student Aelys," Sanvar

1

Gilbain said in the cultured, smooth voice Aelys had always found beautiful—despite the cruelty his words so often carried. "But perhaps you would like to show *some* dignity? This is your final graduation exam, after all. Get up."

"Yes, Sanvar," Aelys said, hating the tremor she couldn't keep out of her voice. She forced her leaden arms and legs to obey, and slowly pushed herself up to regain her feet. With a deep breath, she clasped her hands in front of her waist and dipped her head to signal that she was ready once more.

"Oh, isn't that cute," Sanvar Gilbain said with a chuckle. "No, little Brionne. We've seen enough. I doubt you have the power to survive another attack. You are dismissed. Run along back to your chamber, or to the training yard to gawk at the Ageon candidates, or wherever it is that you go."

"Yes, Sanvar," Aelys said. Her head pounded, and nausea rose up inside her throat, so she was grateful to be dismissed, even in such a backhanded, insulting manner.

She turned on shaking legs and walked to the exit at the back of the large classroom, doing her best to ignore the whispers that followed in her wake. Final exams were always performed in front of an audience of more junior students. Aelys had seen several herself... and listened to the commentary that resulted.

"She'll be back next term. Didn't you hear how the Sanvar spoke to her? He wouldn't speak so to a mage ready to graduate."

"Well, just look at her! She's sweating worse than a first-year Ageon candidate learning advanced sword forms."

"Poor thing, everyone says she's nearly powerless. It seems cruel to let her continue here, but I suppose the Brionne heiress must be trained—"

Aelys hit the heavy oaken door with both hands and forced her shaking arms and legs to push through before she heard anything else.

I don't know which is worse, she thought as the door swung mercifully shut behind her, leaving her in the cool silence of the stone corridor. *The scathing disdain or the ostentatious pity. Mother of Magic, please let my scores be good enough to graduate. I don't know how I'll face them if I must remain here for another year!*

"Student Aelys, is there a reason you're loitering outside the examination room?"

Aelys jumped, sucking in a quick breath of surprise. She lifted her gaze to meet that of her herbalism teacher before ducking her head in the appropriate show of respect.

"Apologies, Sanva Erisa. I just finished and I—"

"Needed to catch your breath?" The Sanva's words and tone sounded kind, but Aelys knew that Erisa had no patience with the lazy, or the weak, or those who gave less than their best effort, or...

"No, Sanva," Aelys said, attempting to marshal her resources and focus. "I-I mean yes, Sanva. I—"

"Well, which is it, child?" Sanva Erisa asked, irritation flashing into her eyes as her aristocratically arched eyebrows rose in impatient inquiry.

"I was just...deciding where to go now, Sanva. That was my last examination."

"I see. Well, whatever you decide, I can think of nothing less useful than standing here blocking the hallway. Aren't you enamored of that one Ageon candidate? Go cheer him on or something. They're doing their evaluation exercises in the training yard. But do get out of my way."

"Yes, Sanva," Aelys said, stepping quickly to the side to let Sanva Erisa by. With a roll of her eyes, the Sanva swept past and into Sanvar Gilbain's classroom.

Once more, Aelys let out a shaky breath.

Sanva Erisa is right, she told herself. *I should go see Halik and encourage him. He has been so patient while I've been caught up in my studies. How selfish of me not to consider that he is facing his graduation examinations too! Stupid Aelys, to abuse the love of such a man in that way!*

With these self-recriminations ringing in her ears, Aelys finally started moving. She told herself that what was done was done, and tried to put the question of her exam performance behind her as she made her way through the Lyceum's twisting corridors and myriad courtyards to the rear of the complex.

The Ageon training yard was a vast bailey surrounded by the outermost wall of the school. Aelys could see the multicolored energetic wards lining the battlements shimmer in the afternoon sunlight as she descended the narrow stone staircase to the first gallery above the training yard.

When it was first founded, the Lyceum Belli existed to train mages to serve alongside the imperial legions. That was the origin of the "Bellator" title used by Lyceum-trained mages. Bellator—or the feminine Bellatrix—literally meant "warrior" in Bellene, an ancient, magical language. In modern times, the Lyceum was, first and foremost, a place of learning and study, but like many ancient imperial institutions, its history hadn't always been peaceful. And to this day, the Lyceum maintained close ties with the Imperial Battlemage Corps, a fact upon which Aelys had pinned most of her hopes for the future.

"Well, look who it is: Aelys of Brionne!"

Aelys looked up from watching her steps—a habit learned from a painful and embarrassing tumble her first year—and caught sight of one of her fellow senior students.

"Tasri." Aelys kept her voice even despite the dread that soaked through her system. Like Aelys, Tasri was the daughter of a powerful noble family, the Courlyns. Unlike Aelys, Tasri appeared to have no problem drawing upon copious magical energies. From their first year together, Tasri had always excelled where Aelys had faltered. This, along with the fact that their families were often trade and political rivals, fostered a mutual antipathy that only grew as the years passed. The fact that Aelys's best friend and roommate, Myara, was one of the few who consistently outperformed Tasri only made matters worse. Aelys couldn't imagine a person she was less inclined to speak to than Tasri Courlyn.

Except maybe her own mother. But that had nothing to do with anything.

"I heard you flubbed your final exam and let Sanvar Gilbain burn your eyebrows off."

"You heard incorrectly," Aelys said coolly. "As you can plainly see, my eyebrows are quite intact. How did you fare?"

Tasri tossed her glossy waves of black hair back over her shoulder. "Sanvar Gilbain has never given me any problems," she said, smirking. "I find his attacks to be rather pedestrian. I look forward to learning to defend against more sophisticated measures once I am inducted into the Imperial Battlemage Corps."

"I'm certain you do." Aelys tamped down hard on the instinctive longing that whipped through her. During her first year, she'd gone through a period of trying to win Tasri over and make her into a friend. One night, she'd confessed to the other girl that her dearest wish was not to take her mother's seat as Head of Brionne House, but rather to follow in her famous aunt's footsteps and serve the empire in the Imperial Battlemage Corps. Tasri had laughed at her and called her a fool. For even at that tender age, it had been readily apparent that Aelys had nowhere near the same access to power as her Aunt Aerivinne, nor even Tasri herself.

But from that day forward, Tasri had used this knowledge to ruthlessly bully Aelys, and to persuade their other classmates to do the same. Only Myara stood strong against Tasri's badgering and remained Aelys's stalwart friend.

"I suppose you're looking for your paramour." Tasri's sneering tone insinuated that there was something wrong with having a relationship with an Ageon candidate, despite the fact that the Lyceum eagerly encouraged such liaisons as the basis for the bond between mage and Ageon.

"I am," Aelys said. "Have you seen him?"

"Oh, assuredly," Tasri said, her smile widening. "You've just missed him, I'm afraid. He was here, and looking around for you, but since you took so long with your examination, he ended up leaving with that little friend of yours. I'm sure you can catch them if you run along."

Aelys snorted softly. "Oh, that's lovely. Myara is such a good friend to us both. I will catch up with them later. Thank you, Tasri. You've been *so* helpful."

With that jab, Aelys turned her back on her rival and started back up the stairs. Behind her, she heard Tasri's annoyed huff that her barbs about Halik and Myara hadn't seemed to land.

That made Aelys smile, despite her ongoing anxiety about her exams.

Several hours later, Aelys took a deep breath and pushed her continuing fears away once more. *Worrying about the exams won't change the outcome. They're done. For good or ill, they're done. Your future is decided, one way or another. Best focus on what you can do now.*

With that self-admonishment foremost in her thoughts, Aelys turned to cast one more look over the bare stone walls and wooden shelves of her room. For the last ten years, this tiny, semicircular chamber had been her home. The narrow bed, now stripped of linens and with her warm quilt packed away, had soaked up gallons of her tears. The shelves had once held the books and scrolls she obsessively pored over, hoping to make up for her lack of power by gaining a deep understanding of magical lore. Every obstacle, every failure of her power and nerve, every disingenuous comment by her peers had sent her here, to the sanctuary of this tower room, where she could weep over the unfairness of being a Brionne heiress with barely enough power to call magelight.

"Aelys! Dear heart, are you in here?"

Aelys schooled her face into a smile and looked up as her best friend burst through the door to their shared chamber. Myara was always lovely, with her soulful brown eyes and wild cascade of auburn curls, but today a flush of excitement stained her cheeks and lit her up from the inside. She always looked so vivid compared to Aelys with her white-blonde hair and blue eyes.

Despite the nervous nausea writhing in her stomach, Aelys felt her smile deepen as Myara caught her up in a spontaneous, laughing hug.

"There you are!" Myara said as she kissed Aelys's cheek and let go. "I've been looking everywhere for you! They've posted the final examination scores, Aelys! You graduated! You're a Bellatrix!"

Aelys's knees buckled, and she sank down to sit upon the bare mattress that had been her bed. She clasped her hands tightly together and let her eyes unfocus as she tried to take in this information.

"I graduated?"

Myara laughed again. "Well, of course you did, silly! I told you not to worry! The Sanvari weren't going to let a daughter of Brionne fail!"

Aelys's eyes locked onto Myara's face. "You think they fixed the exams?" she asked, icy dread joining the roil of nerves in her stomach.

Myara blinked in confusion, before realization dawned, and her eyes went wide.

"Oh, Mother of Magic, no! That's not what I meant at all! Oh, my stupid mouth! No, darling, the practicals were just as demanding as always. I'm going to have nightmares about trying to shield against Sanvar Gilbain's attacks! And *you* withstood him longer than two-thirds of our class. Plus, your herbalism and antidote scores have always been top notch, and you *know* your presentation on the theory and history of magic was well received. Your extra tutoring and additional work are paying off, my love, that's all!"

Once more, Aelys found herself caught up in Myara's embrace, inhaling the light floral scent of her friend's soap.

"I never could have done it without you," Aelys whispered, as tears prickled the backs of her eyes. "Your love and support—and Halik's—those have been the only things that have kept me going some days."

"Oh, dear heart!" Myara's arms tightened around her once more, and then she sniffled. Aelys echoed the sound, and then both girls laughed as they separated and moved to their individual bunks.

"So, what will you do now that you're a graduated Bellatrix?" Myara asked. "Go home and finally tell your mother what a worthless human being she is and force her to cede the leadership of Brionne to you?"

Aelys let out a shaky laugh. "Well, perhaps during our first period of leave from the Battlemage Corps," she said. "Although, I can hardly take over leadership of the house if I'm serving the interests of the empire."

Myara turned from her bed where she'd been removing quilts and blankets prior to packing her own bags. "You...you mean you still intend to stand for selection?"

"I—well. Yes, I thought that if I graduated, I would. Of course I would! It's been my dream since I was a little girl to bond with an Ageon and serve the empire. I can't do that without wearing an Ageon's bracelet."

"I know, it's just...some of the things you've said lately, I thought maybe you'd changed your mind."

Aelys laughed again and bent to fasten the ties on the knapsack that held the last of her belongings. "Oh, that was just my insecurity talking, you know how I get! Besides, it's Halik's dream, too! How could he ever forgive me if I cost him his one chance to move past his illegitimate birth and show his worth to his mother's family and the whole world?"

"Halik...yes, I guess you're right," Myara said slowly. "He does have ambitions. But do you think you could protect him properly? I don't mean to be cruel, Aelys, but you've said yourself that you have *such* a hard time pulling any real quantity of power. And because of that, you lack serious practical experience. How are you going to control the kinds of energies that Battlemages wield? You know as well as I do that if your concentration slips even the *tiniest* bit, it can trigger enough backlash to kill you, *and* anyone connected to you...and you can barely summon magelight! Besides, what if he's wounded? How will you heal him? How are you going to add to his strength if you have no power to give?"

"I—" Aelys bit her lip, her hands going still. She pressed her lips together and blinked rapidly as more tears threatened to fill her eyes. "But I love him," she whispered. "And I know he loves me. Once we're bonded, I know I'll be able to get stronger—"

"Dear heart, not this again! Bellators pulling power through their Ageons is just a legend!"

"It's not! It's well documented in the histories—"

"Right. Ancient histories, from hundreds of years ago. And even then, only the most powerful mages could do it. Your aunt, Sanva Aerivinne, says there's no conclusive data on the topic, and she's the most powerful mage anyone's seen in generations!"

Aelys's face crumpled, and her shoulders hunched inward in the familiar posture of defeat and self-loathing. She lost the battle against her tears, and her vision blurred away under the flood.

"Oh, Mother of Magic," Myara said, her voice instantly contrite. Once again, Aelys felt her beautiful friend's arms come hard around her shoulders. "Aelys, my love, I'm so sorry. Forgive me, I didn't mean to hurt you! Today is a day for joy! You're a graduated Bellatrix! I'm so sorry."

"No," Aelys said, sniffling loudly once again. "*I'm* sorry. I shouldn't dissolve into tears at the littlest thing. What you've said are only facts, after all."

Myara let go and sat beside Aelys on the bed, keeping one hand rubbing gentle, soothing circles between Aelys's shoulder blades. "I wasn't trying to be cruel," Myara murmured softly.

"I know. It's just...I can't not *try*."

"Well," Myara said, standing slowly and turning back to her packing. "Things will work out as they're meant to work out. And today *is* a day for joy, so let's focus on that! I got word from my family. They're arriving in the morning, before the selection ceremony. They send their congratulations and hope that they'll get a chance to see you tomorrow."

"Oh, that's lovely!" Aelys said, sniffling loudly again and using the hem of her sleeve to wipe her eyes. "I *should* get a chance after the selections. My family isn't coming, of course, so I should have plenty of time tomorrow evening."

"They're not coming?" Myara's brows pinched together in a frown. "To your *graduation*? That seems low . . . even for your mother."

Aelys shrugged and ignored the sharp pang of loneliness with the ease of long practice. "Aunt Aerivinne sent me a message. Apparently, House Monterle is proving troublesome again. There have been attacks on some of our trade caravans. They're denying any involvement, of course, but they've been staunchly arrayed against House Brionne since I was a little girl."

"Since your father died," Myara filled in. "Wasn't he a son of Monterle?"

Aelys nodded. "Yes, my grandmother chose him for her heiress, my mother. But then he died, and his death caused a rift between our families . . . but you know all that already." She smiled at her friend, who shrugged and gave her a half smile back.

"I'm sorry," Myara said. "I can't help it. High house politics are so *fascinating*. It's like something you read about in the his-tories . . . which makes sense, I suppose, since that's exactly what it is."

"Well, the histories will all say the same thing we've always said. My father's death was a tragic accident, and the Monterle reaction only compounded the tragedy. But to this day, they maintain enmity with my house, for all the good it's done them. Their fortunes have never recovered from losing us as a trading partner. My mother has seen to that."

Myara snorted indelicately. "You mean your aunt has seen to it. We both know that Lady Lysaera of Brionne is too self-absorbed to act for the welfare of her house. So long as she's got the luxuries and the men she wants, why should she care about anything else?"

"Careful, Myara!" Aelys said, letting out a nervous giggle and glancing toward the chamber's heavy oak door. "You shouldn't say things like that out loud. Someone might hear you! My mother is still a powerful and prideful woman, and she wouldn't stand for being insulted."

"Eh, I'm nothing but a baby Bellatrix from a minor house, she'd never even notice me."

"No, but my aunt might, and she wouldn't stand for it either."

"Sanva Aerivinne is just as contemptuous of your mother as I am, but you're probably right. I just hate Lady Lysaera for how she treats you. You deserve so much better. Is Sanva Aerivinne coming? I wish she had been your mother."

So do I, Aelys thought. Rather than voicing it out loud, however, she focused on Myara's question.

"No, she sent her regrets." Aelys shrugged, though she could feel her smile going sad. "She's at the imperial court and can't get away. Delicate negotiations, she said. She would be here if she could."

"Oh, too bad. I know you've always been close to her... and to Corsin, you lucky girl." Myara winked at her and grinned conspiratorially. "I swear, I'd give quite a lot to have that man in my bed for just a single night!"

"*Myara!*" Aelys gasped, her face flushing red. "He's my aunt's Ageon! You can't... besides, he would never. He's absolutely devoted to my aunt, and an Ageon bond is as binding as a marriage, which you well know!"

"Hmmph. I know that if I were your aunt, I'd take care to give my Ageon the attention and affection he's due! She wasn't even here last season when he won the master class in the Midsummer Tournament!"

"That's because she was advising the Empress Regent! She's on the regency council, Myara, she can't just up and leave because her Ageon is competing in a tournament!"

"Not even when that tournament is one of the most prestigious and long-standing traditions of the very Lyceum where your aunt is a leading instructor?"

"Myara—"

Myara tilted her head back and laughed. "I'm teasing you, Aelys! Goodness, you should see your face! Everyone knows what an honor it is to have one of our own Sanvari on the regency council, and we all look up to your aunt. Her healing prowess, her knowledge of magical theory... I'm just sorry her duties keep her away from your special day."

"It's all right," Aelys said. She took a deep breath and willed her shoulders to drop down and away from her ears. "She sent her love. I'll see her soon enough, I expect. Besides, you said your family is coming tomorrow, and I'm very excited to see them again. It seems an age since we were all together for Midwinter at your mother's estate!"

The graduation ceremony was everything Aelys had dreamed it would be. The entire Lyceum had gathered outdoors in the amphitheater, early enough that the spring dew still slicked the stone seats, and the morning fog hadn't quite burned all the way off. One by one, Bellator Toris had called each of the graduates down to the central stage, where he'd presented them with the dark blue sapphire in the Lyceum's distinctive steel setting.

"Bellatrix Aelys," he'd said when it was her turn. The assembled crowd had applauded.

Afterward, in the echoingly empty space of her room, Aelys relived the moment and let her fingers drift upward to trace the facets of the stone that now sat at the hollow of her throat.

"Graduation day," she whispered. "I made it! *We* made it!" She added this last as her gaze fell upon a folded note lying atop the knapsack she'd left next to her stripped bed.

The note was new, though. It bore her name, in Myara's graceful script. Myara herself had gone to wait for her family, but she must have placed the note after Aelys left in the morning.

How very thoughtful, and just like her to leave a quiet note of congratulations so I would know she hadn't forgotten me, Aelys thought. Gratitude and love soaked through Aelys as she picked up the note and brought it to her lips.

Because, of course, she could never have made it to graduation alone. She and Myara had spent countless night crying on each other's shoulders about the difficult tasks they had been set, about the seeming unfairness and caprice of the instructional staff, and about the strain of being away from everyone and everything they'd ever loved. Together, they'd watched as the Ageon candidates enrolled beside them fought through their own trials and lessons of combat and warfare. They'd talked for hours about the various candidates, and about the varying levels of prowess that they'd each shown... but especially about Halik, and the prowess he'd *always* shown.

Myara had been there when Halik first noticed Aelys. She'd been there as friendship and banter had bloomed into more. She'd been a sister to them both, an integral part of their relationship. Her calm, clear counsel had helped Aelys to get over her too-sensitive nature and see Halik's jocular teasing for the playful flirting it was. She'd encouraged Aelys to use her research skills to help Halik in the academic lessons he hated. In a very real way, Myara's loving advice had laid the foundation for the love that had grown between Aelys and Halik.

Now, all that remained was the binding ceremony. Once she and Halik were bound, they could officially be inducted into the Battlemage Corps: she as Bellatrix, he as her Ageon and protector. Her sword and shield. The warrior who would guard her life amidst the chaos and fog of battle.

Aelys's lips curved in a more genuine, heartfelt smile as she pictured Halik's dark, long-lashed eyes and his wide, full-lipped grin. She imagined him kneeling before her, looking up at her with a smile gone soft as he said her name and publicly declared his choice to dedicate his life to protecting hers. Never again would she have to wonder if she was good enough, powerful enough to deserve his love. Never again would she have to fear that his casual conversations with her friends and peers meant anything more sinister. He would be fully hers.

As she was his, body and heart. She laughed a little and shook her head as she turned to pull her new cloak off the hook behind her door. She wrapped herself up in its blue-embroidered black folds as she remembered the awestruck, awkward teenager she'd been when she'd first met Halik.

He was a few years older than she, and had been at the Lyceum as a candidate for longer as a result. Although, when they'd first met, he'd struggled to retain the information in some of his history and social-dynamics classes, he'd always cut quite a figure on the practice grounds. He'd been so dashing, with his well-developed musculature and deadly fighting skill. And he'd dazzled her with his biting wit and hearty laugh.

Without him and Myara, I would have been fully alone here, Aelys reflected. *None of the other Ageon candidates ever looked at me twice, and none of the mage students had time for me.*

Speaking of Myara . . . Aelys jumped a little as she realized she still held her friend's note, unread, in her hand. *Trust me to get distracted dreaming about Halik! Stupid girl, best focus on today of all days!*

She turned the note over and broke the wax seal.

A chime sounded overhead, and Aelys jumped at the reminder

of the time. She let out a small "eep" and tucked the note into her pocket. *I'll read it after, I'm sure she's just telling me how proud she is of me. I should send her something as well,* she thought as her fingers flew over the ornate, stylized cloak fastenings that bore the insignia of a graduated Bellatrix. Aelys glanced over her shoulder one last time at her old room before opening the heavy oaken door.

Another chime.

With anticipation and joy bubbling in her veins, Aelys pulled her hood up to shield her face and stepped out into the hallway toward the rest of her life.

The booming of the defenders' counter siege engines reverberated in Romik's chest, bringing deep memories roaring up behind his eyes.

Blinding sunlight streaming in through the grate above, casting burning bars on the sand-covered lift. The stench of fear, sweat, and urine. The creaking rattle as the lift began to rise and the grate retracted. The light growing brighter and brighter until it engulfed everything. The roaring of thousands of voices howling for blood.

"Blood on the sand," Romik whispered, blinking away the memory and focusing on the here and now. "His or yours. You decide."

"What's that, Lieutenant?"

Romik looked over at his sergeant and shook his head, careful to keep below the level of the berm currently shielding them from the defenders' arrows.

"Nothing, Sergeant," he said. "Just an old saying."

"From the arena?"

Romik's eyes snapped back to the sergeant's face. But he couldn't see any sign of scorn or disdain there. Just curiosity and something like . . . respect?

He shook his head again. "Never mind. Pass the word. As soon as the sun is halfway below the horizon, the sappers will blow a breach in the wall. When they do, we go. Just as we briefed."

"The men are ready, Lieutenant. They'll follow you into hell itself."

"They're about to." Romik listened for the telltale rattling of the arrows to slacken and turned to squint at the setting sun behind him. They'd have the advantage of the sun at their backs, which would hopefully blind some of those bastard archers lining the walls of the outpost ahead. Between that and the explosion that the company's sappers had rigged, he hoped it would be enough that at least a *few* of his men would make it out alive.

Although I'm sure the commander would prefer if I didn't, Romik thought dryly as he peeked up over the berm again, judging the slope he was about to have to charge. He pushed it aside in favor of another, older voice that lived forever in his memory: *There's always going to be blood on the sand, boy. Will it be his, or will it be yours? You decide.*

Romik glanced over his shoulder at the sunset again, and the world detonated.

The concussive shockwave rolled over him, bringing heat and sound like a hammer. It stole his breath. A high, insistent ringing roared to life in his ears, loud enough that he couldn't hear the pattering of the rock and wood bits that pelted his sheltering arms and back as he buried his face in the berm. He sucked in a deep breath, waited until the stinging rain of debris slackened, and then pushed himself up to his feet with his own roar:

"On your feet, Raiders! CHARGE!"

He gripped the haft of his long-bladed spear and lurched forward and up the slope. His foot caught on the sharp corner of a skull-sized rock that had been flung to the top of his sheltering berm. Beside him, the sergeant kept up a steady stream of bellowed encouragement that just barely managed to penetrate the ringing throbbing through his skull. All around and behind him, Romik's men leapt to their feet, gripping their own knives and spears. They followed his awkward, shambling run into the smoke and debris that had once been a fortified wall.

A skinny figure loomed up ahead of him in the smoke. Romik veered to the side and lunged, driving his spear into the figure's center mass. The figure stumbled toward him, and Romik felt the blade catch on something hard as he pulled to withdraw it. Another figure appeared through the smoke, bellowing as he swung a spear. Romik ducked, and his sergeant drove the wide, flat blade of his spear into the second man's face.

Romik grunted and twisted his wrist, trying to disengage the writhing body of the wounded man from his spear blade. He was only partially successful, but the man's own weight helped, and he slumped to the ground, yanking the spear's haft out of

Romik's hands as blood welled from his gaping mouth. A sharp *snap* echoed through the cacophony of combat as Romik's spear haft hit exactly wrong on a protruding stone and broke in half.

Romik sucked in a deep breath, drew his short sword and his long dagger, and started forward again, following his still-charging men toward the smoking gap in the fort's wall. A few steps ahead of him, his sergeant ran beside two other spearmen, driving forward into the ragged line of defenders scrambling to cover the sudden breach. The ringing in Romik's ears eased enough to allow him to hear the defenders' frantic shouts and the sounds of metal clashing on metal. Screams rose through the smoke, and the stench of blood and shit joined the taint of scorched wood and stone on the air.

As always, time moved weirdly in combat. Romik had no idea how long he spent fighting. The world narrowed down to his immediate vicinity: the desperate, emaciated enemies in front of him, the treacherous mud churned up by the boots of his own soldiers, the feeling of his sergeant's presence close against his left side, covering his flank. Romik followed his men as they pressed hard forward, fighting their way to the breach and through it, until Romik found himself scrambling up over a pile of tumbled stones and jumping down the other side. A defender crouched there, eyes wide and panicked. Romik leveled his sword at the man's exposed throat.

"Yield?" he asked. Or thought he asked. He tried, anyway, but rage suddenly darkened the defender's hollow face and he lunged, stabbing his spear up toward Romik's eyes. Romik parried with his sword, stepping up close and under the defender's guard to bury his knife in the back of the man's armpit. The defender yelped, and turned, but Romik struck again, withdrawing his knife and stabbing up quickly under the man's chin.

Hot, salty blood fountained into Romik's eyes and open mouth. He grimaced, spat, and swiped the back of his arm across his face as he turned, leaving the corpse to bleed out behind him as he continued this mad thrust into the heart of the enemy's fortified position.

The screaming around him had changed, he realized. The crazed bellows of his charging men had given way to the cries of the wounded and the shouted surrender of isolated men.

"Lieutenant."

Romik spun to the side, his blades at the ready, only to come face to face with his sergeant. The man's face was nearly as bloody as his own must be, but his lips stretched wide in a fierce, savage grin.

"We've done it, sir. We've taken the fort."

"We have? Already?"

"Aye, sir, your charge inspired the men and the enemy had even fewer defenders than we thought. Seems this was all they had left. Most of their company fled a few days ago, leaving a green sergeant in charge. He's over here, ready to offer his surrender."

"I'll take it," Romik said, scrubbing his face with the back of his hand again. "Have the men gather up the prisoners and get their parole. Send a runner back to camp with the news."

"Yes, sir," the sergeant said. "Follow me."

Romik nodded, and then looked around to try and get his bearings. The smoke had begun to clear, and he stood just inside the broken wing of the fort's outer wall. Behind him and to the right, the crumpled form of his last opponent slumped against the rubble pile they'd fought over. Romik blew out a breath, bent to wipe his blades clean on a corner of the dead man's tunic, and then sheathed them.

"Sir?"

"Coming, Sergeant."

The garrison's commander was, as the sergeant had described, very green. He couldn't have been more than a pair of decades old, and his sunken, glassy eyes, hollow cheeks, and shaking hands betrayed his complete unreadiness for the command that had fallen to him. He lurched to his feet as Romik approached.

"Sir, I s-surrender—" he stammered, holding out a dented, battered sheath that encased a plain-hilted short sword.

"I accept," Romik said, taking the sword from the youth's shaking hands. "We'll have a verbal parole from each of your men who can speak. Our company's healers will be along shortly to have a look at your wounded. It would be helpful if you could assist with organizing your men and having the most dire cases ready to be seen first."

"Y-yes, sir."

"First time being captured?" Romik asked, raising his eyebrows.

"First time for anything, sir."

Your company officers should be hanged for leaving you in this situation. Romik didn't voice the thought. Instead, he untied the thong on his waterskin and held it out to the young man.

"You're doing fine, kid," Romik said softly. "You did the right thing. Our company commander is a fair man. He'll contact your employer and get your ransom, and you'll all be back in your garrison by the next new moon."

"R-really, sir?"

Romik nodded. "So have courage and go take care of your men. They need your leadership now to reassure them that it's going to be all right."

The kid nodded, then lifted the waterskin to his lips and drank greedily.

"Sir, the commander has arrived."

Romik nodded acknowledgment to his sergeant and turned back to his young prisoner. He opened his mouth to try and say something else encouraging. At that moment, though, one of the nearby wounded defenders let out a loud, moaning sob. As Romik watched, his prisoner's eyes firmed, and his trembling stilled. He handed the waterskin back to Romik with a nod and turned to go to his man, his steps steady and assured.

Romik allowed himself a tiny smile and nodded in return. Then he turned to follow his sergeant back over the scattered rubble of the battlefield.

"Lieutenant!"

Romik squinted into the last rays of sun, and then brought his closed fist to the center of his breastplate as a tall, muscular figure stepped forward out of the sunset's silhouetting blaze.

"Sir," Romik said.

"Well done, Lieutenant!" His commander's voice, bluff and hearty, seemed out of place on the devastation of the battlefield. "We've been trying to break this siege for weeks! How many enemy officers have surrendered?"

"None, sir."

"What?"

"They ran. Left a green sergeant in charge. He's over there with the wounded. They don't have many—they don't have many men at all, but I promised him our healer would—"

"Yes, yes. Of course," the commander said. "Did they take the gold with them when they ran?"

"I don't know, sir. We've only just accepted the surrender—"

"Red Lady's tits, man! That was the whole point! Where is that sergeant?" The commander stepped forward, as if he'd brush Romik aside and charge up to the young prisoner. Before he could really even realize what he was doing, Romik stopped him with a hand on his chest.

"No, sir," he said. "He's busy seeing to his men."

"Lieutenant, you've got some kinda balls on you to—"

"You're not the first to say that." Romik didn't raise his voice, but he met the commander's eyes with his own battle-worn gaze and held them. Eventually, the commander looked away.

"I'll have one of my men make a search, but I think it's likely that the enemy's officers took whatever they could steal, sir. Look at the men they left behind. They're skin and bones. I don't think they had much left in the way of supplies."

"Can't eat gold," the commander said, his voice edged and ugly.

"Fair point, sir." Romik said. "I'll have my men make a search. Would you like to accompany them?"

"I'll be back at the camp, Lieutenant. Find my gold, and then you and I are going to have a chat." With a sneer, the commander turned his back without acknowledging Romik's fist-to-chest salute and stomped away.

"That was a risky move, sir," his sergeant said lowly, just behind his shoulder.

"Not really," Romik said. "He's a fair commander, but he's hated me for years. It's hard to make that worse. We joined the company together. He advanced. I didn't. That's why I'm leading charges against prepared positions and he's strolling around looking for gold to loot."

"You think he's trying to get you killed, sir?"

"I'm sure of it. That's why this is my last contract with the Raiders." Romik turned and met the sergeant's eyes. This was the first he'd mentioned to anyone of his plans. This was the first he'd admitted the plans to himself.

The sergeant, unflappable as ever, nodded. "Well, sir. The boys will miss you. You're a fine officer, and something of a good luck charm to most of 'em. 'Our Demon,' they call you."

Romik snorted. "That was a long time ago."

"Not so long they don't remember, sir. You were famous."

"And now I'm not. C'mon, Sergeant. Let's go search for the gold we're not going to find."

True to his predictions, over the next four hours, they found nothing in the storerooms and magazines of the fort but weaver-webs and dust. Even the rat droppings were partially fossilized, making Romik wonder how long the defenders had been without food. Long enough to put a dent in the rat population, at least.

Not that it was his problem anymore. He made sure his horse and gear were packed and ready to go, and then reported to the commander's tent to give his report and his resignation simultaneously. The commander, already drunk on the sweet wines he preferred and always carried on campaign, didn't seem to understand, but that, too, was not Romik's problem. The man continued to shout confused insults as Romik walked out of the tent, letting the flap fall behind him.

He pulled himself up into his saddle with a sigh and reached into his saddlebag for the folded note he'd received just before they left for this campaign. Once more, his eyes roamed over the text. Once more, he wondered what it meant. Once more, he squashed the treacherous demon of hope that threatened to rise in his chest.

Romik. I have a proposition for you. Something that could be good for all three of us. Meet me and Daen at the inn just north of Cievers on the forest road on the eve of the summer solstice. I'll make it worth your while. Vil.

Romik folded the note and stuffed it back into his saddlebag, and then kicked his horse into motion. The note could have been a fake, of course, but he didn't think so. It had showed up wrapped around the hilt of his short sword one morning. Anyone from the company could have put it there, but no one knew the names of his two boyhood best friends, nor that "I'll make it worth your while" was something of an in-joke between them. As boys, Vil had often used that phrase to talk Romik and their other friend, Daen, into all kinds of adventures...including the one that had ultimately saved their lives and led to their separation.

For just a moment, Romik let his mind drift back to that terrible night. He and Daen and Vil had slipped away in the afternoon to go exploring in the woods they way they often did. Vil had found a cave with a long-abandoned animal's nest, and they'd spent hours playing bandits and Foresters until the sun sank below the horizon. Finally, they slunk home, aware that they were late and therefore most likely in trouble...

They had no idea.

For while they'd been pretending, real bandits had attacked their small village, slaughtering their families and neighbors, setting their homes alight. They smelled the smoke as they drew near and hid while they watched the last of the attackers leave.

Finally, when the Mother had risen halfway to her zenith, the three of them had crept out of their hiding spot, tears wet on their twelve-year-old faces. They went first to their homes, and then to the village sanctuary...but all they found were corpses and destruction.

Romik remembered feeling numb as he comforted Daen and directed Vil to go see if any of the food stores had been left unspoilt. Vil came back with a few withered root vegetables and a single egg, and so that was what they took with them back to the cave for the night.

The next morning, they argued.

They were just boys, scared out of their minds. He could hardly blame his younger self, but as a result, they separated in anger.

For many long years—after being found by more bandits and sold to an arena trainer—Romik thought he'd never see his best friends again. Until he'd found the note wrapped around the hilt of his favorite short sword one morning during his last garrison contract—

The rising Daughter chose that moment to break through the canopy of trees ahead, and the path ahead of him shone silver in the growing night. Romik shook himself out of his memory, clicked his tongue at his horse and touched his heels to her flanks to urge more speed while the light was good.

I hope you do make it worth my while, old friend. I hope you can.

Daen looked up as someone opened his door without knocking and barged on in.

"The Lord Leader wants to talk to you."

Daen curved his lips in a smile that came nowhere near his green eyes. The intruder, a toad-faced, squat little man by the name of Shevik, came to an abrupt halt, folded his arms, and began tapping his toe impatiently. Daen stayed put and swiped his oil rag along the smooth grain of his longbow.

"Did the Lord Leader say what he wants?" Daen kept his tone

mild, mostly because he knew it would irritate Shevik and turn his face red. It was also the professional thing to do, but that really didn't matter. He knew it, and Shevik knew it. There was only one way this was going to go.

"On your feet, lowborn slug!" Shevik growled. "When the Lord Leader summons you, it's not your place to *question* him! Get up."

Daen let his smile fall away from his face. He stood slowly, unfolding his body to its full height: a head and a half taller than Shevik. He took a quick step forward, and the red-faced toady let out a little "eep" and scuttled backward against the doorframe.

Daen stopped and smiled again.

"I'd watch my mouth if I were you, *brother*," he said, emphasizing the honorific. Because, in one sense, it was true. Or should have been. Shevik's green-and-brown leather jerkin was a twin to Daen's own—except for being cut a bit more generously through the middle and less so on the shoulders. They'd both been through the years of training in tracking, hunting, foraging, and survival necessary to live completely alone on the land. They'd both taken oaths to serve the empire and protect its natural resources.

They *should* have been like brothers, but they weren't. And much as he hated to admit it, Daen knew that they never had been. Shevik, like all of the Foresters he'd met, had been born a younger son of a noble, or at least wealthy, family.

He, Daen, had been born a nobody. And they hated him for it.

Shevik opened his mouth as if he would say something else, but he must have thought better of it, because he settled for smirking at Daen instead. He waved a hand at the door, gesturing for Daen to precede him out.

"Bring it," Shevik said, when Daen made to set his longbow down in its rack near the door. "The Lord Leader said to bring it with you."

Daen's grip tightened on the bow. *So this is it then, is it? Well, so be it. I knew it was coming, I just...*

Shevik's eyes darted to Daen's white knuckles, and his smirk deepened. Daen took a deep breath, exhaled through his nose, and forced his hand to relax. Then he turned his back on Shevik and headed out into the narrow stone hallway that bisected the living quarters of the Outpost.

Apparently, Shevik had no intention of being left out of any fun, because he fell into step behind Daen, walking loudly enough that he should have been ashamed of himself. Of course, a heavy tread was but one of Shevik's failings as a Forester, and Daen had yet to see him bothered by any of them, so he had to conclude that Shevik didn't know the meaning of shame.

Which, honestly, made sense. Very few of Daen's so-called "brother" Foresters did.

Once upon a time, the Imperial Foresters had been an elite force of hunters, trackers, and gamesmen dedicated to preserving the empire's natural resources and protecting imperial citizens from the dangers that lurked deep in the untamed shadows. Daen had grown up listening to stories in which the gallant Forester saved the lost little girl from a nest of hungry goblants, or where the cunning Forester tracked the greedy bandit king to his hideout in the mountains and trapped him in a cave. All his life, all Daen had ever wanted was to be one of those brave, hardy men doing epic deeds under the spreading canopy of the Green Lady's trees.

As a boy, he'd dreamed, but everyone told him it was impossible.

Then, through soul-rending tragedy, the opportunity dropped in his lap. Bandits destroyed his village. He and his best friends argued and lost each other in the forest...but he'd been found by a true hero, the man who finished raising him, sponsored him into the Foresters.

And it turned out, being a Forester in this day and age was *nothing* like he'd dreamed.

Instead of a dedicated company of stalwart men, Daen found himself the lone commoner surrounded by spoilt, arrogant, noble children. Rather than husbanding the forest's resources, the senior Foresters exploited them, selling wood and game rights that weren't theirs to sell. Rather than hunting down the bandits that plagued imperial roads, the Foresters made deals with them, bribing them to keep their own interests safe while allowing them free rein to prey upon the less-fortunate merchants and travelers who couldn't pay the unsanctioned "tolls." Worst of all, the bandits would often kick some of their "toll" takings back to the local Foresters, making the organization nothing more than just another enclave of brigands.

Daen knew all these things. Had known them for a while.

Once upon a time, he'd tried to change things, but years of being dismissed, denied, and degraded had taken its toll and shattered any illusions he had left.

There's nothing left to save, he reminded himself as he started down the circular stairs at the end of the hallway. *Nothing but yourself, Daen. You knew this was coming. Now see it through and get out as fast as you can. Before one of your ex-"brothers" figures out which end of an arrow to point at you.*

The Lord Leader's office wasn't far from the bottom of the stairs. Daen approached the heavy oaken door and banged on it twice with his fist.

"Enter!"

He squared his shoulders and pushed the door open, stepping inside with his head held high.

"You wanted to see me, Lord Leader?"

"You needn't pretend you don't know why, boy." The Lord Leader sat behind a massive, intricately carved desk. His smooth white hair and beard did nothing to soften the simmering hatred and censure in his dark eyes.

That hatred and censure crawled up the inside of Daen's skin, bringing an angry flush to his cheeks. Once upon a time, the Lord Leader's approval had been the thing he craved most in the world.

He'd never gotten it.

You don't care, Daen. Remember that. You don't care about what this old predator and his corrupt cronies think or do. They're not worth the energy.

It almost helped.

"The raid two weeks ago?" Daen guessed. And truth be told, it *was* a guess. There were, honestly, half a dozen reasons that the Lord Leader could have called him in here. Some of them might even be legitimate.

"There wasn't supposed to *be* a raid," the Lord Leader growled. He lifted a closed fist and hammered it down onto his desk with a *thump*. "You were *ordered* to stand by and await reinforcements!"

"There were only four bandits in the camp, Lord Leader—"

"*Orders are orders, boy!* That camp was supposed to be a leadership exercise for one of our new brothers—"

"You mean, an easy takedown for some noble whelp who needs to polish his reputation to hide his latest scandal?"

"YOU WILL BE SILENT!" The Lord Leader shot to his feet, knocking into the desk hard enough to make the inkwell on the edge topple and fall. Daen suppressed a smile at the sound of shattering glass and imagined the blue-black stain spreading across the expensive carpet beneath their feet.

The Lord Leader appeared not to notice. He kicked the desk one more time and stalked around it, his face twisted in rage and hatred.

"You will not *speak* to me! You should never have been allowed into our ranks! If not for the pleading of my dear brother Bormer, you would have been left to the wolves and goblants like the filth that you are!"

Daen suppressed a snarl at the mention of his late foster father. Bormer had saved his life, sponsored him into the Foresters. He'd been a good man, and it rankled to have the Lord Leader claim brotherhood with him...even though it was, technically, true.

But still. Bormer would have been the first to tell him to cool his hot head and keep his mouth shut. So Daen pressed his lips together and said nothing.

The Lord Leader strode up to him, coming close enough that Daen couldn't look away from his vitriol-filled eyes.

"You are a disgrace," the Lord Leader said, dropping his volume to a low snarl. "You have never belonged here. Your low blood and insubordinate ways have befouled this organization for long enough. Believe me when I tell you, boy, that I am going to take *such* great pleasure in what I'm going to say next. You. Are. Cast. Out."

Daen had expected the words. He had not expected the piercing stab of pain at hearing them. Still, he had his pride. So, even though a thousand angry retorts hovered behind his lips, he said nothing. Instead, he gave a single nod and took one stiff, formal step backward before spinning on his heel.

"Wait," the Lord Leader said, his voice poisonously smooth. Daen froze.

"That is a Forester's longbow. You are no Forester. Leave it for a more worthy man."

Daen slowly turned back to face the Lord Leader. The man actually smiled at him, looking as satisfied as a mountain cat in a sun puddle. He held out one thick hand and flexed his fingers in a "give it to me" motion.

Daen hesitated for less than a heartbeat before moving. He lifted the bow, but he didn't extend it to the Lord Leader. Instead, he braced one end of it on the carpeted floor. In one smooth move, he bent it as if he were about to string it and brought his booted foot down on the center of the curve, just below the where his hand would normally go.

Crack!

The sound reverberated through the stone room, and the victorious smile on the Lord Leader's face vanished in shock. That bow had been Bormer's, and it was a masterwork. But Daen would rather the Green Lady's creatures tore him apart than let one of these corrupt Foresters ever touch it.

"Oh no," he said, meeting the Lord Leader's eyes and throwing the now-useless fragments of wood to the floor. "Looks like it's broken." Then Daen smiled and ducked as the Lord Leader swung his clenched fist at his head.

He quickly straightened and responded with two fists of his own to the older man's gut. When the Lord Leader doubled over, coughing, Daen grabbed the back of his head and spun him, slamming his face into the heavy oaken desk. By that time, Shevik had come rushing into the office, his short sword extended.

Daen had been expecting him. He sidestepped Shevik's rush and swept a foot out to trip his ex-brother into the Lord Leader as he stumbled back from the desk. Blood poured down the Lord Leader's face, and droplets flew in all directions as he shook his head.

Daen bent and picked up one of the bow fragments, and then bolted for the door. He took a half second to slam it closed behind him and then rammed the jagged remnant of Bormer's bow into the keyhole, jamming it shut. It wouldn't hold forever, but it should buy him a little time.

He took off down the hallway and careened through the doors at the far end, ending up in the Outpost's bustling inner courtyard. Just as he'd planned when he realized this day would come, he made his way to the stables. At this time of day, it should be relatively empty...

Thank you, Green Lady, he thought as the warm silence of sleepy horses and an empty stable wrapped around him. Within a few minutes, he'd saddled his favorite roan mare and led her out into the courtyard. From there, he mounted up and headed for the little side gate near the kitchen. He often used that gate when sent on the menial errands that he was usually assigned.

Less than an hour later, the setting sun glinted through the trees at him, and Daen smiled. He'd done it. He'd made it out. It was a day's ride to the small cave where he'd stashed his second-best bow and his pack with supplies...and the letter.

Daen. I'm surprised you haven't burnt the Outpost to the ground yet, if I'm honest. Ready to leave that creche of mewling children behind and have some real fun? You know the inn on the forest road just north of Cievers? Meet me and Romik there the night before the solstice. We'll talk plans. I'll make it worth your while. Vil.

Daen let his smile grow as he nudged his horse off the road to follow a game trail that wound deeper beneath the spreading canopy of trees. He had no question that the letter he'd memorized was genuine. For one thing, he really *had* been contemplating burning down the Outpost, or something equally drastic, when he'd found the paper stuffed inside his quiver one morning about a month ago. Of all the people in this world, Vil was one of two who knew him well enough to see that. Romik was the other, but the note's style and tone were all Vil. And then there was the promise to "make it worth his while." Vil had always used that phrase when they were kids. And once again, he, Romik, and Vil were the only ones who knew that.

So instead of doing something drastic, Daen had gone against his usual method of operation and began to work with subtlety. He visited the old cache spot that Bormer had shown him years ago and cleaned it out. He started stashing trail food in there, a little at a time. He bought sturdy traveling clothes that bore no resemblance to Forester uniforms and regalia, and locked them in a heavy trunk, along with weapons and a small pouch of gold. Then he took the whole thing to the cave and hid it in a corner of the wall under and behind some loose rocks and dirt.

Then he waited, and caused as much trouble as he could.

He'd thought about just leaving, but if he did, he'd have been labeled a deserter, hunted down, and executed. Getting thrown out of the Foresters took longer than he was expecting, but it was worth it to not have his face plastered on wanted posters all over the empire. He'd started to worry that his plan wasn't going to work, but then he'd been ordered not to attack that bandit camp, and he'd seized the opportunity.

And the Green Lady smiled, he thought as he ducked under a low-hanging branch. *Thank You, Lady, for loving fools and foresters. True foresters, not those... what did Vil call them? "Mewling children." I wish I had burnt down the Outpost. Maybe that's what they need. Kill them all and start again... ah. But there I go being a hothead again. I can't wait to see what Vil has in mind...*

Up ahead, the rising moon shone through the trees, lighting his way like a benediction. Daen leaned forward and patted the roan mare's shoulder. Excitement and joy tangled through him, bubbling out through his lips as laughter. Years of simmering anger and disillusionment fell away, and excitement ran like lightning under his skin as he nudged the mare with his heels, urging her to move faster toward this new adventure.

Vil squinted through the noonday sun as the wagon in which he rode topped a rise in the path and the tavern he'd chosen came into view.

It wasn't much to look at, truth be told, and the harsh glare of the daylight didn't do it any favors. It was a long, low-slung building with a sagging roof and cluttered yard, set a few lengths back from the road. Behind it, up the slope of a hill, another long building crouched under the tree line. Judging by the pattern of wheel tracks, that second building functioned as the inn's stable. Or had functioned at one time, anyway. It stood in serious need of some repair.

Not that any of that was Vil's problem. He wasn't buying the inn; he was merely using it as a meeting place. A quiet, discreet meeting place outside of the city of Cievers and those who held influence there.

He'd been waiting a long time to have this meeting. Years, in fact. Ever since he'd first caught a glimpse of his boyhood friend Daen wearing Forester colors and sullenly watching an archery tournament on the outskirts of Cievers. Ever since he'd first heard whispers about an arena champion they called the Demon.

"This your stop, hey?" The wagon driver's gruff voice held the burr of the northern mountain regions, but his steady hand showed that he knew this more southerly stretch of the imperial highway very well.

"Yes," Vil answered. The driver grunted in return. He was a man of few words; a trait Vil heartily approved. On this particular trip, Vil actually had nothing to hide, but the habits of a lifetime died hard... for good reason.

When one is used to being the premier second-story man in

Cievers, one tends to like one's privacy. Especially because a lack thereof can be deadly.

The ghost of a smile played about Vil's lips as his mind turned these ridiculous thoughts over in his brain. The truth was those days were behind him. Too many bridges burned.

Don't look back, Vil reminded himself, fixing his gaze on the dilapidated building as the wagon driver drew the vehicle smoothly to a stop. He hopped down from the seat, grabbed his knapsack from the bed of the wagon, and tossed the driver a silver coin. The driver snatched the coin out of the air, making Vil wonder if he'd ever been trained as a pickpocket.

Not my place to ask. Not anymore.

The driver picked up his reins, shaking them out as Vil slipped his arms into the straps of the knapsack. Vil raised a hand, and the driver grunted something that could have been either thanks or goodbye...and was probably both. With a sharp *snap*, he urged the team back into motion, wheels creaking on the rutted, uneven road.

Vil watched him go, and then turned his attention back to the inn. He checked to be sure his hood was up and shading his face, and then strode quickly up the unkempt grass slope toward the front door.

At this time of day, he wasn't surprised when the inn's common room proved mostly empty. A sleepy-eyed, buxom woman idly dragged a semiclean cloth across a table in the far corner. The bright morning sunlight filtered through cracked and sagging shutters and didn't do much to dispel the gloom inside. A fire smoldered rather sullenly in the hearth.

"Good day," Vil said as he crossed the floor toward the woman. She blinked, then straightened up, tugging at her strained bodice and smoothing her honey-colored hair.

"Help you, sir?"

"I hope so. I am meeting some friends here today, but I don't know what time they'll arrive. I'll take this back corner table, and food and drink as it's ready." He palmed another silver coin and laid it down on the table with a click. The tavern maid's eyes widened slightly.

"That's for the use of the table," Vil said. He laid another coin next to it. "And that's for you, for ensuring our needs are met and we're otherwise given privacy to talk."

"Yes, sir," the woman breathed, her eyes wide awake now and fixated on the coins. She glanced up at him with an edge of anxiety. Vil gave her a tiny smile and a nod, and she grabbed the coins nearly as quickly as the wagon driver had done.

"Bring a pint of ale and some bread when you can," Vil said then, hoping she would hear the dismissal in his tone. He slipped his arms out of the straps of his knapsack and concealed it on the floor between the table and the wall. Then he folded his thin frame down to sit in the chair that backed up against the corner and afforded him the best view of the common room—and all its entrances and exits.

Nerves and anticipation ran along the underside of Aelys's skin and tangled together in pulsating knots deep in her stomach. She blinked, breathing deeply through her nose as she willed her body to relax.

Chin high, expression pleasant, Aelys! This is a happy occasion . . . a public *occasion! Don't dishonor House Brionne by letting anyone see your weakness today.*

She stole a quick glance around at the other six graduates. Ten years ago, they'd entered the Lyceum together as children. Tomorrow, they would depart as Bellators. Tonight, they stood in a half circle on the speaker's dais at the north end of the Lyceum's grand hall, looking out on the junior students and Sanvari who lined the central aisle. The students all wore the undyed wool cloak traditional for those enrolled at the Lyceum. It made them easier to see than the Sanvari in their Bellator's black. Candlelight flickered in sconces along the walls, providing the only light in the cavernous space. It made the hall look like it stretched for leagues, but Aelys knew that was an illusion. She'd scrubbed every finger width of the hall's stone floors on her knees. Several times.

Soft strains of music floated down from the gallery above and behind her, a dreamy, mystical melody that signaled the beginning of the ceremony. Aelys obediently bowed her head, letting the hood of her brand-new black cloak fall forward to cast her face in shadow. A soft scuff echoed down the length of the hall, signaling the approach of the candidates.

They've been here for ten years, too. Some of them longer, Aelys reflected, trying to distract herself from the renewed burst of nerves in her gut. *What must it be like, waiting to be called, to feel that pull toward a mage that forms the basis for an Ageon bond?*

"Candidates. To your Bellators."

Aelys recognized Agea Giara's voice. She'd been one of the weapons masters at the Lyceum for the last seven years. Though she was old enough to have grandchildren, she still carried herself with a warrior's grace and power...and her reputation garnered respect from all who knew her. At her command, the rhythmic thump of booted feet on stone heralded the approach of some number of candidates.

Officially, no one but the senior Ageon—or Agea, in Giara's case—was supposed to know exactly how many of the graduating Ageon candidates there were. Like the mage students, Ageon candidates had to pass a grueling battery of examinations before they could graduate. But unlike the mage students, Ageons theoretically had one more requirement to fulfill: they had to feel a pull toward a graduating mage.

The bond between Ageon and Bellator is a deep and nuanced one, Aelys recited silently as she recalled one of the texts she'd read often enough to have parts of it memorized. *It is both incredibly simple and deeply profound, and cannot be fully described, as each individual pairing experiences it in slightly different ways. Suffice it to say that it begins with the Ageon feeling drawn to a graduating mage in one way or another. Many conflate that drawing with romantic or sexual attraction, but there is more to it than that. It is a mystical, almost compulsive pull toward the mage in question. In every case, Ageons universally report that when the time came to choose, there was never a question or hesitation in their mind as to* whom *they would choose. Many reported it as being "obvious."*

Aelys risked a glance upward at the short column of warriors marching down the length of the hall toward the half circle of waiting mages.

Practically speaking, the bond provides benefits to both parties in the relationship. Many Ageons report an increase in their strength, martial prowess, and physical constitution which they attribute to the relative power capacity of their mage. And, of course, there are the social advantages to the warrior that come with allying themselves with a scion of one of the noble houses.

For while many Ageons themselves come from noble stock, it is not a requirement, and any warrior of suitable prowess may apply as a candidate.

For the mage, the Ageon provides protection and companionship, as well as a cool head unmuddled by some of the more intoxicating effects of certain spells. No one will ever care for a mage as well as his or her bonded Ageon. This protective instinct appears to be a universal feature of the bond and has resulted in tragic mishaps in the past. For example, if a mage is killed and their Ageon survives, they typically do not survive for long.

This is the reason why a bond is always *the Ageon's choice. Anything else is monstrous and immoral in the extreme. The Ageon must always feel the draw and choose their mage.*

In the past, it *had* happened that a mage was left standing, unchosen by any of the graduating candidates. Officially, it carried no shame. The Lyceum and the empire both recognized that an effective Ageon bond required a pull on both sides. An unbonded mage couldn't serve in battle, but a Lyceum education lent a certain cachet when it came time for one to negotiate a noble marriage alliance... as Aelys's mother had often told her.

But that's not a problem, because Halik is here. In fact... is that...?

Excitement stabbed through Aelys's chest, sending her heart into a pounding race as she recognized the loose-hipped strut of the warrior approaching down the long, candlelit hall. His bootheels rang off the floor's pristine stones in half time with her hammering pulse. Her mouth went dry as her mind frantically tried to remember the words of the oath.

He will say he is called to be my sword and shield. He will say he answers and call me by my name and title. In return, I must say—

Halik came to a stop in front of the circle of mages, heels clicking together in perfect military precision. Per the protocol, he drew his sword and placed it, tip down, against the stone floor in front of him before lowering himself to one knee. Aelys risked a glance up, hoping to meet his gaze for just a moment. But as was proper, he showed no expression, none of the wry, sometimes spiky humor she loved. Instead, he kept his eyes locked, staring straight ahead.

"I am called to be your sword and shield—" His voice, deep

with just a hint of gravel, rolled through her, just as it had done time and again when they lay together in the small hours of the night. Something low and warm clenched deep in her body at the sound.

"—your defender against all harm. I am called, and I gladly answer."

Aelys lifted her head a fraction more, desperate to let him see the love and hope and gratitude shining in her eyes.

"Bellatrix Myara. I am yours."

Myara?

Though it was against protocol, Aelys turned her head enough to see her friend's bright smile for just an instant before she walked forward, her sleeve brushing Aelys's as she stepped past. Nausea roiled into being in Aelys's stomach, and a high, buzzing sound echoed in her ears as she watched her best—and only—friend for the last ten years place her hands atop the crossed hands of the only man Aelys had ever touched.

The only man who ever looked at me twice.

"Ageon Halik, I accept your protection and your call. I am yours."

The only man who ever noticed me. Pathetic, powerless me.

The great bells overhead rang out, three peals of joy in a new union. Halik's stoic expression finally broke open into a wide, joy-infused grin that twisted through Aelys's entire being, leaving acid-soaked wounds behind. He rose smoothly to his feet, moving with that warrior's liquid grace, and bent to press his lips to Myara's. Agea Giara placed the silver bonding bracelets around their wrists as their fingers intertwined. A glint of light showed that the bracelets had magically locked into place, never to be removed. Not even in death.

The rest of the ceremony passed in a blur. Aelys had no idea how long she stood there, rigid, shadowed in her hood as one by one, the Ageon candidates stepped forward and called out a name that wasn't hers. Her feet felt rooted to the stone as she watched her classmates step forward, faces shining with excitement as they accepted the warrior that had chosen them.

Until, finally, no other warrior appeared.

No one else walked down the long hallway.

No one called her name.

Go.

Aelys didn't know where the thought originated, but that didn't matter. Despite the protocol, despite the very public setting, she knew one thing to be true. She could not stay there another second. She had to *go*.

As the bells fell silent and one of the senior instructors stepped forward to address the assembled crowd, Aelys of Brionne turned her back on the entire Lyceum and fled into the safety of the shadows at the back of the hall.

One benefit of scrubbing this floor over and over again. At least I know where the servants' entrances and hidden exits are!

Aelys recognized the edge of hysteria to her thoughts as she ducked behind a large hanging tapestry and let herself through the narrow door waiting there. She took a deep breath and pulled her hood up higher on her head, shielding her face from any of the Lyceum's serving staff who might be using this warren of corridors to complete their duties.

What am I doing?

Aelys shoved that thought away and forced herself to move forward with steady, purposeful strides. She'd get back to her room, grab her knapsack, and then make her way down to the stables. There was a Brionne-owned horse there she could use. She'd ride out and go—somewhere. Home, probably.

Mother will be so smug, but I don't care. She's easy enough to distract with wine or her latest pretty man. I'm used to her. I just hope— She stifled a sob and turned the corner into a crossing hallway with stairs at the far end.

Aelys snuck a quick glance left and right, and then lifted her skirts and bolted toward the stairs. Her boots slipped on the slick stone of the floor, but she managed to catch herself on the smooth, wooden handrail. She hauled herself upright, unable to stop the next sob from coming, and flung herself headlong up the winding circular staircase.

My room. Let me just get to my room, where no one can see my shame . . .

It seemed an eternity before she hauled the wooden door open far enough to slip past, and then let it fall shut behind her with a soft *boom*. Another whimpering sob slipped past her lips. She took a step toward her bed, but her knees buckled, sending her crashing to the floor. Agony came pouring out of her, wracking her entire frame as her deep, wrenching cries echoed off the bare stone walls of the room. She curled into herself, hands like claws clutching at her knees, tearing at her new cloak as the rage and betrayal and grief and self-hatred tore at the fabric of her soul. Tremors ripped through her body as her dreams and hopes shattered into worthless crystal shards that threatened to shred her sanity.

Aelys didn't know how long she lay there sobbing. Long enough that her shoulder and hip felt raw and sore from the unyielding stone of the floor. Eventually, however, the sobs quieted, the shaking stilled, and she found herself with no more tears to cry.

Slowly—for every muscle felt as if she'd been run over by a full baggage wain—Aelys pushed herself up to a seated position. She took one slow, deep breath, and then another. She swiped her fingertips under her eyes, then sniffed and reached down to dig into the pocket of her new cloak for a handkerchief.

Her fingers crinkled against the folded parchment of the note she'd hastily pocketed earlier.

The note from Myara.

Aelys pulled it from her pocket, moving slowly, as if she were underwater. It was almost like she was watching someone else turn the note over in her pale fingers and unfold the nested pages. It was almost as if someone else's voice read the words of the note into the echoing silence of her mind.

Dearest Aelys,

Before anything else, I want you to know that I am so very proud of you. From our very first day together here at the Lyceum, you have always worked harder than anyone I know. Your dedication is truly an inspiration, and I am so fortunate to have had you as my friend. Without you spurring me on, I do not think I would have accomplished half so much as I have here, and for that I thank you.

What I am about to say will no doubt come as quite a shock, but I know you better than perhaps anyone else and you have always been the kindest and most generous of friends. How often have we said that we love each other as sisters? I know that the love and loyalty you bear me will lead you to rejoice in my joy, even if at first it hurts a little.

For you see, my dear friend, I am in love! The deepest, most passionate love you can imagine. I know this will come as a surprise to you, as I have said nothing up until now. I know you have worried for me, that I would not make a connection with any of our Ageon candidates, but rest assured, my dear friend, there is nothing to worry about on that score.

For I have fallen in love with Halik, and he has fallen in love with me. He is the Ageon who will be my sword and shield, my sworn protector as we go out into the world to serve the empire together, as we have always dreamed.

I know... I know you have feelings for him. And believe me, he cares very much for you. We have agonized over how and when to tell you. The last thing we wanted to do was to jeopardize your chances of graduating by distracting you prior to the final evaluations, and so we decided to wait until today. I know you may have thought that perhaps he might choose you, but darling, you know your power limitations better than anyone. And though you did so well to graduate here, I know that you must see that you would never be effective as a part of the Battlemage Corps. Halik saw this too, and neither of us want to see you get hurt.

So today, during the bonding ceremony, he will choose me, and I him. We wanted you to know first. And we want you to know that we both love you so much. We know this must be very difficult for you, but we also know that in time, you will come to understand the difficult choice we've both had to make.

Congratulations, my dear friend. You deserve the title you've earned. I pray to all the Divines that They may guide you toward a good marriage and a wonderful, fulfilling life of safety and comfort.

With all my love, I remain your dearest friend,
Myara

Aelys watched from a distance behind her own eyes as she let the note fall to the floor. A tiny, dispassionate corner of her mind congratulated her on the steadiness of her hand as she reached back into her pocket for the handkerchief and methodically wiped her eyes and nose with it. She refolded it neatly before laying it beside the discarded note.

Then she pushed herself up to her feet and refused to let the trembling start again as she reached for her packed knapsack.

With quick, staccato movements, she slung the bag over her shoulder and settled it under her cloak. Then, for the last time, she reached for the door to her room and let herself out.

Nothing remained in that tiny, cold sanctuary but her folded handkerchief, and the note warning her of an impending broken heart.

◆ CHAPTER TWO ◆

THE NOONDAY SUN WARMED ROMIK'S NECK AND BARE HEAD AS HE urged his horse up the slope of a hill. This close to Cievers, they were too far south and east to be in the foothills, but Romik could feel the gradual increase in grade as the road wound its way north.

His mount could feel it too, and she tossed her head in annoyance.

"Settle down now, Bay," Romik said, patting the side of the mare's neck. "It's not much farther. Look, you can see smoke coming from just beyond this rise. I bet that's our place."

He touched his heels to Bay's flanks, and she moved obediently into a trot. Sure enough, as they crested the rise, Romik could see the low-slung outline of a building on the next hill ahead. Just for fun, he urged Bay into a run, and let her have her head as she raced toward the sweet feed he would have bet a hundred Imperials she smelled in the tavern's barn.

Romik let her charge past the tavern with the thin ribbon of smoke rising from its chimney. She ran all the way up the slope toward the stable yard before he reined her to a stop. She stamped her feet as he dismounted and looked around.

"I don't see anyone, do you?" Romik asked the mare. She ignored him in favor of sniffing at the overgrown grass that ringed the stable yard. Romik snorted a soft laugh—whether at himself or at Bay, he didn't know—and clicked his tongue to lead her into a walk around the yard.

A few minutes later, once Bay had cooled down, Romik led her into the ramshackle barn. A swaybacked nag looked up from the feed bucket hung on his stall door. The stall next to his was empty, as were the tack hooks on the wall. Despite the rough appearance of the roof and the daylight Romik could see through some of the wall slats, the stalls appeared well-enough constructed, and the feed was full and fresh.

"This will do for an old wargirl like yourself, won't it, Bay?" he murmured softly as he led her into the stall. "Nothing wrong with taking care of you myself, I suppose. Let me get you brushed down and we'll get some feed and water for you. Then I'll head down to the tavern and... Well... I guess we'll see."

Bay snorted, but she stood docilely enough as Romik groomed and cared for her. Once she was settled in her stall with a full feed bucket and clean water, Romik dusted off his hands, adjusted his weapons belt, and walked to the barn's exit.

He glanced back at Bay, but the mare had her nose buried in the feed bucket and didn't seem to notice or care that he was leaving. Romik shook his head at his own sentimentality and stepped resolutely back out into the stable yard.

The tavern itself sat just down a wide slope from the barn. As he approached, Romik caught the scent of roasting meat and frying onions, and his stomach gurgled in response. He squared his shoulders and pushed the heavy wooden door open with one hand, then stepped in out of the noonday sun.

The food scents were stronger inside and mingled pleasantly with the aroma of barley and hops. Out of habit and self-preservation, Romik let his eyes sweep the place before he entered further. Patrons sat at several of the tables, eating and drinking and carrying on enough conversations to produce a low, burring murmur of sound. Mostly working men, by the look of their clothing. Probably locals—

Romik's gaze collided with a figure in the far corner wearing a dark cloak and a hood that shadowed his face. The figure lifted his head, and a shaft of light from a nearby window fell upon his mouth and chin.

The figure smiled, and Romik felt like he'd taken a spear to the gut.

"Vil," he whispered. Before he realized that he meant to move, Romik had crossed the tavern floor and stood staring down at his childhood friend.

Slowly, Vil raised a pale hand and pushed back his hood, revealing the white-blond hair and shadowy dark blue eyes Romik remembered so well.

"Hello, Romik," Vil said, the corners of his mouth deepening in the tiniest of smiles. He offered a hand for Romik to clasp.

"Red Lady's ruin... *Vil!*" Romik grabbed Vil's long fingers and hauled him up to his feet. His other arm came hard around the slighter man's shoulders in a tight embrace as Romik squeezed his eyes shut against the emotions that threatened to engulf him.

"It's been the better part of twenty years," Romik ground out, his throat thick with the tears he refused to shed. "I never thought I'd see you again."

"Likewise," Vil said, pounding Romik on the back. "By the Shadow, it's good to lay eyes on you up close."

Romik let go of Vil and cleared his throat, trying to ease the tightness there. "Up close?"

"Good day, sir. Some food or ale for ye, then?"

Romik blinked rapidly to dispel the wetness threatening to flood his eyes and turned to look at the woman who'd spoken. Then he blinked one more time and took a better look in appreciation.

She had honey-colored hair, braided back from her face and coiled against her skull, but heavy enough that Romik knew it would fall to her waist when unbound. She was buxom, with a delicious curve at belly, hip, and ass. She angled her body away from Vil and returned Romik's look boldly, her tongue flicking out to wet her bottom lip before she smiled in unmistakable invitation.

"Romik, this is Mirandy," Vil said, his tone dry with what Romik recognized as amusement. "Mirandy has been taking care of me while I've been waiting."

"Fancy having me take care of you, too, sir?" Mirandy asked, adding a saucy wink.

Sudden joy bubbled up within Romik, curling his lips and escaping in a deep, appreciative chuckle. "That I would, Mirandy," he said.

"We've business just now," Vil put in. "And we're waiting on our other friend. So, we'll be here quite a while, and probably spend the night."

"I could bring you some ale and food," Mirandy offered, her eyes still boldly locked on Romik's.

Romik nodded. "Perfect," he said. Mirandy returned the nod, her smile growing. Then she spun slowly and sauntered away. Romik didn't miss the swing in her hips when she walked. The look she threw back over her shoulder said she noticed him noticing.

Vil chuckled darkly. "Well, that didn't take long."

Romik returned his attention back to his boyhood friend. "She's nice," he said, with half a smile. Vil snorted and lowered himself into a chair, waving a hand to indicate that Romik should do the same.

"I see you've come a long way from the big farm boy too shy to talk to girls," Vil said.

"I see you haven't lost a bit of your smart mouth," Romik shot back as he took a seat. Vil laughed, a dark, almost bitter sound.

"I've lost many things, but never that," Vil agreed. "A lot can happen in two decades. I imagine we both have stories . . . as will Daen, when he arrives."

"By all the Divines," Romik leaned forward and held his head in his hands for a short moment before pushing his fingers through his short hair and meeting Vil's eyes again. "I can't believe this is happening. I can't believe you found us both."

"I'm just glad you came. I hope—" Vil broke off and looked up as the tavern door swung open. Romik followed his gaze to see a lanky man with wide, muscular shoulders step into the tavern. He wore a green hood and a brown leather jerkin. For the second time that day, Romik fought the urge to let his eyes fill with tears. Moving as one, he and Vil pushed up to their feet once again.

Romik took a step forward. "Daen," he whispered through the sound of his own blood pounding in his ears.

Daen stood just inside the door to the tavern, letting it swing shut behind him. He surveyed the crowd, taking in the rough edges, the scent of cooking meat and onions, the sound of myriad conversations over generous tankards of ale.

Common folk, midday gathering. Ten gets you twenty that more than half of the men in here are poachers. That kind of crowd. Not my business, not anymore. A man has a right to feed his family.

With that thought, Daen stepped further into the room, letting the heat from the crowd and the large hearth in the corner wash over him. Two men stood up at a table close to the fire.

The taller of the two had dark hair and eyes and a nose Daen remembered being straight and fine. It had obviously been broken several times since. The other man wore a dark cloak hanging from his shoulders and had a shock of short, white-blond hair.

Vil. And Romik. Daen kept himself motionless as his heart pounded wildly in his chest. Romik took a step forward, and Daen recognized the compact grace of a warrior in the way the bigger man moved.

"Daen," Romik said. He sounded dazed, unsure. It didn't fit with the overall competence of his fighter's mien. Daen took a breath and threaded his way through the tables until he came face-to-face with his childhood best friends.

"Hello, Romik," Daen found himself saying. "Hello, Vil."

Hello? The sarcastic voice that inhabited his mind sniped. *You haven't seen them in twenty years. The last time you did see them, the three of you screamed at each other. You've dreamed of this moment for decades and all you can say is* "Hello"?

"Hello, Daen," Vil said, his smooth voice empty of emotion. "Will you join us? Romik has made friends with the barmaid, and she's headed this way with ale and food."

Daen glanced over his shoulder and saw a buxom woman carrying three tankards of ale, atop which she balanced a tray holding three plates of stew and a loaf of brown bread. Despite her load, she put a little sway into her hips and winked at Romik as she approached their table.

"So, you're the third friend, hmm?" she said in a saucy tone. She deftly maneuvered the tray onto the table, set down the tankards, and began passing out the plates.

"Seems that way," Daen said, amused despite himself. "And you are?"

"Mirandy. This is my place, and it is my pleasure—" She paused and smiled at Romik before continuing. "—to serve you boys. Sit down now and eat while it's hot. I'll keep your ale coming."

"Thank you, Mirandy," Romik said.

"Thank me later," she shot back with another wink, before she turned and sauntered away.

Daen snorted, and then gave up any pretense of decorum and laughed outright. "My, my, you *did* make a friend, Ro." Romik's boyhood nickname crossed his lips before Daen could think better of it, and he decided just to let it go. Sure, there was a lot to dig into between the three of them, but there was also hot stew and ale. And he was hungry.

With a shrug, he unslung his quiver and leaned it and his bow up against the nearby wall, then eased himself into a chair while the other two did the same.

"So, what did you mean, Vil?" Romik asked as Daen grabbed the loaf of bread and tore off a section.

"When?"

"When you said it was good to see me up close. Have you seen me from afar?"

"A few times," Vil said. He tilted his head slightly until he met Daen's gaze with his own. "A few times for both of you."

"I figured as much when you left that letter in my quiver," Daen said, scooping up a mouthful of stew with a shrug.

"Why didn't you ever say anything?" Romik asked.

"I did," Vil said. "I invited you here."

"But—"

"You want to know what took me so long?"

"Yeah," Romik said. "Almost twenty years... if you knew where we were the whole time—"

"Not the whole time," Vil said. "I first saw you about eight years ago, when you came to Cievers on the Imperial Champions' Tour. Publicity for the tour was full of 'The Demon of Zandrine' who had decimated the southern arena champions. You were by far the odds-on favorite to take the final melee in Cievers. The day after you arrived, my boss sent me to talk to your employer—"

"Owner." Unlike his easy tone of earlier, Romik's voice had gone hard and almost as emotionless as Vil's. Daen looked up from his stew, but Romik kept his gaze locked on Vil's.

"Owner, then," Vil said, inclining his head. "If that's what you prefer to call him."

"That's what he was. I wasn't there by choice. Best to call it what it is."

"As you say. In any case, I was sent to talk to him and offer him a deal to have you throw the tournament in favor of Cievers's champion."

Romik's eyebrows went up, and he snorted derisively. "No one would have believed it. I remember him: big bruiser of a man, but no finesse with a blade. But even if they had, I'd never have cooperated."

"My boss didn't intend to offer you the option," Vil said with a tiny smile. "Which was why when I recognized you, I went back and persuaded him that rather than poisoning you and making a fortune off the upset, he was better served to spread the rumor within the underworld that the melee had been fixed in Cievers's favor...and then make a fortune when you actually won."

Daen blinked. "Who, exactly, was your boss?" he asked around a mouthful of stew.

"No one of relevance to this conversation," Vil said smoothly. "He's dead now anyway."

"I know who it was," Romik said, his voice a low growl. "Only one man in Cievers ever had the power to do what you describe: Bezier Tanithil, Soft Hand of the Thieves' Guild."

Vil smirked, and inclined his head forward, but didn't say anything else.

"You were a thief?" Daen asked, feeling like he was trying to catch up with the words the other two weren't saying.

"I *am* a thief," Vil corrected. "A very good one. But Cievers is no longer my home, which is why I've asked you both here to meet me. I have a prop—"

"No."

Daen heard the hard edge in Romik's voice and looked over to see that same hardness in the man's eyes.

"You haven't even heard the proposition," Vil said mildly.

"That's not what I'm saying no to," Romik said. He took a deep breath, and Daen heard the tiniest shudder in the inhale. "I'm saying no to your diversionary tactics. I've been a mercenary long enough that I recognize a feint when I see one."

"I'm with Romik," Daen said, not realizing he meant to speak until he did. "Like he said, it's been almost twenty years. We each need to know where the others have been, what we've done. The last time we were together..." He trailed off, remembering the shouted insults that had scarred that terror-filled morning so long ago. Daen sucked in a deep breath, and blew it out, shaking his head. "We were kids, and scared. But maybe if we'd actually *talked* to one another instead of flinging insults and blame, we wouldn't have been separated. And then Romik wouldn't have ended up in an arena pit, and Vil wouldn't have ended up working for a ruthless criminal. And I wouldn't have lost the only brothers I've ever really had!"

He closed his mouth with a snap. He hadn't meant to say that last bit, but with every word, the constant loneliness of the past almost twenty years weighed heavier and heavier on him, until it was a struggle just to breathe.

"What about the Foresters?" Vil asked, his voice dropping softly into the silence that followed Daen's outburst. "Don't they consider themselves a brotherhood?"

"Themselves maybe, but never me," Daen spat. He leaned back in his chair, hefted the tankard of Mirandy's ale, drained half of it, and then set it down with a heavy *thunk*. "Fine," he said. "I wanted open speech, I guess I'll start. After losing you both in the woods, I wandered for about three days, surviving on wild berries and onions. A Forester named Bormer found me. Bormer was a good man. He raised me as his own son and when I came of age, he sponsored me into the Foresters. He tried to warn me that it wouldn't suit me, but I've always been hard-headed—" Romik let out a slight chuckle, and Daen met his eyes with a little smile. "—so I didn't listen. He was right, though. The Foresters aren't the heroes we told stories about as little kids. Not anymore. The organization is corrupt from top to bottom, and only ever concerned about appearances and the relative nobility of one's birth."

"Which you don't have," Romik said, his tone sympathetic. Daen shrugged.

"No, I don't. I only have my hard-earned skills. For a long time I thought—I *hoped* they would be enough. If only I was good enough, skilled enough, accurate enough...maybe then my so-called 'brothers' would really, truly accept me. But eventually I learned the truth: they never would, no matter how good I got. In fact, the better I got, the more they hated and despised me, all because I was born in a cottage instead of a grand estate." Daen raised his mug to his lips again and drank, lest the emotions rising up within him begin to spill out through his eyes.

"So, what did you do?" Vil asked quietly. Daen lowered the mug and wiped his mouth, then gave his blond friend a small, savage smile.

"I got even better," he said. "I decided to shove their upturned noses in their own inferiority and outworked them all. Maybe they were never going to embrace me, but by the Green Lady's rut, they *would* notice me."

"And did they?"

"Yeah. And yeah, they hated me even more. Your note was a dead-on bull's-eye, by the way. I *was* close to burning the whole Outpost down out of spite when I got it."

Vil snorted a laugh, and even Romik, who hadn't seen the note, chuckled. Daen remembered his childhood fascination with the art of fire making and joined in as well.

"So, that's where I've been," he said as the mirth died down. "And now I'm here. Older, probably no wiser, but rutting glad to see you both. And maybe I shouldn't say this, but I don't care. I've missed you both. 'Bare is the back that has no brother to watch it,' someone said that . . . or wrote it down, or something. I don't remember who. I just remember that when Bormer taught me that line, it wasn't the Foresters that came to mind, it was you two, and may the Green Lady rot my limbs if I'm lying."

Rather than think too hard on that, Daen drained his mug and set it down again, then twisted around in his seat to look for Romik's friendly barmaid. "Call your girl over, Ro. I need a refill."

Romik leaned back in his chair, and apparently spotted Mirandy, because he jerked his chin slightly, and then smiled. "She's on her way," he said, satisfaction in his tone. "So, did the Foresters grant you leave to come here, then?"

Daen shook his head. "I resigned."

Vil snorted softly. "Foresters don't resign. Did you desert?"

Daen grinned slyly and shook his head. "Nope. If I'd done that, I'd be hunted for the rest of my life. Not that any of them can track worth a damn, but everyone gets lucky sometimes."

"So?" Vil pressed.

"So, I decided to think like you," Daen said. "Little Villaume, always had a scheme or a plan running. I suppose I'm not surprised you ended up on the dark side of the law, but I still want to hear the tale."

"And you shall, as much as I can tell," Vil promised. "But first, tell us why the Foresters let you 'resign.'"

"I got them to cast me out. I can be an arrogant, insubordinate prick when I want to be, and they already hated me. It wasn't hard." *Not as hard as it should have been, may the Green Lady rot their bones.*

"You're not arrogant."

Daen looked up from the scarred tabletop to meet Vil's eyes.

"No?"

"No. Arrogance implies that your confidence is misplaced. From what I've seen, yours is not."

"What have you seen?"

"I saw you put an arrow center target at a hundred paces—four times in a row."

Daen opened his mouth to speak, but Mirandy chose that moment to bustle up to the table and plunk down three more brimming mugs. As she bent to gather up his and Romik's empties, Daen could see that she'd loosened her chemise around her neck, putting her generous assets on display. Her eyes, though, were all for Romik, who thanked her with a smile.

"You're a lucky man, Ro," Daen grumbled, without any heat in it.

"That woman at the table near the door hasn't stopped staring at you since you walked in," Vil pointed out. "The one in the blue coat, sitting next to the older man."

Daen glanced to his right and saw the woman Vil mentioned. She was, indeed, looking boldly at him. An inviting smile spread across her lips as his eyes met hers.

He considered, and then turned back to his ale.

"Bored townwife with a rich husband," Daen said dismissively. "More trouble than she's worth. I'd rather just drink and envy Romik."

"Smart man," Vil said, and clinked his mug against Daen's. "So, Daen's told us his story, Romik. What about you? How did you become the Demon of Zandrine?"

"Killed a lot of men and animals in the arena." Romik's short, blunt answer may have been intended to stave off further discussion, but it didn't work. Daen sipped at his ale and waited. Vil sat silent and motionless. Finally, Romik let out a gusty sigh.

"Fine," he said. "After we got separated in the forest, I found my way to a road. That night I got jumped by a bandit gang. They sold me to a slaver caravan who took me south. I'd fought the bandits, and tried to fight the slavers, and they liked that. So, they sold me to an arena stable down in Zandrine. The arena master was a former fighter himself. He saw potential in me—you know what a big kid I was—and so he trained me personally. It was either get good or die. I chose to get good."

"And then—?"

Romik took a deep drink before continuing. "And then," he said, "I got really good. So good I was able to win enough to buy my freedom. But once I'd done that, I realized I had a problem. I didn't know anything other than fighting. Most fighters who win their freedom end up back in the arena, fighting for themselves, but still risking death for the entertainment of others. I didn't want that. So, I took my winnings and bought myself a place in the Raiders mercenary company."

"I bet that was a shock," Daen said. "Mercenary battles are a different animal than arena combat."

Romik nodded. "Yep. But I'd figured they would be, so I started at the bottom rank like everyone else. I was fit and had great endurance, and I *did* know how to swing a blade and a spear, even if the employment tactics were quite different. So, I did all right, rose through the ranks to become a lieutenant."

"Doesn't sound like a bad life." Daen lifted his mug again. Romik shrugged.

"It was all right. I liked leading men, and they liked me, or so I hear."

"So, what happened?" Vil asked.

"Eh. Word got out as to who I was. I managed to keep it secret for a year or two, but someone found out and rumors spread. My fellow officers got real jealous of the attention I was getting, and eventually, it became clear that they were looking to get rid of me. So, I got your note, and I left."

"I'd think having a celebrated fighter as an officer would be an asset to a mercenary company like the Raiders," Daen said.

"Maybe it would have been, if I'd played their games. Mercenaries play politics just like Foresters. I made the mistake of keeping myself aloof—trying to keep my identity secret, you know—and so I never really made friends with my peers. If they'd liked me, maybe things would have worked out differently. They didn't like me. They resented my fame, and they resented the way my men respected me." Romik snorted softly and lifted his mug again. "Didn't help that they thought respect only flowed one way." He muttered these words softly into the mug, but Daen heard them, and judging by the quick flash of eye contact between them, so did Vil.

"Bare is the back without a brother to watch it," Vil murmured. Romik took a deep drink, then set his mug down.

"You said it," Romik agreed. "So, what about you, Vil? What happened to little Villaume?"

"It's not a pretty story."

"You think being cast into a stable of arena fighters at twelve years old is pretty?"

"No. But I thought it fair to warn you." Vil shrugged, and then reached back to pull his hood up over his head, leaving his face in shadow as he wrapped his cloak around himself.

"After we got separated, I wandered in the forest for a day or so before I, too, found a road. I stayed hidden, but I followed it until it got to a bigger road, and a bigger one. By then I was close to starving, since I hadn't dared stray too far from the road to find food. In my hunger-dazed state, I found myself picking through the midden pile of a large house on the outskirts of a city—Cievers, although I didn't know it at the time. Anyway, the mistress of the house caught me. But she was sympathetic, and kind. She took me into her home, fed me, bathed me, gave me clean clothes. And then she drugged me with a soporific and sold me to a brothel keeper inside the city. This particular brothel was notorious for skirting the age laws. When I woke up, I was informed that it was my duty to service the client, and that if I did not, I would be violated by force, locked up, and starved into submission."

"Red Lady..." Romik breathed. Daen swallowed hard against the nausea that rose within his throat.

Vil took a sip of his nearly full mug.

"Anyway, I agreed, as it seemed the safer option. The client came in...he was the rich son of a merchant family, as I recall. Big, burly man with an arrogant sneer. He never expected me to steal the knife from his boot and sever the artery in his groin. I took his clothes and boots and escaped out the window. They looked for me, of course, but they didn't find me because instead of dropping down to the ground, I climbed up and escaped across the rooftops, deeper into the city.

"I sold his clothes and used the money he'd had on him, but that only lasted a few weeks. Before too long, I was destitute again, with no place to live. I started begging...and that's when they found me."

"Who?" Daen asked, enthralled by his friend's storytelling.

"The thieves. At first, they roughed me up for begging on

their corners without permission, but when I fought back, I must have impressed someone. They took me to meet the Soft Hand."

"Tanithil?" Romik asked. Vil nodded.

"He asked me if I was the one who'd murdered the merchant's son at the brothel. No one had put that together yet, as far as I knew. But he knew it. He asked me if I'd been at the brothel willingly, and when I told him that I hadn't, he nodded, as if it confirmed something. It seemed the brothel keeper had been playing fast and loose with the laws—not Cievers's laws, *Tanithil's* laws. He offered me amnesty for the murder on the condition that I come to work for him and join his family. Others call it the Thieves' Guild, but for Bezier, it was always 'his family.'"

Vil got quiet for a bit, his eyes shadowed by his hood. Daen shared a glance with Romik, who seemed to echo his own cautious concern.

"In any case," Vil said, moving on as if he'd never paused, "I joined the family, and I learned. Tanithil liked my trick of escaping over the rooftops, and so he taught me second-story skills—"

"The Villain!" Romik snapped his fingers, sitting up straight in his chair. "You're the Villain of Cievers!"

Vil's mouth twisted into a curve under the edge of his hood, but he only lifted his mug and sipped at Mirandy's ale in reply. Daen felt his eyebrows rise in spite of himself.

"Even I've heard of the Villain of Cievers," he said, keeping his voice low. "That was you?"

Vil set his mug down. "Once, maybe. Like you both, I've left my former employment. I, too, found that my back was bare without someone I trusted to watch it."

"I never should have left you both, that day in the forest," Romik said, his voice soft with regret.

"We were just kids," Daen said, tilting his mug to tap the rim against Romik's. "You included. We were all scared and angry. But we survived."

"I aim to do more than just survive," Vil said lowly. "That's why I invited you both here. Of all the people in this world, the ones I most trust ... are you two. Twenty years notwithstanding."

"There wasn't a single day in the Foresters that I didn't think about you both," Daen said, surprising himself. He swallowed hard, and then shrugged and plunged on. "Every day I'd look at the mewling pustules—my *peers*—and think how either of you would be worth two, or three, or *four* of them. You two knew the meaning of friendship, of loyalty. They knew nothing but how to kiss the Lord Leader's arse."

"I never wished you both beside me in the arena pits," Romik said. "I wouldn't want to see you in that situation. But in the Raiders... Yeah. I missed you two. I always hoped we'd find each other, eventually."

"And now we have," Vil said.

"Rut yes, we have!" Daen said. He took a deep swig of his ale and plunked it down on the tabletop slightly harder than he intended. A tiny bit sloshed out the top, but he barely noticed. He stretched out his arm and laid it, palm up, on the table as a sudden fierce, ebullient energy surged through his frame. Words from long ago stories and games floated to the surface of his memory, and somehow, he found himself speaking them as he bent his arm at the elbow and raised his forearm, hand open in invitation. "And I don't intend to ever be brotherless again. By the Green Lady's grace, I swear to stand shoulder to shoulder with you both. May She bless our hunts through forest and field and grant us rich quarry!"

"It's been decades," Romik said slowly, "since I've seen either of you. But I still *know* you. My gut says you're still the friends I would have died or killed for, back before we got separated in the forest that day. And in twenty years fighting and killing, my gut hasn't steered me wrong yet. So, I'm in." He leaned forward, planted his elbow, and clasped Daen's hand in a meaty grip. "By whatever tarnished honor I hold, I swear to stand shoulder to shoulder with you both as my brothers. May Fortune, the Red Lady, smile on us and fill our purses with gold."

The restless, reckless feeling inside Daen intensified. He found himself grinning savagely as he gripped his friend—his brother's hand, and turned to look a challenge at Vil.

Vil, too, leaned forward. He lifted one hand to push back the hood that shadowed his face, and then clasped both of his hands around theirs.

"By my own wits and cunning, I swear to stand shoulder to shoulder with you both as my brothers. May Darkness witness our bond and hold us hidden under Her mantle."

Something surged within Daen. A ringing horn—no... A forest wolf's howl—no... The sound of thunder in the trees—somehow, a sound that was all three and more besides echoed through his mind, sweeping up all that reckless energy and twisting it, braiding it together with something searing and hot, and something icy cold.

He blinked and saw his chosen brothers through a green haze. A fierce warrior with braided, blood-soaked hair stood with her mailed fists on Romik's shoulders. A vaguely female shape cloaked in shadows loomed over Vil. And above him...

Daen looked up to see his divine patroness's savage smile and fur-cloaked but otherwise naked body as She looked down at him.

"Brothers you have been," She said. Or maybe it was the Red Lady, or maybe the Dark. Or maybe it was all three of Them.

Daen shifted his gaze to see Romik staring back at him, red fury and fortune in the scarlet pools of his eyes. Vil, too, looked out at them through eyes gone unrelieved black.

"Brothers," They said again, "you shall be. From this day forward, by your own choice and oath, brothers you are."

The sound returned, ringing through Daen's ears as the green haze solidified in his eyes. The center of his palm tingled with icy fire that seared into him. Daen gasped, fought to draw a breath of the leaf-scented air...

And blinked.

Someone called a farewell as they departed the tavern, letting the heavy door swing shut behind them. Someone else cursed at the sound of a metal tankard hitting the floor with a dull *thunk*. The scent of frying meat and onions intensified. The fire crackled, sending a spray of sparks leaping from the hearth not far away.

Everything was normal again.

But he and his brothers—*brothers indeed!*—still clasped hands in the center of the scarred, ale-stained table. Slowly, Vil unclenched his fingers first, followed by Romik. Daen lowered his hand and turned it palm up on the table. All three of them looked at the mark sitting directly in the center of his palm.

Three crescent-moon shapes intertwined to form a knot in the center of his hand: red, green, and black. They looked like the kind of fancywork tattoo he'd heard was popular in certain cities in the south. But he knew deep in the marrow of his bones that this was no tattoo that would fade with age and use.

"I suppose that's what we get for invoking the Divine," Vil said. "You never know when She might decide to pay attention."

"Three of Them, no less," Romik said. He ran his thumb over his own palm, and then angled it to show them his mark. Daen wasn't surprised to see that it was identical to his own. Vil's right hand, too, showed the same mark.

"I've never heard of anything like this happening, though," Daen said. "The brotherhood oath in old stories, sure, but... Divine visitation?"

"Does it change anything?" Vil asked.

"Yes," Romik said. "And no. They said it. We were brothers before by choice, we're brothers now by choice and oath.... And Divine recognition."

"Exactly," Vil said, and for the first time since Daen had walked in, he saw his dark brother's lips curve in a genuine smile. "We all said we didn't want to ever be alone again. Looks like we got our wish."

With that same lightning quickness as before, Daen felt his mood shift from reverent awe to irreverent glee. "By the rut, we did, didn't we? Ha! I'd say this calls for a celebration, wouldn't you?" He nudged Romik under the table with his knee, and slowly, Romik joined them both in a smile.

"Mirandy," Romik called out, getting the buxom barmaid's attention. "Another round, please! My brothers and I are celebrating!"

Romik wrapped his hand around the battered tankard and lifted it to his lips. He'd had plenty of Mirandy's ale, but that wasn't the reason his head felt like it was spinning. Plus, drinking it gave him a moment to try and shut down the treacherous shining hope threatening to bloom in his chest. If life in the arena and in the Raiders had taught him anything, it was that hope was a dangerous, addictive thing, best avoided at all costs. Just when you let yourself start to hope, that's when bad things started to happen.

But seeing his brothers again—and the sudden Divine recognition of that relationship—had rattled him enough that the persistent brightness of hope had begun to break through the walls he'd built to keep it out.

So, Romik drank, and ate, and swapped stories with his brothers. And he fought that feeling, hour by hour. And as darkness rose around the tavern and the moons began to shine through the windows, Romik began to suspect that it was a losing battle.

Meanwhile, Daen was, of course, talking.

"...so, we're tracking this wounded aurochs bull through the woods, hoping to get close enough to bring it down and put it out of its misery. But the thing had the Green Lady's own toughness, and it just kept going, through the entire day and into the night. The whole time, our Point is saying 'just a little bit further, it can't go on much longer...' Derfin. He was an idiot," Daen shook his head and paused to take another long drink. Romik had to give it to him, Daen could hold his ale. Twice, Mirandy had brought trays of food along with her dark, bitter brew. Each time, she winked at Romik in invitation and gave him a look that tightened his body in anticipation. But she seemed in no mood to hurry them along, so the three of them stayed, and drank, and laughed, and talked, and drank some more.

Romik didn't know when he'd ever been happier. And therein lay the problem.

"...so, the bull busts through the wall of this rickety, tumbledown cabin, sending timber and dirt flying everywhere, and we hear, of all things, a woman's scream!"

Romik blinked and focused on his ex-Forester brother's face. "A woman?"

Daen nodded, mischief bright in his eyes. "And not just any woman, but Lord Ulito's youngest daughter!"

"What did you do?" Vil asked. Romik turned to regard his thief brother. *What an odd concept,* he thought idly as Daen took another swig, letting the tension in his story build. *That I would have a thief for a brother. But I suppose it's no stranger than an arena slave turned mercenary lieutenant turned... whatever the hell we are now.*

"I shot the bull," Daen said. "He was stunned from the impact with the wall and the surprise of having the entire roof come crashing down on him, so I put an arrow through his eye and dropped him... which is what I would have done in the beginning if Point Derfin wasn't such a pompous arse. But anyway, the bull was dead, and the girl was screaming, and I'll be a wet briar toad if it wasn't Lord Thiren himself, naked in bed with the girl. Who was also naked, of course."

"Oh, of course," Vil said, dry amusement threading through his tone.

"To the man's credit, though, he kept his aplomb. I hate to say anything good about the nobility, but Thiren seemed all right. He invited us to wait outside while he calmed the girl, and then came out and thanked us for saving them from serious injury. He also paid us handsomely to forget we'd ever seen them there... 'for the lady's privacy,' he said. I guess I didn't forget, but I doubt anyone here cares about Lord Thiren's indiscretions with his neighbor's lovely daughter!"

"Wait, Lord Thiren, he's a young man, right?" Romik asked then, as a memory percolated.

"Younger than old Lord Ulito. Probably no more than five years older than us, why?"

"Yeah," Romik said with a slow smile. "I remember him—the Raiders took a contract with him one summer. Harrying his neighbor's outposts, if I recall. He needed to make a point but still be able to deny our actions, is what he told us. I do remember, though, the terms of engagement. We only attacked guard posts, stole only gold, weapons, and horseflesh. And under no circumstances were we permitted to harass the local civilian population."

"I imagine your Raiders didn't like that," Vil observed dryly. Romik shrugged.

"My men were fine; I kept a tight leash on them anyway. Some of the others balked, but since Thiren threatened to withhold all pay to the whole company if a single one of our men stepped out of line with the local women... well. Let's just say my peers had more incentive than usual to enforce proper discipline."

"*See*," Daen said, and Romik suspected that his usual enthusiasm had been amplified by the ale. "He might be a noble, but he's got *some* honor."

"Did he pay well, Romik?" Vil asked.

"Very," Romik said, lifting his mug to drink. "Otherwise, the commander probably wouldn't have given a shit."

"Perhaps the three of us should go see if he's got any other needs for work that could be eventually denied," Vil said. "I believe I could meet his conditions."

"What do you mean?" Daen asked.

"I mean, that's the kind of thing we could do. Together. This is what I wanted to talk to the two of you about. The proposition. A business venture, between the three of us. I think we could make a good deal of money helping people like your Lord Thiren with certain things they may or may not want to be linked to."

"So, you're saying we just... strike out together and... what?

Do odd jobs?" Daen snorted a soft chuckle as he spoke, but his dark eyes were serious. It was surreal how instantly and well Romik could read his childhood best friend's mannerisms, even after so many years. But from the moment he'd walked into the dingy roadside tavern and seen Vil, the heart Romik hadn't known he still possessed had lurched with joy so painful and profound, he'd had to lock it away.

Just like he had to lock away that bright, treacherous hope. Hope was the fastest way to get hurt. He couldn't afford to forget the lessons of the arena, of war.

But the Divines Themselves blessed our fraternity. That has *to mean something!*

"Odd, perhaps, but lucrative." Vil leaned forward, his hood shadowing his white-blond hair and dark blue eyes. He tapped the scarred tabletop with long, slender fingers. "Think about it. Between the three of us, we've got contacts in every major city and several smaller towns throughout the empire. With our varied skill sets, we're in a position to make money hand over fist doing jobs for the highest bidder."

"What skill sets?" Romik's voice came out rougher than he'd intended. Daen looked at him with a shadow of a frown, but Vil's wide mouth curved in a slow smile. Romik feared no man, but a cold shiver of foreboding whispered up his spine at the darkness in his friend's eyes.

"Well," Vil said, drawing the word out. He sat back in his chair and kept that intense, sardonic gaze locked on Romik's. "We've got you, who was once known as the 'Demon of Zandrine.' Zandrine's favorite son, famous for single-handedly defeating ten other gladiators on the sands."

"That was a long time ago," Romik said, his words a low growl.

"Indeed," Vil continued, apparently unperturbed by Romik's glower. "Since then, you've managed to earn enough to buy your freedom and *then* earn a commission in one of the empire's most well-known mercenary companies. So, what sorts of skills might you have then, hmm? Melee combat? Hit-and-run raiding? Training and doctrine?"

"Supply and logistics," Daen added, leaning forward on his elbows. "Siege warfare."

"All of those," Romik conceded, speaking slowly. Vil's smile grew, and he nodded.

"And Daen," Vil went on as he turned his attention to the third member of their trio. "As an Imperial Forester—"

"*Former* Imperial Forester," Daen said, raising his mug. "I 'resigned,' remember."

"Still, you're the one who split your competitor's arrow in the regional semifinals for the Imperial Games two summers ago."

Daen lowered his mug enough to look over the rim of it at Vil. "How did you hear about that?" he asked, his voice carefully neutral.

"Like I said, contacts. You should have won that purse. You should have gone on to the Games."

"I was disqualified."

"On a spurious charge of tampering with your bowstring. Except that I *know* all the match fixers in that region. If anyone had tampered with anything I'd have heard about it. Your string was legitimate, and so was your shot. They just couldn't countenance an orphan nobody beating out all of those second sons of minor houses to compete for the Emperor's Cup."

Daen said nothing, just lifted his mug again and drank deeply.

"So," Vil went on, "besides being deadly accurate and fast with that bow, you know every length of the imperial forest lands... which means all the caves, crevices, and hidey holes."

"No one knows all of them," Daen said. "And even if they did, things change. Trees fall, streams flood, things like that."

"Yeah, but that's my point." Vil stabbed a finger across the table and leaned forward again. "You *know* these things. Better than any one of those no-talent lordlings in the Foresters, unless I miss my guess. And like you, my talented friend...I *never* miss."

Daen snorted softly, and then inclined his head with a smirk, conceding Vil's point.

"What about you?" Romik asked, letting his earlier aggression creep into his tone.

"Simple," Vil said, turning his gaze back to Romik. "I do the dirty work."

"The Villain of Cievers," Daen said, speaking as if he were a minstrel telling a tale. He waved a hand in an exaggerated flourish at Vil's form. Vil's eyes darkened, but he didn't otherwise move. Daen snorted another laugh, then lifted his mug once more and drained it. Then he set it down with a *thud* on the tabletop.

"What's in it for you, then, Vil?" Romik asked. "What's in it for all of us?"

"I thought that was obvious, Demon," Vil said. "Money. The empire is vast, my friends, and while the emperor upholds the rule of law...he can't peek into the shadows in every corner of every city, now, can he? There will always be jobs to do that require our skills, just as I've said. Mark my words, within four, five years? The three of us will accumulate enough of a fortune to make several noble houses salivate."

"And what would we do with that fortune?"

"Hells, man, whatever you want. That's what's so great about money. It doesn't care what you use it for."

"Equal shares?" Romik asked, his voice low.

"Of course. We're brothers now, as we always should have been," Vil said softly, rubbing the thumb of his left hand across the palm of his right. He looked from Daen to Romik and back again.

Daen, too, lifted his gaze to meet Romik's.

"I'm in," Romik said. He hadn't even realized he meant to speak until he heard the words coming out of his mouth, but as he did, that treacherous gleam of hope surged within him.

Gods above and below, I've missed them! This has to be real, right? With the blessings of three Divines, it has to be real. I can't lose them again. Somewhere, in the back of his mind, Romik realized he'd curled the fingers of his right hand into a fist, as if to protect the brotherhood mark that had appeared there.

"Me too," Daen said. "As long as we're together. I won't be brotherless again."

"None of us will." Vil smiled once more. He held his hand out across the table, in an echo of their earlier oath, and Romik found himself clasping it—and Daen's, as he joined in too—without hesitation. *This is real. This is true. I can trust this. By the Red Lady Herself, I really think I can!*

"I say we stay here tonight, sleep it off, let Mirandy entertain Romik, and then in the morning we can discuss business strategies," Vil was saying when Romik refocused on the conversation.

"Eminently practical," Daen said, not even slurring a little bit.

Romik wanted to agree, but the confusion of hope and joy swirled dizzyingly in his mind. *I need some air.* "I'll be right back," he said as let go of his brothers and pushed up to his feet, careful to make sure he was steady before he stepped away from the table. "Need to drain away some of this ale." Caution and habit had him fastening his sword belt around his hips as he tossed a smile toward Mirandy at the bar and headed out into the night to piss, and think...

And wonder if maybe, this time, that treacherous hope wasn't a liar after all.

Aelys dragged in a ragged, desperate breath as the wind whipped her loosened hair across her face. The night air stung her clenched fingers, cheeks, and ears. Her hood had long since fallen back on her shoulders, and she couldn't spare a hand to pull it back up again.

She needed both hands to keep from falling.

She let out a gasping whimper and bent lower over her galloping horse's bobbing neck. The poor animal was slick with lather, his eyes wide enough that she could see the whites as they hurtled through the darkness. Something caught at Aelys's cloak, yanking her backward hard enough that the horse reared, throwing her off and to the side. She twisted in midair as she fell, but her left side hit the roadside berm hard enough to make her vision disappear in a wash of gray sparkles. Nothing snapped, but agony erupted from shoulder to hip, and Aelys gasped as the air fled her lungs.

A horse whinnied. Booted feet crunched over the road's sparse gravel. Aelys let out a groan as air whooshed into her lungs. She fought to marshal her limbs enough to roll over. She'd just managed to get her hands and knees underneath herself when a large, heavy hand clamped down on her shoulder and flipped her onto her back.

Flash.

She visualized a bright burst of light as she thought the word and desperately pulled at her pitifully weak, tiny reservoir of power. The magelight responded beautifully. It exploded into brilliance inches from the brigand's face as he leaned over her with murder in his expression.

"Qunt!" He stumbled back, his hands clawing at his eyes.

She gulped in a hopeless sob and scrambled backward on her elbows and heels, trying to get away from his terrifying bulk. The soil of the berm crumbled under her weight, pitching her backward onto a softer, grassier surface.

"You'll pay for that, bitch," the brigand growled. Aelys looked up to see him shake his head, then squint at her before stretching his mouth in a leering grin. A terrified whimper slipped past her lips as she tried to coordinate her leaden feet and her slow, weak hands. Once more she reached for her power, but it was no use. One tiny burst of light and she had nothing left to call.

Some Bellatrix I am.

Her attacker's chuckle cut through her like icy steel as he started walking toward her. Behind him, more horses arrived. For one desperate second, Aelys thought perhaps it might be someone coming to help her, but that hope died a quick death when one of the arrivals called out.

"All right then, Varryl?"

"Jus' fine, Dem. Jus' bleedin' fine."

"Remember, we need her alive."

"Oh, she'll be alive, all right..." He let the words trail off suggestively and grinned even wider. Moonlight and firelight from a nearby building flickered over his face and Aelys realized that they were just outside the inn she'd been fleeing toward. She'd nearly made it.

Why is he chasing me? I don't have that much money on me! Is he...he can't be one of the Monterles! He's so dirty and rough!

Varryl lunged, his big hand grabbing Aelys's waist as his weight came down, knocking her flat into the dirt once more. She let out another gasping kind of sob.

"That's it. Cry for me, bitch. Not so rich and powerful now, are you?"

The back of his hand impacted Aelys's cheek, slamming her face to the side hard enough to wrench her neck and make stars explode into her vision. She fought to get her hands free of his pinning weight so that she could protect her face. More blows would come. She knew it. And then—

Unwilling to think much further, Aelys hunched in the dark with her forearms crossed over her face and waited for the pain.

The sky outside glowed deep blue with the rising Mother near the eastern horizon. It shaded into star-studded black overhead, with the bright silver crescent of the Daughter hanging just west of zenith. Romik sucked in a deep breath of woodsmoke-scented air and shook his head. That strange, hope-edged euphoria continued to gild his thoughts in a way that might have been alcohol-induced...but he didn't think it was.

He was pretty sure it was just joy. And he had no idea what to do with such a feeling.

Romik let out a sigh and finished relieving himself in the small, unroofed outhouse he'd found set back from the tavern in a scraggly stand of trees. He straightened his clothing and stepped down off the platform into the crystalline beauty of the night.

How is this possible? Red Lady, I'm afraid to think on it too much, lest it shatter around me. To have my brothers again is...overwhelming enough, but now the prospect of a business venture? It's like the dreams of my ten-year-old self coming true!

That thought startled him into a laugh as he made his way down the slope back toward the tavern. The light from the windows shone golden out into the night, and Romik paused for a moment to take in the sight, knowing that in the future, he would remember this night as the night everything in his life changed.

That moment of reflective pause was the reason he saw the girl.

She bent low on her horse, bright hair and dark cloak streaming behind her. Even at his distance, Romik could see the white lather that flecked the horse's neck and chest glistening in the rising Motherlight. Behind her, three more horses thundered up, and as he watched the closest pursuing rider reached out and grabbed hold of the girl's cloak, ripping her from the saddle and casting her down to the ground hard enough that Romik heard a distinct *thump* and a cry.

He didn't think.

The blissful golden haze around his thoughts vanished as he drew his sword and charged silently—or as nearly so as he could manage—down the slope toward where the attacker and his two fellows converged on the hapless girl.

"...see, I think we head south in the morning. You seem to want to bypass Cievers, which is fine, but we can take ship at Elocar or one of the other ports and head down to Zandrine or Ioletta or one of those big cities—" Daen broke off from his rambling as his pleasantly blurred thoughts suddenly sharpened.

He lowered his mug to the table and met Vil's gaze. Vil, who had been listening with an indulgent expression and half smile shifted forward in his seat, his gaze going dark.

"Something..." Vil said, his tone low in warning.

"Romik," Daen said at the same time. He didn't know how he knew, but he was absolutely certain. Romik was...not in danger, precisely...but he needed them. Now.

Daen pushed up to his feet, grateful that the effects of tankards of Mirandy's fine ale seemed to have vanished. He slung his quiver, grabbed his bow, and bolted for the door.

And the whole time, he could feel his dark brother's presence behind him.

Watching his back, just as he'd sworn to do. As they'd all sworn.

Romik...

Daen kicked the outer door of the tavern open as he nocked an arrow and drew. He blinked to settle his eyes to the sudden change in light, but with the Mother rising and the Daughter high, he had no trouble making out the figure of his brother, sword drawn, charging down the slope toward a trio of men intent on an indistinct, lumpy patch of ground.

Daen took two steps out into the darkness and let fly. His arrow soared down the slope and thudded into the throat of the tallest man. Daen caught the edge of a strangled cry as his target stumbled backward and fell heavily.

He nocked and drew again, but by that time Romik was there, and he didn't want to risk hitting his brother in the uncertain light.

A brief tussle followed, and one of the remaining attackers backed away, and then turned and lunged for the nearby horses. He got himself up into the saddle before Daen could take proper aim and let fly. His arrow thudded into the man's thigh, just above the knee. The man let out a cry and the horse under him took off, hooves thundering down the dirt road in the opposite direction.

"Guard his back while he gets the girl. I'll head back in and warn Mirandy she's got bodies on the lawn," Vil said softly. Daen nodded, nocking another arrow and holding it at the ready as Romik bent over the fallen body of his opponent. Only then did he realize that he had no idea what Vil was talking about.

Girl?

Varryl let out a weird grunt, and his weight made a sudden shift to the side. Something wet and hot pattered down her arms and hands, sending drops splashing onto her face. She flinched, and then his full weight dropped on her, his body going slack and boneless.

Aelys heaved upward, shoving at his shoulders, and managed to worm out from underneath him. Overhead, the Mother hung full and round, just rising over the trees. Her light revealed a wide black gash in the attacker's throat. A slow-spreading, black puddle glistened beneath him in the Motherlight.

Aelys pulled in a breath and tried to quiet the ringing in her ears.

That's not just ringing. That's the sound of a man screaming.

Aelys blinked and scrubbed with unsteady hands at the tacky blood drying on her face.

A bowstring sang out somewhere behind her. Aelys flinched and ducked, and then looked wildly around. She couldn't see who was shooting, or from where. Another scream brought her attention back to face the road, only to see one of the men who'd attacked her fleeing, crouched low over his horse's neck. The third attacker lay nearby, letting out a high, gurgling whine as blood fountained forth around the arrow in his throat.

"Are you all right?"

Aelys whipped her head around again, letting out a tiny scream. While she'd been watching the fleeing attacker, a warrior had approached. His face was grim. His sword gleamed naked in the moonlight, dark liquid glistening as it dripped from the blade.

"Are you all right, demoiselle?" he asked again, stepping closer. He used the toe of his boot to nudge the body of the first attacker, the one who'd taken her to the ground. "Did this trash hurt you?"

"N-not really," she stammered. Without meaning to do so, she raised her hand to brush her bruised cheek. "He only hit me."

With the Mother rising full behind him, the Daughter's quarter light high in the sky wasn't enough to fully illuminate this warrior's face, but Aelys could see his eyes narrow.

"That's bad enough," he said. "You shouldn't be out here alone. There are rough sorts in these woods."

"I know," she said softly, guilt sinking deep in her gut. "But I didn't have a choice."

"Well, you'd better come in and get warm, at least." He jerked his chin in the direction of the inn. "Let's get you something to eat."

"I-I can pay," she said.

"The innkeeper will be glad to hear it."

Aelys wasn't really conscious of him pulling her to her feet or of starting forward, but somehow, she was walking beside this hulking man while he cleaned his sword and sheathed it. She watched him tuck the rag he'd used back into a pouch on his belt.

Then they stood at the door.

"—is she?—"

Another man stood in the open doorway. Almost as tall as the warrior, but leaner, thinner, except for his massive shoulders, a bow held loosely in his hand.

"Demoiselle. *Demoiselle!*"

Aelys blinked and forced her eyes to focus on the face of the warrior. Her rescuer.

"Yes?"

"She's badly shaken up," the other man said. Disgust ran thickly through his voice, and Aelys flinched.

Of course he's mad at you, you're stupid and *weak! First you get robbed, now you're not paying attention!*

A hand on her arm, just above her wrist, interrupted her mental tirade. She looked down, wondering how the hand got there, and then looked up again into the face of the archer.

What she could see of it.

"Demoiselle, I think you should come with us." He had a nice voice, not gravelly and rough like the warrior's. Not overly loud. "We have a table near the fire. My name is Daen, and this is Romik. Our brother Vil is there. I give you my word that you are safe with us."

Safe? How can I be safe when I ruin everything?

She must have nodded, or otherwise indicated assent . . . or done nothing and the archer—Daen—went ahead with his plan. Because next she was in the process of sitting down at table with yet another man. He looked just as rough and angry as the two who'd rescued her.

"So, who is this, then, Daen?" the third man asked, looking up from under the black woolen hood he'd pulled over his head. A wisp of white-blond hair peeked out, but most of his face remained shadowed.

"Romik found her being attacked on the road."

"Not our problem."

"Vil, don't be an arse. She's a young woman who needs help . . . and she said she has money. Maybe she'd like to hire us to escort her, hmm?"

The man in the cloak lifted his shadowed face and Aelys got the impression of dark blue, empty eyes as he studied her. A shiver started under her skin and radiated throughout her body, and the warmth from the crackling fire nearby did nothing to stop it. Those dark eyes narrowed, and the man called Vil leaned forward.

"Where is your Ageon, Bella?" he asked. His quiet voice held an edge of menace that made Aelys round her shoulders and duck her head, curling further into her misery. Out of the corner of her eyes, she saw Romik spin from his watch on the door to stare at her.

"Vil, what are you talking about?" Daen scoffed. "She's not—"

"She is," Vil said, his voice drawing out the last word in a sinister purr. "Look at her clothing, look at her throat. She's wearing Lyceum livery, and only Bellatrices ever wear that type of choker stone."

Before she could stop herself, Aelys looked down at her dress. He was right. In her haste to depart the Lyceum, she hadn't bothered to change her ceremonial graduation gown. Firelight from the nearby hearth glinted off the black thread embroidery winding its distinctive pattern across the blue silk. She reached to pull her outer cloak closed.

Vil's hand shot out like a viper. His long fingers wrapped around her wrist and pulled it forward, pinning it to the table while his other hand shoved her sleeve up past the elbow.

"You wear no bracelet."

"I—I have no Ageon."

"A Bellatrix with no Ageon? How is that possible?"

Aelys pulled against him, afraid to look away from the intense darkness of his eyes. He held her in his iron grip for a long moment, and then let her go. She sank back into her seat and buried her braceletless arm back within her sleeve before hunching further into herself. *Stupid, stupid girl! Of course someone would recognize your dress, and your necklace!*

"I don't understand, Vil," Daen said, his tone cautious. He took the wooden chair next to Aelys and spun it, straddling the seat and leaning forward with his arms crossed on the back. Aelys glanced sideways at him, absurdly grateful for his presence.

"She's a Bellatrix from the Lyceum in Cievers—or at least she's dressed like one," Vil said. "But I've never heard of a trained battle mage without an Ageon protector . . . so, who are you really, girl?"

"Did your protector die?" The big man, Romik, had turned his attention fully back to the conversation. He leaned forward, putting hands nearly the size of dinner plates on the surface of the heavy oak table. His voice, though still gravelly and rough, sounded almost gentle.

But that can't be true. Why would he be gentle with someone as worthless as you?

Aelys glanced up into his severe face with its hard lines and even harder expression and swallowed against the despair that threatened to drown her. She opened her mouth to speak, but nothing came out.

"No," Vil said, drawing the word out like silk in the firelight. "If her Ageon had died, she'd still have the bonding bracelet on her wrist. I don't think she's a true Bellatrix at all. What's the story, girl? Were you a servant? Or maybe a student who couldn't take the training? Did you steal that gown and necklace and run away from the Lyceum?"

Despite the icy fear flooding her veins, something in the hooded man's sneering tone ignited a tiny spark of defiance deep within Aelys's brain. The same impulse that sent her fleeing into the night rather than be publicly shamed had her head snapping up, and she felt something like heat kindle in her eyes.

"I graduated," she snarled. "I *earned* the right to wear this stone! I just...did not bond with an Ageon."

"None worthy of your power, then?" Daen asked, laughter threading through his tone. He didn't sound unkind, though. It was more...teasing?

Aelys's sudden flash of defiance sputtered and died.

"Rather the opposite." Shame had her half muttering, half whispering the words. She lowered her gaze to the scarred tabletop and hunched still further inward, listening to the fire's crackle behind her.

"'Ere now, boys!" A woman's bright, brassy voice cut through Aelys's growing misery, and she peeked up through the wisps of her hair to get a good look at a truly impressive bosom as the serving woman—or proprietress? There didn't seem to be anyone else in the place—leaned over the table to set down three wooden plates filled with some kind of stew. A board with a loaf of delicious-smelling bread followed, and then the woman straightened and pulled at the neck of her chemise, further calling attention to her assets. "Bit of a dust up, Vil says. No matter, I'll have the stableman see to it, and you've my thanks for keeping it outside. And who's this then? Another dinner guest?"

"One more plate of stew, please," Romik said, his rough voice holding a friendlier note than Aelys had yet heard from the man. "And another round of your ale?"

The barmaid winked at him, her lips twisting in a suggestive smile. "Anything for you, big man," she said. Romik snorted, but his gaze intensified, and his smile deepened just a touch as she turned, deliberately swaying her hips as she walked away.

Aelys snapped her eyes back to the tabletop. She hadn't meant to pry.

Daen pushed his plate into her view. "Eat that," he said. "You look like you're about to pass out. I'll have the one she brings."

"I don't want to take your food," Aelys managed to whisper. *Mother and Daughter, Listen to me! Helpless and mewling as a kitten...but what else am I supposed to say?*

"Mirandy will bring another one in just a moment. She won't leave Romik waiting long. Will she, Ro?" Aelys looked up at the archer, but once again, his words seemed teasing and lighthearted, not barbed at all.

Certainly, Romik didn't take offense. He didn't answer, just wrapped one of those big hands around one of the mugs that sat in the center of the table, lifted it, drained it, and put it back down. He swiped the back of his sleeve across his lips, his eyes steady toward the long bar across the room. Aelys peeked over that way, and sure enough, the barmaid emerged with three mugs in one hand and a fourth plate of stew in the other. She saw Romik watching her, and her smile grew.

Stop staring! What is wrong with you?

Aelys bit her lower lip and looked down again, this time finding the plate of stew that Daen had pushed in front of her. Since his was clearly on its way, she pulled her spoon out from the pouch on her belt and dipped it into the thick, meaty gravy.

She tried not to notice the interplay. She focused on eating the surprisingly good stew and keeping her head down. But her eyes seemed unable to resist peeking out, so she knew when the barmaid arrived and set down her burdens. Aelys saw when Romik wrapped his arm around the busty woman and leaned in to whisper in her ear. Aelys heard the barmaid's throaty giggle at whatever he said and caught her saucy wink as she turned to do that same hip-swinging walk away.

"So, I take it you're in favor of staying here the night, then?" Daen said dryly. Aelys did look up then. Had they been planning to leave?

Romik shrugged. "Might as well. Bandits in the woods." He picked up one of the fresh mugs and tilted it in Aelys's direction, as if to say that she was proof.

Which, I suppose, I am.

"Um, excuse me," Aelys said before she fully realized she was about to speak. Her eyes went wide, and cold terror sliced through her as all three of the men turned the full weight of their attention to her. Behind her, the fire crackled and snapped, making her jump as her nerves flashed to life with a jolt.

"Ah, sorry," she said, forcing herself to go on. "B-But Daen said . . . perhaps I would like to hire you? I would. To escort me. Home."

"Would you, now?" Vil asked. Aelys fought not to quail as she met his dark, empty gaze again.

"Y-yes. I could clearly use the help in getting home safely. And I can pay."

"Where is home?" Daen's voice was kinder, less sardonic. Aelys felt a bit like a mouse turning its back on a mountain cat, but she switched her focus to him and took a deep breath.

"Brionne," she said. "In the mountains. My family lives there."

"Does your family work for the House?" Daen asked.

"Not exactly."

"What, exactly, then, *Bella*?" Vil's question cut through Daen's polite interest like a blade, and the sneering way he said Aelys's title made her stomach clench in fear . . . and anger.

She laid her spoon down beside her plate and turned back to face him, though it felt like all of her muscles might lock up and refuse to move. Vil continued to stare at her with that unnerving intensity. Next to him, Romik watched the interplay in between glances over toward where the barmaid had gone.

"My family *is* the House," Aelys said softly. "My name is Aelys of Brionne."

Vil didn't move, but Romik turned his full attention back to the conversation. "As in Aerivinne of Brionne?"

Aelys nodded. "She is my aunt. My mother's younger sister."

"So, you're related to the famous and most powerful Bella-trix in the past century, and yet you don't have enough power to attract an Ageon?" Vil said. The clear disbelief in his tone sparked that tiny flicker of defiance in Aelys's mind once more.

"Yes," she said, straightening her spine. "My family has a long association with the Imperial Battlemage Corps and the Lyceum Belli, but not all of us are...born suitable..." She trailed off as her throat closed up in shame and mortification. She swallowed hard and looked down at her meal, unwilling to let these rough men see her cry.

"Vil, what does it matter?" Daen asked. His voice carried an edge of exasperation. "Either she is who she says she is or she's not. Either way, it's a few days' travel to take her to Brionne. We can leave her at the gate and let the House's guards figure it out. But we could use the work."

"And I *can* pay," Aelys added.

"How much?" Romik asked. She looked at him and then glanced away quickly.

"I...I don't know—"

"Fifty Imperials," Daen said, making her jump again. Aelys blinked up at him. "Half now, half when we arrive at Brionne. Acceptable?"

It was extortionate. Aelys knew that. But she also knew that he'd inflated the price to help convince his friends to take the job. And really, what choice did she have? If they were going to hurt her, they could just as easily left her to the bandits.

They didn't know I was rich when they rescued me, fed me.

"Agreed," she said.

The three of them glanced at each other.

"Let's see—" Vil started to say, but Aelys had already reached into the inner pocket of her cloak.

Open, she thought as she brushed her fingers across the enchanted seam. She pulled out the flat pack of coins she kept on her person and counted out twenty-five of the big silver Imperi-als. She called a hint of magelight to her fingers as she closed the wallet and resealed it back inside her cloak.

A warning? A demonstration of what little power I do have?

Both, probably. It just felt like something she needed to do.

Vil's hand shot out again, and the neat stack of coins disap-peared. Neither Romik nor Daen protested. These three obviously trusted one another. Romik leaned forward, put down his ale, and reached his beefy hand across the table toward her.

Is that a tattoo on his palm? What kind of—

"We'll take your contract, Lady Aelys," he said.

Aelys swallowed hard and clasped his hand in the ancient gesture of a bargain sealed.

"Bellatrix Aelys," she said, though she felt slightly ridiculous in doing so. But she *had* graduated, so the title was hers to use, even if it was little more than an honorific. She would be Lady Aelys as soon as she returned home to take up her new life as a noble breeder for her family, so she might as well be a Bellatrix as long as she could.

"Bellatrix Aelys," he said. He squeezed her hand lightly, his thick fingers swallowing her hand whole. Then he let go and picked up his mug again. "We'll leave at first light, if that suits you. Does anyone see Mirandy? I'll see if she has a pair of rooms available."

"One for the Bella, one for Vil and me?" Daen asked. He smiled widely and winked at Aelys. She felt her face flame as her sudden courage deserted her. She looked back down at her meal.

Stupid girl. What have you gotten yourself into with these three?

As the evening wound down, Mirandy's ale spread a sunny warmth through Romik's body, and he continued his earlier trend of feeling pretty good about things. Not only did he have his brothers back, but there had been a nice little fight and a chance to help someone desperately in need of it. Even better, it turned out that she was rich and wanted to hire their newly formed band to escort her home!

And to top it all off, he still looked forward to a long, comfortable night with the buxom, willing Mirandy to warm his bed. Maybe hope wasn't a lie after all.

As if his thoughts had conjured her, the barmaid/innkeeper stepped out from the kitchen and approached the table, two keys dangling from her hand. Her gaze locked onto Romik's and his body stirred in response to her knowing smile.

"Everyone else is gone, and I'm closing up. Big man 'ere said you lot wants to stay the night," she said. "I've two rooms upstairs, both clean. Ye can have them both for two Townies apiece. And I'll throw in hot water for a bath for free...since we're such good friends and all." She winked at Romik, and he lifted his mug in salute.

"Bring the water in the morning and you've got a deal, Mirandy," Vil said. He produced four small copper coins from somewhere inside his jerkin and clicked them down on the table. Then he gave her a tight, tiny smile as she dropped the keys into his hand and picked up the coins in one swift motion.

"I'm going to go lock up," she said, pocketing the coins into her apron and turning her full attention to Romik. Her eyes wandered over his chest and shoulders, and her tongue darted out to wet her bottom lip. "I'll be right back." Her lips curved in a slow smile before she turned and sauntered back toward the kitchen.

"Here, Daen," Vil said, holding one of the keys out across the table. "You can take our client upstairs and get her settled into her room."

"Good idea." Daen took the key and stood, then gently put a hand on the girl's chair. She startled, as if she'd been half asleep, and shot to her feet. "Easy mi—Bella. It's all right. I'm just going to see you upstairs to your room. So you can rest."

The girl, her pale blue eyes wide and panicky, nodded. Daen gave her the smile Romik had seen him give to any number of young, frightened animals when they were kids and held out his arm for her to take. Next to Romik, Vil snorted softly, but Romik stayed silent.

Romik watched as she took Daen's arm and let him lead her gently toward the stairwell along the back wall of the tavern. He had to fight the urge to shake his head.

"That girl is damned lucky I was outside," Romik muttered. Next to him, Vil nodded.

"The world is no place for unsheltered, unescorted noblewomen. Which makes me wonder... *why* was she all alone?"

"Who knows? Running away from something, probably. She's young."

Vil grunted but made no other answer.

"So, probably three days—maybe four at most to see her home." Romik went on. "Daen will know better, I don't remember much about the roads around here. I've not been to Brionne, but I don't think it's farther than that. And afterward, where do you think—"

Vil shot to his feet, his skinny daggers flashing into each hand.

Romik stood and reached for his short sword just as a scream ripped through the crackling sounds of the dying fire. He spun toward the kitchen where Mirandy had gone.

A man burst through the kitchen door, holding Mirandy across his body, his fist tangled in her pretty blonde hair.

"Mirandy!" Romik shouted, ripping the sword from its sheath. A feeling like cold iron settled in his belly at the sound of her whimper. The cloaked, hooded man holding her yanked her head back against his shoulder and set the edge of his knife against her throat.

"Give us the girl, and this one lives," the brigand growled.

"Give us *that* girl, and we'll let *you* live," Vil shot back, his voice a silky purr of menace.

"Not the deal I offered," the brigand said. "Too bad, sweetheart." And he stabbed his knife into the side of Mirandy's slim white throat.

White, sun-blasted rage roared to life inside Romik's chest. The pleasant buzz from Mirandy's ale vanished in a steam explosion deep in his mind. Romik kicked his chair, sending it sliding across the room, and leapt at the murderous bastard. He stabbed low, taking the brigand high in the groin. He screamed and fell, his body crumpling around Mirandy's.

Some instinct warned Romik, and he ducked just in time to avoid losing his head as two men rushed through the kitchen door, followed by two more. Romik sidestepped, not wanting to get tangled up in the corpses or slip in their blood as it mingled and pooled in the rushes that covered the stone floor. He parried another blow and glanced around for Vil. He didn't see him, but he did see a blur as a bowstring twanged and an arrow buried itself in the throat of the next man directly in front of him.

"Daen," Romik shouted. "Get the girl out of here!"

"They've set fire to the roof!" Daen called back. "This is the only way out."

Romik sliced his sword across another bandit's unprotected face while he drew his off-hand dagger and stabbed still another one in the gut. That one cried out and crumpled, as did the one behind him, felled by Vil's knife severing the tendons behind his knee.

More bandits came boiling in through the kitchen door. Daen's bowstring sang out again and again. Romik kept hacking and swinging, trying to fight his way toward the front door, only to hear Vil yell that it was blocked and couldn't be opened.

Sweat coated Romik's hands and beaded along his hairline. Daen shouted something about the windows as he ducked a thrust and took off the arm of yet another black-cloaked assailant. He turned to look behind him, but smoke stung his eyes. Flames licked their way up the window shutters. Romik heard a breathy scream, and a small, lithe body stumbled into his back.

"Stay behind me!" he growled to the girl. He reached back with his dagger hand and felt her grip his arm to steady herself. On his left, Romik glimpsed Vil drawing nearer through the smoke. Daen's bowstring sang out on the right.

The bandits broke off their attack, retreating through the kitchen just as a mass of flaming timbers fell from the ceiling directly in front of them. Heat blasted Romik's face and he stumbled back, nearly taking the girl down underneath him. Daen grabbed his sword arm, helping him to stay upright as the three of them shuffled backward away from the flames.

"We're trapped," Vil said, his voice calm and completely empty as he spoke over the increasingly loud roar of the flames overhead. "That was our last way out."

Soft sobs rose behind Romik. He lowered his sword to turn and see the girl kneeling on the blood-tacky floor. She had her arms hugged tightly about herself, her head down as she wept.

"Idiot," she whimpered, rocking back and forth. "Too weak to break through. Break through!"

"We can't, Bella," Daen said, coughing. Holding his bow in his right hand, he knelt beside her and lightly touched her shoulder with his left.

More smoke stung Romik's eyes, burned his throat. He, too, lowered himself to one knee, sheathing his dagger and holding his sword loose in his right hand. He pulled in a breath and coughed, but the air was marginally clearer down low...for now.

"Not you," the girl whispered. "Me. Too weak...but I have to try...break through. Break through it!"

"She's lost her mind," Vil said. He, too, crouched below the building layer of smoke, his shoulder just touching hers.

"Can't blame her," Romik said. Vil looked up and gave Romik one of his rare, savage grins.

"Me neither, brother," he said. He clapped Romik's shoulder with his right hand, and with his left, he covered Daen's hand on the girl's other shoulder. Flames ran overhead, sending a wave of scorching heat cascading down. Another section of the ceiling collapsed, this one over the fireplace, crushing the table where they'd been sitting.

"Break through!" the girl cried harder, rocking faster and faster. Her head slammed forward into Romik's chest. Some instinct had him reaching up with his left hand and cradling the back of her skull, holding her as if she were a weeping child... which wasn't far from the truth.

"It's okay," he said, knowing it was a lie. Unable to help himself, he squinted over to the pile of bodies where Mirandy lay like a broken doll. Deep regret joined the smoke stinging his eyes. *I'm sorry, sweet lady. You deserved better.* "It won't be much longer," he murmured, half to Mirandy, half to the crying girl. "You're not alone. We're all here with you."

Her rocking stopped. Her head snapped up, her tear-wet blue eyes glistening in the burning light of the flames.

"With me?" she gasped. "You choose to be with me?"

Romik couldn't help himself. Of course, he wouldn't *choose* to be trapped in a burning building with anyone, let alone some slip of a rich girl he'd never met before. But in that moment, knowing that it would be among the last things he ever did, he smiled. Maybe he couldn't save Mirandy, but he could comfort this girl.

"Bella," Romik said, grinding the words out against the smoke. "Right now? With you and my brothers? Absolutely."

Vil let out a harsh laugh. "Same," he said.

"Me too," Daen added. Romik caught the white flash of his teeth as he grinned. "Wouldn't miss it."

"You *all* choose me," she whispered, and it sounded more like a statement of wonder than a question. A shudder ran through her tiny frame. Romik lowered his hand to the back of her neck in concern, and her head snapped backward, her eyes falling shut.

A deep *crack* reverberated above them, like the sound of an axle snapping. Romik squinted up into the billowing smoke and flowing flames as the wood timbers overhead began to groan. The girl started crying again.

"Break through," she whimpered. Romik tightened his grip on her neck and pulled her closer against his chest. His brothers crowded in close as well.

None of us want to die alone.

"Break through," she said again, louder this time. For just a moment, Romik wondered if she was willing the ceiling to break, willing the torment to end. He supposed he could agree with the sentiment, but still...

"BREAK. THROUGH!" she screamed, and her whole body tensed in their tangled arms. Something not cold, not hot, but somehow both flowed into Romik's hand where it touched her neck. He grunted, and the scalding, freezing power—for that was what it was, though he didn't know how he knew that—exploded out of his mouth and reached up for the flames dancing above their heads. Next to him, Romik felt Daen scream and Vil gasp, and somehow, he knew they felt it too.

This strange power that invaded their systems *reached.* Somehow, it gathered all the heat and flame of the fire and pulled it down, funneling it into three separate strands of pure energy which flowed right back the way it had come.

Through them.

Agony worse than anything Romik had ever felt wreathed each nerve. Someone screamed. Him? His brothers? All of them? The girl?

With a wrenching exertion of his will, Romik forced his eyes open to slits to check on her. Sweat and blood ran down his face. She lifted her head to stare at him, though he could see her eyes were still tightly closed.

"Give it to me."

He didn't know if he actually heard the words or just imagined them, but Romik's brain screamed its assent. Something opened between him and the girl, and the nerve-searing agony rushed toward her, flowing through the connection of his hand on her neck like water racing toward a drain.

Romik reeled, panting. His hand felt welded to the skin of her neck, but his body bowed backward away from her, breaking the contact. As he watched, Vil and Daen collapsed on either side of her as she lifted her hands toward the still-groaning, flame-damaged timbers of the ruined tavern.

"Break through," she whispered.

And the night exploded.

Get up.

Long years of training had Vil opening his eyes without moving the rest of his body. He blinked, willing the picture to come into focus, but the Dark Lady lay thick and heavy over everything, and he couldn't see for shit.

Vil inhaled, tasting smoke and death. It coated his nose and tongue, made him want to cough and spit. He forced the impulse down, for the moment. He couldn't hold it off forever, but Darkness take him if he didn't have enough control to wake silently after—

What had happened?

Images flashed across his mind, almost too rapidly to be recognized: Smoke on the ceiling, blood on the floor. Black-cloaked bandits pouring in through the kitchen. Mirandy's white throat opening up to an attacker's blade. Romik's savage scowl as he attacked. The ceiling collapsing in flames and more black smoke...

We fought, and were trapped, until the ceiling fell in, and we ended up all huddled around...

The girl. The hapless noblewoman with the too-wide eyes and skittish nerves.

Bellatrix after all, I see. My mistake.

Vil heard nothing save the soft shushing of the rising wind during all those ruminations, so he pushed himself up to a seat. Every muscle in his body ached as if he'd been beaten by ten men with clubs... but he'd survived that before, so he should be all right now.

The girl knelt, centered between where he'd lain and where Romik and Daen still lay, radiating out from her position. She slumped forward, still on her knees, her head resting on Romik's thigh. Daen let out a groan, his fingers twitching toward her form.

"Daen. Brother," Vil called out, his voice raspy from the smoke. A fat drop of water splashed down onto his cheek. Another followed, and he lifted his aching arm to pull his hood up to shield his face. "Daen. Wake up."

"Are we dead?"

The corner of Vil's mouth deepened in a half smile. Daen was all right.

"Not yet. At least, I don't think so. Check Romik. Then get the girl."

Daen rattled off a string of rather creative profanity as he pushed himself up and crawled over to inspect their warrior brother. More drops pattered down, and Vil looked up to see the rising wind blow away the obscuring fog—no, not fog, smoke— that hid the Mother's full, round face.

The tavern is gone. With this realization, Vil pushed himself up to his feet and looked around. Debris spread in all directions, stained here and there with the blood of the men they'd killed. But no structure stood taller than Vil's knees, not even the stone hearth. No fragment of wood or stone that remained was larger than a hand's span. Of the bodies, there was no sign but blood. It was as if it had all been...obliterated.

Vil turned back to look at the girl. She lay in Romik's lap as Daen helped him sit up. Romik squinted in pain and held his left hand to his head, though his right hand still gripped his sword. That, too, made Vil smile. Daen's bowstring had snapped, but the bow itself appeared unhurt, lying beside where he crouched.

"We should get moving," Vil said. "We don't know how many of those bandits there were."

Romik and Daen both looked up at his words, and only Vil's strictest training kept him from flinching as he met their gaze.

"Vil—" Daen said, sounding strangled. "Your eyes!"

Vil held himself to stillness, counting through the calming, freezing exercises he'd learned as a child thief hiding on the streets of Cievers.

"What about them?" he asked, keeping his tone even and empty. "Have they become a ghostly, almost glowing blue?"

"How did you know?" Daen's words sounded sick, like he already knew the answer.

"Because ours are that way, too." It was Romik who answered, turning back to meet Daen's gaze. "See?"

"All of us?" Daen breathed. "What happened? Is this another brotherhood thing?"

"I don't know," Vil said. "But I know I don't want to be sitting here trying to figure it out when those bandits return. Or when someone else comes to investigate the fire and explosion at the old tavern."

"Right." Daen shook himself and picked up his bow, frowning at the snapped bowstring. He sighed and pulled a spare cord from a pouch at his belt and restrung the weapon with neat, economical movements. Then he reached a hand down to help Romik up.

Romik hadn't moved.

"What about her?" he asked, looking down at the girl lying on his thigh. Vil watched, something dark curling deep in his belly as Romik's big fingers tenderly brushed a curl of her wispy, white-blond hair away from her cheek.

"Bring her," Vil snapped more curtly than he meant to do. "She's our client, after all."

"Help me lift her."

"Daen will help. I'll go see if the bastards left our horses in the stable." Vil knew that there was no way the bandits had done any such thing, but he couldn't take another minute of seeing the look on Daen's face as he bent to cradle the girl's limp form close, or the way Romik had touched her hair... or the way the rain splashing onto her pale face had twisted like a knife in his own chest.

Especially not that last.

Instead, Vil focused on the dark shape of the stone stable set back amongst the trees. It occurred to him that while it was unlikely that the bandits had left the stable unplundered, there *was* a chance that one or more of them might have sheltered there from the inn's explosion.

At least, I hope *they have...*

The Lady Darkness wrapped the night's shadows around him as he angled to the side and wound through the trees and around behind the back of the stable. This forest was quite old, so it didn't take him long to find a tree that stretched high enough for his purposes. Vil pulled his hood close to hide his white hair and hauled himself up into the tree as easily as if it had been an open second-story window in Cievers's merchant district. Darkness smiled on him, and a remaining wisp of smoke flowed over the Mother's bright face as he reached the branch he sought. Vil seized the moment and leapt across the short gap to the small opening in the hayloft. He hit softly, as he'd trained for years to do, and pulled himself in.

Once inside, Vil crouched in the musty hay and listened for the stamp and whinny of horses, or the footfalls and voices of men. Nothing. The place was quiet as a tomb.

Well, of course the bandits took the horses. They'd hardly be proper bandits otherwise. Still, there's something...

Without a sound, Vil climbed down the ladder. It wasn't until his soft-soled boot touched the packed earthen floor that he realized what he was sensing.

Or smelling, to be specific. Quiet the barn may have been, but it reeked of blood and shit—the scents of death. With a step, Vil faded back into the embrace of his Lady, sliding against the walls, avoiding the Mother's light as she shone through the open barn doors.

The bandits *had* left men. Four of them lay roughly in a circle just outside the door. Enough dagger-sized shards of stone and wood riddled their bodies that they looked as if they'd been flayed. The debris from the inn's explosion must have perforated lungs, arteries, and by the smell of it, bowels.

With nothing left to do, Vil sidled past the bodies and out into the night. Once he was outside, he could see the extensive damage to the front of the barn from the inn's explosion. He didn't backtrack fully, but he kept beneath the sheltering trees in the Dark Lady's embrace down the slope for as long as possible and watched as his brothers carried the limp form of the girl toward him. Again, he pushed away the odd wrenching he felt at the sight of her.

Once they had come within earshot, Vil lowered his hood and stepped forward, letting the Mother paint him. Romik's and Daen's strange eyes seemed to glow in the Motherlight, and Vil spared a thought to wonder if his did the same.

"They took the horses and left four men, but they were dead before I got there," he said without preamble as he skidded down the slick grassy slope toward them. "Shards from the explosion killed them."

Romik blew out a breath and hitched the girl higher against his chest. He'd apparently taken her back into his arms after he stood up, though Vil noticed that Daen continually wound his fingers through a loose strand of her pale blonde hair. Vil's own fingers twitched, and it took more effort than he wanted to admit to keep from reaching out to touch her for himself.

"Without the horses, we can't get far," he said, gritting his teeth at the effort it took to focus on what they needed here and now. The rain continued to pelt down, rolling off his woolen cloak—for the time being. "And we need to get her out of this storm."

Her? Us! All of us—what is wrong with me? What is wrong with them?

"I know a place," Daen said, his voice rough. He continued to play with her hair, his eyes locked on her face. "It's not far."

"Daen. Daen!" Vil snapped his fingers in front of his brother's face until Daen blinked and looked at him. His ghostly blue eyes had gone glassy, but they sharpened again as they focused on Vil.

"Where is this place?" Vil asked.

"Not far," Daen repeated, but this time without that eerie dreaminess. "A cave. Just a little ways into the forest. I can take us there."

"Good. You lead, I'll guard our rear. Romik, you've got her?" Vil leaned in until his warrior brother looked up and met his eyes.

"I do," Romik said softly. "It's the damnedest thing. I couldn't... she's..."

"I know, brother," Vil admitted, almost in a whisper. "Something's shifted. We all feel it. Let's just get to Daen's cave and we'll figure it out."

At least, I hope we'll be able to figure it out, Vil thought as he fell into place guarding Romik's—and the girl's—back.

◀ CHAPTER THREE ▶

THE CAVE WASN'T FAR FROM THE INN AT ALL, WHICH WAS WHY Daen had chosen it to cache his gear for his departure from the Foresters. He *did* find it harder than it should have been to find the thin game trail that would lead him to the creek that wound next to the entrance. He had to keep fighting the urge to look back and drink in the sight of her.

Her.

Aelys of Brionne. A rutting noblewoman, of all things. What have you done to me, Bella?

Daen was no stranger to women, nor to the ways in which they would sometimes use their pretty faces and lush bodies to twist men up and bend them to their feminine wills. He'd seen plenty of Foresters distracted and duped by tricksy women, and he swore that he'd never be like that. He'd never compromise his honor, or lose his focus, just to get a woman in his bed.

Not that I've ever had to work particularly hard on that score, he reflected with a smirk as he started up a sloping hill. Women seemed to like his rangy build and chiseled face well enough that he typically had no trouble finding bed partners.

Is that what I want? Her in my bed?

Daen ducked under a low-hanging branch and glanced back over his shoulder at her pale form cradled close in Romik's arms. The thought didn't seem *wrong* exactly...just...incomplete. She was beautiful, it was hard to take his eyes off her; he *did* want to hold her and caress her skin and...

And. There's never been an and *before.*

But he couldn't ignore the twisting anxiety in his gut whenever he looked at her unconscious and vulnerable form. His hands itched to cup her face and urge her to come back to awareness, to come back to *him.* Every time he turned away from her to focus on following the trail, it felt like some amateur bard was sitting in his head, sawing away at a lute to make the most benighted noise.

Once more, Daen glanced over his shoulder.

"I'm right here," Romik said, his low rumble of a voice edged with irritation.

"It's not *you* I'm worried about," Daen said before he could think better of it.

"She's right here, too."

"Is she all right?"

"How should I know? She's breathing. Red Lady grant that she's only sleeping." Romik hitched her up higher in his arms.

"Do you need a break?" Daen asked, trying to keep the question casual, even as his heartbeat accelerated in sudden need. "I can take her for a while."

"No," Romik said. "We need you to follow this so-called trail. It's all but invisible to me. I'll carry her. She's not that heavy."

Daen clamped his mouth shut and turned back to the forest in front of him, and the perfectly visible game trail they were following. Either Romik was a complete, blind idiot or...

Or I just really want to hold her.

The thought startled Daen so much he stepped unwisely, and a twig cracked under his foot. Immediately, his face flushed red, and he shook his head angrily at himself.

Idiot! Now you sound like the two cobbleheads behind you! Pay attention, Daen. Get the girl out of your head and focus!

But he couldn't. For the rest of the way to his cache, Daen alternated between glancing back at her and following the correct path. Romik sighed a little louder every time Daen turned around, but he didn't say anything.

Which was good, because Daen was getting more and more antsy with every step. By the time he led them across the thin trickle of water from the natural spring and down into the cave entrance, his hands visibly trembled with his need to touch her.

"Down here," he said, skidding down the rough-hewn stairs

that generations of Foresters had once used and then forgotten. With hurried, half-absent motions, he unslung his quiver and bow and hung them on the hooks provided. Then he turned and raised his arms toward where Romik crouched in the narrow entrance.

"Hand her through to me."

"No, I—"

"Romik, this isn't a city staircase. These steps are narrow and uneven. Hand her to me, lest you trip and break both of your necks!" Daen didn't bother to disguise the impatience in his tone. He couldn't see his warrior brother's face, but Romik hesitated long enough for Vil to mutter darkly behind him.

"Romik. Do it. So we can all get inside out of the cursed rain."

Slowly, Romik crouched and lowered the girl down. Daen stepped up beside the stairs and put his arms under her slender form. He drew her in to his chest, marveling at the warmth of her, the way her weight felt *right* in his arms. Like drawing a fine bow, or the whistle of an arrow flying true.

"Daen—" Romik broke off, sounding strangled.

"I've got her," Daen breathed. He stepped backward into the cave, his eyes never leaving her face. "I won't let her go."

"Daen. Is there light down there?"

Light? Of course there's light. Don't you see the Mother shining on her face, in her hair?

"Daen!"

Daen jumped and cradled her closer to his chest, looking up with a growl. "What?"

"It's darker than the Red Lady's humor down there! Have you got a lantern or something? Like you said, I don't want to break my neck!"

"Oh. Right." There were lanterns, but he would need both hands free to light them, and Daen had no intention of letting the girl—Aelys. He should use her name—go long enough to light either them or the fire that lay waiting on the hearth.

Though she *would* need a fire's warmth. Her cloak was soaked through, and her face felt clammy when he laid his cheek down upon her forehead to check.

"Here," Daen said, energy and purpose flooding into his body, his tone and movements. With the toe of his boot, he nudged a mirror set near the floor so that it caught the thin stream of Motherlight that filtered down into the cave. This reflected stream shot across the space, bouncing off another mirror, and hitting a carved crystal that dispersed the pale light through the space. It didn't quite dispel the gloom entirely, but at least they could see what lay directly in front of them.

"She's freezing," Daen said, turning to kneel in front of the pallet of blankets set up against the far, curving wall of the cave. "There's a fire already laid in that hearth there. Get it lit and I'll get these wet clothes off of her."

Romik let out a growl that had Daen turning to look at him, eyebrows raised in a half-mocking challenge.

"Red Lady's tits you will!" Romik snapped.

"Do you want her to die of hypothermia?" Daen shot back. "Her clothes are soaked. If we don't get her out of them, she'll just get colder and colder, no matter how big you build the fire!"

"But—"

"Romik. Just light the damned fire. Daen's not going to take liberties, he's just going to strip her down and get her under the covers so she can warm up." Vil's voice filtered down through the dimness from the entrance at the top of the stairs.

"Someone should get in with her—" Daen started to say, but Romik's growl warned him, and he fell silent as Vil jumped off the side of the stairs to stand between the two men.

"No. Daen, just put her in the bed and cover her up. Romik will build the fire. And then we need to talk."

A part of Daen wanted to protest. No one had elected Vil their leader. But just as had sometimes happened when they were kids, he found himself obeying before he really thought about it. Such was Vil's force of will. When he cared enough about something to take a stand, he was nearly impossible to defy.

So instead, Daen turned his attention to the woman in his arms. With great care, he knelt and tenderly laid her on the pallet of blankets before unclasping her sodden cloak from around her neck. He pulled it out from under her and found to his surprise that the gown beneath wasn't really damp at all. He'd give Romik credit; he must have made sure Aelys was well covered and protected from the rain.

Moving slowly so as not to jar her, Daen pulled the topmost cover down, noting with satisfaction that it was one of the tanned furs that some long-ago Forester had taken from a large forest animal—likely a bearcat, based on the rosette pattern of the fur.

As Romik's fire caught and began painting the cave walls with warm, flickering light, Daen got the fur out from underneath Aelys, removed her boots and stockings, and then pulled the fur back up to cover her, gown and all, from the tips of her toes to her ears. Only the top of her head and the tip of her nose peeked out, and Daen couldn't resist leaning down to brush his lips against her forehead.

"Daen," Vil said, his voice a warning.

"I'm coming," Daen said, and tucked a stray strand of wet hair away from Aelys's face. Then he straightened and turned to see both of his sworn brothers staring at him with those eerily blue eyes. He couldn't read Vil's expression—no surprise, that—but Romik's pinched brow and curled lips weren't hard to interpret at all. Defiance rose, hot and spiky within his chest, and Daen let his lips curve in the slow smirk he'd perfected in the Forestry Service. He stepped away from Aelys's bed but let his fingers trail across the top of her hair.

Mostly because he didn't want to stop touching her. But it didn't hurt to see Romik's big hands clench into fists.

Gonna fight me for her, big man? So much for sworn brothers, hmm? The thought twisted agonizingly inside Daen's chest, but he only straightened his shoulders and held his ground.

"For the love of all the Divines, will the two of you quit? You're acting like a pair of bull moose posturing over a cow!" Vil's words weren't loud, but they were cutting. Romik blinked. The pain inside Daen's chest eased, and he let his shoulders relax. He did wink briefly at Romik, just to let him know that he hadn't won outright, and then turned to drop down to sit on the floor beside Vil.

The cave wasn't exactly spacious, especially not with all three—four, if he counted the sleeping woman—of them crowded inside. But it was a decently configured space. Shelves lined the walls on either side of the hearth, some carved into the stone like the fireplace itself, some built out using thick wooden planks. A small, scarred table sat below the side of the stairs they'd come down, with two chairs directly across from the pile of blankets where Aelys slept. Romik's fire threw a warm, cozy light throughout the cave, and Daen reached out a hand to adjust the mirror alignment, which amplified the light still further.

"All right," Vil said after a moment's silence, when it became clear that neither Daen nor Romik intended to speak first. "What have we got?"

"What do you mean?" Romik grumbled, still glaring at Daen.

"I mean, the situation has changed. So, we need to take stock, figure out what we're working with. So, what have we got?"

"Here? In this cache?" Daen asked.

"To start."

"Well, I've been laying in supplies here for the past little while," Daen said. "So, there's some food in that trunk under the table. But I was only planning for myself, so it won't last long. The spring outside the entrance is pure, so we've got drinking water for as long as we want it, and there's enough wood there to get us through probably two nights before we have to collect more." He waved a hand at the lowest shelf on either side of the hearth, which held rows of neatly stacked logs and branches.

"Can we hunt here?"

"Legally? No. This is imperial forest. But that's good, it means that game will be more plentiful."

"Unless you get caught poaching," Romik said. Daen snorted.

"My former 'brothers' couldn't catch an amateur poacher if he pissed on them. Let alone get even a whiff of me. We'll be fine for game. It's not a concern."

"What about medicines, tonics, healing herbs?" Vil asked. Daen grimaced and shrugged.

"Eh. Not much. Some basic first-aid herbs, maybe. Arrowroot, probably, to poultice a cut until we can get to a healer, but I don't think there's more than that."

"Brandy or spirits?"

"Some," Daen said, with a ghost of a smile around his lips. "There on the shelf behind Romik."

"Perfect. Romik, grab it, will you?"

"Why?"

Vil turned to glare at their glowering brother, and Daen stifled a chuckle.

"Because I need a fucking drink, and your sullen ass does too! What in Darkness's name is *wrong* with you?"

Romik let out an inarticulate snarl in answer, but he also reached up and grabbed one of the bottles of brandy on the hearthside shelf and tossed it. Vil's hand shot out with that unnerving quickness of his, and he snatched the bottle out of the air, uncorked it, and took a long pull.

Daen felt his eyebrows rise. He'd noticed, back at the inn,

that while he and Romik had both consumed many mugs of poor Mirandy's ale, Vil had nursed a single mug for the whole night until...

Well, until whatever happened, happened. I'm still not sure what that was.

"Drink," Vil said, his voice roughened by the spirits. Daen hadn't said it was *good* brandy, after all.

Romik leaned forward, took the bottle from Vil's outstretched hand and took a long, deep drink. When he lowered the bottle, he looked over at Daen and paused.

Daen raised an eyebrow and waited.

"I know what's wrong with me," Romik said as he slowly held the bottle out. "I just don't know what to do about it."

Daen took the bottle and let himself relax. "The girl?" he guessed as he accepted the bottle for the peace offering it was.

"Yeah," Romik said, letting his eyes drift over to her sleeping form.

Daen thought about answering, but just took his drink instead. Heat like a sunburn erupted throughout his mouth and seared its way down into his gut. He lowered the bottle and let out a cough, then handed it back to Vil.

"I think you're right," Vil said, corking the bottle and putting it firmly to one side. "It's the girl."

"Aelys," Daen said, and though he didn't consciously intend it, his voice held a clear warning.

"What?"

"Her name is Aelys, not 'the girl.' It's not like we don't know her."

"It's not like we *do*!" Vil said, narrowing his eyes. "She just shows up at the tavern—"

"No, she showed up on the road being chased by bandits. Romik brought her to the tavern."

"That just further proves my point! She could be anyone! She claims to be a battlemage, but she has no protector, but she's apparently from one of the richest families in the empire and wants to hire us. All right, well and good, but then the bandits come back and *try to bargain with us for her?* What about that sounds normal to either of you?" Vil leaned forward, looking pointedly at Romik and Daen both.

"It all seems normal, compared to the rest of it," Romik grumbled. "Compared to what happened after."

"What, exactly, did happen? After?" Daen said. "I still don't really know."

"I don't either." Vil's tone said clearly that he intensely disliked having to admit his lack of knowledge. "Romik?"

Romik shook his head but couldn't resist shifting closer to the pallet where Aelys lay sleeping.

"Romik."

"What?" the big man's head snapped up. "No! I don't know what happened! All I know is we were kneeling there with her, about to burn to death, and she asked if we'd stay with her and we said yes, and then all of a sudden it felt like she pulled the fire *through* me...and then the building exploded and since then I feel like I'm going insane because it feels like my skin itches or aches or both unless I'm actively holding her!"

"Me too." Daen spoke quietly, but it was loud enough for Vil and Romik to both look sharply at him. He met their eerie blue gazes and nodded. "That's exactly how it feels."

"Yes," Vil said. "It does."

"You too?" Romik's question carried an edge that was something between relief and despair. "You didn't say anything, so I hoped..."

"Hope is a lie, brother. Whatever she did, she did it to all of us. I feel the pull as well. It's like the world shifted and she's at the center of it. I...I *have* to protect her, like she's somehow *mine*. And when you—either of you—protect her instead of me... it's hard. Harder than it should be. Not like I'm jealous, just that...it should be me."

"That's exactly it," Daen murmured again.

"So, yeah," Vil said. "I feel it too. I'm just...better at hiding."

For the first time since they'd arrived in the cavern, Daen turned and really *looked* at Vil. Sure enough, there was a tightness around his eyes that hadn't been there the night before. His hands remained rock steady, but as he looked, he noticed Vil subtly leaning forward, closer to the pile of blankets, almost as if he were being pulled by an invisible thread.

"Vil. Touch her," Daen said.

"What?" Romik asked, the warning back in his voice.

"Not like that," Daen said, disgust with the idea churning in his stomach. "Just...Vil. Trust me, it gets better if you do. What you said...that's why I didn't want to put her down, probably

why Ro here didn't want to give her to me. Just touch your fingertips to her forehead. It will make it better."

"I'll be fine," Vil said, his voice icy.

Daen rolled his eyes. "Are we going to do this? Really? All
right. You're leaning toward her so far you're about to fall and
bust your pretty face on the floor of this cave. Your hands haven't
moved from where you have them placed oh-so-casually on your
knees, which means you're holding them there with a consider-
able amount of will. You glance at me but stare at Romik, only
I bet it's not really at Romik, because you're talking to both of
us equally. Even now, as I'm running down this list and pissing
you off, you can't help but look over there. But not at Romik.
At her lying next to him.

"You said it yourself. You feel the pull too. Like she's *yours*.
Like she needs you. Like you're going to go mad if you don't
touch her. So, touch her."

Vil did look at him then, his blue eyes ablaze with an intensity
that might have been hatred, or rage, or maybe even gratitude.
Slowly, he closed his hands into fists on his knees, his gaze
locked on Daen's.

"It makes it better, Vil. I swear." Daen half expected Romik
to protest, but instead, the big man just reached out and drew
the fur cover back enough to expose Aelys's face.

Vil shot forward like a viper striking. In a blink, he knelt
beside her head, his right hand out, fingers hovering over her
brow. Daen watched as his sworn brother's chest rose and fell
rapidly, as if he were gasping for breath, though he made no
sound at all.

Bit by bit, Vil lowered his hand until his fingertips brushed
along the arch of Aelys's eyebrow. Daen saw his voice box bob
as he swallowed twice, thrice while he traced the lines of her
face with a touch that looked feather light. Vil closed his eyes,
and finally, Daen saw the tension leak out of his sworn brother's
cloak-clad shoulders.

"Enough," Vil whispered. Daen blinked in confusion, then
looked over at Romik.

"Vil, what—we're not doing anyth—"

"Not you," Vil said, pulling his hand back suddenly, as if her
skin had burned him. "Me. Enough. You were right. It did make
it better. I can...think, now."

He stood up, still staring down at her sleeping face, and then spun back toward the fire.

"If she's only sleeping, we should be all right without much in the way of healing herbs, but we will need food. I don't think we'll have a plan and be ready to travel tomorrow, and I have... questions for her."

"Vil," Romik said, his voice a rumbled warning.

Vil snorted softly and turned to look sidelong at him. "I will be civil, brother, don't worry. But she did *something* to all of us to cause..." Then he waved a hand toward Aelys without looking in her direction.

Is he afraid? Daen wondered. *Am I afraid? What* did *she do?*

"I'll go out hunting tomorrow. Romik can come with me. With the two of us, we'll get enough to last a couple of days. Enough time to figure out a plan, anyway."

"But—" Romik started to protest.

"Romik," Vil said, turning to the big warrior. He crouched down and looked directly into Romik's eyes. "Listen to me. I know you feel like she's this precious crystal jewel that will shatter if you leave her unattended. Didn't you hear me earlier? We all feel it. Every impulse you have is raging through both Daen and me, too. Whatever she did—"

"She did to all of us," Romik finished, nodding. "Like...like maybe she needs all of us to keep her safe. All right. You're right. I'm sorry, it's just..."

"I know. But I am your brother, sworn so before three Divines. Whatever she did doesn't change that." Vil stripped the black glove he'd been wearing off his right hand and held his palm up, letting the light from the fire illuminate the brotherhood mark there. "*Nothing* will change that. You can trust me to protect her while you help Daen bring her—*us* something to eat."

"Wait. Vil. What is that?" Daen asked, pointing at the dark band that circled his brother's wrist. "You didn't have that before, in the tavern, when we swore..." Certainty flooded his body, and Daen reached down to pull up the sleeve of his jerkin, exposing his own wrist.

And the two-finger-wide band that circled it. Like the brotherhood mark, it was embedded into his skin. He rubbed at it, though he already knew it wouldn't smudge, or wipe away. *Dark blue*, he realized as he angled it to catch the firelight. *Not black, not green nor red. So, none of our Divines' doing? Then what—?*

"It's like the eyes. Something to do with the girl. Romik has it too," Vil said softly.

"Ro?" Daen asked.

Romik nodded, casting his gaze down on the floor. But he moved slowly to lift his sleeve and show off his own blue band. "She marked us, changed our eyes. It's like she owns..." He trailed off. Vil reached out to grip his shoulder as silence filled the cave, broken only by the crackle of the fire.

"I'll take first watch," Daen said, needing to change the subject and clear his head. He pushed up to his feet, and even though a corner of his mind screamed at him to go to Aelys, to stretch out beside her and cradle her sleeping form close, he turned his back and focused on grabbing his bow and cloak from the hook by the stairs. "I'll be up by the entrance."

"I'll take the second and then Romik can wake you before sunrise for your hunt," Vil said, straightening up and moving toward the small trunk. "In the meantime, I'll see what I can make from the provisions you stored here. I'll bring you something in a bit."

Daen nodded, then started up the stairs toward the cave mouth. Like Vil had done, he avoided looking at the girl sleeping on the pallet.

Because if I do, I won't be able to leave her side.

Somewhere above her head, flames crackled.

Flames crackle overhead. Fear and smoke choke me. I reach, slamming up against the barrier of my own weakness. I scream, raging against the pain and knowledge that keeps me bound and helpless, alone.

"You're not alone. We're all here with you."

A tiny thread of hope. They are here with me? They choose to be with me?

They choose me?

A new energetic pathway—three new pathways open. Tiny, treacherous, but there. I let my consciousness slip down all three at once, squeezing through passages stretching little by little to accommodate my presence... and there...

A conflagration of energy, twisting and dancing, right at my fingertips. Power, so much power, more than I had ever dreamed possible. Waiting for me to take it, and twist it, and make it my own.

I pull it...and it comes to me! In a triple strand of ecstatic agony, the power flows through those virgin pathways into my mind. For the first time in my life, I take the knowledge I'd fought so hard to accumulate and I use it. I shape this power, I make it my own. And with it I...

"Broke through," Aelys whispered. The words feathered against her chapped, dry lips. Awareness returned in a rush, erasing the fading wisps of memory—or dream? She ached, but it was the ache of remembered physical exertion, a pleasant warmth throughout her body, rather than true pain. Woodsmoke scented the air, and she was deliciously warm, lying on something soft, covered by fur.

Boots scuffed behind her. Aelys held herself still and listened.

"How is she?" The warrior from the tavern—Romik. His voice still held its distinctive gravelly sound, but he pitched it softly, almost a whisper.

"The same." That was Daen. "Breathing easily enough, just... sleeping."

"It's been a whole day. The sun is setting."

"I know, but I didn't want to wake her if she needed the rest. Who knows how much power it took to do...what she did?"

What exactly did I do?

"I know." Vil's silky voice came from slightly farther away, but Aelys could hear him drawing nearer as he continued speaking. "Or at least I have a good idea. As do both of you. Didn't you *feel* it, when she pulled the fire right through us? Of course she's exhausted. Let her sleep."

"I'm awake," Aelys said. She opened her eyes but couldn't see much. She squinted against the stinging behind her eyelids and rubbed at her face, pushing herself up to a seated position.

"Welcome back, Bella," Daen said, and it sounded like he smiled. Aelys pushed her hands up to run them into her hairline and pushed back the tangled mess of her hair.

"Ugh, I'm so sorry. I must look an absolute mess. What ha—" She lowered her hands and blinked, then froze as she got a good look at the three men. Daen crouched in front of her, handsome with the smile she'd expected. Romik sat with his elbows resting on his knees in a rickety wooden chair that creaked every time he shifted. Behind him and a little off to the side, Vil stood leaning against a set of uneven stairs that appeared to lead up into the late evening sunshine. He had his arms crossed over his chest and his eyes fixed firmly on Aelys's face.

All three of them stared at her.

With bright, almost glowing blue eyes.

Just like mine.

"What happened?" Vil asked, his lips twisting in something that might have been intended to be a dark kind of smile. "Why don't you tell us?"

"Your eyes—" Aelys whispered, her fingertips coming to touch her lips in awe and dawning horror.

"I think you mean *your* eyes," Romik said, a gruff edge in his voice. "They're exactly the same as ours. What does that mean, Bella? What did you do to us?"

Aelys swallowed hard, looking from him, to Daen, and finally to Vil. Chill dread crept through her being, and she swallowed once more against the dry ashiness coating the inside of her mouth. With trembling fingers, she pushed the sleeve of her cloak up her left arm.

Three rings circled her wrist, each a finger's width. The fire snapped, sending a flare of brightness washing over her skin, illuminating their colors: scarlet, viridian, and deep, deep black.

"Could I have some water?" Aelys whispered, playing for time. Romik reached for a waterskin sitting on the table beside him, and handed it forward to Daen, who extended it to her. Aelys took it with murmured thanks. Her hands continued to shake as she removed the stopper and lifted it tentatively to her lips.

Gloriously cool water teased at her tongue. Aelys closed her eyes and tilted her head back, drinking greedily, even as her mind raced.

How could this have happened? What did I do? This...how is this possible?

Their eyes. My eyes...Seeing with my eyes...

Dusty words on an ancient parchment floated forward from the halls of her memory. In all of her studies, Aelys had only ever read of such a phenomenon in one source, and that source was so old as to be relegated to the category of legend. It was an ancient Bellene text that predated the Lyceum entirely. It hadn't even been a proper book, just a scroll translated from an even older text translated from an ancient inscription found in a temple destroyed by the Bellenes in the days long before the empire arose.

Aelys lowered the waterskin and looked down at her hands, slowly whispering the Bellenic words she'd remembered.

> "Bind ye, workers, thy swords and shields.
> "See then they, with thine eyes.
> "Deeds defend, thy needs to mend.
> "Through death the *geas* realized."

"What is that?" Daen asked. He spoke gently, but his words had an edge of anxiety and ... not quite trust.

Not that I can blame him. If I've done this ...

Aelys's vision blurred, her eyes filling with liquid shame. She ducked her head down, curling into herself.

"I am sorry," she said, afraid to meet the accusing stare of her own eyes looking back at her. "I'm so sorry. I don't know how this could have happened. I didn't even know it was really *possible*—"

"You didn't know *what* was possible?" Romik asked, his voice far less patient than Daen's had been. Aelys swallowed hard and forced her chin up, forced herself to look at the horrifying thing she'd done to these three men who had never been anything but kind to her.

"I bound you," she whispered, feeling the words staining the air with her guilt. "Not in the usual way, where you choose me, and we make oaths in front of witnesses ... but in the old way. The ... ancient way. It's been all but forgotten, or maybe suppressed. It's—" She stopped as her throat closed up, choked by tears of remorse.

"It's what?" Romik asked.

"It's horrible. It's evil. I ... I somehow bound you using energy—magic. It's how the old mages used to take warriors for their protectors ... whether the warriors agreed or not." The tears overflowed her eyes, running in a hot line down her cheek.

"Just now?" Daen asked. "When you said those words?" Confusion creased his handsome face, and Aelys shook her head, hunching further into herself.

"No," she said. "I was just remembering the old text. Ancient, really. From a civilization that predates the empire. No one even remembers their proper name. They were conquered by another people, the Bellenes, who developed much of what we know about magical theory and practice before the empire defeated them and assimilated them into our culture. Most mages think it was the Bellenes who pioneered the practice of linking mages to warriors and using them in battle, but they're wrong. They learned from that other, older culture. Anyway, when the empire finally conquered the Bellenes, imperial mages studied their records and methods. Those lines are part of a larger historical text explaining how when a mage took a protector, the power of the mage's binding—or *geas*, as they called it in the ancient language—would change the color of the warrior's eyes. It was... it was how they knew the *geas* had been a success." She looked down at her hands again, picking at the fur that still covered her lap. The green ring peeked out of her sleeve at her, as if it were taunting her with her own incompetence.

"That's why your eyes have changed," she said, hearing the misery in her voice. "And... do you have marks? On your wrists?"

"Like manacles," Romik growled, and a spike of fear shot through Aelys's stomach. "Yes. All of us."

"Th-they're not manacles," she whispered, curling further into herself. "They're b-bracelets. They symbolize our bond, and your role as my p-protectors."

"What does that mean, 'protectors'?" Vil asked.

"It means... you're my Ageons. A-as if you'd chosen me at the Lyceum. It means you are responsible for keeping me safe. And I, in turn, am responsible for your social standing and your well-being—"

"We never agreed to that!" Romik ground out, anger flaring in his face. Aelys gulped back the rest of her words and nodded.

"I know," she whispered. "That's why it has to be a *geas*. It's the only way it makes sense. But I didn't mean—I would never—"

"Is there a way to break it, this *geas*?" Vil's voice carried no emotion.

"I don't know," Aelys whispered. There was, of course, one obvious way. But she wasn't about to suggest her murder to the three violently capable men in front of her.

"What do you know?"

Aelys looked up at Daen, prodded by the gentle encourage-ment in his tone. His eyes, although so eerily blue, looked at her with compassion, rather than anger. Aelys felt more tears welling up within, and she sniffed loudly to try and hold them back.

"Not much, unfortunately." She focused hard on the words, trying desperately to calm her trembling voice. "The barbarian records don't speak of any particular way to dissolve the *geas*, but logic dictates that there must be one. What is done by magic may usually be undone by magic, after all. That is one of the first things we learn. My aunt might know. If . . . if you're still willing to take me home, perhaps she can help us."

Misery flooded up from deep within as Aelys's mind started down the all-too-familiar spiral of self-recrimination and hatred. Her shoulders shook, and she couldn't suppress a sob as she col-lapsed into herself again.

"Shhh," Daen said softly. Furs rustled, and hard, callused hands gripped her shoulders, pulling her into an embrace. She stiffened and flinched back out of his arms.

"It's okay, Bella," Daen said, his voice carrying a touch of hurt. Guilt for that lashed Aelys's mind even further. Especially because he let her go, but his hand lingered on her shoulder.

He's still trying to comfort me. Even now. Even after every-thing I've . . .

"Let her be, Daen," Romik said. "Let her cry about it if she wants to. Her plan is sound, we'll take her home and see her aunt about breaking this *geas*. Then we can all get back to our lives."

Aelys bent double over her knees, arms wrapped tightly around herself. More tremors wracked her thin frame as Romik's disdain rolled toward her on a near-palpable cloud.

And why not? Why shouldn't he despise me? Too weak for a proper Ageon, and yet I have the gall to accidentally *bond three* unwilling *protectors? I would despise me too.*

As I do. As I always have.

More rustling of furs meant Daen rose to his feet. She heard Romik join him. Their booted steps echoed on the stairs as they left the tiny forest cave. Only then did Aelys let go of what little control she'd been holding.

All of her agony and self-hatred and misery began to flow from her eyes in scalding tears. She opened her mouth in a soundless scream and buried her face in the fur blanket beneath her. Her entire body shook, spasming and trembling until she lay weak, wrung out.

Wasted. Just like mother always said.

"Are you done?"

Vil's voice shivered through Aelys with a jolt. She startled up to her knees, blinking in the dimness. The fire had burned down, leaving a bed of smoldering coals that put out heat, but not much light. Outside, the sun must have set. She looked toward the stairs to see the vague shape of a darker shadow sitting sideways in the chair where Romik had earlier been.

"I—I think so."

"Good. They will be back soon, with food. You'll eat, then sleep. We'll leave in the morning."

"Why—why did you stay?" She reached for the waterskin that still lay beside her in the furs.

"To protect you," he said, his voice a low murmur as she drank. "That is what I am, am I not? Your protector? Your sword and shield? Or in my case, I'm more like your knife in the dark."

"Y-yes," she said, lowering the flask. "I suppose so. For now. But I'm not going to hold you to anything, obviously. If you don't want to—"

"I can't seem to help myself. You have suddenly become very important."

Aelys swallowed hard and pushed back against the spent remnant of her misery as it weakly tried to rise again. "I know," she whispered. "I'm so sorry. That's the *geas* at work."

"That is why they're called Ageons, is it not? Same root word as *geas*?"

"Yes," Aelys said, blinking in surprise at this turn of conversation. "It meant 'bound one' in the barbarian tongue."

"What do they do currently? For the binding?"

"Um," Aelys reached up to push her tangled hair back out of her face. "Well, there's a ceremony."

"What kind of ceremony?"

She took a deep breath, inhaling the smoky, woodsy scent of the fire. "All right," she said. "I suppose. It isn't secret or anything. Um, so at the Lyceum Belli, there are two kinds of candidates. Mage candidates and Ageon candidates—"

"Yes, I know. They train there together. I lived in Cievers for many years. I'm familiar with the Lyceum."

"Right. I'm sorry," she said. "Um, so the idea is that while we're learning, we'll learn about each other, too. So, we can form attachments . . . to be formalized after we graduate."

"Formalized by this ceremony."

"Yes." She shifted in her seat. "Right. Um, so after graduation, we—the new mages—all wait, kind of in a circle, at one end of the grand hall. Behind and around us, in the galleries, the instructors all stand as witnesses, so it's a big occasion. The Ageon candidates line up and one by one, they walk down the length of the hall toward us and kneel in the center of the circle—" She paused as memory thickened her voice with more shame.

No. Enough. You've cried enough today.

"And then what?"

"And then they choose." Aelys forced the words out, blinking furiously to keep from weeping again.

"And the bracelets?"

"After the Ageon chooses, they both swear the oaths. One of the Sanvari comes forward to put the bracelets on their wrists and seals them shut with magic. It's symbolic of the Lyceum and society recognizing the bond between them."

"Sanvari?"

"Sanv—oh, our senior instructors. It's their title."

"So, this Sanvari magically welds the bracelet onto your wrist and that formalizes the attachment you made in training and that was reinforced by the Ageon's action of choosing you, yes?"

"Well, choosing *their* Bellatrix or Bellator, but yes. And it's Sanvar, singular. Or Sanva, if she's female. Sanvari is plural."

"Sounds like a wedding."

"It is, for all intents and purposes. Imperial law recognizes the binding, and if an Ageon bears a child to her Bellator, the child is considered legitimate."

"What if an Ageon sires a child on his Bellatrix?"

"Well, yes. But powerful Bellatrices do not usually bear children. It . . . can be dangerous. Especially in late pregnancy."

"Why?"

Aelys shifted, straightened her spine. Maybe she wasn't powerful or useful, but she *did* know quite a lot about magical theory. In *this* at least, she could answer his questions.

"Wielding magic requires a great deal of concentration and focus. The Bellator, or Bellatrix in this case, utilizes her conscious mind to shape the energy and channel it through her body into what she wishes to achieve. This is why we study for so long at the Lyceum before we graduate.

"The problem with pregnancy is that in a manner of speaking, we utilize our bodies as a...a kind of energetic fulcrum when we perform magic. It is not harmful to us, so long as we retain control and focus—"

"And if you do not?"

"The energy can backlash and cause extensive damage. *Lethal* damage in some cases."

"And so you don't bear children because of the risk of backlash? What about your years of training in focus and control?"

"Recall that I said we use our bodies as fulcrums? When a woman is pregnant, hers is not the only consciousness inhabiting that fulcrum. The child itself could instinctively affect the energy flow, which could interfere with the mother's control and cause the backlash, no matter how well trained she is."

"So why not just refrain from using magic while pregnant?"

Aelys licked her lips. "Have you ever known an addict?"

Vil snorted. Aelys took that to mean he had.

"Magic is...addictive, to a certain degree. When one is used to channeling energy, it becomes very difficult *not* to channel it. It would be like...like intentionally removing one of your senses for the nine months required. It can be done, but it is very difficult and most unpleasant. Most of us use magic to keep from becoming fertile."

"So, you've been magically sterilized?" For the first time in the conversation, Vil shifted, leaning forward enough that the firelight caught his newly blue eyes and glinted back at her.

"No!" Aelys shook her head and let out a nervous parody of a laugh—though it was mostly nerves, rather than humor. "Nothing so drastic. Just a tiny pulse of power at the right time every month, to eliminate the risk of conceiving. My family would never allow me to be sterilized...especially..."

She trailed off, her face heating up as she realized just how personal the conversation had gotten.

"Especially?"

Aelys pressed her lips together for a second, and then shrugged. *Why not? He is my Ageon, after all...even if only temporarily.*

"Especially because I'm not actually powerful enough to serve in the Battlemage Corps." Aelys heard the truth of the words as she said them and accepted them for the first time in her life. "I was trained, yes, because education is important, but I was never really going to serve. When I get home, my family will arrange a suitable marriage, and I will need to be able to bear healthy children to carry on the Brionne legacy."

Vil said nothing for a long moment. The silence stretched between them, broken only by the crackle of the fire and the whistling of the evening wind across the cave mouth above his head.

"Is that what you want?" he asked, after long enough that Aelys had figured they were done speaking. She'd pulled herself out of the bed and begun to pull the blankets straight. She stopped and turned to look over her shoulder at his silhouetted shape.

"I want to be useful," she said, letting her lips curve in a little smile that probably looked as pathetic as she felt. "I want my life to have purpose. Without an Ageon, I'd be useless on a battlefield, even if I *did* have enough power to make any kind of impact."

"But you have an Ageon. Three, in fact."

Aelys startled herself with a laugh. She let it ripple out of her, though, figuring it was better than crying again.

"I suppose I do, for the moment. But that doesn't change the fact that I'm nearly powerless. And we *will* find a way to break the *geas*. It's not as if it's a real, legal binding."

"No, we're only accidental husbands and protectors."

"I'm so sorry," Aelys whispered.

"Stop. Apologizing." Vil's words slipped into a furious growl. He opened his mouth to say more, but a scuffing sound at the top of the stairs had Vil stepping back away from her with that near-preternatural quickness of his.

Romik and Daen clattered down out of the rapidly darkening forest into the firelit cave, each carrying a brace of waterfowl.

"Evening," Daen said. "We had a fair bit of luck out there." He hefted his prey, and his teeth flashed white in the firelight as he smiled. "These should make a tasty stew. I don't suppose you're the kind of noblewoman who knows how to cook, are you?" He turned to look at Aelys, and she couldn't suppress the shiver that snaked up her spine at the sight of his blue eyes. They looked so odd and...unnatural in his face. She hadn't known him long, but suddenly she felt a pang of loss for the warm, smiling hazel regard he'd turned on her back in the tavern.

The tavern. What in the Divines' names had happened at that tavern?

"N-no," she said. "I never learned..." She trailed off, unsure how to ask her questions. Unsure what questions to ask. Unsure even where to stand as Vil pushed past her to perch on the stairs.

"It's all right." Daen flashed his sunny smile at her as he maneuvered his way to the fireplace, followed closely by the silent Romik. "I'm a fair hand if you don't mind trail food."

"I—of course I don't—" The anxious bewilderment in her tone set Aelys to cursing in her head. *Can't I, just for once, sound like someone who knows what she's doing?*

"Have a seat, Bella," Romik said as he handed Daen his own birds. "We've got some things to discuss while Daen cooks."

"I—all right." Aelys pressed her lips together to keep from stuttering. She glanced around, but the only chair in the place was the one where Romik had been seated earlier. She couldn't imagine taking his chair, so she sank back down to the pile of furs where she'd awakened.

Romik watched her, then glanced over at Vil, who had settled himself on the stairs. Daen hummed softly under his breath as his hands flew over the bird carcasses, neatly plucking their feathers with a minimum of fuss and feathery fluff. But his long-fingered hands paused as Romik settled himself back in the chair and cleared his throat.

Trepidation crept up the insides of her throat, but Aelys forced herself to turn and look at the big warrior in the eyes. She did her best not to flinch at his blue gaze, but she couldn't help a small shiver at the deep intensity of emotion she saw there. Her mouth went dry with fear or pain...or maybe just the knowledge that these men who had so gallantly rescued her the night before must thoroughly hate her now.

"You said we're your protectors now. Responsible for your well-being. Who or what are we protecting you from? Who was chasing you last night? Who attacked us at the inn?"

Aelys blinked. *That was not what I expected him to say.*

"I-I have no idea," she stammered. "I don't have any enem..."

"You've thought of something," Vil said.

"Maybe...No. I'm being silly."

"Tell us," Romik growled. "We have a right to know what we're up against."

"I— It's just that my family is powerful. We have enemies. But I shouldn't think I'm important enough—"

"Who are these enemies?" Romik interrupted, slicing a hand impatiently through her protestations.

"The Monterles," she said. "My father's kin. They've hated my family since I was a little girl."

"Why?"

Aelys swallowed hard. "They accused my mother and grandmother of having my father killed. It's ridiculous slander, of course. My father died in a hunting accident. But they've hated us ever since. Although the men who chased me were not Monterle men. They were far too rough and dirty. They had to be common bandits. They stopped me not far up the road from the inn and ordered me to dismount. I assumed they wanted to steal my horse, and so I ran."

"Could they have been hired by the Monterles to capture you?"

"N-no—" she stuttered again, and shame heated her cheeks. She forced her spine straight. "That doesn't make sense. Why would they want to capture me? How would it help them?"

"Didn't you just tell me that you're the Brionne heir?" Vil said. "If I were an enemy of your House, I imagine that capturing or killing you would be useful in a number of ways."

"If they killed me, it could bring my House to an end," she admitted slowly. "It could destabilize the whole empire, particularly since we're still under a regency until the emperor comes of age. But how would they know it was me? I told no one of my plans when I fled the Lyceum. How would anyone even know I'm rich or noble..." She trailed off as all three of them looked at her with expressions that ranged from blank, to condescending, to vaguely amused.

"Anyone with eyes in their head would know," Vil said, his dark, smooth voice a strange counterpoint to Romik's rough grunt of agreement. "Your cloak alone costs more than most families see in a month."

"I see," Aelys whispered. "That could be it too, I suppose. There may not be any political motive."

"We thought of that, as well," Daen said. "The forest roads aren't as safe as the Imperial Foresters like to pretend, and this area is known to be lightly patrolled. You might just have picked a bad day to try and ride home alone."

"I know," she said, looking down at her hands. Her knuckles had gone white with tension. "I'm sorry. It was a stupid thing to do. I just...I couldn't stay—"

Romik slashed his hand through the air, cutting her off again. "It doesn't matter now," he growled, and despite her best intention, Aelys felt her spine wilt, her shoulders curl forward.

"Of course not," she murmured. "I'm sorry."

Vil's boot shifted on the stone of the stairs: a warning and a reminder. *Stop apologizing.*

But how can I, when everything I do is wrong?

"Sorry or not," Romik went on, "we have a problem. The bandits took our horses, all of our supplies, everything we will need if we're to make it all the way to Brionne."

Cold dread solidified in her chest and sank into her gut like a wet stone. "Please," she said, her voice barely above a whisper. "I am sure that taking me home is the last thing you want to do, but I...I cannot do it on my own! And I don't know how to break the *geas*—"

"No one said anything about you doing anything alone, Bella. That's what got us into this mess in the first place." Vil's silky words slithered through the dark, smoky air.

"Of course not," Aelys said once more as her body collapsed further inward. "How stupid of me. I'm sor—"

"*Don't!*"

Romik's demand cracked out like a whip, making Aelys jump and close her mouth with a snap.

"Romik," Daen said, a warning in his tone. Metal clanged against stone, and something began to sizzle, sending a mouth-watering aroma through the cave. "You're scaring her."

Romik let out a huff and dropped his head into his hands.

"We've already spoken about the Bella's irritating habit of apologizing all the time, haven't we, Bella?" Vil spoke from his perch.

"Yes," Aelys said in soft misery. "And I'm—" She fell silent, not sure what to say if apologizing for her infinite shortcomings wasn't allowed.

"We know." Something that felt a lot like disdain threaded through Vil's voice, and it made Aelys's shriveled insides quake. "You're sorry."

Aelys pressed her lips together and stared down at her hands, wishing she could just disappear.

"We will take you to Brionne," Romik said after a long, uncomfortable silence. His tone sounded measured, as if he were keeping himself under tight control.

He probably wants to strangle me. And I certainly cannot blame him. How he must wish he'd just let the bandits have me!

"Thank you," she whispered.

"But we can't go directly there, not without gear, provisions, horses. There is a town not far from here. Mageford. Daen says he can lead us there through the forest, keeping us off the road and hopefully away from any other bandits. It will take a few days on foot, but when we get there, we can find work, buy supplies. Get what we need to take you home."

Aelys nodded without looking up. She didn't trust herself to speak, but she determined to keep careful track of what they spent, so that she could have the Brionne steward reimburse them for their funds. She still had some of her gold, but Romik was right, it wouldn't be enough to outfit them all for the trip.

"We'll leave in the morning." The chair creaked. Aelys looked up to see Romik leaning toward her. "Early. So, get some rest tonight."

Despite the fact that she'd apparently slept for over a day, Aelys nodded, unwilling to say anything and make the whole situation worse. She scooted herself back to sit against the wall of the cave and drew her knees up to her chest, trying to take up as little room as possible while the men turned their conversation to the route they'd take in the morning.

After a little while—long enough that Aelys's stomach had started to audibly grumble—Daen brought her a rough-hewn wooden bowl filled with a steaming liquid.

"Not going to be as good as Mirandy's, I'm afraid," Daen said, his smile slightly sad. "But I put in a few dried herbs, so it shouldn't be totally flavorless."

"Thank you," Aelys said, taking the warm bowl from his hands. Her fingers brushed his, and a tiny frisson of energy rippled under her skin at the touch. Daen jumped a little, as if startled, and his gaze flew up to hers.

"What—?"

"The bond," she whispered.

"What about it?" Daen asked, his voice patient.

"Because it's a magical bond, energy flows between us. More if we touch. I mean, there's always *some* energy flow between Bella and Ageon, but this seems different. Stronger than what is commonly described. There are legends...histories. According to a few sources it's one of the ways the Bellene mages used their protectors. As a conduit for more energy than they could pull alone. But I didn't mean to... I didn't realize. I'm sor—" She cut herself off at his raised eyebrow. Apparently, he wasn't going to tolerate any more apologies from her, either.

"It didn't hurt."

"No," she said. In point of fact, it had felt deliciously good, better than Halik's touch had ever felt, but she wasn't about to tell Daen that.

"Hmm. Interesting," Daen said, pulling her back to the present. He gave her a kind of lopsided smile. "Well, you eat, and there's plenty more when you're done with that. Build your strength, tomorrow's going to be a long day."

Aelys nodded, and obediently lifted the bowl to her lips. Daen's smile deepened, and he winked one blue eye at her before turning back to the fire to ladle out three more bowls.

Tomorrow's going to be a long day indeed. Here's hoping I can keep from making any more mistakes...not that there's any chance of that, I suppose.

Tears prickled behind Aelys's eyes again, but she didn't want to further upset the men with her crying. So, she ducked her head, lifted her bowl, suppressed a shiver that ran under her skin, and let the tears silently leak from her eyes.

The day was long, but not, Daen felt, unpleasant.

Romik had shaken him awake just before dawn, pulling him from a strange, formless dream involving walking along tightropes of solid light over an abyss of darkness. It had put him out of sorts at first, but by the time they got packed up and climbed out into the gray light of false dawn, the dream-induced foreboding dissipated, and Daen felt his usual cheer reasserting itself.

Only I'm not usually this cheerful, he thought sometime in the afternoon as he reflected on the journey his thoughts had taken throughout the day. Most of his attention had been on their path and route through the forest, and on making sure they were traveling in the correct direction toward the town of Mageford. All Foresters learned certain landmarks and features, and long familiarity with this part of the imperial lands had helped Daen to find his way to the trail. It had once been a proper road but had been overgrown and forgotten as the empire expanded outward into newer, less unforgiving lands than the old forest.

The trail would lead them north into the foothills and most of the way to Mageford. They would have to leave it and go cross-country through the hills for a bit on the second day, but he would worry about that when the time came. Until then, he was just as happy to have a relatively easy path to follow.

A path that left his mind free to wander, and to examine the events of the past few days, turning them over in his head the way he would inspect a fresh kill, looking for flaws and damage, trying to decide the best way to put it to use.

Fleeing the Foresters, meeting up with his brothers, finding himself bonded to a Bellatrix...

But he actually felt *happy*. Daen couldn't fully remember the last time that had happened. He'd laughed, of course, but it was usually sardonic and cutting. He'd smiled, but it was hardly ever a genuine expression of joy. The last time he remembered feeling actual joy was... well. He couldn't remember how long it had been. Before Bormer died, certainly.

And even then, Bormer always chided me for being too serious, for not playing with the other boys around the outposts where we lived. He never understood that I could never be one of them. I didn't have the birth for it.

Daen felt his thoughts start to slide down the old, familiar path of brooding cynicism. He inhaled and shook his head, willing that cycle to break. By the Green Lady's grace, he was *happy*. He wasn't about to squander it on old sorrows.

"All is well?"

Aelys's voice, quiet and tentative, came from just behind his shoulder. Between Romik's glowering silence and Vil's sinister stares, Daen could see why she'd gravitated toward him during their trek, and he slowed his steps and smiled down at her while inwardly congratulating himself on earning her attention.

"It is," Daen said, speaking just as quietly. "It is better than well, in fact. I was just thinking about how fine today seems."

"I am glad the rain stopped."

"Yes, that's part of it. Traveling is always better done when dry. And the forest does show her best self after a good rain."

"You...you shook your head like something was bothering you. I was afraid I—" She cut herself off, pressing her lips together as he raised his eyebrows.

"You were afraid you had done something to upset me?" he said, keeping his voice and his face neutral.

"Well...yes."

"Why would you think that?"

"Well, because I usually—" She stopped, closed her mouth. Then took a deep breath and opened it again. "I make a lot of mistakes," she said, squaring her shoulders. "Most of the time—well, often, anyway—I have no idea I'm doing it, but I make them anyway. I thought perhaps this was one of those times. Maybe I was walking too loudly, or too close to you, or—"

"I don't think you could ever be too close to me."

Daen hadn't intended to say the words out loud, but he didn't wish them back.

"Oh." Her voice got smaller, quieter. "I see. I suppose that's the *geas* as well."

"Must it be? Cannot I just like you? Like having you near me?"

Aelys looked up at him, a flash of heat in her eyes. "Are you making fun of me?"

"Not really." He gave her a smile. "Men do, occasionally, decide that they like pretty women, you know."

Aelys snorted, but then her shoulders drooped and she looked down again in what he was coming to think of as her "collapsed" posture. "At least I have that going for me, for a time."

Daen let out a snort of his own. "Many women would—and do, in some places—pay quite a few Imperials to look half as beautiful as you. Perhaps you should consider a bit of gratitude for your natural luck, Bella."

She sighed. "I know, and I am grateful. And thank you for the compliment. It's just that...as you said. *Anyone* can be pretty. I wanted...something else."

"And what was that?"

"Power."

Daen blinked. He would not have guessed that answer from her.

"Bella, you're a scion of one of the most powerful of the noble families of the empire. I'm not sure you can get much more powerful than being a daughter of Brionne." For all he'd come to hate his brother Foresters, their conversations over the years had given Daen a fairly complete picture of the political games that members of the empire's twenty noble families played.

"But that's my family. That's not *me*. I wanted to serve in the Battlemage Corps. I wanted to help expand the borders of the empire and defend her citizens from threats. I wanted to be more than just a noble broodmare trying desperately to bear a daughter with talent and a son to trade away for a favorable marriage alliance!"

Daen let her have her outburst and walked in silence for a moment or two while she collected herself. He listened and glanced out of the corner of his eye to see her take a deep breath, and then another, before collapsing inward again and training her eyes back on the path in front of them.

"So why didn't you?" he asked. Because he was watching, he saw the jolt as she flinched from his words.

"I can't. Not without an Ageon."

He thought about pointing out that she now had *three* Ageons but decided to leave that part unsaid. For one thing, Ageon or not, he was fairly certain that the Imperial Battlemage Corps wouldn't be any better than the Foresters. For another, he had further questions.

"Why didn't you have an Ageon? Before us, I mean."

"I wasn't chosen," she said. "None of the candidates felt... drawn to me."

"I thought you said that the modern oath didn't involve magic."

"It doesn't, at least not until after the choice is made. But it's a...a relationship. It's basically a marriage, Daen. And none of the candidates wanted to be bound to me like that."

"Why not?"

Her head snapped up, and that tiny spark of heat returned to her eyes. "Now you are making fun of me."

"May the Green Lady's beasts tear me in two if I am," he said, his voice serious. "I genuinely do not understand."

"Because I have no power!" she said, loudly enough that a small flock of songbirds exploded from the trees overhead and wheeled, screeching, into the sky. "I can *feel* the energy all around me, but I cannot seem to...harness it."

"With your magic?"

"Yes. With my magic. That is what magic is, Daen. It is just energy directed by the will of the mage."

"I thought magic involved spells."

"Spells are the mechanism by which the mage directs the energy. Like a certain shape of lens can direct sunlight into a point hot enough to burn," she said, her tone distinctly exasperated.

He thought for a second about taking offense, but in the end, he decided not to do so. Truth be told, he was enjoying this conversation, and this strange feeling of being happy, far too much to let it go so easily.

"Apologies, Bella," he said, keeping his voice light and teasing. "I'm afraid I know nothing about magic. You might have to explain it to me as if I were a child of five years."

"No, *I'm* sorry," she said on a sigh. "I shouldn't have snapped at you like that. Why should you know anything about magic? It's not as if you've spent ten years of *your* life at the Lyceum Belli chasing an impossible dream."

"No. But I did spend longer in the Foresters, surrounded by men with half my skill who barely tolerated my company because I wasn't part of one of those noble families. I'm not trying to be cruel, Bella, but I really don't think you know how good you have it."

Aelys tilted her head to look up at him. "You were a Forester?" she asked softly. "How did that...? I mean. If you're not a noble son...?"

Daen smiled tightly as the old, familiar pain contracted inside his chest. "The man who raised me was a Forester. The best man I ever knew. He sponsored me into the organization as his son by adoption. It was enough to get me in the door, but never enough for some of my so-called 'brothers' to accept me as one of them."

"That's terrible," Aelys said, her voice thick with sympathy.

"Eh," Daen shrugged. "It wasn't fun, but I stopped caring what they thought a long time ago."

"But what did you do?"

"I practiced. A lot. All the time. I got good enough that while they could complain about my lack of noble blood, they couldn't say a word about my skill. Of course, that caused other problems, but that's the way it always is, right? Solve one set of problems, another challenge arises. Keeps things interesting." He grinned at her and winked.

She responded with a tentative smile, and Daen felt as if someone had kicked him in the chest. His hand twitched out toward her, but he kept it down by his side, mindful of her reaction to him in the cave the other night.

"How much longer?" she asked then. "I mean, I can go as long as we need, I'm not complaining—"

"It's okay, Bella. I'm not going to bite your head off for asking a simple question."

"I—well, thank you. I was just wondering..." She trailed off, ducking her head again.

"There's a good place to camp a little way off this path. We should get there soon. Always better to set up camp in daylight."

"Will it be another place like..."

"Like the cave? Not quite. Just a small clearing next to a stream. But there's some boulders where we can set up a campsite. Easily defensible. We'll keep you safe, Bella, don't worry."

"I'm n-not." She looked up at him, alarm flashing across her face. "I never thought you wouldn't—"

"I'm teasing you, Bella."

"Oh! I-I'm sor—"

"Uh-uh. Nope. No apologies, or you'll make Vil irritated."

She pressed her lips together, and despite his lighthearted tone, misery continued to swim in her eyes.

"Bella...hey. Aelys, what's wrong?"

"I just...You're so nice, even after everything I've done. I can't, I don't deserve it, but I am grateful that at least one of you—"

"Hey," Daen stopped and turned, reaching out and taking her hand before he could think better of it. "Listen. I know Romik is like a growling bearcat and Vil can be scary—"

"He terrifies me," she whispered, looking down. But she didn't pull her hand away.

"It's how he survives. It's how we've all survived. But I swear to you upon everything I hold dear, he won't harm you. None of us could possibly harm you. Don't you know that?"

"Because of the *geas*," she whispered.

"Maybe," he said. "But in the end, does it matter? You're safe with us. Who cares what the reason is, all right?" Daen waited for a beat, and then reached with his free hand to tilt her chin up so that she looked him in the eye.

"All right?" he asked again.

"All right," she whispered, nodding. He didn't miss the way she blinked rapidly, or the moisture that pooled at the corner of her eyes, but he figured he'd pushed her enough, and so he let it go.

"Something wrong?" Romik asked, approaching up the path. Daen released Aelys, then turned to smile easily at his sworn brother.

"No. Just thought I'd let you guys know. Campsite isn't far ahead. We'll be there in less than an hour."

"All right," Romik said. Daen's smile grew at his brother's unconscious echo of their words. Vil materialized out from the shadow under a nearby tree.

"Let's move on, then, shall we?" Vil asked, his voice barbed. Daen deepened his smile, winked at Aelys one more time, and then continued on down the trail.

At the camp, Vil watched Aelys.

To be fair, he'd been watching her all day. He'd listened in from the shadow of the trees as she spoke of her frustrations with Daen. He'd watched how his normally cynical, bitter brother treated her with relaxed, mildly flirtatious teasing. He'd also felt the clenching in his gut as she gave Daen more and more of her tremulous smiles.

True to his word, Daen led them into a small clearing shortly after their conversation along the road.

"We'll set up over here by these boulders," Daen said, his casual expertise clear in his body language as he pointed to a clutch of partially rounded stones maybe twice the height of a man. They made a rough semicircle, and Vil could see a smaller circle of stones laid out for a campfire in that space.

"Romik, if you can get the fire going, I'll grab us something to eat. There was a nest of groundoons nearby the last time I was here. I should be able to get one or two for tonight's dinner." Daen walked over to the boulders and dropped his pack, then unslung his bow and reconfigured his quiver to ride on his back.

"What can I do?" Aelys asked, her voice quiet but eager. "P-please. I'd like to contribute."

"I was just getting to that," Daen said with a grin for her. He crouched and flipped open the top of his pack, removing a small, much-dented cooking pot. "We're going to need some boiling water to cook those groundoons...or whatever I get. Romik's got a bigger pot in his pack. Take this over to that creek there and collect as much water as you need to fill it."

"I can do that," she said, her voice strengthening. She gave him another one of those smiles, and Vil gritted his teeth and steadfastly refused to let his knees buckle.

"Fire will take me a minute," Romik said, dropping his own pack. He took out a small hand axe he must have taken from Daen's cave and stomped over toward the tree line. Vil watched Aelys look after him, her shoulders slumping a little.

"Don't worry about him," Daen said, his tone gentle. "Big men get short-tempered when they're hungry. The stream is that way." He pressed the pot into her hands, and nodded, his expression encouraging. Aelys nodded back and took the pot, then squared her shoulders and turned toward the stream.

Daen stayed where he was and looked at Vil, their twin blue gazes connecting almost as if they could communicate silently.

Protect her.

Vil nodded once, letting the corner of his mouth deepen in acknowledgment. Not that he needed Daen's silent prodding; that had always been his plan. He turned to follow her slim figure as she crossed the clearing and knelt on the bank of the stream. Not far away, the sound of Romik's axe echoed through the otherwise serene woods.

He didn't say anything, just watched her as she peered down at the water, her face creasing in dismay. The creek may have had a current, but it wasn't a quick one. A thin film of plant debris and insect webs sat on the surface, making the water glisten a deep green in the fading light. Aelys reached out, tentatively touching the water before snatching her hand back as if someone might scold her.

"You can filter it," Vil found himself saying. He hadn't even really meant to speak, but he held himself steady as she jumped at the sound of his voice.

"What?"

"Do you have a handkerchief or something? You can use it to filter the big stuff out of the water. Boiling will take care of the rest."

"Oh! That's a great idea," she said, her face lighting up. Vil held himself still, refusing to let the jolt her happiness gave him show on his face or body. He watched her fill the pot, then followed her as she carried it back to the fire ring and their packs. She pulled a thin scrap of fabric out of an inside pocket of her cloak, and he held it over the larger pot as she poured the creek water through it. When she'd emptied the small pot, she looked up at him with a smile.

"Shall we go again?"

"If you want to fill the cooking pot the way Daen said, then probably." Vil didn't mean to sound cutting, but she flinched anyway, her smile vanishing.

"Of course. How stupid of me." She dusted off her hands, gathered up her things, and headed back to the creek. Vil watched her go for a second, and then followed a few steps behind her.

"I can do it," she said softly as he approached. "You don't have to watch me."

"Yes, I do."

She looked up at him, her brow creasing in irritation. "What? Why—"

"To protect you, Bella. I'm your Ageon. Is that not my role? Protecting you?"

She blanched, her slight show of temper disappearing as her eyes went wide and her cheeks paled. "Oh," she said.

"This forest has always had bandits, like those who attacked you on the road and at the tavern."

"Of course," Aelys said, ducking her head down and staring at the water. She dipped the pot back into the murky water.

"Unless you know of a reason they wouldn't be in this area."

Her head snapped up again. "What? No! Why would I know—"

Vil shrugged one shoulder. "You tell me."

"I don't!" Her irritation was back, or maybe it was just agitated fear. Her eyebrows slammed together in a frown and a fine tremor started up in her hands. "I don't know anything."

"A random attack on the forest road I could understand, especially when you present such a tempting target: a noblewoman, obviously rich, traveling alone? Naturally someone would attack. What I don't understand is why they would return to the tavern after being thwarted by someone as formidable as my brothers and try to bargain with us for you."

"*What?*" Her eyes went wide, her spine snapped straight.

"You didn't know?" Vil allowed himself to smirk. "Before they killed Mirandy, they offered a trade: you for her."

"Oh no," Aelys breathed. She brought her fingers to her mouth, horror filling her expression.

"You're losing your pot," Vil said, nodding toward the handle of Daen's pot as it disappeared beneath the murky water.

"Oh no!" Aelys repeated, crying out. She plunged both hands in, leaning forward so far Vil thought she might just totter headfirst into the creek herself. She searched, her movements frantic, until she paused, relief clear on her face, and pulled the pot from the murk.

Vil watched her swallow hard and carefully set the full pot on a flat stone near the bank. Then she closed her eyes for a moment and took three deep breaths before blowing her air out and turning to meet his gaze.

"I don't know why they would have done that," Aelys said. Her voice trembled, but her chin lifted, and she didn't break eye contact. "I have the feeling you would know more about that than I. Other than a ransom—or a plot by the Monterles, I suppose—I haven't got the faintest idea why someone like that might want to take me."

"If you say so, Bella."

Despite his sardonic words, Vil actually believed her. She had none of the tells of someone lying, though her tense shoulders and staccato movements betrayed her agitation. She stared at him for a minute longer and opened her mouth as if she had more to say . . . but she closed it with a snap and let her head and shoulders wilt forward in her habitual posture. He watched her pick up the little pot once more. She rose but didn't turn to go back to the fire right away. Instead, she paused, her brow furrowed as she looked intently at some of the weeds growing next to the water's edge.

"That's salicress," she murmured, sounding as if she'd just made a discovery.

"What is salicress?" Vil asked, when it became clear she wasn't going to say more without prodding.

"Salicress is an herb, and it's actually rather rare. But it has several healing properties. I . . . I could make it into a tea. It helps with muscle fatigue and inflammation. I don't know about you men, but *I'm* not used to hiking through the woods all day, and I'm surprised I'm not sore alread . . ." her eyes darkened, and she fell silent.

"Why aren't you sore already, Bella?" Vil asked.

"Hmm? Oh! Well, I...I just realized. Or I guess I knew this; I just hadn't thought about it because...well...everything was so unexpected and not the way things are usually done—"

"You're rambling."

"I— I am. I'm sor—"

"Don't apologize. Just answer my question. Why aren't you sore already, when you think you should be?"

"B-because of the bond. The Ageon bond."

"This *geas*?"

"Well, yes. But even if we had a...a more usual type of bond, it would still have an effect. This appears to be stronger, because it's a *geas*, or it may be because there are three of you. Or—"

"What effect, Bella?" Vil kept his voice empty, though he could feel his patience wearing thin.

"Th-the energy. There is energy flow between us. Daen experienced it earlier, on the trail. Because you are my Ageons, your energy flows to me, strengthens me. You're all such strong men... I imagine that's a large part of why I don't feel worse than I do."

She looked down at the salicress, and then held the pot of water out to him. "But still, my herbalism Sanva would never forgive me if I passed up the opportunity to gather salicress. And one never knows when herbs might come in handy."

Vil took the pot, and watched as she used a nearby twig to help her dig out three of the broad, flat-leaved plants. Then she stood and wiped her right hand on a corner of her cloak while she clutched her harvest in the left.

"There are more," he said, jerking his chin at a patch of four or five more of the plants nearby.

"Yes," Aelys said. "I'll leave those be. Salicress is rare because it's hard to grow in gardens and greenhouses. It really only thrives in a wild environment. It's not really responsible to take it all, and this is more than enough for what we need." She lifted the bunch of leaves with a smile. "Shall we go back?"

She's like a different person when she talks about the herb, Vil thought as he followed her back to the camp and watched her filter the water and lay out the herbs by the fire. *It's like there's a glimmer of confidence there. Interesting.*

He remained silent for the remainder of her trips to the creek. Instinct had him fading into the growing shadows as he followed her back and forth, watching her, watching the woods around her, trying to get to the bottom of the many puzzles she represented. Sadly, he'd not made any further progress by the time Daen returned. He called out a cheery hello, and then joined the rest of them next to Romik's merrily crackling fire.

"A bit of luck," Daen announced. "The groundoons had moved on, but I got us a couple of wood pheasants instead. You'll like these, Aelys. They're very flavorful birds!"

"Thank you," she said, giving Daen one of those smiles that lit her up, even if it didn't fully reach her eyes. For just a moment, envy stabbed through Vil's guts like a particularly vicious knife. Not that he wanted any harm to come to Daen. The man was his brother, after all. He just wanted her to look at him that way, instead of with fear in every glance.

That's not you, he snarled silently at himself. *Daen's content to fall head over heels for the girl, but you gotta be smarter than this. Someone has to keep his head and figure out just what she's done, who she is, and why we're all in this damned mess! Keep it together!*

Vil savagely ripped every shred of longing or desire away and forced himself to stare at the girl's face. Warmth bloomed in his chest, but he fought it, wrapping his emotions in ice as he'd learned to do long ago on Cievers's streets.

For good measure, he faded back into the trees once more, content to watch from the shadows as she talked and laughed with Daen, brewed her tea, and even gave Romik a smile or two as he tended the fire and helped Daen prep the birds for stew. Vil remained there until the savory scent of their dinner wafted toward him, twisting in his belly. He waited until Romik served the girl, then stepped out and strolled nonchalantly toward the fire, accepting the bowl that Daen held out to him.

"Something I've been wondering, Bella," Daen asked after they'd all eaten in silence for several moments—hiking was hungry work, after all. Vil glanced up through his eyelashes at Aelys, who swallowed her latest bite of stew and turned to Daen, her expression open.

"I know you insist that you've got no power," Daen went on, spreading his hands as if to say that he didn't mean to cause offense. "But if that's true, then how do you explain what you did at the tavern?"

"W-what?" Aelys's eyes went wide in what Vil was beginning to recognize as her major tell of surprise or discomfort.

"You know, after you bonded us?"

"She doesn't know," Romik rumbled. "She passed out, remember?"

"We all passed out," Vil put in, just to see how she reacted. Her lips pressed together, and her eyes stayed wide.

"Yeah, but she didn't wake up until the next night, and we were already in the cave by then. She has no idea what happened."

"What did happen in the tavern?" Aelys asked, her voice trembling and high, as if she dreaded the answer.

Daen reached out for her hand, opening his mouth, his face gentle. Vil cut him off before he could speak.

"You destroyed the tavern, and everyone in it," Vil said, his voice hard and empty. "Everyone but us."

She shook her head, her eyes filling with tears. "I don't underst—"

Her obvious distress ignited a rage deep in Vil's chest, and he leaned forward, baring his teeth as he elaborated.

"You used the power you insist you don't have to pull the fire *through* us, and then exploded it outward, annihilating every piece of timber or rock larger than a pebble, and turning the bandits into nothing more than a fine, red mist."

As she'd done at the stream, Aelys covered her mouth with her fingers, her eyes going even wider. Tears spilled over her lower lashes. She shook her head.

"N-no," she said, her words muffled. "No. That's not possible."

Romik snorted. "Neither is this," he said, pointing to his eyes. "But here we are."

"B-but I don't under—"

"For all you insist on the honor due your education, *Bella*," Vil said. "There certainly seems to be a lot you don't *understand*."

Aelys flinched as if he'd struck her. The fire in between all of them surged, reaching up higher than Romik's head with a roar. Heat slammed into Vil, rocking him backward hard enough that he had to lean into it, tuck his body, and take the roll rather than sprawl helpless on his back like Daen and Romik had both done. Only Aelys stayed upright, her tear-filled eyes overflowing with horror.

She gasped loud enough to be heard over the flames and flung her hands forward, palms down. Instantly, the fire subsided, settling back down into the ring of rocks and letting out a single *snap* as one of the thinner branches broke.

Vil stared into Aelys's eyes.

"Not quite powerless after all, it seems."

Aelys let out a sob and surged to her feet, her forgotten bowl tumbling from her lap to spill the remainder of her dinner in the ash-laden dirt.

"Bella, wait!" Daen called out, picking himself up from where he'd fallen. He started after her, only to have Romik stop him with a hand on his arm.

"Where do you think you're going?" Romik growled. Daen yanked his arm away.

"After her! She could get hurt or—!"

"She's not going far," Vil said, his voice low. "She's just shaking her bedroll out and lying down."

"But she's upset! Why do you have to be such a horse's ass, Vil?" Daen rounded on Vil, his brow tight with rage that sent foreboding shivering down the length of Vil's spine.

She's got her magic in you deep, brother. Romik too, it seems.

For Romik, also, was scowling at Vil.

"These are things we need to know," Vil said quietly. "She says she's powerless, but she's obviously not. Why would she want us to believe that if it weren't true?"

"*She* believes it," Daen said, nearly spitting the words in anger. "When you spend your entire life being told you're not good enough, eventually you start to believe it. And then you come along and *push* at her—"

"It wasn't me who asked the question about her power, *brother*," Vil said, emphasizing their relationship in hopes of reminding Daen where his loyalties should lie.

Where mine should lie . . . where they have to lie. Darkness damn it all!

Because even while he faced off with his brothers, Vil couldn't help but watch over Daen's shoulder as Aelys curled into a small, blanket-covered ball on the ground. The air had cooled as the sun set, and he might have imagined it, but he thought he saw her start to shiver.

"She's cold."

Vil wasn't sure who said it, whether it was him, or Daen, or even Romik. All he knew was that no one said anything else, but suddenly, all three of them had gathered beside her. Romik bent down in a crouch, and gathered her up, blanket roll and all. She let out a muffled sound of protest.

"Shhh, Bella. We'll leave you alone, I promise," Daen said, pulling the blanket aside enough to stroke her hair. "We're sorry we upset you, but you can't sleep that far from the fire. You'll freeze. We're just going to move you closer where you'll be warm."

Vil didn't say anything, just closed his suddenly shaking hands into fists and hoped neither of his brothers noticed the tremors. Just as had happened when they first arrived in the cave, he *ached* to be near her, to touch her, even if it was just a strand of her hair.

No, he told himself. *Lock it up. Dark Lady, for the love of all that is hidden, please help me keep a clear head!*

The shaking eased as Romik laid her down, situating her between the fire and where the three of them had laid out their bedrolls. As Aelys's shivers stilled, so did Vil's hands. The tightness in his chest relaxed, too, as he watched Romik and Daen fuss over her.

So. She's safe and comfortable. Protected. That seems to be the key, even if I'm not the one protecting her... interesting.

"What are we doing?"

Vil blinked, tearing his eyes from Aelys's sleeping form and turning to look at Daen. His Forester brother stood nearby, staring into the fire, his unnatural blue eyes glowing in its reflected light.

"Protecting her," Romik said on a sigh, after a long, silent moment had stretched between them. "Anything else is secondary to that."

"How are we—you going to protect her from herself?" Vil managed to keep his tone empty, but only just. *If I can't figure it out, maybe they can.* "She's her own worst enemy."

Daen bristled, but Romik just shook his head.

"I don't know," Romik said. "I just know I have to try." He lifted his head and met Daen's gaze, and then Vil's. "We *all* have to try."

CHAPTER FOUR

ROMIK COULDN'T REMEMBER WHETHER OR NOT HE'D EVER BEEN to Mageford before.

At some point during his mercenary career, all the little towns and villages had started to look the same. Mageford was maybe more picturesque than most, with a couple of mountain streams converging to form the headwaters of the mighty Zetsi. The Zetsi river was a major waterway down by Cievers, but up here, it was narrow enough to be forded.

Thus, the town's name, I guess. Clever.

Because of its location, Mageford controlled the northernmost major imperial road crossing in the empire. For that reason, there was a garrison of imperial soldiers stationed just inside the walls, ensuring that no one noble family gained too much control over the town and the all-important river crossing. Other than its strategic location, however, Mageford filled all of Romik's criteria for a little town of almost no importance. A cluster of steep-roofed buildings huddled together, encircled by a tall, stout stone wall. A pair of stone spires near the center of the cluster jutted toward the sky. Probably a shrine of some sort, though Romik had no idea which Divine they honored this far north. Below the rise on which they stood, Romik could see the imperial road meandering west, following the foothills as they curved away toward the horizon. At this distance, he could just make out the shapes of the various carts and wains that creaked their way along the well-trafficked road.

The girl stepped up next to him, breathing heavily from the walk. "Pretty town," she said. Before he could think better of it, Romik looked down at her. As always, the delicate lines of her face and those piercing blue eyes struck right to the core of him. He opened his mouth to reply but couldn't think of a single thing to say.

So, he just grunted a vague affirmative and looked over her head at Daen.

"Contact's got a shop down in the market square," Romik said, ignoring the way Aelys wilted next to him. "You want to come with me to see him? Might have better luck with two of us. Vil can take the girl to the inn."

Daen's eyes darkened a little, and he looked rather pointedly down at Aelys.

"Is that all right with *you*, Bella?" he asked.

"Oh! Of... of course. Whatever you all think is best. I don't want to be any trouble."

Shoulda never been caught alone on the road then, Bella. The thought was uncharitable, perhaps, but Romik didn't push it away. It was true. The girl had been nothing *but* trouble since he'd first laid eyes on her panicked, Motherlit face in the tavern yard several nights ago.

And yet, I have to protect her. She's so vulnerable... It's like I can't think of anything else! All these years of freedom, and this chit has me bound again!

Romik blinked and *did* push that thought away. He turned to meet Vil's eyes, raising his brows in a question. Vil gave him a nod and stepped forward to take Aelys's hand from behind. The girl jumped and let out a squeak of surprise.

"Come with me, Bella," Vil said. "The inn isn't far. I'll keep you safe."

"Oh! Um. Of course," she said, her voice trembling. Romik held himself still, even though his instincts screamed at him to wrap her up and hold her close. He gritted his teeth instead and looked away, concentrating on breathing through his nose the way he would to calm himself before a fight.

Back when he had to do such things.

"You don't have to always be such a prick to her, you know."

Romik blinked, and looked up to see Daen had come closer, his brows pinched in irritation. Behind him, Vil led Aelys down the slope to intercept the imperial road heading into the town.

"I'm not," Romik protested, even though it felt like a lie. "I'm just . . . blunt."

Daen just stared at him. Romik let out a sigh.

"Fine," he said. "I'm being a prick. But I don't want to get close to her. I don't want to be her friend."

"Horseshit. You can't keep your eyes off her."

"Doesn't mean I like her."

Daen snorted and started down the hill. "Yeah, suck on my other nut, Romik. That one's empty already. I *saw* you! That first night, you were like a damn bear, growling at anyone who got near her!"

"Exactly." Romik followed Daen, his longer legs catching up and outpacing his friend before they'd gotten halfway to the road. "She said it herself. That . . . magic whatever of hers that she did. It made us want to protect her. That's not natural. It's her spell."

"So?"

Romik felt his eyebrows jolt upward. He turned to stare at Daen and nearly tripped on a rock sticking out of the hillside as they descended.

"*So?* So, it's horseshit, as you said! I don't want some witch messing around with my emotions."

Daen threw his head back and laughed. "You sound like every man who's ever dealt with a woman."

Romik shoved his friend's shoulder and glowered at him. "This is different, and you know it."

"Why? Why is it different?"

"Because she used *magic*! We don't really feel this way, it's just her spell or whatever you call it."

"The *geas*," Daen filled in for him. "And she didn't mean to do it."

"Still. It's not right."

"Green Lady's tits, Romik. You'd think you've never made a mistake in your whole fucking life! So, she bound us to her with magic? So what? It's not hurting us at all. The blue eyes are weird, but I'm getting used to you and Vil having them. And so what if we feel like we need to protect her? Here's a concept for you: Maybe that's our job! She *did* hire us, after all."

"Not for this."

Daen let out a gusty sigh and shook his head. "You're a stubborn ass, you know that?"

"It's not right. I'm in control of my emotions. Me. No one else."

Daen opened his mouth then but stopped and looked oddly at him.

Red Lady fuck me running, Romik cursed himself and his too-revealing words. *I should have known better than to try and explain to mooncalf over here.*

"It's not like that," Daen said, pausing at the bottom of the hill. Romik stopped beside him as he drew a deep breath and continued on. "She's not trying to control us. She's just scared and...a bit lost. She just needs us to get her home. The thing is, I've never seen anyone with worse self-confidence than our Bellatrix. So, when you're short with her, it makes it worse."

"She's not my problem," Romik said through gritted teeth.

"Except that she is. You may not like it, but you don't want to hurt her any more than I do. And when you're surly or mean, it hurts her."

I take it back, Red Lady. Fuck him *running!*

Romik swallowed hard and glared at Daen, his jaw clenching. Daen stared right back, his eyes sober and devoid of any humor. There was challenge there, though. Lots of it.

"Fine!" Romik spat. "I'll be nicer." He barely resisted the urge to kick at the dirt mounded up by the side of the cobblestone road and started walking toward the town instead.

"Good," Daen said. His long stride brought him up alongside Romik within three steps, which didn't do anything to dispel Romik's foul mood.

They walked in silence for a bit, and then Daen reached out and clapped Romik companionably on the back. Romik didn't say anything, but as they passed into the village proper, he felt his shoulders ease with the knowledge that at least he had a brother by his side.

Aelys expected Vil to drop her hand as soon as they reached the bottom of the slick, grassy slope and stepped onto the worn cobblestones that wound their way into the tiny hamlet nearby. She stumbled, rolling her ankle and pitching forward. Vil's grip on her hand hardened, and next thing she knew, Aelys felt herself being hauled into him, her free hand slapping against his black-cloaked chest.

"All right?" he asked, his voice like cold silk. Aelys nodded, her pulse hammering in her throat. She risked a glance at his face. Unlike Romik or Daen, Vil wasn't much taller than she, so the intense searching in his blue-eyed stare was close enough to bring heat to her face.

"I'm s— Yes." Aelys managed, then looked down as Vil's iron-hard arm eased across the small of her back, and she stood on her own two feet again.

But he didn't let go of her hand. In fact, his fingers curled around hers so tightly, she could feel the heat of his skin through the thin black leather of the gloves he wore.

"Do try to remember how to walk," he said, holding her with that stare for a moment longer. Then he let go of her hand and turned away, pulling his hood down lower over his face.

Aelys swallowed, and then shook herself out of the daze he'd left her in, and hustled to catch up with him as he strode toward the gatehouse that guarded the entrance to the town.

Foot and cart traffic increased once they passed beneath the towering gatehouse structure. Imperial guardsmen carrying pikes stood on either side of each of the three arched entrances, but only one made eye contact with her. She saw his gaze alight on her—battered, dirty, but apparently still distinctive—cloak, and watched as his eyes tracked up to the Bellatrix stone at her throat. He inclined his head but said nothing as she and Vil moved with the flow of people, animals, and vehicles through the arch and into the town itself.

Mageford wasn't nearly as grand as Cievers, but it was certainly larger than the small village outside Myara's family's home estate. The imperial road was wider than a simple cart track, but Aelys recognized the architectural style of the buildings that lined the street. The stone foundation and ground floor housed warehouses and workspaces for merchants, butchers, tanners and the like, while the timber structures perched above provided housing for the families who worked there. Here and there on the sides of the road, occasional vendors hawked colorful fruits and flowers to passersby as the traffic carried them deeper into the heart of the town.

"Pretty place," she said as they turned from the main road onto a crossing thoroughfare. "It reminds me a little of Myara's..." she trailed off as memory flowed in, replacing her reminiscence with misery as she recalled her "friend's" deceit. "I—I mean, it reminds me of home...of Brionne—"

"It would be better if you didn't chatter on." Vil's icy words cut through hers. Once again, Aelys felt a spike of anxiety slam down the length of her spine, even as the sound of his voice made things low in her body curl in pleasure.

"Oh, I'm ... oh."

"You never know who might overhear."

"Of course."

"It isn't wise to advertise our destination."

"No, of course. I understand."

Aelys looked down at the path in front of her feet and pressed her lips together. *Don't cry,* she ordered herself. *He's no doubt sick of your tears. I'm sick of your tears. Don't you dare cry!*

Her eyes filled in defiance of her internal orders, and she stumbled again. Vil's hand shot out like a viper striking, but she flinched away.

"I'm all right," she said, hoping he couldn't hear the thickness in her voice. "I'm just clumsy ... and tired."

"The inn isn't far," he said. She nodded, and blinked away the traitorous tears, then spent the rest of the walk focusing on following him closely, and on not stumbling again.

They made another turn onto a quieter street less filled with creaky-wheeled carts and half-shouted businesses. Aelys took a deep breath and let it out slowly, then glanced up to see that they'd entered a clean neighborhood. Several shops still fronted the street, but they were the kinds of shops where artisans sold their finer goods and lived with their families on the second and third floors of the buildings. Her shoulders eased down away from her ears, and she smiled as a small child came running out of one doorway, trailing a length of brightly colored fabric and followed by a harried-looking young man.

"Good day," she said, stopping and crouching in front of the little one. Aelys could feel Vil standing close behind her, and she noticed that the other people in the street stepped around them, giving him a wide berth. "That is very beautiful fabric you have there. Does your family sell it?"

The child—a little girl with reddish-blonde curls who couldn't have been older than four—stopped and nodded, after popping the side of her free hand into her mouth.

Aelys glanced up with a smile at the man as he approached, winding up the fabric with every step. "Do you like the bright colors? I always do," she said.

The child nodded again, and then squeaked as the young man picked her up from behind and settled her on his hip. Something warm and sunny bloomed in Aelys's chest as the little girl tucked her head into the junction of the man's shoulder and neck. He smiled down at her, dropped a kiss on her tousled curls, and finished winding up the length of fabric with his free hand.

"Thank'ee," he said, speaking with a hint of the regional mountain accent that Aelys knew well from the servants back home. "This one likes to try and get away from me when I've customers in the shop. It's a game to make me chase her through the neighborhood."

"You're very patient with her," Aelys said, her smile growing with approval.

"I'm too indulgent," the man said with a self-deprecating shrug. "But she's my girl, aren'tchee, baby? I ought to swat yer bottom, but I just can't. Come on back to the shop, now. Let's let the fine lady and her man be about their business. If ye've a need for fabric, Lady, come see me. I'll give ye a good price in thanks for your help."

"Thank you," Aelys said as the man inclined his head and headed back to the open door of the fabric shop. She watched him disappear inside, and then turned to Vil, her smile fading.

"I'm sorry," she said, not bothering to censor her apology this time. "I know you want to get to the inn; I just couldn't let—"

"It's fine," Vil said. "You're right, the streets of a town are no place for a small child unsupervised, especially one that pretty. That man had better keep a closer watch on his daughter, or else... well. He should watch her."

Aelys fought to keep her face neutral. For the first time since she'd met him, Vil sounded... emotional. Angry, even. She opened her mouth to ask what prompted this change, but he cut her off by grabbing her hand again and pulling her into motion down the street.

As they continued on their way, more and more people seemed to take notice of them. More than once, Aelys heard a whispered "noble" or "magic" as they passed. With Mageford designated under imperial protection, and without a major noble seat nearby, Aelys realized that these common people rarely saw anything that had to do with magic. Though it wasn't unheard of for commoners to have an understanding of herbalism and basic medicine, the ability to work true magic lay exclusively within noble bloodlines and had for as long as anyone remembered. So, it wasn't any surprise that a Bellatrix in their midst might cause a stir—even if it was one who made as many mistakes as she did. Vil seemed less and less happy about the attention, though, and so Aelys did her best to follow him quietly and not meet any of the curious gazes that turned her way.

However, Aelys did notice something else that piqued her interest. At the corner of one of the intersections they crossed, a small, brick building stood next to an open yard with a stable and several horses already saddled.

"What is this place?" Aelys asked as they passed. Vil glanced over, and then turned his attention back to the wagon traffic currently crossing in front of them. He waited until the intersection was clear, and then pulled her across the dirt road over to the other side.

"Imperial posting house," he said. "For sending messages to other locales. Never seen one before?"

"I may have," Aelys said. "But I—my family has its own couriers. When they send me messages, I just send my replies back with them."

"Efficient." Vil's voice had regained its blankness, and Aelys furrowed her brow as she wondered if he was making fun of her.

Not that it matters if he is. It's not as if you're going to do anything about it. You're ridiculous, with your spoiled rich-girl ways and ignorance of the real world!

Aelys ducked her head back down and focused on the road while tugging her hand free. She didn't say anything else. Before long, Vil came to a stop and pushed open a narrow door set inside yet another brick wall.

"Stay close," he said, his voice pitched low as he held the door open and gestured to her to proceed past him into the building. "And say nothing."

He didn't wait for her to respond, but just walked in and pushed his hood back off his head as he approached the matronly woman standing at a high counter just inside the doorway.

"Two rooms," he said, reaching into his cloak and pulling out a pair of coins. He set them down on the counter with a *click*. "Meals and baths for four."

"How many nights?" the woman asked.

"Just the one for now," Vil said. "I'll let you know if we need more."

"Bathhouse is out back," the woman said, tilting her head at a hallway that continued behind her to end in a large, wooden door. "From now until sunset, it's women only. After sunset, it's men only until middle night, when we close. Opens up in the morning for couples only, but you must reserve a time."

Aelys felt her face heat up, but the woman either didn't notice, or was too professional to remark on it. She reached under the podium and brought out a box, which she unlocked with a key worn on a bracelet around her wrist. She withdrew two more keys, and handed them to Vil.

"Adjoining rooms. Through the taproom, up the stairs, take a right. Last two rooms are yours. There's a door in between that can be locked or not. Mealtimes are posted in the taproom, along with the menu. Cold meats, cheese, and bread are usually available at all hours, just ask Eldin behind the bar. He's my husband."

"Thank you," Vil said, taking the keys with a nod. "Our two friends will be joining us shortly. Please send them up."

"Of course. Let Eldin or me know if you need anything else. My name is Wircy. Welcome to the Mageford Inn."

Wircy gave them a smile that crinkled the skin at the corner of her eyes. Aelys smiled back, but Vil just inclined his head and turned for the open doorway that led to the taproom. Wircy nodded once, and then turned her attention back to the open ledger in front of her, and Aelys had no choice but to follow Vil.

It wasn't until they had crossed half the length of the taproom that Aelys's knees buckled.

Flames flowed across the ceiling in a roaring ripple of dancing orange and blue. Smoke choked her nose, making her cough. Her eyes burned like coals as more flames licked up the sides of the walls and heat wrapped her up in a vise of pain...

"Not here."

Vil's voice flowed into her like cooling water. Aelys blinked and realized that once again, he held her in a grip like iron. She looked up to find him staring into her eyes.

"It's just a memory," he murmured. "It can't hurt you now. Let me get you to your room, all right?"

She nodded, and he let go where he'd been holding her around the waist. He caught her right hand with his left and, just as he'd done outside, pulled her behind him the rest of the way to the stairs and up them.

As promised, the end of the hall had two doors that opened to Vil's keys. Aelys let him lead her into the one on the end and sit her down on one of the beds that lined either wall. With his help, she shrugged out of her pack, which he set on the floor next to the foot of her bed.

"Just sit there for a moment and breathe. Feel the floor solid underneath your feet. I'll open the window to let fresh air in. Just breathe and remember where you are."

Aelys nodded and closed her eyes, trying to follow his instructions. She turned her mind to the sensation of the floor solid beneath her boots, to the softness of the bed upon which she sat, to the darkly glowing line of energy pulsing into her from Vil as he moved about the room—

Her eyes snapped open, and she gasped.

"What?" Vil said, turning toward her. "You're all right, Aelys. It's just a memory."

"No, I know," she said. "It's not that."

"What then?" His voice sounded the same as it always did, but she could *feel* his impatience as his energy surged toward her.

"It's... I'm not sure how to explain it."

"Try."

"I can...I can feel you. Or not you, precisely. But energy. Through you. More than I should."

Vil's eyes narrowed. "Through me?"

Aelys nodded. "All magic is a form of energy, right? Well, technically *everything* is a form of energy. Magic is the manipulation of that energy to create a desired effect. When a mage does a spell, she utilizes energy that has to come from somewhere. So, she pulls it from the environment through that part of her brain that can sense the magic. Then she shapes it with her will and focuses it with the steps of the spell to create the desired effect. That's what magical talent is: the ability to sense and access the ambient energy." Despite her best intentions, Aelys heard the wistful note in her voice as she spoke and had to fight not to look down and away.

"And you don't have this talent?"

"Well, I do, of a sort. I have always been sensitive to ambient energy. It isn't uniform, you know. It pools and builds up in some places, and in others it's scarce and thin. But no matter how much energy I can feel around me, I've never been able to channel more than the barest trickle."

"And you're sensing this energy from me? I'm creating it?"

"Well... not exactly. There's a theory that says that energy cannot be created or destroyed, simply moved around. I told you before there's always *some* energy flow between Bellatrix and Ageon, due to the bond. And the old texts said that ancient mages could intentionally pull energy through their Ageons, but I'm not... that's not what's happening here. For one thing, the flow is far greater than it should be, especially if we're not touching. I'm not pulling it from you, and it's not that you're creating the energy. It's more like you're... siphoning it. Or funneling it, maybe."

"Funneling it?"

Aelys took a deep breath, let it out slowly.

"Into me."

Vil's blue eyes intensified somehow, as if the light behind them had brightened. He didn't move a muscle, but Aelys became suddenly very aware of his body position. He knelt on one knee in front of her, his hands resting on the mattress on either side of her. His fingers slowly curled into fists, bunching the thin coverlet on which she sat.

"Right now, I'm doing this? Funneling more than the usual flow?"

She closed her eyes, unable to withstand the intensity of his stare. A dark, velvet pulse surged into her, sliding against the underside of her skin.

"Yes," she whispered.

"Is it hurting you?"

"No." She shook her head rapidly. "No. It feels good."

Another pulse, and Aelys let out a gasp. Her nerves sang with liquid pleasure that rippled throughout her system. She felt her lips part and opened her eyes to see Vil's gaze fixed on her mouth.

"Don't touch me," she whispered. "I'm afraid—"

"I won't."

"This is too much; I've never pulled this much energy before."

"How do I stop? Giving it to you?"

"I don't know. Please don't, though. I..." Aelys closed her eyes again, pushing back against the intoxication swirling in her brain. Her fingertips and the tips of her ears tingled. *Think. He's feeding you energy. It has to go somewhere. Use it.*

"Flash," she whispered, focusing her will. Light bloomed throughout the room, bright enough that the insides of her eyelids flared orange. Vil cursed and ducked away from her, his hands releasing the bedclothes. He'd been so close that Aelys could feel his body's heat, and its sudden absence struck her like a cold wind. She opened her eyes to see him crouching in front of her, head down, hood up, as her magelight painted the entire room in stark relief. And her magelight...

She'd worked for *years* to be able to conjure a simple ball of light the size of her head. It had always taken all that she had, all the power she could pull to do just that simple task. But now...

The *entire* room glowed, the light coming from everywhere all at once. There were no shadows, only the sharp, coldly burning light leaching the color from every surface, every object. And unlike her pitiful lights of the past, this conjuration actually *brightened* as she watched. The flow of energy continued its path through Vil, into her, and out via her focused will into the field of light, pumping it brighter and brighter—

"Stop!" Vil ground out, pain wreathing his usually silken steel voice. Aelys gasped, and quick as a thought, extinguished the light, throwing the room into near darkness by contrast.

"Oh, Divines! I'm so sorry! It was too bright, wasn't it? I didn't realize—"

"Stop," he said again, raising his head. His blue irises burned against scleras gone red with burst capillaries. His skin pinkened as she watched. Her magelight might not have hurt her, but its radiance had ravaged her defenseless Ageon.

Aelys sucked in a breath, her fingertips flying to her mouth. "Oh no! Oh, Vil, I'm so so—"

"Stop. Apologizing."

"No, but I hurt you!"

"I've had worse."

"But this is my fault, I—" Without meaning to, Aelys reached her hand out toward his face. Once more, he moved quicker than a viper strike and captured her hand in his own black-gloved one. Her words died in her throat as another pulse of energy rolled from him to her, shivering under her skin once more.

"Is that it, what you feel?" he asked, his voice a low murmur, barely above a whisper.

She nodded, unable to speak. Another pulse hit her, harder

this time, and she couldn't suppress a tiny gasp as her entire body tightened with sensation.

"Do you know what I'm doing?" He shifted forward, still crouching in front of her, but drawing nearer. He still held her hand captive.

"No," she whispered.

"I'm thinking about you."

Another wave of dark silk slammed into her, and Aelys couldn't stop herself from crying out. Her eyes rolled closed, and her head fell back, and only Vil's iron grip on her hand kept her from falling back onto the bed. Delicious pressure built within her as his energy—her energy now, but flavored with him—swirled and eddied in her mind, under her skin, pooling in her core. Once more, her fingertips, nose, cheeks, toes tingled with it. She opened her mouth to beg him to stop, to beg him to never stop, but words were beyond her grasp as she drowned in the flow of pure power flooding her system.

Vil raised her hand, brought her fingertips to his lips.

Aelys cried out again, her whole body shuddering as the energy rushed through the skin-on-skin connection out of her and into him. She snapped her eyes open to see Vil trembling too, his eyes closed, his head tucked down, hood shadowing his face.

As she watched, the shadow deepened, until she couldn't see anything but darkness under his hood.

And then he opened his eyes.

Burning ice stabbed into her brain, holding her paralyzed for a heartbeat that stretched on for moments.

He blinked.

She blinked.

He let go of her hand. It fell to her lap between them.

"That—"

"You—"

Aelys swallowed, waited to see if he would try to speak again. When he didn't, she took a deep breath and tried again.

"Your eyes are better. Your skin, too."

"They don't hurt anymore. Did you heal me?"

She shook her head, and then changed her mind and shrugged.

"N-no. I don't think so. True healing requires a whole series of very complex spells that I never had enough power to learn."

"That seemed like a lot of power."

"You felt it?"

Vil stared at her, then flipped the corner of his cloak back to reveal a wet spot high on the inside of his thigh.

Heat flooded Aelys's face. Nothing like the energy transfer—but enough that she knew she'd blushed crimson in mortification.

"Oh, Divines! I'm sor...forgive me. I think...It's the *geas*. I...somehow, I was able to pull power through you...or you fed it to me. And when I touched your lips, I pushed it back to you and it...healed you. And...other things."

"It's the *geas*." Vil's voice had regained its emptiness. Aelys nodded.

"That's the only reason I can think of for...what just happened. I am so... Please forgive me." She pressed her lips together as guilt and worry rose up in her brain, chasing away the memory of his power and her bliss.

"The only reason."

She nodded again. "I *am* truly sorry, Vil. I'll find a way to break it, I promise you. This...this won't happen again."

Vil remained motionless for long enough that Aelys had to fight not to babble another apology. The twin serpents of guilt and worry tangled together, squeezing around the inside of her chest until she felt like she might burst.

Vil's cloak snapped as he surged to his feet, moving with even more lightning quickness than usual.

"I must go clean up. When the others return, I'll fetch you for the evening meal."

Aelys tried to smile, but she could feel that it didn't touch her eyes. *A weak, tremulous, pitiful excuse. Just like you. Divine Breath, look how badly he wants to be gone! He hates you. He really hates you. And he has good reason!*

With these thoughts echoing in her head, Aelys didn't even hear the door close behind Vil as he left.

"So, who are we going to see?" Daen asked, following Romik around yet another corner into yet another narrow laneway. Mageford wasn't a large town—certainly not as large as Cievers or Bameny—but the buildings still loomed over him, blotting out the sky. It made something in his chest tighten just the slightest bit, and Daen found himself breathing deeper as they wound further into the center of the town.

"Gormren. Trader who had the supply contract for our company a few summers ago. He's a skinflint, but mostly honest. I worked with him to set up some of our logistics, and he told me to let him know if I ever came through this way. I told him I didn't think it likely...but here we are."

"If he was providing supply for a major mercenary company like the Raiders, what under the Green Lady's leaves is he doing way out here on the edge of the mountains?"

Romik turned to him with one of his rare grins. Daen pushed back his agitation to answer it with a smile of his own.

"I asked him that. Turns out, Gormren has a very pretty young wife who has a very demanding mother who lives here. She apparently wouldn't quit nagging about having her grandchildren nearby, and so when he made enough money from our summer campaigns, he bought a place out here near town and set up a mercantile business."

"Gotta think that wasn't a great business move."

"You know what they say. Happy wife, happy life."

Daen smirked at Romik's dry tone, then angled his body so as to fall in behind his friend as their route narrowed even further. Years of pulling a longbow had widened Daen's shoulders to match Romik's warrior build, and Daen tried not to notice how often his sleeves brushed the stone of the buildings on either side of him.

In the woods, it was different. He never minded closed-in places out in nature. But leaves and branches and even natural stone caves felt less restricting than worked stone and wood. In the woods, he could move silently, naturally. Bormer had taught him that and it had become his whole life. In towns, though, he felt out of place, uneasy, like he didn't fit there.

Or anywhere. But especially between buildings.

Fortunately for Daen, they soon stepped out of the alleyway into a more-open oblong market area. Wooden stalls formed two concentric rings in front of the buildings, many of them topped with brightly colored canvas tarps. On the far side of the area, Daen could see the twin spires of the town's sanctuary reaching up into the blue-and-white sky. Sunlight filtered down through the patchy clouds, glinting off the glass window set high in the front spire. A murmur of sound—hundreds of individual conversations punctuated with the enthusiastic cries of market hawkers—tightened Daen's shoulders once again. Once again, he fought to breathe in a slow, controlled manner.

Romik wove his way between the stalls, heading for the low, square fountain in the center of the space.

In the center of the noise. And the thronging people. Daen pressed his lips together and pushed on, following his brother's broad back as the crowd got tighter and tighter. Someone lurched into him, and Daen reacted without thought, gripping the man's bony wrist and twisting it around and down. In less than an eyeblink, Daen had the assailant flat on his back, his emaciated chest creaking under Daen's knee as he drooled, seemingly unaware of Daen's large knife at his throat.

"Daen," Romik said. "Easy, brother. He's just a vaporhead. He's not going to hurt you. Look at his eyes, he's so fogged he can't even see you."

Daen licked his lips and slowly sheathed his knife, and then stood. The vaporhead didn't seem to notice but remained lying on his back as the crowd just naturally flowed around him.

Romik's big hand landed on his shoulder and squeezed. "Come on," he said, pulling his brother into motion. "He'll get himself moving soon enough. It's best just to leave them be."

"What causes that? Is he ill?" Daen asked, feeling like the worst of rubes. Buildings and crowds notwithstanding, maybe avoiding towns his whole life hadn't been the best idea.

"In a manner of speaking," Romik said. "He's a vaporhead. They mix certain plants together and then steam them, inhaling the vapors that result. It makes them drunk, and worse than drunk. After a while, they can't live without it. It's . . . not a great life."

"Why would someone do that?" Daen asked, shivering.

"Some see it as a way of escape. Same as drink, I imagine. Come on, the fountain's just this way."

"Does your friend hang out at the fountain?" Daen asked, sidestepping quickly as a group of small children careened out of nowhere and crossed in front of him at a breakneck pace.

"Not exactly."

"So . . . are you just thirsty, or what?"

Romik turned to look over his shoulder at Daen, his eyebrows pinching together.

"Maybe I am. What does it matter?"

Daen blew out his breath in a huff. Romik's low, patient voice confirmed what he'd already suspected: He was acting like an arse. *But damn it, I hate towns!*

"I just don't want to be wasting time, I guess."

"We're not. I don't know where Gormren's set himself up, but there are always people in these markets we can ask. It's their business to know these things." Romik turned fully toward Daen and reached out to grab his forearm. "Hey," he said softly, the words almost buried under the market's ambient noise. "What's going on?"

"I don't . . . I'm fine." Daen tried to pull away, but Romik tightened his grip and leaned even closer.

"As you so eloquently said earlier, horseshit. You look like a green slave hitting the sands for the first time."

Daen swallowed and looked around briefly before answering. "There's just . . . a lot of people. More than I'm used to. I don't . . . I haven't spent much time in a town in . . . a long time."

Romik pursed his lips for a second, his eyes narrowing. "You don't like crowds?"

"I don't like *towns.*"

Romik nodded. "All right." He let Daen's arm go and stepped back but stayed close enough to keep talking in that undertone. "I get it, a little. I think. It's hard to see where everyone is coming from, right? Hard to keep track of the possible threats?"

Yes, partially. "Something like that," Daen forced himself to mutter.

"That makes sense. So, here's what we're going to do. We're sworn brothers, right? So, I'll watch your back and you watch mine. This market has six exits that I can see from right here. How many do you see?"

Daen sucked in a deep breath and looked around again, forcing the panic away from the edges of his mind as he concentrated on identifying the routes out of the milieu of stalls and people. "Five," he said.

"The sixth is behind us, it's the way we came from," Romik said. "Keep taking those deep breaths, all right?"

Daen nodded.

"Right," Romik went on. "Here's the plan. We're going to head toward the fountain. You keep an eye on the approaches off my right shoulder, and I'll take care of the ones off your left. I'll do the talking; you just stand there and look intimidating.

You're not as good at it as me, but I'll wager you can put on a good face when you want to. You've certainly got the height and shoulders for it."

That surprised Daen into a tiny grin. "Longbow," he said by way of explanation. Romik nodded.

"No surprise there. So, you follow my lead and watch my back. We'll have our conversation and find Gormren, and then we'll take the long way back to the inn, around the perimeter of the town so we stay off the main thoroughfares. Right?"

Daen nodded again. "I'm good."

Romik reached out and squeezed his shoulder once more before turning back toward the center of the market. "I know you are, brother. Let's go."

Concentrating on his breathing helped, Daen found. As did keeping his focus sharply on the avenues of approach Romik had assigned him. He felt the panic in his chest draining away.

Still feels wrong to have so many people here...but I can handle it. Romik is right, having a true brother makes all the difference.

It didn't take Romik long to find one of these alleged information brokers. A woman sat on the edge of the fountain, leaning back on her elbows and staring at the two of them with frank appraisal in her eyes. Despite the silver strands glinting in her dark brown hair, her face still held a kind of luminous sensuality, with wide green eyes and full lips that curved knowingly as the two of them approached.

"Well, hello, gentlemen," she said, rolling the sounds around in her mouth in a way that made the corners of Daen's mouth curve up despite himself. "What can I do for you...both?" She arched one dark eyebrow and deepened her smile in a clear invitation.

"We're looking for someone," Romik said, his tone flat and all business.

"I could be someone. Especially for two men with such gorgeous eyes. You must be...brothers?"

"Yes," Daen said, earning a scowl from Romik. He shrugged and closed his mouth, but then returned the woman's smile. *Better to flirt than to hyperventilate, right, Romik?*

"How delightful." The woman sat up, leaning forward enough to showcase her lovely swell of bosom.

"We're looking for someone specific," Romik said. "A merchant by the name of Gormren."

"Oh." The woman pouted, her eyes glinting playfully. "Well, that's much less fun. Though perhaps more lucrative." She put out her hand, palm up, and tilted her head to look up through her lashes at Romik.

He said nothing, simply reached into his pouch and placed a few copper Townies in her hand. When she remained perfectly still, he sighed and added a few more. She weighed the coins in her hand and then cut her eyes to Daen.

He winked.

"Fine," she said with a long-suffering sigh. "But only because I'm a sucker for a pretty face. Doubly so for two, it seems." She stood up, and for the first time, Daen noticed that the simple gown she wore appeared to be made of fine, figure-hugging, silken material. She met his eyes and he realized she'd noticed him noticing. He gave her a tiny shrug.

"Be still, my loins," she murmured.

"Gormren?" Romik asked, his tone dry.

"Not nearly so fun to look at as you gentlemen," the woman said pertly. "But he's this way." She turned, flipping her long, dark hair, and began to sashay her way through the people milling about the fountain.

"Feeling better?" Romik asked Daen as they stepped up to follow her.

"A little," Daen said. "Watching the approaches helps."

"Oh, it's the *approaches* you're watching?"

Daen snorted in acknowledgment of the hit. "Among other things."

The woman looked back over her shoulder to make sure they were behind her, and then turned back to her route, her hips swinging in a full strut as she walked.

"Wish I could watch other things," Romik said, so softly Daen almost didn't catch the words.

"I think she's hoping you will."

"It's not that." Romik let out a huff of air. "I can't... I can't help but think of *her*."

Daen said nothing as the crowd shifted and thinned around them. The woman appeared to be leading them toward one of the exits he was supposed to watch, so he gave himself time for a long, thorough look and threat assessment while he considered how to respond.

"Me too," he finally murmured. *Truth is always the simplest option.*

He didn't like it though. Deep in his gut, Daen felt a dark twisting at Romik's admission that he'd been thinking about Aelys. He clenched his jaw and forced himself to take several deep breaths before he spoke again.

"I thought you didn't like her."

"I don't."

"So don't think about her." He couldn't help that it came out as a growl.

"Believe me, I'm trying not to."

Romik's muttered resentment sparked a low burn of anger within Daen. It tangled up with the dark jealousy twisting through his gut and threatened to ignite into a full-blown firestorm of temper.

"Are you boys coming?" their guide asked. Daen blinked twice and focused on her, happy to have something else to think about.

"How much further?" Romik asked. Daen didn't miss the soft threat in his voice, and judging by her smile, neither did their guide.

"Not far. My son-in-law's business is just there," she said, pointing to a good-sized building made mostly of stone, with a wide, curving avenue leading to the entrance.

"Son-in-law?" Romik asked, his eyes narrowing as he stopped walking. Daen paused too, his eyes flicking back and forth between his brother and the woman smirking at them both.

"Yes, of course! Gormren married my beautiful Olisa several years ago. They've given me seven strong grandchildren to carry on our family's legacy here in the mountains."

"You're Olisa's mother?"

She put one hand to her chest and curtseyed like a fine lady. "Sabetha, at your service. Wisewoman, midwife, and business partner to Gormren the trader."

"You could have said."

"But I chose not to. Would you like me to take you in, now? I believe Gormren is in his office."

Romik glowered at her, then nodded. Daen suppressed a smile as they started moving forward again.

You never did like surprises, did you, Romik? Not even when we were kids. No wonder this whole geas *thing is pissing you off.*

The interior of the building was just as nice as the exterior.

Sabetha led them through a small but comfortable-looking entry-way, down a short hallway, to a room with a heavy, oaken door. She pushed open the door without knocking and gestured for the two of them to go on inside.

"Sabetha, what—*Demon*?"

"Hello, Gormren," Romik said as he walked in. The office had wide windows that looked out on a fenced area dotted with sheds and corrals. In front of those windows, a large wooden desk sat, behind which a lanky man was getting to his feet, his expression something between delight and disbelief as he held out his hand.

"What under the stars are *you* doing here? I know the Raiders didn't take a contract out here in the middle of nowhere!"

Sabetha snorted behind Daen. He looked over his shoulder to see her standing with her arms folded, smirk still firmly on her face as she watched the interplay.

"I've left the Raiders," Romik said, shaking the man's hand with a smile. "This is Daen, one of my business partners. We happened to be in the area, and I thought I'd stop by and see if you had any work for us."

"Work?" Gormren's eyebrows rose up. "What kind of work are you looking for? I could absolutely use a caravan guard command—"

"Short term only, I'm afraid," Romik interrupted him smoothly.

"What kind of skills do you have?"

"Well, you know my background. Daen, here, was an Imperial Forester until recently, so he's a deft hand with woodcraft and archery. And our third brother, Vil . . . well. He's ruthless."

"I like the sound of 'ruthless,'" Sabetha said, her voice almost a purr. Daen looked over his shoulder again with a smile. She lowered one eyelid at him in a wink.

"Hmm. Well, I'm not sur—"

"Gormren. Have them look into the Browervon shipment," Sabetha said then, her tone changing to something crisp and businesslike. "We can't spare any more of our own men, not with that big caravan departing in five days. Let these boys go chase it down and figure out what happened."

The frown that had been building on Gormren's face cleared, and he smiled at Romik. "Ah! My beloved mother-in-law has a point. That might be ideal for both of us."

"What is the Browervon shipment?" Romik asked.

"We had a small shipment, mostly farm implements but some luxury goods, go missing two days ago. It left here at dawn, but never made it to our factor in Browervon, downriver. The rapids are too dangerous this time of year to transport goods by boat, so we sent the shipment overland along the forest road."

"Did you send someone after it?"

"We did," Sabetha said. She pushed off the doorframe where she'd been leaning and walked over to Gormren's desk. "But they haven't come back. Something dangerous is in those woods, and we need to know what happened . . . and then there's the matter of the correspondence."

"What correspondence?" Romik looked at Gormren, who pursed his lips and gestured for Sabetha to continue.

"Accounting details for our Browervon factor, mostly. But also . . . our buying strategies for the upcoming season, complete with sourcing information. It's the kind of thing that if found by our rivals, could hamstring us for the next several years. Everything else in the shipment can be lost, but we *need* that correspondence back!"

Romik looked over at Daen, a question in his eyes. Daen grinned and nodded at his brother. *A dangerous assignment in the forest? Yes, please, Green Lady!*

"Sabetha is right, the correspondence is paramount, but we'll pay you for your trouble, as well as a twentieth share of any other goods that you recover," Gormren said. "Three Imperials apiece, shall we say?"

"Ten apiece, plus the share, and you have a deal."

"Ten—! You're mad! You can't think I'm about to pay thirty Imperials—"

"I think you'll pay forty. There are four of us, total, counting our mage."

Gormren's eyes narrowed. "You have a mage? How did you . . ." He shook his head. "You know what? Never mind. Forty Imperials is highway robbery."

"No. Highway robbery is not getting any of your shipment back, and never knowing what happened, and probably what will happen to any further shipments you send out that way, added to the loss of business you'll take if you can't use that route at all. Not to mention the loss of your important correspondence and all that entails. Compared to that, forty Imperials is a bargain."

Sabetha threw her head back and laughed, and Daen grinned at Romik's savage smile.

Gormren blew out a breath.

"Fine," he said. "Forty it is. Half now, half on your return with a *full* report. And you're crazy if you think I'm giving you more than two percent of the value of any recovered goods!"

"Two percent sounds more than fair," Romik said, extending his hand to Gormren. The merchant took it with a glare, and then burst into his own laughter.

"I should have known you'd be a demon at haggling, too."

"You pick up a few tricks here and there," Romik said. "We've just arrived in town. We'll take the first installment now to repair some of our gear and head out in the morning."

"That's fine," Gormren said. He pulled out a chain from inside his shirt and used the key on it to unlock one of the desk drawers. From this, he removed a small box, which he then unlocked using another key from his neck chain and counted out twenty of the big silver coins bearing the emperor's profile on one side and the Imperial Seal on the other. "Twenty Imperials," he said as he dropped the coins one by one into a small fabric pouch, which he then handed over. "If you find my wagons, there's a hidden compartment under the driver's seat. Use the key in that pouch to open it. The orders will be there."

"Thank you," Romik said. "It was good to see you again, Gormren."

"You too, Demon," Gormren replied. "Don't get yourself killed, hey? I'd like a return on my investment."

"We'll do our best," Romik said, causing Sabetha to laugh again.

Daen stayed silent until they'd exited the building and fallen into step on a mostly empty path that ambled toward the town's walls and then curved back toward the inn. But when he could stand it no more, he threw his head back and laughed.

"By the Green Lady's grace, Romik! I had no idea—"

"Shh," Romik said, cutting him off. But he smiled as he looked over at his brother. "Let's talk about it when we join the others. Not out here in the open."

"Right," Daen said. *Stupid towns. So much noise, you can't even hear if someone is trying to sneak up on you!* "Still. Well done."

"Thanks, brother," Romik said. He reached up and clapped

Daen on the shoulder blades, and for just a moment, everything felt right.

It took Aelys the better part of an hour to collect herself. Between the shame of losing control of her power—*again*—and the mortification of having caused pain—and then embarrassment— to one of her long-suffering Ageons, Aelys felt lower than the smallest, slimiest worm to ever crawl its miserable way through the mud and muck of life.

But, eventually, she managed to dry her worthless tears and convince herself to get up and wash her face. The water in the washstand by the small window was tepid, but it did the job, and she took a deep breath as she used the thin towel to dry her skin.

"Okay," she said out loud, as she used to do occasionally at the Lyceum. Silly, perhaps, but it *did* help her focus. "You've gotten yourself into this mess, stupid girl. The least you can do is get yourself out of it.

"What I really need is to learn to *use* this new power," she said, turning her back to the washstand. She lifted her hands, then ran her fingers over the triple band that encircled her left wrist. "What I wouldn't give to have access to the library right now! Of course, I'm certain I would be in immense trouble if the Lyceum got word that I'd created a *geas*. I hope Aunt Aerivinne knows how to break it . . . but will I still have the power once she does?"

The thought struck her like a hammer blow to the forehead. Because, of course, if the only reason she could channel more power was because she was pulling it through the men, then it stood to reason that breaking the *geas* would render her just as she had been before: pitiful and weak, barely able to call magelight.

Dread flooded in from the edges of her mind, and she swallowed hard to keep from drowning.

"That's a problem for another day," she whispered, and then squared her shoulders and forced her head up. "That's a problem for another day," she repeated, stronger. "One thing at a time. If we break the *geas* and I'm rendered powerless again, well, at least I'm no worse off than before. But it's certainly something I must ask Aunt Aerivinne."

Aelys turned and peered out of the window, her gaze falling on the street she and Vil had walked earlier. A tiny idea sprung to life in the back of her mind as she watched a young man on a horse trotting past.

"The posting house!" she gasped, clapping her hands together in excitement. "Of course! That's it!"

Vil had said that they were for sending messages to other locales, and surely Brionne was included in that. Her family *was* one of the most powerful families in the empire, after all, they must receive messages like that all the time.

And, if I'm honest, they're probably quite worried about me. Well... perhaps not Mother, but Aunt Aerivinne certainly! It really was irresponsible of me to just leave the Lyceum with no word or warning like that. Just the sort of stupid, inconsiderate move I'd make! But if I can get a message to Aerivinne, then she can come here and help us break the geas, and then I can set the men free and pay them handsomely for their trouble... and I've certainly been plenty of that!

Aelys turned toward the door and took a step toward it before freezing again as doubt seized her by the insides and squeezed.

But... Vil doesn't want to see me right now. He couldn't get out of here soon enough. Not that I can blame him. Daen would take me, I'm certain, but he's not back yet with Romik. And Romik... well. I'm certain he's got better things to do than to squire me around town. So does Daen, for that matter.

She spun back toward the window and looked out at the sparse foot and wagon traffic that flowed down the avenue.

Ugh! I hate being such a useless, needy thing! If I were any kind of real adult, I would just go down there myself instead of hiding up here, shaking in my boots at the thought of stepping foot out of doors unprotected!

Aelys craned her neck and considered the sun's angle as it slanted through the buildings.

It's not yet sunset. Surely I've time to walk down the street to the posting house, send a message, and walk back! It's not even a complicated route, just the one turn at the intersection there, and then I remember it's another intersection up. Such a lovely town, this, with its well-laid-out grid!

Excitement and daring tangled up in her chest, but Aelys took a deep breath and forced her emotions down. She made herself reach slowly into the magically sealed pocket inside her cloak and count out her coins. She had no idea how much it cost to send a message, but she *did* have her family's ring. Perhaps she could trade on the Brionne name for credit.

And I'll be sure to make good and then some if needed, she promised silently. With hands that trembled only a little bit, she reached up to rebraid her hair back so that she looked less like she'd been sleeping in the woods for two days and more like a presentable young woman, and then she turned the handle of her door and stepped out into the hallway beyond.

Her pulse thundered in her ears as adrenaline surged through her at the sight of the empty hallway. Aelys swallowed hard and stepped lightly out, trying to make as little noise as possible as she walked past the door next to hers and headed for the staircase.

At the bottom of the stairs, the memory of the fire threatened to rise up and overpower her again, but this time she was ready for it. She'd spent several painstaking years at the Lyceum learning to use the tiny bit of energy she *could* channel and weaving it into a mental shield. Her instructors and fellow students had taken an almost sadistic pleasure in bombarding the weakest student with energetic attacks. As a result, she'd become quite proficient in shielding, and doing so quickly.

This time, as she stepped foot into the common room of the inn, Aelys took a deep breath and wove an impenetrable, impervious, flexible barrier around the scent of smoke and the taste of terror, and then she shunted the memory away to the back of her mind and forced herself to keep moving. She trained her eyes on the floor a scant length in front of her feet and before she knew it, she was through the common room and reached the initial foyer where the woman—Wircy—smiled up at her with a questioning look.

"Thank you," Aelys breathed, and then, before her nerve failed, she bolted through the main door and out onto the street.

Vil heard her tentative footsteps pause outside his door, and then move on down the hallway. He waited until she had started down the creaky staircase, and then eased the door open and followed her out into the hallway.

For just a moment, when she'd paused, he'd thought that maybe she'd found the courage to come and talk to him about what had happened between them.

I should have known better. Courage isn't exactly her strong suit.

Of course, that didn't explain *why* she'd left her room, nor did it give him any hints as to why she was walking back down toward the inn's common room. He'd have wagered good money that she'd not willingly set foot there again, not after the panic that had overwhelmed her on the way in.

But to his surprise, Vil watched from the shadows at the top of the stairs as she paused once more, took a few deep breaths, and then squared her shoulders and stepped into the common room like a bull aurochs charging onto the sands of a gladiatorial arena.

She even has her head down like a bull. Courage enough, it seems. Once again, you surprise me, Bella.

Curiosity tangled up with amusement and irritation as he watched her say something to the innkeeper, and then dart through the door as if all of the Dark Lady's hounds were after her. Vil descended the stairs, and then rather than go through the common room as well, he let himself out of the side door half hidden behind the stairs.

Once outside, it didn't take him long to find her. She either had no concept of how to move unnoticed through a crowd or didn't care to try.

Both, probably, he reflected as he watched her walk down one side of the road, smiling tentatively at people and looking around herself furtively. The setting sun glinted in her white-gold hair, drawing the eyes of men and women alike.

As do your damned expensive clothes, Vil thought. *Dirty as they are, the cut is still distinctive, Bella. You're impossible to hide.*

Vil, of course, had no such trouble. He kept his blond hair covered with his hood and slipped easily into the growing shadows at the base of the buildings. Just as he'd learned to do years ago in Cievers's streets, he followed closely enough to track the mark, but not closely enough to be noticed doing so. He watched Aelys proceed down the main thoroughfare, then turn onto a side lane he recognized from the path they'd taken getting to the inn.

The posting house? Within the privacy of his hood, Vil let his eyebrows raise in curiosity. *Whom are you contacting, little Bella? And about what?*

He waited until she went inside and then continued his own path around the side, so that he could approach the front of the business from an angle that kept him safe in the shadows.

Just as he stepped up close to the building, however, a pair of horsemen approached at a dead run, both riding lathered, blowing mounts. The combination of the horses' shod hooves on the cobblestones, and the shouts of the riders and the grooms that appeared at a run to answer them drowned out whatever conversation was happening inside the building. Vil curled his lip in a silent snarl and crept closer to the building, sliding along the wall toward the front window, but it was no use. Another pair of grooms appeared, leading two fresh, spirited mounts and carrying waterskins and pouches of food for the riders, who called out their thanks as they leapt into the saddles and took off at another noisy, hell-bent-for-leather gallop.

Vil pushed his back against the brick front of the posting office, levering himself closer to the window. He tilted his head, just barely catching the lilt of Aelys's voice and a man's low murmur in response.

The posting clerk, Vil told himself, pointedly ignoring the stab of vitriol that arrowed into his gut. *She's obviously talking to the posting clerk to send a message. But where is the message going?*

He inhaled slowly and held it, concentrating on the sound of her voice, trying to pick it out of the ambient noise of the posting house yard.

"'Ere, now pretty girl! That's a good girl! Gave ye a good run, didn't he? A good long run? Yes, that's it. Walk it off, pretty girl, ease those tired legs. Let's get'che cooled down and then we'll get a nice brush, all right? No, no food yet. Ye've gotta walk first. Walk it off and cool it down. There's a pretty girl. There's a good girl . . ."

Vil pressed his lips together and fought the urge to whip one of his throwing knives into the throat of the noisy groom who was, after all, only doing his job. Instead, Vil pushed himself up higher and risked a look through the window, only to see Aelys clasping the posting clerk's hand and nodding her farewell before turning toward the front door.

Vil turned and slid back down the wall, curling into a crouch in the shadows and wrapping his dark cloak around himself lest she see him there. He watched from under his hood as her boots stepped out onto the front step, paused, and then continued down to the street level and turned to go back the way she'd come.

He waited a beat, sparing a thought of thanks to the Dark Lady that the sun had finally fully set, and the shadows waited with open arms to welcome him as he unfolded himself and commenced following her once again.

Aelys kept her arms down by her side and did her best to unobtrusively shake her hands and wiggle her fingers as she started back up the road toward the inn. The sun had set, and all around her windows lit up with lamps and candles as the town's inhabitants closed up their businesses and started their evenings, but the buzzing under her skin made it impossible to focus on taking in the sights of the town around her.

This damned magic... after so many years of wishing and dreaming for it, now *it finally comes to me, and I can't even control it enough to keep my skin from tingling! By all the Divines, I really am useless.*

Cold, wet coils of shame tightened in her throat as Aelys recalled the way she'd lost control in the inn, first by burning Vil with her magelight, and then when she...

I can't even think the word. I didn't mean to—but ineptitude is no excuse. My magic, my responsibility. I... took advantage of him. In trying to take away the hurt I... caused a sexual response. I'm no better than...

Tears flooded her eyes as she forced herself to think about her actions, to face the magnitude of what she'd done. She had forced Vil's body to an unwanted orgasm. There was really no other way to look at it.

No wonder he left so suddenly. No wonder he looked so angry. No wonder he hates me. No wonder they all hate me.

Conscious of the fact that she was walking on a public street, Aelys ducked her head down and swiped at the tears overflowing onto her cheeks.

Someone grabbed her upper arm and pulled, spinning her off balance and sending her careening to the side. A hand clamped down over her mouth and nose, cutting off her air. She stumbled as her feet tangled each other and she fought to stay upright. The hands holding her tightened.

"That her?"

Another hand grabbed her wrist, stripped her glove off, and shoved her sleeve halfway up her forearm, baring the ring with the Brionne sigil she always wore on her first finger. A sudden, deep fear lanced through her. *Will they take my ring?*

"It's her. Let's go."

The hand on her mouth shifted enough to uncover her nose, and Aelys pulled air into her starving lungs. She felt herself lifted, her feet barely dragging in the dirt as the one holding her moved to the side, ducking into a narrow alley between the rows of buildings on the block. Darkness settled over them as she lost sight of the still-glowing western sky. Panic clawed its way up her throat, and she reached up to pull at the hand still clamped over her mouth.

No response.

Desperate, she started to scratch, and then lifted up her feet and tried to kick the one carrying her. That got the hand to move, but only enough to slap her hard enough that bright stars erupted into her vision.

"You fight me, I'll fight back," he growled into her ear as he pulled her up hard against him and clamped his hand over her mouth again. The scent of fried meat and strong drink wafted into her nose, making her fight the impulse to gag. "And I'm a mean fighter. I'll win."

His other hand, which had been like an iron band around her stomach, suddenly reached upward, skimming over her ribs to the swell of her breasts.

"But if you're nice," he went on, adding a cold thread of terror to the nausea swirling in Aelys's stomach, "then I'll be nice, and we'll both win." She felt him bend and press his thick, wet lips to her neck, and she couldn't help but flinch away.

He opened his mouth and started to speak, but he could only get out "D—" before letting out a strange gasping noise. He stumbled forward, which made her trip on the rough dirt of the alley. His arms went slack, and she managed to scuttle ahead and keep from going all the way down as he slowly collapsed behind her.

Aelys spun and looked back over her shoulder. A pale hand emerged out of the shadows there, beckoning to her. She gaped as a hooded figure followed, who then reached up to push his hood back enough for her to recognize her own blue eyes in Vil's face.

"Let's go."

"He had a friend," Aelys whispered as she put her hand in Vil's.

"Already dead. But he has more friends waiting. Come. We're out of time." Vil stepped over the body of her would-be abductor and pulled her further down the alley toward the far end.

Behind them a shout echoed off the walls, and Vil broke into a run. Aelys managed to mostly keep up, but that might have been because of Vil's steely grip on her hand.

Just as Aelys started to see the flicker of lamplight at the far end of the alley, Vil stopped. Aelys stumbled to a halt next to him, unprepared for the way he suddenly went from running to complete stillness.

"Vil—" she whispered.

"Shh." He raised his other hand and gently touched her lips. The tingling she'd been feeling in her hands jumped to the place where his fingertips rested. He stepped backward, up against a large bin piled high with refuse. With a tug, he pulled her up against his chest, facing him, and then let go of her enough to wrap his cloak around them both.

"Tuck your chin and lean into my shoulder," he breathed in her ear. "I'll cover us."

The tingling spread, her entire face buzzing as if crawling with honeybees.

"Are you . . . thinking about me again?" she asked.

"Don't speak. Whispers carry."

"Are you?" she insisted as the tingles spread.

"Always," he answered, almost absently. "I'm always thinking about you."

And sure enough, as soon as she considered it, she could *feel* the conduit of energy between them. It was wider, stronger than before, as if using it had exercised the connection somehow. That dark, silken trickle had become a murderous current of sensation that rubbed along under her skin and filled her energetic pathways with acute, almost painful decadence.

"Stop, please," she whispered, risking his wrath. *I can't risk losing control of the energy again. I can't!*

"I've tried," he said, leaning back enough to look down at her face, his eyes intense. "I can't. Why?"

"It's . . . too much. I'm afraid I'll lose control. Again."

"Too much energy?"

"Yes."

"Use it."

"I can't. They'll find us if I conjure magelight."

"Do the other thing, then."

"The other—"

"Where you push it back to me. The thing that you did in your room that horrified you so much you ran out into the streets of a strange town without anyone to protect you and almost got yourself taken...again. Do that thing."

Aelys risked a look up at him in surprise. He looked down at her, expression hard.

"Do it quickly. They're coming," he murmured.

She swallowed and nodded, and then tucked her head into his shoulder. With her eyes closed she could almost *see* the energy flowing like a dark river into her. She took a deep breath, and consciously opened her energetic pathways to the flow. Hot, silken sensation began to pool low in her belly, spiraling out along her nerves to mingle with the pressure and tingling already there.

Aelys felt Vil shift the cloak around her and duck his own head down over her shoulder, shielding them both within the depths of his voluminous hood. To feed energy to her Ageon, she needed to touch his skin, that much she knew from her experience earlier. After a moment's thought, she turned her face so that her forehead brushed against the bare skin at the base of his throat.

Aelys froze as she held the energy still, balancing on a precipice between bliss and annihilation. Then the flow reversed and became a raging torrent, rushing along every nerve toward that tiny patch between her eyes where her skin met Vil's.

His chest under her hands flexed as he inhaled sharply, almost gasping. She didn't hear anything, and though she opened her eyes, she couldn't see at all. Even when she lifted her head away from his chest, the shadows around them had become inky, impenetrable. She couldn't even see the curve of his jaw inches from her face.

"Dark Lady..." he breathed, the words nearly soundless as his lips brushed her ear. "Goddess of shadows, what have you done to me?"

"Did I...does it hurt?" Aelys couldn't help but ask. Her words, too, sounded muffled to her own ears.

Vil's chest shook in something that might have been laughter...or might have just been shudders.

"No."

The word rolled through her, bringing with it a new wave of that dark, silken energy she was learning to associate with Vil. She tried to step away, to give him space, but his arms held her close like silk-encased steel.

"They're still out there. Getting closer. I can hear them com-ing up the alley now."

"Should we run?"

"Not yet," Vil said, turning his face so that his lips brushed hers as he spoke. The energy leapt between them like an eager puppy, and Aelys felt her knees buckle as pure, sinful pleasure washed through the nerve endings just under her skin. "You've made the shadows darker. They won't see us if we don't move."

I made the shadows darker? She lifted her head again, turning away from his face to try and peer out...but there was nothing. The darkness surrounding them had grown so absolute that she couldn't see the wall of the building he leaned on, nor the crates of stinking garbage her nose told her were right there.

"It's you," she breathed as understanding crept into her mind. "It's—the legends said—"

"Shh." He reached up to cup the back of her skull, gently pushing her head down, tucking her face back into his neck. "Here they come."

Aelys held herself still, barely daring to breathe. Every inhale carried the scent of Vil's skin: he smelled like clean wool and a hot, sweet spice she couldn't name. He turned toward her, brush-ing his lips against her ear again. Once more, the energy surged. She caught it, trembling as she fought not to move, and pushed it back to him through the places where their skin touched.

"Anything?"

The voice that called out sounded muffled and far away, but Vil's chest muscles tightened under her fingers. They must be close.

"It's dark as your mother's arsehole back here! I can't see anything!"

"Get out of there, then. You'd see her if she were there. She probably went out the far end! Hurry up before we lose her!"

"What about them?" Aelys heard a wet thud, as if someone had kicked the corpse of her would-be captor.

"Leave 'em. They're dead. They won't mind."

Whoever was looking for them started muttering an unbro-ken string of profanity as he started picking his way back out of the alley. Vil's hand on her waist tightened in a warning not to move. She nodded, an infinitesimally small movement that slid her skin across his where they touched.

They waited there in the darkness until the footsteps faded, and then still longer. Eventually, Vil's iron-hard arm against her back softened, and she stepped back, away from the warm folds of his dark cloak.

She risked a glance up to find him watching her face, his eyes unreadable.

"I—" she started, then faltered. "Thank you," she said, finally, unsure what else to do.

He nodded once, and opened his mouth as if to speak, but then stopped and just stared at her. She swallowed, shivering as the night air whispered over her skin.

"Come," he said, reaching out to take her hand again. "It's not safe here."

Aelys nodded, and once more found herself being pulled down the alley. Vil kept to the shadows, moving between the buildings and streets as the night rose all around them. They didn't have far to go, and Aelys could see the inn's windows glowing with warmth as Vil urged her across the open area of the mostly deserted street.

"There they are!"

Vil stopped dead and whirled, putting himself between her and the voice that rang out. A cacophony of running steps filled the space, and by the uncertain light of the street lanterns, Aelys caught the flash of a blade as two men ran toward her from the rear.

A bowstring sang out, followed quickly by another. The closest man to her fell, gasping, as blood fountained forth from the arrow in his throat. Someone screamed, and lights bloomed in the buildings on either side as the remaining townsfolk ran from the disturbance.

The dead man's companion leapt over the body, his sword going high, blade turned so that the flat swung toward the side of Aelys's head. She let out a little scream and ducked, just in time to see a dark figure rolling toward her. Another blade flashed upward, glinting in the uncertain light before skewering the leaping attacker high on the inside of his thigh.

He let out another scream that rent the night, but before she could react, Romik uncoiled from his roll and grabbed her free hand.

"With me, quickly. Daen's watching from above. Vil?"

"With you, two dead here." Vil's voice came from right behind Aelys, but she didn't dare turn to look, lest she lose her footing.

"That's four."

"Six total. That's all of them that I saw earlier."

"Good. Let's get her inside."

Romik said this as his heavy hand hit the oaken door and swung it wide. The innkeeper looked up, startled. Romik whipped Aelys forward, propelling her over the threshold and moving to block as much of the doorway as possible. Not so much that Vil couldn't squeeze in under his arm, though, which he promptly did. Romik let him get inside, and then backed in before letting the door swing shut.

Vil grabbed her shoulders and turned her to look at him, his blue eyes intense. "You need to be upstairs. Can you make it?"

Aelys nodded, steeling herself once more for the journey through the taproom. As before, she used the energy still coursing through her system to weave a barrier to hold back the memory of fire. This preparation made all the difference, and she was able to follow Vil as he once again took her hand and led the way through the tables and up the stairs at the back of the room, leaving Romik to follow and guard their rear.

Daen met them on the landing at the top of the stairs.

"Is she—"

"Safe, well." Vil said, and a look of relief washed over Daen's features. He reached out, as if to grasp her hand, but Vil pulled her past without pausing and headed straight for her door. He stopped before entering, though, and motioned Romik forward.

"Check it. Just to be sure."

Romik nodded, and burst through the door, sword in hand. No one waited within, but he took the time to go and pull the thin curtains closed over the tiny window before turning to motion them inside.

Aelys let out a shaky breath and obeyed Vil's silent urging to sit. He let go of her hand then, though his fingers slid slowly off hers, as if he loathed to let go. She glanced up at him, startled, but he was already turning away.

"Thanks," she heard him say to Romik. "You saw them chasing us?"

"Not exactly," Romik said. He opened his hand and angled it so the light from the window illuminated that strange palm mark they all shared. Vil closed his own hand into a fist and nodded.

"Aelys," Daen murmured, pulling her attention to him. Her mattress dipped as he sat beside her, putting one arm gently around her shoulders. Her shudders grew, spreading throughout her body, and she clamped her lips shut to keep from sobbing aloud. "Shhh, it's all right. You're all right."

Aelys leaned into the warmth of him, breathing in the scent of woodsmoke and pine that always seemed to cling to Daen. He pulled her close, his muscled longbowman's arms tightening around her.

"She is all right," Vil said, in a tone that suggested he was reassuring the other two men. "Despite her best efforts."

"Go lightly, Vil," Daen warned, but Aelys sucked in a deep breath and sat up.

"No," she said, her voice wet with tears. "He's right. It's my fault. I should never have gone out alone. I just never thought that bandits might attack travelers in Mageford!"

"That's because they don't," Romik said, his voice rumbling lowly from where he leaned against the window frame. "Bandits don't, as a rule, come into towns. Towns have watches and militias to keep order and protect their citizens."

"But then why—?"

"Why don't you tell us, Bella?" That was Vil again. And once again, his voice edged into hostile territory. Aelys recoiled, her eyes going wide.

"Me? I don't know! I—"

"Where did you go?" Vil pressed.

"I-I went to the p-posting station. To send a message."

"To whom?"

"T-to my aunt."

"Why?"

Aelys opened her mouth, and then closed it, peering at him. Vil's eyes were locked on her face, but there was a tightness in his expression she hadn't noticed before. She glanced down at his black-gloved hands and noticed that they remained curled into fists.

"I . . ."

"It doesn't matter," Daen said, heat threading through his tone. "It's her business, Vil."

"Not if it puts her in danger, it's not."

"She just wanted to let her family know she was safe, right, Bella?"

Aelys nodded and pressed her lips together before looking away from Vil's piercing gaze.

"It was stupid of you to go out alone," Romik put in. "Even

in a town. You're too conspicuous. You should have told one of us, we would have taken you, or sent the message for you."

"I-I'm sorry," Aelys said, and this time, no one objected to her apology.

"She won't do it again, will you, Bella?" Daen said. He reached out to take her hand.

"Stop. Don't touch her."

Daen froze, then slowly looked up at Vil, murder in his face. "Who in seven hells—"

"Stop. This isn't about jealousy. Are you thinking about her, right now?"

Daen frowned, and Romik turned to face them from where he'd been looking out the window.

"What are you on about, Vil?" the big man rumbled.

"Can you feel them, Bella? Or is it just me?"

Aelys jumped as she realized what Vil was asking. She felt her mouth open in a little O of surprise for just a moment before she closed it with a snap and shook out her hands.

"Let me see," she said, and then mentally kicked herself for saying something so stupid just as she closed her eyes.

The dark current of energy continued to flow in from Vil, but it had gentled from its earlier torrent and settled into a steady stream. However, Vil was right, there were two other conduits there. One burned red with fire and ecstasy, searing where it touched. The other shone cool and green, like the ringing silence beneath a forest canopy. As soon as she noticed them, both of the new currents opened wider, pouring energy into her until she felt like she might just levitate off the bed.

"Yes," she whispered, and opened her eyes, fully expecting to see the world through a dark haze, or a green or red one.

"What?" Romik asked. "What do you see?" Daen moved again to take her hand, but this time it was Aelys that stopped him by pulling back.

"It's more what I *feel*," she said, her voice breathy and raw from the strain of holding so much energy in her system. "Each of you is pumping energy into me—"

"Like in the forest?" Daen asked. "You said that was part of the Ageon bond."

"Y-yes. And no. *Some* energy flow is normal with a ... a normal Ageon bond. But the *geas* bond seems to allow for ... more.

When you think about me, each of you, it pushes energy into me at a rate like nothing I've ever experienced. That's probably why I took no ill effects from the fire and the explosion at the tavern. My body was using that energy to heal from the exertion and so I didn't notice before."

"But you're noticing now?" Daen asked, confusion threading through his tone.

"Oh, yes."

"Tell them what it feels like," Vil said, his tone empty.

"It's...like a river, like three rivers of pure magic rushing into me, each flavored with the essence of one of you. Like I can *feel* part of you under my skin, flowing along my nerves..." she trailed off and shook her head. "It's too much. I...I'm afraid..."

"When we think of her, focus on her, that's when she feels us most." Vil picked up the explanation. "It feeds her magic, and she's afraid to lose control of it."

"So, what do we do?" Romik asked, his tone hushed, as if hoping Aelys wouldn't hear him.

"I don't know. So far, she's been able to use the energy to create her light, but it was like someone put the noonday sun in this very room. It burned my skin and my eyes like I was crossing a desert naked. But then, afterward, I touched her, and the energy reversed its flow back into me...and that healed me."

"Did it help her?" Daen's intensity echoed through the question.

"It seemed to."

"Then what are we waiting for?" Before anyone could stop him a third time, he reached out once more and threaded his fingers through Aelys's. The cool green flow intensified, paused, and then reversed, draining from her fingers into his like water bubbling out of a natural spring and cascading over a rock cliff to plunge into a hidden forest pool.

Daen's fingers tightened on hers, and a deep, aching moan rippled up out of him in response.

"Aelys," he whispered, his voice rough with need. He pulled, leaning closer, as if he couldn't help himself from kissing her—

Then he stopped, and his eyes narrowed as they stared into hers.

"What—" he asked, and wonder joined desire in his tone. "How is this... I can see *into* your eyes!"

Vil edged forward, his boots soundless on the wooden floor. "What do you mean, Daen?"

Daen turned to look at him. "I mean... I can see *inside* her eyes! Her iris, it's like a thousand petals all overlapping the opening of her pupil... and I can see yours, too."

"Can you see far away too? Or just minute detail?"

Daen turned toward the window, his own pupil contracting as he looked out into the growing night. "I can—Green Lady! I can read the inscription stamped on a coin that some woman is handing over to a man in the marketplace! How is this possible?"

Daen turned back to Aelys, a smile completely devoid of his usual cynicism spreading over his face. Wonder and guilt rolled through her as he brought her fingertips to his lips in a kiss.

"I—" she whispered. "It's the magic. It enhances your natural talents. I made Vil all but invisible in the alley outside when those men were chasing us. I seem to have given you even more of a raptor's eye."

"I could hit a bull's-eye at fifty yards like this," Daen said. "I can even see the effect of the wind through the trees outside and know what it would do to my arrow... this is... is this permanent?"

He turned from his study of her face to look at Vil, who shrugged, and then shook his head. "I don't think so," he said. "When she did it the first time, the shadows got deeper around me, but then she had to do it again in the alley to help us hide."

"And there are no ill effects?" Romik asked, from his post by the window. Aelys looked over to see him watching her with typical suspicion.

"Goddesses, no," Daen said, squeezing Aelys's fingers again. "It feels amazing. Like she's touching me inside my skin. But like—"

"It feels like sex," Vil said, his voice clinical and cold, and Aelys closed her eyes in shame. "She made me ejaculate the first time."

"I'm so sorry," Aelys whispered. She dropped her head and shrank inward, pulling her hand back. "I never meant for that to happen."

"That was clear," Vil said, his tone short. She glanced up at him only to see him turning back to Romik. "The second time, I was better prepared, and so I controlled my response better. What about you?" he asked Daen. "Any... physiological repercussions?"

"It was a damn close thing," he said, smirking a little. "But no. I got distracted by how beautiful her iris is up close. And then by wondering how in seven hells I could *see* that."

Vil nodded, and then turned to Romik. "You need to let her do it, too. Now."

"Me? Why?"

"Because you heard her. Her power enhances our natural gifts: mine for stealth, Daen's for sight and therefore accuracy with his bow. Especially with your gifts, we need to know how this is going to manifest for you."

"My gifts?" Romik snorted. "I have no gifts."

"Shall I enumerate them, Demon of the Arena?" For the first time, Aelys heard Vil's scathing tone directed at someone other than herself, and her eyes went wide as Vil went on. "Strength. Agility. Tactical perception and understanding. The ability to read your opponent. Body awareness. Pain tolerance... Shall I go on?"

"None of those were gifts, Vil. I worked my arse off to earn those skills."

"And you don't think I worked mine off to learn how to move silently, to disappear into shadows, to kill without being detected?"

"Which of those did she enhance for you?"

"All of them."

"*All?*"

"Every one."

In the silence that followed, Aelys risked another glance at Romik. He turned from Vil to meet her gaze.

"Is this just another way to bind us closer to you, Bella?" he asked, his lip curling in a bit of a snarl. "To strip our will away and make us even more yours?"

"N-no," she said. "At least, I don't think so. I wouldn't— I didn't even know that pushing energy to you would enhance your gifts. It's how we help Ageons heal faster, but nothing in the books said—though there *are* a few songs, and a legend or two. But they're just *stories*! There isn't a mage alive who knows how to deal with... all this, I'd stake my life on it!"

Aelys dragged in a deep breath and closed her eyes for a moment. *Think!*

"However," she said, opening her eyes but refusing to meet any of their gazes. "Now that I know the increased energy flows are there, I can work on a way to slow them down, so that I'm not pulling so much energy through you that I... have problems."

"After you reverse the flow through Romik," Vil said. "We

need to know what it will do. I don't want our first time trying it to be in the middle of a fight."

Romik grunted, as if this was a valid point. Then he let out a sigh and pushed away from the wall.

"Fine," he said. "Let's get this over with, then. What do I have to do?"

"Um...think about me," Aelys said, turning her body on the bed so she could more fully face him. "And then, when I say, I need you to...touch me."

"Touch you."

Aelys swallowed hard and reached her left hand toward him. "Just a little. I'm sorry."

"Stop apologizing," Vil and Daen said together. It should have been funny, but no one laughed.

"Fine. Let's just do this."

"Okay," she said. "Are you thinking about me?"

He laughed, and the sound of it carried notes of despair. "Yes, Bella. I am thinking about you."

"We're always thinking about you," Daen whispered next to her. "We can't help it."

"I'm—"

"Don't say you're sorry," Vil snapped. "Just reverse the flow."

Aelys pressed her lips together and nodded, and then closed her eyes and reached for the red current searing its way through her nerve pathways.

Unlike Romik himself, the energy flow leapt for her with joyous abandon. Aelys welcomed the burn, opening her mind and her energy to receive the inflow.

"Take her hand." Vil's voice, urging Romik along. Aelys kept her eyes closed, kept her focus on that pulsing red river as it scorched its way through her system.

Slowly, a warm hand enveloped hers, the touch soft despite the myriad calluses along each finger.

Aelys inhaled, and then willed the flow to reverse, pouring back through her and into Romik. His careful grip tightened spasmodically on her hand until she cried out. Her eyes flew open just in time to see him let go of her as if she'd burned him, then he stumbled backward.

Only he didn't really stumble. He should have; it looked very much like he overbalanced from where he'd crouched next to the bed in order to take her hand. But he moved like water, or like fire itself as he pivoted, sidestepped, and stayed upright.

"Enhanced agility," Vil said, a note of satisfaction in his tone.

"And strength, too," Daen said, tilting his head at where Aelys cradled her hand to her chest. "You damn near crushed her fingers, Ro."

"Red Lady! Bella, did I hurt you?"

"N-no," she breathed. "No, I just...I didn't expect it."

"Right. So...are you happy now?" Romik asked, turning to glare at Vil. His rugged face was stained red, as if the blood flowed very close to his skin.

"Not remotely," Vil said. "But I think I have the information I wanted. Bella, will you be all right for the night now? No more uncontrolled light spells?"

"I'm fine," she said. "I...I think I know how I can close the flows down to a trickle, now that they've been established and... Well. Now that we've done what we've done."

"Fine," Romik snapped. He stomped past her without another word and slammed open the door, retreating to the room the three of them intended to share.

"Bloody tree bole," Daen muttered.

"Go lightly," Vil said, echoing Daen's warning from earlier. "Aggression is likely one of the things she enhanced. He's not going to be fully himself. Just as you are a lot less of a hothead than usual right now."

"I am?"

"Yes. Focus is one of your talents, is it not? Something you've worked hard to develop?"

"Huh. I guess so." Daen turned to Aelys with a smile. "Thank you, Bella, for this amazing gift."

"I didn't...I...you shouldn't thank me."

"I do what I want," he said, and leaned forward to press a kiss to the top of her head. "Sleep well, Bella. We've got a busy day tomorrow." He, too, stood and walked out of the room, though he looked back at her with a smile and a glint of longing in his eye before he exited.

"You're all leaving me alone tonight?" Aelys said, before she really realized she meant to speak. Vil went very still, his eyes locked on hers.

"Do you want me to stay?" he asked, his voice empty.

Yes. "N-no," she said. "I just...I wasn't sure if...the bandits..."

He looked at her for a long moment before his lips curved in a smirk. "Bella, you have never rested safer in your life than you will this night. You have three Ageons bound to your protection. And not one of us is going to sleep tonight."

Inhale, one, two, three. Hold. Exhale, one, two, three, four. Hold. Inhale...

Romik sat on one of the two narrow cots, his elbows on his knees as he shoved his hands through his hair and forced his mind to focus on the breathing exercises he'd learned decades ago in the bowels of the gladiator training arena.

It had been years since he felt rage coursing under his skin, hazing his vision, driving him forward to slash and tear and rend. Discipline had always been his watchword, his bulwark against that destructive urge, and so the ritual, the routine of his breathing kept the rage from driving him into a frenzy...

But just barely. Red Lady damn that girl...

Romik couldn't complete the thought before the door opened and he heard Daen and Vil walk in. He didn't look up right away, afraid that the rage might leak through and let his brothers see how close he'd come to the edge.

"See," Vil said. Romik tensed and was about to demand clarification, but Daen responded before he could.

"Yeah, you're right."

"Right about what?" Romik growled.

"Vil said that aggression is another one of your gifts, and so it got enhanced along with everything else." Romik felt the thin mattress of the cot dip as Daen sat not far away.

He looked up to see his ex-Forester brother leaning back on one elbow.

"You look supremely unconcerned," Romik said, nearly spitting the words.

"Nothing to be concerned about," Daen said. Romik glanced over at Vil, but their third brother said nothing, merely leaned against the closed door with his arms crossed.

"No? I could kill you with my bare hands, Daen. I've done it before."

"But not to me. And besides, no matter how angry and aggressive you feel, you'll never lose control accidentally."

"Why are you always so fucking confident?" Romik hated the bitter way his words sounded, but he didn't seem to be able to make them come out any other way.

Daen let out a little laugh. "Because, Romik. You heard Vil. Aelys enhanced *all* of your skills and gifts. So not just your killer instinct, but also the discipline to keep it in check."

Romik blinked in confusion, which elicited a smile and a wink from Daen. He turned his head to look inquiringly at Vil, who stayed predictably silent. He did incline his head slightly, which Romik took to be a nod of agreement.

Inhale, one, two, three . . . Red Lady's blade, he's right!

Romik straightened his spine and scrubbed his hands over his face before willing his hands to drop to his sides. He blew out an explosive breath and shook his head.

"That girl—"

"But it would be good in a fight, wouldn't it?" Vil's interruption startled Romik, and he snapped his head over to look in his direction.

"What do you mean?"

"The increased aggression, the agility, the strength. It's like she made you better. Think about how effective that would be in a fight."

"But at what cost?" Romik swallowed hard, hating the rough vulnerability that leaked into his words. "What is she doing to us? I can't—I could barely keep her out of my head anyway, and now this?"

Daen let out a snort and rolled his eyes. "Romik, be reasonable. It's not as if she's hurting us. Everything she's done has felt really good, in fact." He grinned and the glint in his eyes made Romik have to curl his hands into fists.

Maybe I won't kill you with my bare hands, brother, *but I'll happily rearrange that pretty face of yours . . .*

"You've never been enslaved," Vil said, his icy voice cracking through the red haze of Romik's anger. "Don't belittle what you don't understand, Daen."

"I'm not—"

"She commands our very bodies with a thought," Romik blurted. "I've spent years, *decades*, perfecting my emotional control and she takes me to the ragged edge of it every time she looks at me. Don't you see how that's dangerous, Daen? Don't you see how easily she could break us?"

"But she hasn't!" Daen sat up, his good-natured expression falling away to be replaced by a look of dark intensity that Romik instantly recognized. He'd seen it on his own face reflected in the polished bronze doors of a thousand arenas. "She hasn't done anything except need our help. She asked that we take her home—a job she *hired* us to do, I might add! Our Bella isn't your old master, Romik, and she's not a master criminal. *She is not our enemy!*"

"She isn't our friend," Romik shot back. "She's a noble lady, and you know as well as I what those types are like."

"Aelys is—"

"Different?" Vil asked, his voice mocking. "How many times did you think that about one of your would-be friends in the Foresters, Daen? And how many times did they end up stabbing you in the back?"

Daen stiffened, his intensity turning to anger.

"Don't belittle what you don't understand," he snarled back at Vil, heated temper in his words. "How many times did your thieving would-be friends do the same?"

"Once."

"Only once?"

"Yes. Once was enough to teach me not to trust 'friends' at my back. That is why I swore to be brother to you both. Friendship isn't enough of a bond."

Romik watched as Daen and Vil stared at each other for a long, silent second. Then Daen exploded up off the bed and wrapped his arms around Vil, pulling him in for a tight, rough hug. Because he was looking for it, Romik saw Vil's hand twitch toward one of his hidden knives. But his brother didn't draw. Instead, he returned Daen's embrace and pounded him lightly on the back.

"I'm sorry." Daen let go and stepped back. "I didn't mean to snap at you. I've got a temper...but I trust you. I trust you both at my back, and beside me. We *are* sworn brothers. I meant every word of that oath."

"So did I," Romik said. "So did we all. And that's why I think we need to be careful with this girl."

Daen opened his mouth as if he would argue, but then he closed it again. "I understand you're trying to look out for us, Ro," he said after a moment. "I respect your need to do that."

"And I know you're drawn to her. Seven hells, *I'm* drawn to her. We all are, we know that. And we have this... *need* to protect her. So, fine. We'll protect her, but I'm not going to let anything, not even her, tear us apart. I..." Romik swallowed again; his throat felt thick and uncomfortable. "Brothers are a new luxury for me. I have missed you both. And I'm not about to lose you again."

"I won't let that happen," Vil said, drawing Romik's gaze. "We've all been through too much alone. I won't let us be separated again. Even if—" He broke off.

"Even if what?" Daen asked.

"I hope you're right about her, Daen. For the record, I hope she's as good and innocent as she appears. But we've all lived enough to know that hope is not a strategy. So, if she *does* try to tear us apart, or betray us, or use our bonds to her against us or each other—I will kill her."

Romik stiffened as a sudden urge to wrap his fingers around his brother's throat swept through him. He gritted his teeth and fisted his hands in the threadbare coverlet beneath him.

"How, brother?" he scoffed. "Even hearing you say that makes me want to strangle you. That's the worst part! With the way we... feel... about her, how do you think you could manage to do that? Daen and I would be driven to stop you."

Vil looked at him with those icy, intense blue eyes and a shiver ran down Romik's spine. "It's what I do, Romik. You'd never even know until it was done. I swear to you."

"And what about *your* compulsion?" Daen pressed. "Are you saying you don't feel the same things Ro and I do, about her?"

"No, I feel them."

"So then... how?"

Vil smiled, though it didn't touch his eyes. The chill running down Romik's spine suddenly spread throughout his body, and for the first time, he realized just how much of a predator his brother really was.

"It wouldn't be the first time I've killed someone I loved."

CHAPTER FIVE

DAEN RUBBED HIS EYES AND SCOWLED UP AT THE CRYSTALLINE blue of the sky and the frustratingly cheery sunlight that bathed the marketplace like a benediction. The sun beamed back, unconcerned with Daen's lack of sleep, hatred for towns, and building impatience to be on the road.

"Last stop," Romik promised him as they paused before yet another shop and pushed open the door to the accompaniment of tiny bells.

"Good morning!" an older woman's voice sang out to them from somewhere in the back. "I'll be right out, my dear ones."

Daen groaned. "I can't handle this," he whispered to Romik. "I'm going to wait outside."

Romik nodded and clapped him on the shoulder, squeezing lightly and looking a question at his friend.

"I'm okay. Just need some air."

Romik nodded again and let go just as a tiny woman with a cloud of white hair emerged from the rear of the shop. She said something else, but Daen didn't register it as he pushed the jangly door open and stepped back into the street outside.

It wasn't much better out there; the buildings still loomed too close. But at least he could see the sky, and both ends of this short street just off the marketplace. He drew in a deep breath and let it out slowly, focusing his eyes on an object in the road at the end of the lane. It glinted, and he was pretty sure he could hit it, if he had to. That was about twenty yards away. Which meant that his eyesight was back to normal.

The memory of Aelys's sleeping face rose up in his mind. She'd been exhausted, and still sleeping off yesterday's exertions when he'd looked in on her before he and Romik left to gather supplies for their job. Her face had been pale, with dark circles under her eyes, and her hair loose and tangled around her bearing mute testimony of the restlessness of her sleep. He'd wanted nothing more than to crawl into the cot beside her, draw her head to rest on his chest, wrap his arms around her and reassure her that she was safe, he was there, and nothing was ever going to harm her again.

But then Romik had growled at him that it was time to go. He'd hated to leave, but he'd shared a look with Vil, who gave him one of his silent nods. As much as Daen loathed the idea of not being the one to look after Aelys, at least he knew his brother would keep her safe, would protect her as well as he himself could.

He didn't like it, but he could live with it. At least long enough to help Romik buy the things they'd need for this job.

"That's it," Romik said over the jingle of the shop door's bells as he stepped out, slinging his pack over his shoulder. "Those herbs were the last things we needed. Let's go get the others and we can head out."

Daen nodded and released the thoughts of Aelys to the back corner of his mind where she'd taken up permanent residence. Just turning his steps toward the inn lightened his mood, and he glanced up at the sky with a tiny, self-deprecating smile.

By the time they returned to the inn, Aelys had risen, packed, and eaten, and she and Vil were ready to leave. They redistributed the food and supplies that he and Romik had acquired and headed back out of the town on foot—their advance had been enough to buy supplies, but not horses and tack—following one of the many small roads that branched off the imperial highway leading out of town.

That route took them into the tree line just as the sun reached its zenith. They'd follow this small, little-used forestry track until it intersected the imperial road Gormren's shipment had used, then follow it in parallel until they found the shipment itself. Daen drew in a deep lungful of air and rolled his head on his neck, feeling the oppressive weight of the close-packed buildings and lives lived on top of each other melt away.

"Feeling better?"

Aelys's tentative question brought his attention snapping down to her, and something almost painful twisted in his chest as he met her blue gaze.

"A little, yeah. I don't really like towns."

"I could tell," she said with a small smile.

"Oh, it was obvious?"

"Not really. Probably not to anyone else. I could just tell. Your energy felt different. Like the flow was constricted, just a little. Around the edges—" She broke off and shook her head. "I'm sorry, I'm explaining this badly."

"No, that made sense," he said, adjusting his stride to match hers. "And how does my energy feel now?"

Aelys smiled, and the twisting in his chest ratcheted up a notch, followed by a flood of warmth that spread throughout his body. He smiled back, leaning toward her as she considered her answer.

"You feel...more free. Like a river current that's had obstructions removed from its channel. And green, alive. You always feel like living things to me."

"Do I? That's interesting."

Aelys nodded. "It's probably just my mind making an association, because of what I know about you. The texts on the subject are nonspecific, but from what I gather, it's not uncommon for mages to feel their Ageons as a unique sensation in their minds."

"Because of the energy flow."

"Yes. The descriptions of what that feels like are not very helpful, though. I suspect it varies depending on the pairing and the strength of the flow between them. It seems that most mages simply feel a vague kind of energetic tether to their protector. They're really not descriptive at all."

"But you feel me, distinctly? More than 'a vague tether'? Separate from Vil and Romik?"

"Yes, to me, you feel like the forest, like sun-dappled soil under a leafy canopy. Like game grazing in a meadow and predators watching from within shadowy branches."

"Predators? So, I don't feel...safe?"

She looked up at him again, hitting him with the full force of those intense blue eyes that he now shared.

"Not safe for everyone," she said, her voice going quieter. "I know you're a dangerous man."

"Not safe for everyone," he echoed. "But for you?"

He watched her swallow, and then look down and away. "Yes," she whispered, so low he could barely hear you. "You feel safe for me. I know you can't hurt me."

"Hey," he said, reaching out to capture her fingers lightly with his. "That's a good thing, isn't it?"

"It would be," she said. "If you had any choice in the matter."

"Bella, I'm not a child." Daen squeezed her fingers gently until she looked up at him.

"I never said—"

"No, listen. I'm not a child, I'm an adult. And like every adult worth the name, I've discovered that I can, in fact, do things I don't want to do. Even really difficult things. You're right, I am safe for you. But I am that way because I choose to be, not because you compel it. Do you understand the difference?"

"But you choose it because of the bond! Because of the way I *make* you feel."

"Trust me, Bella. I can ignore my feelings. We all can. We're men of will, and that means no emotion is ever going to over-power our agency. So, you can stop torturing yourself, all right? It's unnecessary. And it's not doing what you think it's doing."

"I don't—what?"

Daen let his smile fall away. "You're hoping that if you pun-ish yourself enough, you will earn the love and respect of the people around you. But trust me, it doesn't work that way. I should know, I tried hard enough as a young kid. But it never worked. Instead, you know what I learned?"

"What?"

He let himself smile again and lifted their joined hands to brush his knuckles against her cheekbone. "I learned that people will value you exactly as much as you value yourself. And that anyone worth having in your life will respect you for respecting yourself."

Aelys swallowed and pulled her fingers free. He let her go, watching as she shut her emotions down and put them behind a blank mask of politeness.

"That's very interesting," she said, her voice calm but for the tiny flutter of a tremor along the edges.

"Something to think about, at least," he replied, letting his own voice go neutral. "But you're right about one thing, Bella."

"What's that?"

"You're safe with me. You're safe with the three of us. But even Romik, Vil, and I can't keep you safe from your own cruelty to yourself. Only you can do that."

Vil lifted a hand and gently pushed a branch aside, ducking his body low enough to pass under it without it catching on his hood. Romik's plan of staying off the main road and following it in parallel had sounded good back at the inn, but there were drawbacks to tramping through the forest for most of a day.

Though, naturally, he did his best to avoid "tramping" anywhere. He might not be as natural as Daen in this environment, but any burglar worth his salt knew how to walk on uneven surfaces without making too much noise.

Though I'd be even more silent if I had her reverse the energy flow again.

The thought rose up out of the back of Vil's brain. Not that it surprised him. Any provocation, any association was enough for his thoughts to turn to Aelys. She was a mystery he couldn't fully unlock, a safe he couldn't quite crack...

And an addiction waiting to happen. Vil felt his fingers twitch in her direction as she stepped toward him and maneuvered her way around a thick tree trunk. He curled his gloved hands into fists and held himself still as she passed, her eyes intent on the ground in front of her.

In the back corner of his mind, where his darkest thoughts held sway, a sudden savage wish erupted.

If someone attacked, right now, I could grab her, I could hold her, I could make us disappear again...

"Hold."

Daen's murmured command cut through Vil's dangerous imaginings. He blinked and focused on his brother, who now beckoned him, Romik, and Aelys closer.

"I heard cursing up ahead," he said, pointing. "The road comes up over this same rise we're on, and then drops down into the bottom and turns sharply."

"Sounds perfect for an ambush," Romik put in.

"Exactly. What I heard could have been anyone taking the

road, we've heard several groups already this afternoon. But at this spot, in particular...well. It could be nothing. Or it could be something."

"Can we get closer without being seen?"

"I can," Vil said. "Especially if—" He turned to Aelys, watching her pale eyes widen as she realized what he was asking.

"Oh! You want me to...reverse the flow again?"

"Can you do it?" Romik asked, his voice harsh.

"Y-yes. Yes, of course! I'm just... Never mind. Yes. Yes I can."

Vil leaned forward, looking into her eyes. She glanced away, but before he could say anything, she squared her shoulders, looked back at him and nodded, holding out her hands.

Vil stepped closer, taking her bare hands with his gloved ones. With his left hand, he reached up and pressed her palm to the exposed skin on the side of his neck. He braced his feet, took a deep breath and nodded.

Tingling, buzzing heat poured into his system from her touch. He clenched his jaw and used every trick he knew to impose control on his body, but he couldn't keep from inhaling as pleasure sang along every nerve, gathering and tightening low in his groin.

Vil's right hand threaded through Aelys's fingers. He slid his left down along her arm, cupping the back of her neck as he leaned closer.

"Bloody goddess," Romik gasped. "The shadows—you've almost disappeared!"

Vil froze, his lips hovering just above Aelys's. He tasted her breath.

"I'll be right back," he said, letting his lips brush hers as he spoke.

And then he let go and stepped away, pulling his cloak around him as he sank back further into the shadows beneath the trees.

Now he could move silently as he wove his way through the undergrowth back toward the road. He kept his hood up and stayed in the lengthening afternoon shadows, but looked around as he walked, searching for something in particular...

Perfect.

He stepped beneath the spreading branches of the ancient tree and leapt up, his hands gripping the rough bark of the lowest branch. Aelys's energy rippled through his muscles as he pulled himself up with hardly any effort at all. His lips curved in a small smile as he scaled the tree up to the thinnest branches that would hold his weight.

The road wound through the trunks beneath him, sunken into the curve of the terrain by centuries of human and animal traffic. Thanks to his vantage point, Vil had a bird's-eye view of the curve Daen had described. As Romik had surmised, it was, indeed, perfect for an ambush.

As the drivers and guards of two overturned carts could attest. It looked like someone had gone through the contents, as smashed remnants of crates littered the ground between the twisted bodies of dead horses, guards, and carters, but not everything had been taken. Vil could see several farm implements scattered alongside the road.

The harsh, hacking sound of someone coughing reverberated up from below, and Vil shifted his stance so he could look in that direction. Sure enough, a furtive figure leaned out of the scrub brush that lined the road and slowly got to his feet. He looked around, paused for several heartbeats, and then let out a low whistle. More men, all skinny and ragged like this one, emerged from the undergrowth and began picking their way toward the overturned wagons.

Vil stayed long enough to count ten of them before easing back to the central trunk of his tree and climbing down. A few moments later, he emerged from the shadows next to Aelys and pulled his hood back far enough that she could see his face.

"Did you find anything?" she asked, unsurprised by his presence. Behind her, Romik blinked and stiffened, and Daen snapped his head in their direction, startled. But Aelys seemed to have known where he was the whole time.

The geas. *That's all it is. She's made it plain that it isn't . . . anything else.*

"It's our shipment," Vil confirmed. "Someone attacked it. But something is off. The caravan had guards; I saw their bodies. And something killed them all."

"So, was it bandits I heard?" Daen asked.

"Scavengers, more like," Vil said. "I counted ten. Armed. Nothing fancy, knives and such. Mean, but not organized or equipped to take on caravan guards."

"Scavengers can be dangerous," Romik said, his expression grim. "We always had to watch for them after a battle. They'd come out and knife the wounded to rob them of their gear."

"Desperate men are always dangerous," Daen said. "But then, so are we."

"So, we are." Romik smiled a little smile and then nodded. "And Gormren was clear that he'd pay well for that correspondence alone. Do we take them on?"

Romik looked first at Daen, who nodded, and then at Vil. Vil didn't say anything, just let his lips curve in a tiny half smile. Romik snorted softly and rolled his shoulders, as if getting ready for action.

"All right, here's what I want," the big warrior said. "Daen, you're on overwatch. Get up in a tree or on a rise or something. Vil, you come at them through the trees, but wait until I arrive."

"How are you getting to them?"

Romik's smile grew, and Vil recognized an echo of his own inner savagery glinting in his brother's eyes.

"I'm going to walk down the road. Whistling. Like an unwary traveler."

Daen chuckled softly, and Vil felt his own smile emerge.

"What about me?"

Aelys's soft voice made three sets of eyes snap to her pale, earnest face. She flinched backward from their sudden attention, and then swallowed and squared her shoulders.

"You? You will stay here, away from any trouble," Romik growled.

"No, I—"

"I can't have you distracting us—" he started to say over her protest, but he stopped when Vil held up a hand.

"That won't work, Romik. What if one of the scavengers gets around us back here and finds her? Put her up in the tree with Daen, she'll be safe enough there with him."

"Can you climb, Bella?" Romik asked, his voice hard.

Aelys hesitated, and then swallowed again and nodded.

"I'll help her," Daen said, winking at Aelys. "It's a good plan, Ro. She'll be safe with me while you and Vil stir up mayhem and I pick them off from above."

"Fine," Romik said on a gusty exhale. "Then let's go—"

"No, wait," Aelys said, breaking into the conversation again. She lifted her hands. "I . . . I've pushed energy at Vil, but—don't you all want some?"

Vil fisted his hands and kept them firmly by his side as Daen strode over to take Aelys's hands in his own.

"Always." Vil barely heard Daen's soft reply, and the intimate note in his voice reverberated through Vil, releasing a shockwave of desire in its wake.

Stop, he told himself, unable to tear his eyes away as Daen, too, lifted Aelys's hands to the bare skin of his neck, pulling her close in an embrace. *Jealousy is useless. Daen is her Ageon. He is* your *brother. She needs him as much as she needs you . . .*

And therein lies the problem. Vil kept his face icy and blank, but the epiphany ignited in his mind and burned through him like a firestorm as he watched Daen's blue eyes close in ecstasy. *Maybe she needs a knife in the dark, but she doesn't want one. She needs Daen . . . and she wants him, too.*

Vil didn't do unrequited love. Either someone wanted him, or they didn't. He saw it as a waste of time to pursue a liaison where one wasn't wanted by both parties. In any other circumstance, he would walk away, leaving Daen the victor and willing the girl out of his head.

But I can't. Not with her. The geas *has made that impossible. And she* does *need me, whether she wants to admit it or not.*

He exhaled, forcing his shoulders to relax away from his ears, his fingers to uncurl as Daen bent his head and brushed his lips against Aelys's, so similar to how Vil himself had done earlier.

She needs him, she needs me, she needs Romik. She needs us all, she needs protectors, and we are hers. I am hers, and so is Daen, so is Romik. She needs us all, and we are hers.

Vil whispered these words silently in the privacy of his mind. Daen smiled against Aelys's lips and stepped back, shoving a hand into his hair and gesturing to Romik.

"Go now, Ro, or I'll kiss her again and never let her go."

Romik growled a response that Vil didn't hear and stepped carefully toward Aelys.

"Y-you don't have to, if you don't want," she said, something that looked like worry crossing her face. "I just thought—"

"I want to," Romik said. "To my core I want to, I just wish I didn't." And he took her outstretched hands in one quick motion and slapped them to the sides of his throat. Daen came to stand by Vil, his back to Romik and Aelys. The archer's hands visibly trembled as he shook them out, and then he reached back to unsling his bow.

"You all right?" Vil asked quietly. "It didn't feel different this time, did it?"

"Stronger," Daen replied just as softly. "Better. I . . . It was harder to let her go."

"Same. But your focus, your vision?"

Daen looked up at Vil. "Better than when we tried it in Mageford. Are *you* all right?"

Vil nodded.

"It's hard, isn't it? Watching her with either of us? I know Romik and I . . . well, I'm pretty sure he was holding himself back from pummeling you before you left to do your recon."

"She needs all of us," Vil said, echoing the mantra that still filled his mind. "I keep trying to remember that. She needs what each of us brings to her. Without any one of us, she's less safe, less . . . powerful. We're *all* hers."

"That's what I keep telling myself."

"Is it working?"

"Not really," Daen said, flashing him a wry, self-deprecating smile. "Or, maybe a little, but not as quickly as I'd like. I just . . . *want . . .*"

"I know. Take comfort in the fact that she wants you too. More than me or Romik. *We* terrify her. You delight her. It's good, though," Vil said, ignoring the feeling that he was talking in an attempt to convince himself. "It's better that way. When this is all said and done, she will still need a protector. I'd rather it be one of us than anyone else. If she bonds with you romantically, then maybe . . . and then at least we'll know she's safe." He turned back to watch Romik, who stood with eyes closed, motionless in the tiny clearing with his hands wrapped around Aelys's wrists.

She swayed forward, off-balance from having to reach up to Romik's neck, and Vil watched as his sworn brother moved faster than thought to catch her, holding her tightly against his chest.

She needs us all. We are all hers.

"How can you give her up?" Daen whispered next to him. "I don't think I could."

"Let's hope you don't have to make that choice, brother," Vil said in a parting shot over his shoulder as Romik carefully set Aelys back on her feet and backed away from her.

It felt a little like being drunk, only instead of his reactions being slower, clumsier, the opposite was true. Romik felt energy coursing through his body like heat lightning, giving him a strength and vitality he hadn't felt since he'd been a youth of a score-and-one years. His senses felt sharper, his mind quicker, and it was almost as if he could *feel* the presence of his brothers in the trees around him as he walked.

Vil, he knew, would be off to the side, crouching in the shadows beyond the overturned carts, ready to strike as soon as Romik provided the perfect distraction. Daen, perching high on one of the overhanging branches that crisscrossed above, nearly blotting out the sky.

And Aelys, crouching close to Daen, pulling energy through each of them only to turn it around and feed it back into their systems, making them stronger, smarter, faster...

Better. She made them better, and it made him hate her all the more.

Except I can't really hate her, can I?

Romik stepped down from the tree line to the mud-soaked surface of the road itself and shook his head. He was literally walking into an ambush. He didn't have time to remember the way her fingertips had trembled against his skin, or the heat of her tiny body as she collapsed into his chest...

Red Lady's blade! Focus, Demon! You're like a green kid about to step onto the sands, hoping his latest ladylove is watching. Get her OUT of your head!

Muffled cursing and the sounds of a scuffle drifted through the trees toward him, and Romik blinked and turned his attention to the curving road in front of him. Fortunately, the moment he stopped fighting to forget about her, the tactile memories of Aelys's skin faded into the background of his mind. He squared his shoulders and started walking forward, whistling, as he'd promised.

The unmistakable sounds of men hissing at each other to be quiet reached him just as he started into the curve of the road. He continued forward, unhurried, and stopped in his tracks when a dirty-faced, stick-skinny man darted out of the underbrush to stand in front of him, knife drawn.

"'Ere now, what're ye doin' down this road, ye?"

"I...was just traveling."

"Where ye goin', then?"

"I...Cievers, eventually," Romik said. Movement drew his eyes to the side, where he spotted two more men emerging from behind the overturned wreckage of a wagon. "I'm just passing through."

"Passin' through got a price though, don't it?" the first man said, opening his mouth in a stinking grin that was probably supposed to be sinister.

"This is an imperial road—"

"Emperor ain't here, though, is he?" The man brandished his knife, gesturing with it to his own chest before pointing it at Romik's throat. "Just ol' Tev. And ol' Tev says passin' through definitely got a price."

"I don't have anything for you."

Tev looked down the line of Romik's body, eyes narrowing as he caught sight of Romik's sword hilt.

"Got a pretty fine-looking sword there. Be worth a Muni or two... or your life." Tev's grin stretched wide again, and a chuckle rippled through the men now arrayed on both sides of them.

"It's worth more than a Muni or two," Romik said, and he struck, lunging forward to knock Tev off-balance and the outstretched knife hand away. He spun, drawing his sword and taking the first of Tev's men high in the gut, interrupting the scavenger's shout of fury.

Romik twisted the hilt and ripped the sword out of the man's body, and then danced to the side as another scavenger attacked from his right.

A coughing gasp behind him had him spinning just in time to see another attacker drop midstride, revealing Vil standing behind him, both knives out and bloody.

"Behind you," Vil said in a conversational tone, and sent his right-hand knife flying through the air, tip-over-hilt, to bury itself in ol' Tev's eye. Tev let out a howl and collapsed over the eviscerated body of his moaning companion. Romik raised his blade and lunged at the attacker next to Tev, covering Vil as he retrieved his knife, and together the two of them proceeded to cut down the rest of the ragged opposition.

A red haze clouded the edges of Romik's vision as he moved in concert with his brothers. With every sword thrust, Vil was there, covering his offside. Time and again, Daen's bowstring sang out, piercing shoulders, skulls, torsos, filling the air with a fine, red mist as the ragged, desperate, dangerous men fell again and again—

"Romik! Ro! It's done! That's all of them!"

Romik blinked rapidly, dispelling the red haze and focusing on Daen's smiling face. His chest heaved with exertion, but he still felt the power of Aelys's energy coursing through his veins. Daen reached out and slapped him on the shoulder.

"Where's the girl," he croaked out. "Our Bella?"

"I'm here," she said, her voice tentative as always. A shy, small smile played about her lips as she stepped out from behind Daen. As always, her skin shone pale in the light of the setting sun, and Romik immediately noticed that she was determinedly not looking at the bodies strewn in his wake. But she was there, whole, and smiling at him.

Relief and joy swept through him, followed by swelling irritation.

"Shoulda stayed in the tree," he growled.

"I came down, so she did too," Daen said, his own voice shaded with annoyance. "We agreed she's safest with us, rather than alone. Besides, I don't think any of this lot"—he nudged the bloodied torso of a dismembered scavenger "—is going to be giving anyone any trouble again."

"Daen. Come over here."

Vil's voice didn't sound alarmed, per se, but Romik felt his battle readiness snap back into place. As Daen turned and stepped off to answer their brother's call, Romik reached out with his left hand and grabbed hold of Aelys's wrist, drawing her to his side.

"Stay close to me," he said, not looking at her. Nevertheless, he could feel her eyes on his face. He gritted his teeth and tried not to imagine the fear she always got in her eyes whenever he got close to her.

I'm too gruff with her, but what in the Red Lady's halls am I supposed to do? This bond is already too much! I can't get attached . . . or at least not more attached, anyway. Bloody blades, I hate this mess!

"Look here," Vil said, pointing to one of the bloated bodies on the ground. This one wasn't one of their kills. Probably the cart's driver, judging by his dress and the angle of his body where it had been half buried and trapped under the overturned wagon. It had obviously been out there for a few days. Romik could taste the stench of putrefaction coating his nose and mouth, and Aelys let out a little moan of distress as they approached behind Daen.

"The scavengers must have kept the wildlife away," Daen said, straightening up from where he'd been collecting arrows from the bodies. "Otherwise, this poor guy wouldn't be in such good shape."

"That's what I thought, too," Vil said. "But it looked very much like they arrived just before I did to recon the area. And then I noticed these marks here." He pointed to the unfortunate driver's throat, which gaped open in a ragged wound. "It's like a knife cut, but not exactly. I don't know what kind of weapon would make a mark like that."

Romik leaned in to look and realized that his brother was right. The ragged slash didn't look quite like a knife wound, but it definitely wasn't the work of teeth or claws.

"Nothing I've seen would make a cut like that," he said. "But Gormren said the orders he wanted would be in a hidden compartment under the driver's seat." He reached into his shirt and pulled out the thin strip of leather he wore around his neck. The tiny brass key the man had included with their payment dangled from the strip. "Let's find it and go."

Together, he and his brothers did their best to step carefully around the driver's corpse, but it took several long, uncomfortably noxious moments before he finally found the false panel and pried it loose to reveal a metal strongbox with a keyhole.

"Got it," he said as he opened the box and pulled out a thick packet wrapped in waxed cloth and sealed with Gormren's sigil.

"Give it to me," Aelys said behind him. "I've a pocket in my cloak with a magical seam. It will be safe there."

Romik turned and looked at her for a long moment, and then nodded, handing it over.

"Here's another odd thing," Vil said, pointing to an Imperial that lay in the shadow of the inverted driver's seat. "The driver's strongbox tipped over and spilled, but no one bothered to pick up these coins until our friends here showed up. This shipment's been missing for how long? Why hasn't anyone looted it before now?"

"You're right," Daen said. "We should go—"

"Look!" Aelys screamed, pointing to her left. Without thought, Romik moved, pivoting and pulling her behind him as he drew his sword once more to face the threat. He felt, more than saw, Daen nocking an arrow behind him, and Vil crouching in the cart's shadow with his knives out.

For two heartbeats, nothing moved.

Then the ground under the far tree line started to boil.

The undergrowth itself writhed and twisted as scores of short, squat, horned nightmares with beady eyes emerged into the clearing, rushing toward them with strangely glinting black knives held high in their first two limbs.

They emitted a weird insectoid clicking sound that sent fear shivering down his spine, but he raised his sword and forced himself to speak calmly.

"Nasty creatures coming in from the left," he said, his voice empty enough to make Vil proud.

"And right," Daen said. "Goblants. Watch the knives, they poison them."

"We're surrounded," Vil added. "This was the trap. Not the scavengers."

And the creatures attacked.

In one rushing wave, they charged, limbs clicking and black knives glinting like glass in the setting sun. Daen's bowstring began to sing out again and again, and Romik lunged, sweeping his blade to the side to mow through the vanguard of the seething mass reaching for them.

His blade caught on a slick, tight juncture in one of the creatures' exoskeletons. He pulled, but the creature's corpse was light enough that it stayed on the blade and just moved with him.

"Red Lady!" he cursed, and then felt Aelys's fingertips on the back of his neck.

Fire poured into him, searing along every nerve. He lifted his sword high and brought the corpse down on one of its fellows like a hammer. The blade sheared through the both of them, coming away streaked with green ichor.

Daen's bowstring sang out once more, and then fell silent.

"I'm out," he called, his voice empty. A hiss of steel on leather told Romik that his brother had pulled the short sword he carried as a backup weapon. Aelys's touch vanished, and Daen let out a grunt behind him.

"Bella! Make the shield! Like at the tavern!" Vil said, his tone like iron. Behind Romik, Aelys gasped.

"I—I can't. Not that big. I don't know how I did that!"

"You pulled the power through us, you said. Pull it now. We're not going to last much longer if they keep coming!"

"More on the right," Daen called out.

"Bella!"

White agony erupted in Romik's thigh, just above his knee. He stumbled, sweeping out with his blade and took the head off the creature that had just buried its weird black glass knife in his thigh. He reached down to pull the knife out, but instead the edges of his vision closed in, and black nothingness enveloped him.

Who is screaming? Aelys thought for a surreal split-second. Then reality came rushing in.

Oh, it's me. I'm screaming.

"Romik's down!" Daen shouted.

"Bella! Pull your power! Do it now!"

"I don't know any spell but magelight!" she sobbed, dropping to her knees beside Romik.

"Do your magelight spell, Aelys! Look at the size of their eyes! These creatures are nocturnal, that's why they didn't attack until dusk," Daen gasped as he slashed and lunged to cover the hole in their circle where Romik had fallen.

"But—"

"Bella! Do it now or we're all dead!"

Vil's words, the desperation in his normally empty voice, the sight of Romik crumpled on the ground...it all ripped through her, making her sob harder.

Idiot, useless girl! You bonded these men against their will and now you can't even protect them! They're all going to die because of you...because you're too weak and mewling to even learn ONE useful spell. You're such a pathetic waste of air. They deserve so much better than you. The WORLD deserves better than you!

"I know you can do it, Aelys," Daen called.

"Bella," Vil breathed as he stumbled back toward her, his knives flashing in the fading light. "Aelys, please. Let go of your fears and try."

Let go of my fears?

Break through.

Let go. Break through.

You can't do it. You're just going to fail. You're powerless and weak. You—

"Shut! UP!" Aelys cried and threw her head back as she *pulled*. Both of her conscious men gasped, and even the unconscious

Romik twitched as she channeled torrents of power through all three of them, filling up her neural pathways and theirs with searing, buzzing, frenetic energy.

"Bella," Vil groaned.

"FLASH!" she screamed.

The growing night detonated in an explosion of agonizing light. The trees around them bled to white and faded from view as the magelight dazzled her eyes to blindness. All around them, the goblant creatures let out a high, wailing keen that stabbed into the interior of Aelys's ears and made her teeth ache. She swallowed hard and lifted her hands, willing the epicenter of the sphere of light to rise and illuminate the clearing all around them.

The goblants lay crumpled in chaotic circles radiating out from their position. Some of them clicked and moved weakly, but it was clear that most of them were dead. Many of their bulbous, red eyes leaked the viscous green ichor that stained the men's blades.

"Vil," Aelys said, her voice ragged and hoarse, as if she'd been screaming for a week. "Pull the knife from Romik's thigh. Don't let it touch your skin, all right?"

"Bella," he acknowledged, his own voice rough, but layered with respect. He slowly got up from his crouch and stepped toward where she knelt next to Romik.

"Are you hurt, Bella?" Daen asked, likewise getting to his feet. He moved as if much of his body hurt, but he wiped his sword on a rag from his belt and resheathed it, and then joined her on the ground, where he wrapped his arms around her shoulders.

For just a second, she allowed herself to lean on him and draw comfort from his presence. But then she shook her head, pushed herself back and up, and turned to watch as Vil carefully wrapped his gloved hand around the hilt of the knife.

"Might want to be ready with a bandage," he said. "This is going to bleed a lot."

"Use this," Daen said, pulling another, cleaner rag from his belt pouch.

"How many of those do you have?" Aelys couldn't help but ask. He gave her a half smile that didn't reach his exhausted eyes.

"As many as I can carry. They're always useful for something or other."

Aelys smiled back and folded the rag up to make a pad large enough to put pressure on Romik's wound.

"I'll pull the knife free, and then you put that on there and hold it in place while I tie it off, all right, Bella?"

Aelys started to nod, and then paused. "Wait," she said. "Let me try..." She closed her eyes, and although she'd already pulled so much power, when she reached for it, more flowed to her in a steady trickle. "Flash," she whispered, and opened her eyes to see a tiny ball of magelight hovering just above Romik's leg, illuminating the dark stain of his wound.

"Good," Vil said. "That's helpful. Here we go." He steadied himself with his free hand and took a deep breath. Then, in one smooth motion, he yanked the knife free of Romik's leg.

Aelys slapped the pad down over the wound, using both hands to lean her body's weight onto it. "Wrap the knife up in another cloth and save it if you can," she said. "If it is poisoned, I might be able to work up an antidote."

"Daen's got it," Vil said as he leaned close a moment later, wrapping a length of leather around Romik's thigh. She didn't ask where he got the leather, but they looked an awful lot like the reins of the overturned cart.

He tied the dressing off, and then leaned over to peer under Romik's half-closed eyelids and listen to his faint breath as Aelys relaxed and let the magelight fade back into the rising gloom of night.

"How's he doing?" Daen asked, shifting his weight so he, too, could see his brother's face. "Is he—"

The ground shifted beneath them. A quiet rumbling sound started and slowly built to a deafening roar as the earthen road gave way and they fell down into darkness below.

CHAPTER SIX

ONE THOUGHT CRYSTALLIZED IN VIL'S MIND.

Aelys.

He reached out like a whip striking and grabbed hold of her arms, hauling her body against his chest as the ground crumbled.

Thud.

Vil's back hit something hard. Air exploded from his body an eyeblink before Aelys slammed down on top of him. He gasped like a fish, fighting against his stunned diaphragm.

Get up. You're the top-tier second-story man in Cievers. You know how to fall. You know how to move with the wind knocked out of you. Get. Up.

Aelys made a noise, pushed up, scrambled to get off him. He let her but captured her fingers in his. Very little light filtered down into the pitch blackness from above, and he was not about to lose her in the dark.

Her movement spurred his. He rolled, got his feet under him, came up in a crouch as a rush of air finally poured into his lungs. He drew his knife with his free hand.

"Stay close," he murmured to Aelys, even though he could feel the warmth of her skin beside his. "There may be more of those things. This is probably their tunnel."

"Flash," Aelys whispered, and a slow, steady glow emerged from between the cupped fingers of her free hand. It wasn't a lot of light, but it was smooth, controlled. It rose above their heads and hovered there, illuminating a large, uneven cavern. He glanced at her in approval before taking a better look around.

Rubble lay strewn everywhere, as did the crumpled bodies of the goblants.

"Daen!" Aelys gasped and let go of his hand.

"How is he?" Vil asked, carefully keeping his voice neutral.

"Breathing," Aelys said. "Looks like he hit his head on a rock. I need energy. Can you—?"

He looked around, searching for passageways branching off the cavern where they'd landed.

Two. Straight ahead, and back to my right.

Vil angled his body and took a step back, then another, until he could see both approaches, as well as Aelys bent over Daen.

"Of course," Vil said, and let his eyes trail over the sweep of her hair where it fell like a curtain in front of her face. She'd had it braided, but obviously, it had come loose in the fall.

He thought about her pale skin, and how warm she'd been pressed next to him in that alley back in Mageford. He thought about the warmth of her lips when he'd brushed them with his own earlier. Like a living flame, hot enough to burn him with a touch.

She let out a tiny gasp and shuddered, making her hair flutter in the dimness. The sound shot through him like lightning, and he swallowed and imagined what it would be like to more fully taste that sound directly from her lips.

Aelys laid her hands on Daen's forehead. Daen gasped, then coughed, his eyes fluttering open.

"Bella," he said, his ragged voice tender. Vil swallowed back his instinctive desire and watched silently as his brother reached up to trail his fingertips over Aelys's cheekbone.

"You're hurt," she said, her voice broken.

"I'm all right." Daen grunted and slowly pushed himself up to a seated position. "A little sore, but I'll heal."

"Did you fall on Romik?" Vil asked, before Daen could say any more of those tender, sweet words that he, himself, couldn't seem to manage.

"I tried to cover him from the debris before it all went black," Daen said. He shifted to the side, and sure enough, there was Romik, looking even paler in Aelys's magelight.

She let out a little cry of distress that twisted through Vil like a knife. He reached down with his free hand and pulled

Daen to his feet while Aelys pushed away the stones and laid her hands on Romik's face.

"Help me guard the passages," Vil said quietly, as Daen clutched at him while he figured out if he was steady enough to stand, "and think about her."

"Think—oh. She needs energy."

Vil nodded, and Daen clapped him on the back before drawing his short sword and angling his body so he faced the passage to the right. Vil noticed that Daen kept Aelys and Romik in his eyeline, though.

But then, I'm doing that myself. I can't help it and . . . she needs the energy.

He ignored the way that felt like an excuse and drew his other knife. And then he licked his lips and imagined taking her mouth with his own, lips and tongues tangled in passion and wanting and need.

Her body jolted, and she cast him a startled glance over her shoulder before turning her attention back to Romik. Daen also cut his eyes sideways at him, and Vil felt, more than saw, that the look wasn't entirely friendly.

He let his lips curve, just the tiniest bit. *That's right, Daen,* he thought, savagely. *You'll win her smiles with your smooth words and easy manner, but it's* my *energy that's making her shake with power right now.*

Aelys let out a long breath and closed her eyes, lifting her hands from Romik's face before turning to look at him, and then at Daen.

"He is badly hurt," she said. "First the poison blade, and now this. I can . . . I can stabilize him, but I don't have the skill to perform true healing magic."

"Just do what you can, Bella," Daen said. "Vil and I will give you whatever you need."

"I hate to ask—"

"Name it," Vil snapped, his voice cracking through the darkness. "Whatever you need, we'll give you."

"More," she whispered, meeting his eyes with her own. "You've given me so much energy already, but I—I need more."

In answer, Vil stared unblinking into those blue eyes and imagined running his fingertips down the length of her throat, savoring the texture of her skin, which he knew would feel softer than the finest spiderweave silk.

"Yes," she gasped. Her head fell back and her eyes fluttered closed. "More like that, from both of you."

"How are you— What are you doing?" Daen asked, frustration clear in his tone. "How are you giving her so much energy?"

Vil licked his lips slowly, his eyes never leaving the curve of her face, her throat bared to him.

Would you look like that if I had my hands on you for real, Bella? Would you gasp in ecstasy for me then?

"Think about her," Vil said.

"I always—"

"No." He gritted his teeth as he spoke lowly, unwilling to give up this secret. Unable to stop himself. "*Think* about her. Make—make love to her in your mind."

"Oh." Vil glanced up just in time to see a startled look flow over Daen's face, only to be replaced by one of determination. Daen met his eyes and nodded, though a muscle jumped in his cheek and his hands curled into fists.

"She needs us all," Vil said.

"She does," Daen agreed, and shifted to look at her.

Aelys let out another gasp. While they'd been talking, she'd turned her attention back to Romik, and now she tore open his shirt to put her hands on his bare chest. Vil watched her long, slender fingers, imagining what they might feel like tearing *his* shirt open, flattening against *his* naked chest. She jerked again, drawing in a shuddering breath as she received the combined energy from both him and Daen at once.

Romik twitched under her hands. His chest rose, and he coughed. Vil abruptly realized that his brother's face was covered in dust from the rubble. His own must be as well, and Daen's dark hair looked gray in the flickering magelight.

Aelys let out an explosive breath and slumped, her spine curving forward.

"He'll live," she said. "At least for a while. His body may heal some of the damage.... I just don't know. But he will live for now."

Vil swallowed and nodded. He forced his mind to turn from the thought of that light silvering the curves of Aelys's bare skin and focus on her words. She'd done it. She didn't need his energy, his thoughts anymore.

But I want to give them to her. I want to give her all of it.

Romik coughed again and started to push himself up. Vil

moved quick as a thought, grateful for the distraction as he knelt beside Aelys and helped hold Romik back.

"Easy, brother," he said. Years of practice at maintaining a smooth, empty voice kept his ragged emotions out of his words, despite the tantalizing scent of her hair...

Focus, Vil.

"Need to...get up. Bella..."

"I'm here, Romik," Aelys said, bending close enough to speak softly in his ear. Vil pushed away the now-familiar twisting sensation he got whenever she touched one of his brothers and forced himself to listen to her words. "I'm here, but you've been hurt. Please, you need to lie back."

"Can't," Romik said between gritted teeth. "Bad spot. Dangerous."

"He's right," Daen said, his voice grave. "This isn't exactly a defensible position."

"Can he be moved, Bella?" Vil asked, looking at her. Willing her to look at him. Steeling his nerves, in case she did.

"I—I think so. Yes. But he needs help. He's terribly weak."

Vil sheathed the blades he still held as Daen, too, bent to help pull Romik up. Together, they got him mostly vertical, though each of his arms sat heavily across their shoulders.

"Where can we go?" Aelys asked. "Can we climb out?"

This time there was no warning. The ground shifted beneath Vil's feet and slid, taking his feet out from under him. He dropped hard to a seat, and just barely managed get his hands under Romik's head, to cushion it from hitting the rolling cascade of rocks beneath them as the floor collapsed toward the suddenly yawning gap to the right of the chamber.

Aelys's high, breathy cry cut through the rumbling, grinding sound of the rockslide.

"Bella!" Daen shouted.

"I've got Romik," Vil ground out between clenched teeth. "Get Aelys."

Vil fought to keep his face upright, but his sense of orientation disappeared as they passed through the gap, leaving the last rays of sunlight behind. Sharp stones dug into his body from heels to crown, and it was all he could do to keep hold of his brother's arm in the twisting, unstable darkness.

And then he stopped moving. And heard nothing but silence.

"Flash." Aelys's voice was frightened, but near. Light bloomed, but at first Vil couldn't see anything but dust filling the air.

"Ro—" he coughed, fighting to sit up. "Romik? Brother?"

"Vil!" More rocks scrabbled, and Vil braced, but it was only Daen crawling to him from behind. "Is he—?"

"I'm alive," Romik groaned. "Bella?"

"I'm here," she said, and the light grew stronger and steadier, until Vil could make out the shape of her scrambling over the shifting gravel toward them. He exhaled with relief and slowly got to his feet and looked around. The rockslide had dumped them in a long, narrow cavern perhaps twice the height of a man. To the left, a deeper shadow revealed a narrow cleft in the rock.

"Can we get back to the surface?" Aelys asked.

"Rockslides are dangerous," Daen said. "We got lucky. Best we can do is get away from here, find another way out."

"What about—" Romik coughed and shifted his position. Vil heard him quickly stifle a groan. "Those creatures—goblants?"

Daen shook his head. "They must all be dead. Their nests usually don't hold more than a few dozen individuals, and there were at least that many on the surface. If there were any left, they'd have attacked us by now."

"Can you get up?" Aelys asked Romik, bending toward him. "I can—"

"I'm fine," he said, cutting her off as he got slowly to his feet. "Daen's right, we need to move."

"There's what looks like another tunnel going off that way, to the left," Vil pointed out.

"Then that way it is," Daen said, his voice assuming his usual good cheer. Aelys looked over her shoulder at him and smiled.

Vil swallowed and pushed away the stab of envious longing that shot through him and shrugged under Romik's arm.

"Let's go," he said, and stepped forward beside the brother he couldn't help but hate just a little bit.

They didn't make it far before Aelys stumbled, nearly falling to her knees on the uneven ground.

"Bella!" Daen's voice echoed in the small space as she reached out, catching herself on the rough walls, scraping her palms in the process. She held herself still, panting for breath and trembling as she fought to regain her composure.

"I'm all right," she said. Her voice sounded reedy and thin. She cleared her throat and tried again. "I'm all right; I just tripped."

"You're not all right." Vil's voice came, as it always seemed to, out of the dark. For one tiny second, she wondered savagely why he hadn't been leading the way. He always seemed to see so well, even without light.

Because he's helping to carry Romik, the Ageon you nearly got killed. You can't exactly help with that, now, can you?

"I am. I'm just ... tired."

"You're exhausted. We all are. This is a good enough spot. We can stop here and sleep for a while. It's nighttime, after all."

Daen was right, Aelys realized. It had been dusk when the goblants attacked, and the sun had just set when they'd fallen into the tunnel. She didn't know how long they'd been walking, but it couldn't have been long. Still, her muscles trembled with fatigue, and she wasn't carrying anyone. She steadied herself on the wall once again and turned, calling magelight once more.

They stood in a narrow passageway that curved away behind and ahead of them. The path sloped down, growing more and more broken and uneven with every step ahead of them. But this spot here was slightly wider, almost flat.

"This will work," Vil said, and together he and Vil lowered Romik to the ground. The big warrior let out a sigh but didn't say anything. Aelys picked her way back over the rubble to press a hand to his forehead.

"I'm fine," he grumbled, jerking his face away. She snatched her hand back.

"I'm sorry," she said, and then immediately regretted it as he turned to glare at her with his eyes that looked so much like her own. "I just wanted to check."

"Can you heal me?" he asked. "Real healing?"

"N-no. But I can give you more—"

"No. I don't want any more of your energy. You're already exhausted."

And he doesn't want to feel me like that, Aelys realized abruptly. *Of course he doesn't. He hates me. How stupid can I be?*

Still, her energy transfer had saved his life. She couldn't regret that. He might hate her, but he was still her Ageon, her responsibility.

"All right," she said mildly. She rose from her crouch and

immediately regretted it as her head swam and bright sparkles danced in the darkness before her eyes. Daen's arms appeared out of nowhere and wrapped around her, drawing her in to his chest.

"Easy, Bella," he said, his voice a low murmur in her ear. "I've got you."

"I-I'm sorry."

"No apologies. Saving Romik's ungrateful self obviously wore you out."

"And you," Vil said from the darkness. "She channeled energy into you first."

"No wonder, then, that you're spent. We all need rest. Here, I'm just going to lay you down—"

"Not by Romik," she said quickly. "I-I mean . . . He doesn't want me to disturb him."

"He's an idiot," Daen said. "And he knows it. I'm just going to put you right here, all right? Not touching him, but close enough if he needs more of your magic touch."

Romik didn't say anything, although Aelys was certain he'd heard Daen's words. She waited a moment and then nodded, unable to do much else. Fatigue pulled at the edges of her mind, fraying her thoughts.

She felt herself being lowered to sit on the ground, and then Daen shifted and helped her lie back until her head rested on some kind of balled up fabric—someone's jacket? It was a constant temperature under the ground, so she supposed one of them had volunteered it for her use.

"Thank you," she whispered.

"Thank you, Bella," he said. She felt his fingers trail along her cheekbone, and she fought to open her eyes. Daen bent over her, silhouetted by her magelight that still glowed steadily above them. She saw the vague shape of his face as he gave her a brief smile, and leaned in.

For one heart-stopping moment, she thought he might kiss her, but he just pressed his lips to her forehead.

"Lie down with her, Daen. She'll get cold. I'll keep watch." Vil's voice came out of the darkness again, somewhere beyond Romik. Aelys felt her eyes drift closed.

"If I sleep, the magelight will fade," she warned, the words bleeding into one another as oblivion called to her.

"I don't need it, Bella."

Of course. Vil can see in the dark. He sees everything.

That thought should have bothered her more than it did. Especially since she felt Daen settling in beside her, drawing her close against that massive chest of his. Vil always watched her. He would be watching even as she let out a sigh and let her body melt into the warmth of Daen's.

But for some reason, the thought of him watching her wasn't bothersome at all.

It was comforting.

She closed her eyes and let herself fall to the demands of sleep.

Aelys woke into darkness.

Her shoulder ached, and her left arm and hand had gone numb, but she was warm. Behind her back, the rhythmic rise and fall of someone's breathing told her that one of the men lay with his back hard against hers. Her right hand rested on the swell of someone's chest. An arm lay over her waist.

"Daen?" she whispered.

"No," Vil answered. The arm lifted, leaving her colder for its absence. "Daen took the watch. Romik is behind you. He seems to be breathing easily."

She blinked, then shivered as the chest under her hand rolled away. The air felt cool and damp, and for one wild moment, she wanted to reach out to Vil, pull him back to her, huddle inside the warmth of his body and that cloak he wore.

Idiot, she chastised herself. *It was kind of him to keep you warm while you slept. Now he obviously has better things to do. And so do you.*

"Flash," she murmured, calling her magelight. It bloomed in her hand, steady and controlled. With a thought, she brought the brightness down enough so that she didn't have to squint and sent it up above her head.

Not far above her head, because the passageway wasn't particularly tall, but enough that the ball of light wasn't in the way.

"Good morning, or whatever it is, Bella," Daen said. Aelys turned with a smile to see him sitting behind her. She watched as he reached for a small metal box and blew out the flickering flame inside.

"Good mor—oh! You had a lantern! I didn't realize."

"It's Vil's," Daen said, lifting the top of the box and removing what looked like a miniature candle from inside. He then proceeded to unhinge the box and fold it down to a flat rectangle of metal, which he held out for Vil to take.

"Thief's lantern," Vil said, taking the box and candle and tucking it away inside his cloak. "Useful for skulking in dark places. This is why I wasn't worried about losing your magelight, Bella. Even I can't see in pitch blackness."

"Oh—of course not," Aelys said, hoping the heat in her cheeks wasn't visible from her dim little light. She glanced upward at it, noting with a tiny surge of pleasure how it continued to steadily shine.

My control has gotten better, she admitted. *And I barely feel the drain. I could probably sustain this light all day, longer if I pull energy through the men. Finally, after all these years, I'm making progress.*

Bolstered by this thought, Aelys straightened her spine and stood up. She stretched her arms up over her head, feeling her spine pop after the uncomfortable night on the rock, and then turned to look at her third Ageon.

Romik lay still sleeping. Aelys considered him for a moment, biting her lip in uncertainty. He hadn't wanted her to give him more energy last night, but he'd been really badly hurt, first by the poison and then by the fall. The energy she'd given him had been enough to even out his breathing and ease the creases of pain between his eyes that she didn't think he realized he had.

He's strong, she reminded herself. *And he's a warrior. His body is hardened to injury and privation. He's used to healing wounds. More energy will help his body naturally do what I don't know how to do and repair whatever hurts he has. And he's my Ageon. My responsibility.*

Aelys let out her breath in a huff and stepped closer to him. She crouched and laid her hand on the side of his sleeping face.

"I respect your wishes," she said quietly. "But you're mine to protect and care for, and so I'm going to give you this energy so your body can heal itself. I am sorry about the ... side effects."

Romik opened his eyes, and his blue gaze locked onto hers as she reversed the flow of red warmth that ran from him into her. His lips parted, and he sucked in a breath, but she refused to falter.

The dark flow and the green flow both intensified, meaning

that she had Vil's and Daen's attention as she worked. They weren't the torrents of searing ecstasy of the night before, but that was all to the good. She wasn't trying to haul Romik back from the brink of death, she was just trying to feed his body's healing processes. She pushed on a moment longer, and then sat back on her heels, lifting her hands from Romik's face.

"How do you feel?" she asked, pleased to hear that her voice held none of the nervous tremors currently coursing through her stomach.

"Better," Romik admitted. "Thank you, Bella."

"You're welcome."

"We should go," Vil said, his quiet voice breaking the silent interlude. "If Romik's well enough to walk, we should keep moving."

"Where are we going?" Romik sat up with a tiny grunt, but it was one more of effort than pain. "Do we even know?"

"There's moisture in the air," Daen said. "That means we're close to a water source. There's an underground lake that feeds a spring not far from the road and the ambush site. I think we may be headed in that direction."

"An underground spring? Doesn't sound like much of a way out," Romik said. Daen turned and grinned at him, his teeth flashing in the cool magelight.

"Luckily for us, we're strong, strapping men. We can dig."

Romik rolled his eyes, but he snorted a soft laugh. Aelys found herself chuckling, and even Vil quirked the corner of his lips in a tiny smile. Daen winked and let out a low laugh, and then stepped up beside Romik.

"I'm good to walk," the big man protested.

"Sounds good," Daen said. "I'll walk beside you. Aelys, you stay with Vil up front with your light. Can you keep it going all day?"

"I can," Aelys said, her newfound confidence ringing through her words.

"Excellent. That will be our marching order then. Stay close to Vil in case we encounter any of those goblant things, and don't be afraid to fry them with your light. Boys, if you hear 'flash,' duck."

"Good plan," Vil said. "Let's get moving. I'm feeling a powerful need to dig."

Vil's dry humor had Aelys smiling as they headed down the

rocky, sloping passageway. She increased the brightness of her magelight, noting the tiny increase in energy pull. It still felt almost negligible, and certainly nothing to the constant triple inflow of power from the men. Aelys was used to hoarding her power like a miser, but with the wealth of energy coming from her Ageons, she judged it worth the additional drain in order to avoid breaking ankles—or necks—as they descended further beneath the earth.

The passageway got tighter and steeper with every step. Aelys looked back and noticed that both Romik and Daen had begun to walk hunched over, lest they bang their heads on the rock above. Her light painted the ceiling in stark lines and shadows, showing the uneven, jagged texture rife with stalactites waiting like hanging traps. The floor of the passageway wasn't much better, with razor-edged loose rock that rolled under each step, threatening to bring them crashing down onto the spiraling stalactites that stabbed upward toward the roof.

Before long, Aelys found herself scrambling on hands and knees over boulders and ancient rockfalls. Vil would reach back and take her by the hand to help her through, and then together they'd do the same for Daen and the injured Romik.

They paused at one such point. Despite the cool, damp air, sweat beaded her brow and trickled in a line down her spine.

"How are you all not out of breath?" Aelys complained softly. "I feel like I can't breathe in here."

"You're breathing too fast," Romik said, and for once his voice didn't sound irritated with her. "It happens to some people in enclosed spaces. Close your mouth and inhale through your nose to a count of four, hold it for a second, and then let it out slowly through your mouth for a count of six. Then hold for another second before repeating."

"And breathe down into your belly," Daen added. "Pull with your diaphragm, not high into your lungs."

"How do you all know this?" Aelys asked. She swallowed as a buzzing, tingling sensation started to spread over her cheekbones and toward the tip of her nose.

"New recruits hyperventilate all the time," Romik said. His teeth flashed in the dim light, and shock rocked through her. Had he smiled at her? "It's a common reaction to stress. And if you don't like tight spaces, it can get worse."

"I've never been in a tight space like this before," Aelys said, trying to put his advice to work.

"Don't dwell on it," Vil added. "It makes it worse. Concentrate on the air on your face. Can you feel the humidity in it?"

She nodded, and then realized that he probably couldn't see that . . . or maybe he could. He was Vil, after all. He saw everything, even if he needed a thieves' lantern to do so.

"Good. Keep breathing like that, down into your diaphragm."

"That's how we breathe when we're aiming, too," Daen said, his tone conversational. He stepped forward, rocks sliding and crunching under his feet, and reached out to squeeze her shoulder. "It helps with concentration and focus."

"Oh, I'm an idiot, I knew that," she said, letting out a little laugh. "They actually taught us this at the Lyceum, to help us focus on our incantations in the midst of chaos. I just never really got to practice it because I'm too weak to do a full incantation. It doesn't take much focus to summon magelight, and 'flash' isn't all that difficult to remember, even for a useless mage like me." She laughed again, and then trailed off when she realized that none of the men joined her in laughter.

She looked up to see all three of them staring at her with their eyes that matched her own.

"What?" she asked, her voice faltering. She felt her spine curving inward, withering under their scrutiny.

"Don't say that," Romik growled, breaking the silence.

"I'm s—"

"Don't."

Aelys shut her lips with a snap, unsure what she'd done to cause the sudden shift in mood. She turned to Daen with a question in her eyes.

"You're not useless," he said, his voice intense, and carrying the same edge of anger that she heard in Romik's. "And you're not an idiot. You shouldn't say things like that."

"I only meant—"

"It doesn't matter," Vil cut in. "We should keep moving. I think— Daen would be better at this, but I thought I heard the sound of water running up ahead."

Daen straightened up, nearly smashing his head on a stalactite. He reached up a hand to steady himself. "Where?" he asked. "Can you show me?"

"Through there," Vil said. "The same way we were going. Can you hear it?"

Daen made his careful way forward to stand beside Vil. Despite the hurt his reprimand had caused, Aelys focused on the green ribbon of warmth flowing from him into her and reversed it. Maybe if she heightened his senses...

Daen inhaled sharply and looked over at her. She snapped her eyes down to her feet, unwilling to meet his gaze, but she increased the energy flow into him.

"Yes," he said quietly. "I—uh—I hear it now. I think you're right. Let's head that way. If nothing else, we could use some water to drink."

Aelys had been trying not to think about either her growing thirst or her empty stomach, but his words made her realize just how dry her mouth felt. So, she reached out a hand and steadied herself on the slick, treacherous wall of the corridor and started walking carefully forward again.

The way didn't get any easier. Aelys fell twice, thanks to the loose rock under her feet. After the second time, Vil reached down and hauled her up, and then kept hold of her hand as he steadied her with every step. Daen remained in the lead, using his heightened senses of hearing and smell to lead them toward the water. That left Vil to see to Aelys and the injured Romik.

"You don't have to hold my hand," Aelys said lowly.

Vil didn't say anything. But he didn't let go.

"If you let go of me, you can better help Romik."

"Romik is fine, it's you who keeps falling."

"I'm sorry," she said. "I will do better."

"You will," Vil said, his voice going colder with every word. "Because I am helping you. When it's level ground again, I will let you go."

Aelys closed her mouth and sunk back into herself. She'd felt so confident when they'd awakened, but it was obvious the more the day dragged on that she continued to be a drain on the group.

Poor Aelys, weak Aelys, pathetic Aelys! So proud of yourself because you managed the bare minimum of control over your stupid magelight! Can't even walk without needing help not to break your fool neck! He should let you go, then maybe you'd fall and bash in your skull and they could finally be free of you.

Lost in these vitriolic thoughts, Aelys stepped unwisely and stumbled, her ankle rolling as her weight came down on it. As he'd done before, Vil caught her, pulling her in against his chest and supporting her full weight while she untangled her feet.

"Oh!" she exclaimed, closing her eyes in mortification. "I'm sorry."

"Like it or not, Bella, I'm never going to let you fall."

Her eyes flew open, startled. *How did he—*

Before she could complete the mental question, Vil set her back on her feet and pulled her forward into motion again. She shook her head, pushing away all thoughts except those focusing on where she stepped, and how she crouched as the passageway got smaller and tighter.

Eventually, she, too, heard the rushing sound of water echoing off the stone. They pressed forward, even as the ceiling dropped low enough that even she had to duck, her magelight hovering beside her ear.

"Hold here," Daen called out. "Got a small problem."

"What is it?" Vil asked as they came up behind him. Daen crouched in front of a rockpile. The passageway continued off to his right, though it got even smaller as it went.

"The water sound is coming from behind these rocks," Daen said. "And there's even air moving between them. If we go up the passageway any further, we leave it behind. Even if that's the way out, I'm thinking we need water. So, I think we need to clear this."

"Can we do it without bringing the entire cavern down on top of us?" Vil asked.

"Let me see," Romik said. Aelys shifted backward, doing her best to flatten herself to the side to let Romik pass. Vil still wouldn't let go of her hand.

Romik squinted at the rockfall, and with a thought, Aelys sent her magelight forward to shine on the debris, illuminating its composition.

"Thanks," Romik grunted without looking at her. She swallowed and nodded in return but didn't dare say anything as he raised his fingers to the barrier and pushed here and there.

"I think we can probably dig out these here," he said, "and make an opening below this larger slab that fell at an angle. Stones sometimes fall like that when we're sapping a castle, and it's always best to leave the big ones alone. It will be tight, but I think we can probably squeeze through."

"Vil?" Daen said, his grin flashing white in the light. "You said you had a powerful need to dig."

"After you, brother," Vil shot back. Daen laughed and Romik shook his head at both of them. Then he turned and looked at Aelys, a muscle jumping in his cheek.

"We need to be stronger," he said. "Can you—?"

He waved his hand in the air, in a gesture that wasn't, quite, dismissive. Aelys swallowed, nodded, and turned her attention inward to the three separate energy flows that she'd become accustomed to feeling.

She'd reversed Daen's flow without touch earlier, and so she concentrated on the lush, warm green of his energy first. She heard his quick intake of breath as he felt the power pouring back into his system.

Can I keep his flow going and pump energy into Vil and Romik at the same time? Her eyes tracked upward to her glowing magelight. Where once she would have had to concentrate to keep it glowing at such constant brightness, now it was like background noise. A tiny pull on her power, one she was aware of, but didn't have to think too much about. Could she keep Daen's power flow open the same way?

Because it was sometimes useful to use mental imagery, she closed her eyes and built the picture of a sluice gate in her mind and latched it open, keeping the current of green power pulsing in a constant river from Daen to her and back out to him again.

"Bella," Daen groaned. "What are you doing to me?"

"She's making you stronger," Vil said, his voice low. "Start digging."

Aelys heard this exchange, but didn't pay it much mind. Instead, she turned her attention to the red torrent of rage and aggression coming in from Romik. Once again, she built a sluice gate, this time of metal rather than wood, lest the heat from the current catch the imaginary gate on fire. In the back of her mind, she knew that didn't make any sense, but she let it go. The imagery was just there to help her focus, to help get the job done.

The flow reversed, and Romik exhaled loudly. The next thing Aelys heard was the rattle of stone on stone as he joined Daen in his labors.

Aelys locked the red gate open, paused for a second to ensure that both red and green currents remained strong, and then turned her attention to the dark current.

In some ways, the dark current ran stronger and faster than the other two. Perhaps because it was the first one she'd worked with, the searing heat of dark energy that flowed in from Vil seemed almost eager to do as she willed. After a moment's consideration, she built her imaginary dark sluice gate out of stone. Not natural cavern stone like what surrounded them, but worked stone, masonry like you'd find on the streets of a city.

"You're not touching my skin," Vil said, and for once his cool tone carried a breathy, ragged edge.

"I don't think I have to, anymore." Aelys opened her eyes. "The flows are so well established now; I don't need to touch you."

Vil opened his mouth as if he would say something else, and then closed it and turned away, going without another word to help his brothers dig through the rockfall to whatever lay beyond.

It took longer than she would have liked. Long enough that Aelys felt her own muscles start to shake with fatigue as she continued pumping energy to her men. Long enough that when Daen finally broke through with a joyous shout, she slumped against the passageway wall in relief and slowly let the gates close in her mind.

"Bella? Bella? Are you all right? Aelys, look at me."

Daen's voice penetrated the aching fog that wreathed her mind. Aelys slowly forced her eyelids open, saw worry and fear swimming in those blue eyes she'd given him.

"She gave us too much," Romik's gravelly voice said from somewhere Aelys couldn't see. She couldn't see anything but Daen's eyes.

"Come on, Bella," Daen said, bending toward her. She felt his arms go under her, cradling her like a child as he picked her up. "You shouldn't have done that, you know."

"You needed strength," she whispered, her words slurring together. *And I should be strong enough to give it to you without passing out.*

"You gave us plenty," Daen said, and she felt a shiver work its way through his chest. "I've never felt anything like that. It was like you were touching me, but you weren't. And I felt like I could shovel rock with my bare hands all day."

"I'm glad . . . it worked."

He bent and pressed a kiss to her forehead again as he hoisted her higher into his arms. "But look at you," he said, his lips moving against her head. "You can't be giving us so much that you collapse. I need you to promise me you won't do that again."

"I—"

"He's right." Romik's voice came from somewhere ahead of her. Aelys didn't have the energy to turn her head and see. "We had more than enough to do the work, but you've wrecked yourself. Not efficient at all."

"I'm sorry," she whispered, knowing he likely couldn't hear her. If he had, he probably would have yelled at her for apologizing. "I will...be okay. Just give me...a minute."

And she would, she realized. Though her thoughts felt like they swam through thick syrup, that one revelation crystallized in the forefront of her mind. All three of her men were tightly focused on her, and the floodgates of energy had opened for all three of them, allowing the torrent to flow into her once more.

She was exhausted, yes, but she could feel her breathing ease, her tremors still. She inhaled deeply, drawing in Daen's scent of green, growing things, of sunlight on leaves, and shadowy places beneath. The green energy in her mind pulsed in response, spilling warmth throughout her body.

"Hand her through to me," Romik said. Daen bent nearly double, his torso curling around her as he crouched in front of the hole the men had made in the rockfall.

"Watch her head," Daen said, and Aelys felt him extend his arms. One large, strong hand came up to cradle the back of her skull. Another slid under her hips, and then she felt herself being pulled through the rocks and up against Romik's chest.

Where Daen's green warmth had spread, now Romik's red fire blazed. Aelys couldn't help but let out a gasp as the red river in her mind ignited, sending fire racing along every nerve. His fingers tightened in her hair, and he pulled her into his chest, holding her to him as he continued through the short passageway into the large, open chamber beyond.

"I...I can stand," she said, grateful that her voice sounded stronger. Romik didn't answer, but his arms tightened around her. The red torrent raging through her system intensified, and she swallowed convulsively in response. She closed her eyes in order to focus on mastering the influx of energy, but that just brought her other senses to the forefront. The heat rolling off Romik's skin, the unyielding iron of his muscles, his unique scent of heated metal and cool stone.

Romik straightened, lifting her higher in his arms before turning and walking to the side. Aelys kept her eyes closed, fearful of losing control of either the energy or her stomach. Eventually, Romik crouched again, and Aelys felt herself being set down on the ground with a gentleness that surprised her.

"How do you feel?" Romik asked. His voice, while gruff, lacked the anger she'd expected, especially given the raging inferno of his energy as it engulfed her.

"I—better," she said. "Much better. Thank you. I'm sorry I overdid it. I just needed a minute—"

"You and Daen holding her helped," Vil said, appearing next to Romik, his face shadowed beneath his hood, even this close to the magelight that still hovered near her ear. "Didn't it, Bella?"

"I—I think so, yes," she said. "Just as I transferred energy to you, when you held me it opened the flow from each of you wider, and so I...recovered." *And almost made a fool of myself by losing control.*

"Don't do that." Vil's voice was demanding, causing Romik to turn and look at him with a confused expression that Aelys thought probably matched her own.

"Don't do what?" Romik asked.

"Not you. Aelys. She's got that look she gets when she's mentally blasting herself or calling herself unworthy or useless. Don't do that, Bella. I—*we* don't like it."

"I..." She fell silent. *I can't help it,* was what she was about to say, but that sounded too pathetic even for her. So, she closed her mouth.

"Hey, Bella, how bright does your light get?" Daen's voice echoed to them over the roar of water falling some distance away. Aelys blinked and started to stand, but Romik surprised her by grabbing her hands and pulling her up to her feet. Then he held on and stared into her eyes for a moment.

"Steady?" he asked, his voice a low rumble.

She nodded. He nodded back and then let go, leaving her hands feeling cold in the darkness. She swallowed hard again and turned to look where Daen had gone.

"With you three feeding me power, I can probably make it

outshine the sun," Aelys said. "But I doubt that would be good for any of us."

"No, thank you," Vil murmured from just behind her. He was close enough that it should have made her jump . . . except that she'd already known he was there.

"Can you make it bright enough to see the other side?" Daen asked, pointing into the darkness in front of him. He stood on a flattish rock ledge, water lapping at the toes of his boots. He met her eyes and smiled. Aelys smiled back and lifted her hands.

The little ball of magelight that had hovered next to her ear rose up, growing brighter and larger as it climbed. Soon, the cool white light illuminated what had to be thousands of stalactites growing from ledges that ringed the chamber, forming layers upon layers of incomplete ceilings. The rock glittered as bits of mica and other reflective minerals caught the light and flashed it back tenfold. The swelling light spread, illuminating the black, rippling surface of a wide lake that stretched ahead of them, broken here and there by outcroppings of rock that jutted out from the walls. Directly across from where they stood, a cascade flowed down from high among the stalactites, catching on two ledges before spilling into the inky lake.

"It's beautiful," Aelys said, and then immediately blushed and looked down, hoping none of the men heard her.

"I don't think this is the lake I was thinking of," Daen said, his voice troubled as he stepped carefully back toward them. "The water's flowing in here, not out. That's the bad news. The good news is that *this* water has to come from somewhere."

"Yes, up there," Romik said, stabbing a thick finger at the distant opposite wall that rose up out of sight. "And I didn't exactly bring any climbing gear, did you?"

"One problem at a time, brother," Daen said, clapping him on the shoulder. "It can't hurt to go over there and see, right?"

Romik grumbled something unintelligible.

"Daen, is this water safe to drink?" Vil asked.

"Safer than anything you'll find in the city," Daen said. "This is about as pure as water gets."

"Good. Come here, Bella," Vil said.

Aelys jumped. She hadn't been expecting him to call her, but she picked her way over to where he crouched next to the water's edge. He cupped his hands, dipped them, and filled them with water as if he would drink. She started to follow his example, but instead of lifting the water to his mouth, he lifted it to hers.

"Drink slowly," he said. "It's cold and could upset your stomach if you guzzle it."

His gloved fingers rested against her lips, and the black river of energy that flowed inside her swelled with searing fire that rubbed under her skin like hot, silken fur. In contrast, the water that flowed into her mouth was cool, wet, and faintly sweet, tasting of minerals. Her parched mouth and throat soaked it in, immediately demanding more. Her tongue darted out to capture the drops that dripped down her lower lip toward her chin, and the energy flow from Vil exploded throughout her synapses, igniting a desperate *wanting* deep in her body.

She gasped as he lowered his hands, and before she could think better of it, she reached out and grabbed his wrist. He froze, lifting one blond eyebrow in a question.

"Please," she whispered. "I want—"

"More?" His voice was a low murmur that rolled through her. Something dark and primal moved in his blue gaze.

"Yes."

Vil kept his eyes locked on hers as he slowly pulled away from her hold, then bent and caught more water in his cupped hands. Once again, he lifted his hands, his leather gloves brushing her over-sensitized lips. Once again, she drank greedily, pretending that it was the cool water and not the searing darkness flowing from him that had her gripping his wrists, barely holding back from whimpering in ecstasy.

"Enough?" he asked.

No. Never.

"Yes," she said. She swallowed and then nodded, as if she could convince herself. "Th-thank you."

He stepped back, pulling out of her grip again and the dark torrent slowed, receded. She swallowed against the sudden sense of loss; the chill left in the wake of that searing fire.

"Better, Bella?" Daen asked. His voice carried a tiny note of strain that caught her attention. She turned to see him glaring at Vil for a split second before he turned to her, his usual easy smile flowing into place. "The water is good, isn't it?"

"Yes," she said, more than a little breathless. She didn't dare look over at Vil. "It's very good."

"So, the question, then, is how do we get across?" Romik's voice cut through Aelys's scattered thoughts.

"There's a ledge there," Daen said, pointing. "It looks like it goes most of the way around, and when it thins out, there's another just below. I bet we could skirt around the cavern like that."

"How do you know this is all one cavern, and those ledges don't lead to other branching passageways?"

"I don't, brother, but that might be interesting information to have too, right? And we won't know unless we go look."

Romik shrugged. "True enough, I guess."

"Bella, can you send another light up there?" Daen asked, turning to Aelys. "I want to light up that ledge."

"I should be able to," Aelys said, happy to have something useful to do. She walked over to Daen, who held his hand out to steady her. She slipped her fingers into his and let him guide her to the vantage point he wanted.

"Right up there," he said, speaking softly and pointing over her shoulder with his free hand. The fingers of his other hand threaded through hers, curling around her palm as if to say that he had zero intention of letting go. Inside her mind, the flood-gates opened and the buzzing green vitality of him flowed in.

Use it, she told herself sharply. She lifted her free hand to point alongside his. "Flash," she said, channeling the delicious warmth of Daen's energy into her command. A new globe of light appeared at the tip of her finger and shot away across the cavern, toward the ledge he'd indicated. As it flew it swelled, glowing with a greenish hue and casting the rocks in their way into sharp relief.

"Perfect," Daen murmured, his breath warm against the back of her neck. He stood close enough that she could feel the heat of his body all along her back, and the clean, woodsmoke-and-leather scent of him swirled through her senses.

"We could use that rockfall there to climb up, do you think, Vil?"

"I could."

"Could you, Bella?" Romik asked, staring at Aelys with the blue eyes she'd given him.

"I—I think so. If . . . I might need some help."

"You know we'll always help you," Daen said softly. "What-ever you need."

The heat in his tone made it seem very much like he was talk-ing about more than just assistance in scrambling over boulders and stalagmites. Aelys swallowed hard as the green river pulsed within her, sending heat spiraling down low in her body.

"I know," she whispered, before she could stop herself. She closed her eyes, fighting to keep control of herself, of the triple courses of energy swirling into her system.

Breathe. Focus. Get a hold of yourself. They don't really want you like that. You know that. It's just the bond. You have to master this!

She inhaled to a count of four as she'd been taught, and then exhaled and opened her eyes to a standoff. Vil stared at Daen, his eyes cold. Romik, too, glared, though she couldn't tell if she or Daen were the object of his heated ire.

Aelys stepped away from Daen, but he refused to let her hand go.

"Vil..." she said, and then trailed off, because what could she say?

Her voice snapped his eyes down to her face, and all emotions quickly disappeared behind his shuttered, masklike expression.

"All of us," he said, his voice empty. Under her skin, the dark current slowed, easing back from the raging torrent it had been.

"I know," she said again. "I know you will all help me. You three are...I couldn't wish for better Ageons. You've already protected me from so much—"

"Enough," Romik said, his voice gruff. "We're wasting time. If we're going to do this, let's do it."

The red river of heat and light inside Aelys also contracted, slowing and settling to a smaller, but constant flow. She inhaled deeply, pushing it to run alongside the green and the dark streams.

There, she thought as she nodded, following Romik to the rockfall Daen had indicated. *Maybe that will help me get a better handle on this. Their emotions...the energy is intoxicating, but I have to retain control. None of this is their fault. They didn't choose this.*

This plan is terrible, Romik thought, not for the first time, as he reached out to steady himself on a boulder the size of a small house. His leg throbbed with dull agony, and scrambling up and over wet rocks made even more treacherous with the addition of loose gravel wasn't helping matters. His ribs hurt also, though long experience told him that he'd probably just bruised them. If he'd broken a rib, he'd hardly be vertical.

Although I shouldn't be vertical at all, should I? I wouldn't be, if not for the Bella and her energy.

Despite his best attempt at control, Romik's skin shivered up in goosebumps at the memory of Aelys pushing her magic into his body. He was no stranger to women and the pleasures of the flesh, but he'd never felt anything like that. Even badly hurt by a poisoned blade, she'd brought him right to the edge of release and kept him there, drowning in sensations that were somehow *inside* his skin.

And every time she does it, I feel it more. And I crave it more, like a vaporhead begging for coins to feed their need. I should tell her no. I should refuse any more energy pushes, or whatever she calls them . . .

But the facts of the matter were that he *was* hurt. Years in the arena and then serving on campaigns with the Raiders had taught him to know his body. That goblant blade had put something into his bloodstream that his system struggled to suppress. And deep in the darkest parts of his mind, Romik knew that his body would have failed before now if it hadn't been for *her*.

Without really meaning to, Romik looked upward, searching for her slim figure. She climbed just ahead of him, her slender fingers fighting for handholds on rocks worn smooth by ancient waters. As he watched, her hand slipped, jarring her backward.

In less than an eyeblink, Vil was there, his hand wrapped around her wrist, hauling her upward until she found a better hold. She looked at him and said something—probably another damned apology—so quietly Romik didn't hear. Vil nodded and then let go, continuing his own ascent just ahead of her.

Romik swallowed against the hot, instinctive envy that rose inside his throat. Without meaning to do so, he clenched his hands into fists, enough that the handhold under his right fingers started to crumble.

"Go easy, Demon," Daen said quietly beside him.

"I'm fine."

"Are you? Because you look like I feel."

Romik shifted his grip, clenched his jaw and said nothing more for a few moments while he concentrated on getting himself on a more stable footing. Only then did he turn his head to watch Daen following him up.

"And how do you feel?"

Daen shot him a grin that didn't reach his eyes and declined to answer right away. He, too, focused on his arms and legs until he finally pushed himself up to the spot where Romik waited.

"How do I feel? Like I want to shove my brother out of the way and take his place every time one of you touches her. But Vil said something back in the forest that made me think. She needs all of us, to keep her safe, to protect her. From herself if necessary. And we are brothers, aren't we?"

"Sworn and witnessed by three goddesses," Romik said. "If not for this *geas* of hers, I'd say it's the strongest bond I know."

"Same for me." Daen reached out and clapped Romik on the shoulder. "So even though part of me wishes I could be Vil because he was fast enough to take her hand first, the rest of me knows that he's my brother, and she needs me. She needs all of us, Ro. It helps, I promise."

"Does it?"

"It better," Daen grimaced. "No, it does. It's just . . . It doesn't help as much as I'd like. But I don't know what else to do."

Romik swallowed, then nodded and reached out, returning Daen's reassuring shoulder squeeze.

"Maybe it will get easier as we go," he said.

"Maybe." The look in Daen's blue eyes said that he didn't think that was true. Romik gave him a half smile. Squeezed his shoulder once more, and then let go to focus on continuing the climb.

Once they made it up the rockfall to the ledge, they took a short break, and then followed the ledge around the perimeter of the cavern. They were able to stay on that ledge for about three quarters of the way around before they had to drop down to another ledge. There were, in fact, other passageways that branched off here and there. Romik saw Daen noting every one, looking around for distinctive landmarks that would identify the openings for him again, and once even building a trail cairn of small rocks beside a particularly hidden cleft.

By the time they reached the edge of the second, lower ledge, Romik's stomach was audibly grumbling. He didn't bother to say anything about it, because he was pretty sure that no one had any food on them. They hadn't exactly planned on a multiday cave-exploring expedition, after all.

"Ledge ends here," Vil called out ahead of them. Daen lengthened his stride to move up to join him, and Romik stepped up alongside Aelys.

"Doing all right, Bella?" he asked. She looked up at him, her eyes wide and startled.

"Oh! Um—yes. I mean I'm tired and . . . well. I'm fine, thank you."

"Hungry?" he asked.

"Why? Do you have something to eat?" The hope that flashed in her eyes made his stomach clench with self-directed anger. He shook his head.

"No," he said. "I just . . . thought you might be."

"Well, I am, a little," she said. "But I didn't think anyone had brought anything, so I just kept quiet. No use in complaining if we can't do anything about it, right?"

Despite himself, Romik snorted quietly and smiled. "You're tougher than you look."

That caused *her* to snort a soft laugh. "You are teasing me." She smiled, just a little, and it felt like someone had just driven a fist into his solar plexus.

"No," he said, his voice rougher than he would have liked. "I'm not. Toughness doesn't mean you don't feel pain. It just means you move forward in the face of pain. Trust me. A lot of young recruits would have been nothing *but* complaints after not eating for this long."

Her smile grew. Slowly, tentatively, but it grew until it touched the blue eyes that were a mirror of his own.

Red Lady, but she's beautiful. Not my usual type, but right now, I could slaughter armies for that smile—

"Romik, Bella. Over here. We found a way down."

Romik swallowed hard and held a hand out to her. "Careful near the edge," he said, his voice still gruff.

She looked up at him, still with that surprised, tentative look. But she laid her palm atop his. He curled his fingers around hers, her fine-boned hand nearly disappearing in his own meaty grip. He glanced down at their joined hands, and then back up into her eyes.

"I won't let you fall," he promised.

"I know."

"Romik!"

Daen's flash-fire temper threaded through his voice, and Romik tore his gaze away from Aelys to glare at his brother. Sure enough, Daen stood near the edge, his eyes hard and hot. Something primal and competitive reared up from the depths of Romik's mind, but he shoved it away and forced himself to lead Aelys over there at a steady, even pace.

When they reached Daen, Romik took Aelys's hand and put it in Daen's. Daen blinked, irritation and anger bleeding into confusion in his eyes.

"All of us, right?" Romik said softly, for Daen's ears alone. Although judging by the way Aelys's brows furrowed for a second, she'd heard and wondered what he meant.

A muscle jumped in Daen's cheek, but he nodded. "Right," he said. "Right. All of us. Vil's already on his way down. It looks vertical except for right over there, where the ledge meets that crease in the wall. It's slick, so be careful."

"I'll go next, then," Romik said, ignoring the way his leg and his ribs twinged at the thought. "And then she can follow with you at her back." After a moment's thought, he cut his eyes back to Aelys.

"All right with you, Bella?"

She nodded, pressing her lips together.

Romik turned before she could say anything else and started down.

It wasn't an easy descent. The twinge in his thigh quickly became a sharp, stabbing pain as he used his legs to brace himself in the narrow, not-quite-vertical chimneylike structure they descended. His ribs throbbed, sending waves of agony radiating through his body until his arms and hands shook with effort.

Still, this wasn't his first time being injured. Romik knew that he had to keep going. If he stopped, it would only hurt worse. So, bit by bit, finger length by finger length he descended, until his trembling boots touched the ground. His knees buckled, but Vil was just suddenly *there*, in that unnerving way of his.

"Come on, Demon," Vil said. "Easy, brother. I've got you."

"I'm . . . okay."

"You're not. But she's right behind you. Bella! Romik needs you."

Red Lady help me, I do.

Vil helped him lie back on the slick, wet rock. As soon as the back of his head touched down, Aelys's cool hands appeared, pressing against the sides of his face. Romik opened eyes he hadn't realized he'd closed and saw her bending over him, concern writ large on her face.

"See," he said, pain roughening his voice. "Toughness."

"Is it tough if it gets you killed?" she whispered, with just the smallest touch of asperity. Before he could answer, she looked up at Vil. "Please?" she asked.

Romik also turned to his cloaked brother, just in time to see him nod. Aelys bent her head, and so she didn't see the naked longing that flickered across Vil's face, but Romik did.

Aelys gasped, then let out a breathy little whimper that shot through his body like lightning. Her fingers flexed against the sides of his face, and an onslaught of sensation swept through him. The underside of his skin ignited, and his back bowed in ecstasy.

Heated pleasure tangled with the stabbing, grinding pains in his body, twisting them up, dissolving them under her touch—which was somehow everywhere, along every nerve, all at once. Romik let out a gasp of his own as his body exploded in release, leaving him reeling, panting on the cold, wet cavern floor.

"I—oh! I'm so sorry," Aelys said, snatching her hands back from his face. "I didn't mean to...but you looked so hurt and I—"

"It's all right, Bella," Vil said. "He's all right, aren't you, Romik?"

"Fine," Romik panted. His chest heaved as he fought to slow his breathing. "I'm fine."

And he was. The grinding in his ribs, the stabbing pain in his thigh were gone, lost under the buzzing, postorgasmic fog. Somewhere in the back of his mind, he thought he should probably be embarrassed. He hadn't come in his pants like that in... well, ever. But right now, he couldn't care about that.

Romik closed his eyes and forced his breathing to slow down, even out. When he had that much control back, he opened his eyes and pushed himself up to a seated position. Aelys had backed up, her hands over her mouth, her eyes wide and disturbed. Daen stood behind her, holding her by the shoulders, whispering something in her ear. Even in the midst of his brain's euphoric state, Romik felt a small, muted, but still hot surge of envy.

Daen raised his blue eyes to meet Romik's and the message was clear.

All of us. All.

Romik inhaled through his nose and nodded, once, and then let Vil help him up to his feet.

There wasn't much to do about the state of his breeches, so he let it be. Each of them had been wearing the same clothes since the inn in Mageford anyway.

"How can she think she has no power?" he muttered softly, so that only Vil could hear him. The nearby roar of the waterfall helped, as it echoed off the stone walls as they approached it.

"What do you mean?"

"Aelys. She always says she's powerless, but she killed all of those goblants back on the road, she brought me back from the Red Lady's grasp twice, she can undo a man with a single touch—"

"Not any man." Vil's voice dipped lower, colder.

"No. You're right. Only us. Ever."

Vil let out a low growl that Romik interpreted as vehement agreement. Not that he could blame the man. If the idea of Vil or Daen touching Aelys stirred his envy, then the thought of anyone else doing so threatened to push him over the edge into an abyss of scorching rage. For just a second, a scarlet haze clouded his vision, and he stepped unwarily and slipped on the wet rock. Once more, Vil grabbed him, kept him from collapsing while he cursed his own clumsiness and forced himself back to a calm state of mind.

"Your leg?" Vil asked.

"No," he said. "I just slipped, thinking about...never mind. But that's another thing, isn't it? If she's got the power to bind all three of us to the point where we're irrationally obsessed with her—"

"Irrationally? Seems a bit harsh."

"Are *you* rational about her? Can you tell me that she doesn't get under your skin and make you feel...extreme?"

Vil said nothing. After a moment, Romik nodded.

"So, you see what I mean. Our Bellatrix can do all of these things... So why does she insist that she's powerless? Is it a ploy?" Even as Romik said the words, a cold shiver of denial swept through him. *No,* he thought. *It can't be a ploy. She really means it. She thinks she's weak.*

"It could be a ploy," Vil said. "But my gut says it isn't. But with her...I'm not sure I can trust my gut."

"Yes! That's exactly what I mean. I don't know if I can trust mine either, when it comes to her."

Vil blew out a breath. "And there lies the trouble."

"So, what do we do about it?"

"You're asking me, Captain?"

"I was only a lieutenant, Vil, which you know very well. And yes, I want to know what you're thinking in the shadows under that hood of yours."

Vil flashed him a grin, brief and wide like lightning piercing a summer night sky. Gone before he'd even really registered its presence.

"I like my hood," Vil said. "It comes in handy."

"I imagine it does, for a thief. What do you think?"

"I think we do what we're doing. We protect her, we watch her, we keep her safe. And we find out why she's being stalked by bandits."

"And if she betrays us?"

"Then we do what we have to do."

Could I? Romik wondered, but he let the matter drop and turned his attention back to Daen and Aelys. The two of them had walked closer to the cascade hammering down from above and were intently staring up toward the top of the falls.

"There's no way up," Aelys was saying as Romik and Vil approached. "It's completely sheer."

"Well," Daen said. "Not completely...but I think you're right, it would be very tough without proper climbing gear, which none of us have."

"We should just turn back," Romik said. A wave of irritation washed over him, and so the words came out sharper than he intended. Enough that Daen frowned at him and even Vil looked at him sidelong. He shrugged. "It's just...there's nothing to see here. We're wasting time. We should just go back to that first tunnel."

"We only just got here, Demon," Vil said, his voice low. "Why do you suddenly want to leave?"

"There's nothing here."

"You're probably right, but still, we should at least take a look around."

"It's a waste of time!" Romik said. He shifted his feet uneasily as the urge to turn around grew stronger. "Let's just go."

Daen looked from him to Vil and back again. "Maybe we should—"

"Hold on."

Of all people, Romik would have least expected Aelys to speak up just then. But her voice held a clear note of authority as she interrupted Daen. She stepped toward him, peering up into his eyes, and then abruptly turned and looked at Daen.

"You're thinking of leaving too, right? After all the work we did to get here? When it was your idea?"

"I mean . . . Romik's right. It would be a waste of time. There's nothing here." He reached out to touch her shoulder. She caught his fingers before they came to rest. She gave him a tiny smile that Romik couldn't quite interpret. The now-familiar jealousy burned around the edges of his mind at their interaction, but it was like background noise compared to the itchy, uncomfortable feeling overtaking his system. He wanted to leave. It wasn't the same as his survival instinct giving him the kind of gut feeling he couldn't ignore . . . but it wasn't nothing, and he wanted it to end.

"And you, Vil?"

Romik turned to see his thief brother shrug. "I agree. I think it's a waste of time. We should head back."

"There *is* something here," Aelys said, her blue eyes fierce. "And you've just confirmed it for me. I thought I felt it, but it was just a whisper, so I wasn't sure—"

"What are you talking about?" Romik asked.

"A ward," she said. "It must be. It's the only explanation."

"Explanation for what, Bella?" Daen asked. "We really should go."

Aelys narrowed her eyes and sensation bloomed under Romik's skin, sending hot lines of need racing along his nerves, pooling in his groin. He gasped and shook his head before adjusting his suddenly too-tight breeches.

"Red Lady's tits, Bella! Warn a man next time!"

"Sorry," she said, and for once, she sounded like she didn't entirely mean it. "But I had to. Do you all still want to leave?"

Leave? Romik cut his eyes to Daen and then to Vil, both of whom looked as flustered as he did.

"No," Romik said slowly. "Not . . . really. I guess not. What happened?"

A slow smile spread across Aelys's face, lighting it up from the inside. Romik's recalcitrant cock stiffened again, defying his attempts to settle himself.

You're pretty even when you're sad, Bella. Divines help us all when you're not. Your joy takes my breath away.

"It *is* a ward," Aelys said. "I knew it! I have no idea why, or when, but at some point someone decided that they really didn't want anyone looking around down here near this waterfall. I can feel the energy pooling there, which wouldn't ordinarily be that unusual. Energy often collects in places where natural phenomena meet—shorelines, storms, things like that. But the fact that all three of you immediately wanted to leave meant that someone very skilled wove a spell designed to turn people's attention away."

"Away from what?" Vil asked.

"I don't know," she said, her eyes snapping with excitement, and maybe even a little bit of mischief. "But if they went to all that trouble to hide it, I feel like maybe we should find out."

Romik watched his brother's face answer her in a slow, savage smile. This time, the kick of jealousy wasn't overshadowed by the magically induced—if he understood her correctly—desire to leave. But as he fought to keep his hands from curling into fists as he watched their silent interplay, another thought occurred to him.

She's good for him. He needs her as much as she needs us... *as much as I need her. Daen, too,* he realized, cutting his eyes to watch his forester brother. Daen also watched Vil and Aelys. And though his mouth was set in a hard line, as Romik watched, the set of his eyes softened. Daen blinked, and then looked at him.

Maybe it wasn't an accident that caused her to bind all three of us. Maybe, hell, I don't know. Maybe the Divines heard our brotherhood oath and took it to the next level or some such. But if she can put that look on Vil's face, if she can soften Daen's bitter temper... if she can put up with me after what a horse's arse I've been...

Red Lady, I know Your gifts have two edges. This, though—

"You all right, Ro?" Daen asked, interrupting the thought that Romik was almost afraid to finish. He rolled his shoulders, unclenched his jaw, and nodded.

"Yeah. Fine. All of us, right?"

"Every single one," Daen replied, smiling. It was the dark,

sardonic smile Romik had quickly gotten to know. Only Aelys seemed to get Daen's soft smiles.

Which, even as I hate it, I have to admit that I understand it. If I could be soft, I'd be soft for her.

"Everyone what?" Aelys asked, pulling their attention back to her. Not that it ever wandered far.

"Nothing," Romik said. "So, what? We're just going to go check out the waterfall that some mage went to a lot of trouble to turn us away from? That doesn't seem risky to you?"

Daen laughed. "It does to me," he said. "Which is why I'm in. C'mon, Ro. You can handle anything we find."

Romik snorted, but just shook his head and rested his hand on the hilt of his sword. A twinge in his ribs told him that if he was going to be handling anything, he'd best do it quickly. Despite the energy Aelys kept pumping into him, he wasn't fully healthy.

"The energy is pooling just above where the cascade hits the surface of the lake," Aelys said. "Don't most waterfalls carve out depressions behind them? I think the ward is centered back there."

"We're going to get wet," Vil said.

"It's all right," Daen said. "We'll dry, and we could all use a bath, I'm sure."

Aelys snorted a laugh, and then covered her hand with her mouth. But her blue eyes smiled above her fingers, and Romik felt the corner of his mouth turn upward in response.

"Let's go, if we're going," he said, and reached out his free hand to her. Her gaze flew to his, and her smile grew just a little bit. "Careful, Bella. Wet rocks are slick."

Aelys laid her hand in his. Her fingers were cold, but the excitement that sparkled in her eyes told him that she was well. He wrapped his hand around hers, helping her step carefully forward toward the cascade that pounded down from impossibly high above.

As they drew closer, the roar of the falls got louder and louder until the reverberations from its echoes felt like a pulsing throb in his chest. Vil led, picking his way over rocks and through the blankets of mist that plastered Romik's hair to his forehead and soaked through his clothes.

Aelys slipped once, but Romik kept her from falling, and the grateful smile she flashed his way sang through him like lightning. He swallowed hard and considered trying to say something—though he had no idea what—when Vil let out a shout of triumph.

"Here! There's a gap right here between the rock and the cascade itself. I almost didn't see it, but if you look up, you can see that someone engineered it so the water would fall exactly this way!"

He pointed upward. Aelys's lips moved—presumably to say "Flash," although Romik couldn't hear anything over the roar of the falls. A red-tinged globe of light appeared, and flew upward to show that, indeed, someone had managed to shape a kind of rock lintel and gutter arrangement that provided a tiny opening in the curtain of water near the base of the cliff.

Vil ducked through, and then came back out and waved to them to follow.

Romik helped Aelys make her way up and watched closely as she slipped through. He jerked his head to tell Daen to go next, while he brought up the rear.

Once behind the curtain of the falls, a dark, nearly round opening beckoned. Aelys flicked her fingers, sending her magelight forward to illuminate what turned out to be just another short passageway that dead-ended in a blank wall.

Romik watched as her eyes narrowed. She stepped forward, but Vil stopped her, stepping in front of her before she could breach the threshold of the passageway.

"We're your protectors," Daen shouted, not out of anger, but just to make himself heard over the torrent of water behind them. "Let one of us go first, Bella!"

Aelys pressed her lips together but nodded. Vil returned her nod and stepped into the passageway. He disappeared into the darkness for a moment, and then, once again, reappeared and waved them forward.

As soon as he stepped into the passageway, the noise of the falls abated significantly, enough that Romik let out a sigh of relief.

More magic? Or just acoustics? I suppose it doesn't matter.

"There has to be something here," Aelys said. "There's no reason to expend the energy to set a ward over an empty chamber."

"Bring your light here, Bella," Vil said, as he crouched next to the blank wall. "I think maybe . . ." He reached into his cloak and removed a pair of long, thin pins.

"Lockpicks?" Daen asked, incredulity in his tone. "Where is the lock?"

"Right here," Vil said, pointing to a spot on the stone that looked completely unremarkable from Romik's perspective. Aelys's magelight obligingly hovered closer, and Vil went to work with his picks. Romik just had time to wonder if his brother might not trigger some kind of magical trap when Vil let out a satisfied grunt and a deep *ker-thunk* sounded in the small space.

Quicker than a thought, Romik shot his hand out and grabbed Aelys, hauling her back behind him as he drew his short sword. There wasn't much room to maneuver in the passageway, but that was all to the good. If something came at them, he'd be better able to shield her.

"Daen! Rearguard!" he snapped out as the wall in front of Vil began to move. It slid backward, away from them as if it were on rails, and then dropped down into the floor, leaving an opening as wide as the passageway itself.

"Vil. Check it out," Romik said. "Bella, light it up, please."

The magelight moved forward into the revealed cavern, and then disappeared upward out of view. A warm orange light burst into being, and then began to cast flickering shadows on the floor.

"Bella?"

"That's not me," she said. "That's something else."

"It's a fire," Vil said, stepping forward, bared knives gleaming in his hands. "But fortunately, it seems to be confined to the fireplace."

Fireplace?

"Is it safe?" Romik called out.

"Seems to be," Vil said. "No one's here, but it's . . . cozy."

Romik edged forward, his sword at the ready. He stepped up next to Vil, who sheathed his blades, and took a good look around.

The chamber wasn't large, but it wasn't cramped either. Roughly oblong in shape, it had a hearth at the far end, where, indeed, a fire burned merrily away. As he watched, a hearth hook with a black pot hanging from it swung into place over the flames, and the scent of cooking meat and vegetables soon followed.

On the wall, above the fireplace, a strange, twisty design glinted copper and green in the light.

The rest of the wall space had been dedicated to shelves. They ringed the entirety of the chamber from door to hearth on both sides, stretching up higher than Romik could reach. Most were crammed full of books and scrolls and odd items of curious workmanship. Two squashy, fabric-covered chairs stood on a threadbare rug in front of the hearth, and a curved table stood in the center of the room, piled high with more books and strange bits of machinery.

"Oh, Divines," Aelys breathed as she walked in behind him. "This is unbelievable." She tilted her head back, letting the hood of her cloak fall as she looked around with wide eyes. "Is that..." She pushed past Romik and Vil and walked as if in a daze toward a section of shelves next to the fireplace.

Instead of books, these shelves held jars and boxes neatly labeled in some language Romik didn't recognize. Aelys reached out and ran her fingertips along the small clear space on the widest shelf, then picked up a small mortar and pestle there.

"What is it?" Romik asked. "Is it safe?"

"It's...a study," Aelys breathed. She set the mortar down and turned back to face them with wonder in her eyes. "A laboratory of sorts. I thought they were all accounted for!"

"What do you mean, accounted for?"

Aelys walked to the table, running her fingers lightly over the pages of an open book there. "It's part of our history. Ages ago, before the Battlemage Corps was organized and the Lyceum was built, powerful mages would construct their own places where they would go to do research, to study, to experiment and learn. They were always very well hidden and protected. Only another mage of equal power to the founder could ever have found this place..." She looked up, her eyes wide.

"Yes, *Bella*," Daen said with a smile. "You found it. You're not as powerless as you think you are."

Aelys's throat jumped as she swallowed hard, and she blinked rapidly for a few seconds before shaking her head and continuing on.

"Anyway. Yes, Romik. Once we're inside, this place is safe."

"What's this?" Vil asked, pointing at the pot bubbling away over the fire. "It looks like stew, but it sounds like this place has been locked up for years."

"Centuries," Aelys said. "But yes, it is stew. That's probably an enchanted pot. They're quite useful. As long as you keep it charged with magic, every time you set it over a magical flame, it will cook whatever recipe was wrought into it when it was created. There aren't many of these left."

"Why not? It seems useful," Daen said.

"It...they're complicated to make, as I understand it, and we lost that knowledge ages ago," Aelys replied.

"The flames are magic. That explains why there's no chimney, and no smoke," Vil said.

"And why the fire started up when we stepped in the door," Aelys said. "Once we made it in, the magic in this room welcomed us."

"You talk like it's a living thing," Romik said. He sheathed his sword and limped over to one of the two chairs, but didn't sit down, though the throbbing in his leg and the growing pain in his ribs told him he soon would have no choice.

"Magic? It is alive, in a way. In another way, it's just a tool. Energy directed toward a goal, guided by the mage's will and incantation. It can't think or act for itself. The mage who built this place must have laid enchantments on the room to start the fire and get a meal cooking whenever someone arrived. That's all I meant." Aelys smiled up at him, but her brows quickly drew together in a frown.

"Romik?" she asked, stepping closer. "Are you in pain?"

"I'm fine. I've had worse."

Her eyes narrowed. "We talked about this," she said, and for the first time, Romik thought he heard the barest thread of anger heating her words. "Toughness alone—"

"Bella, I'm fine. I once faced a pair of wounded bearcats in the arena with broken ribs and blood from a scalp wound leaking into my eyes. I can handle it."

Aelys blinked. "You...were an arena fighter?"

He nodded. "For close to a decade. And if I can survive the Aldemer Commemorative Games, I can survive this."

She straightened her shoulders and drew in a breath. "Well, that may be, but now you are my Ageon, my responsibility. If you're in pain, I can help, and you need to let me do that. So, I'll ask again. Are you hurting?"

"A little," he said after a moment. He stifled the urge to smile. She looked so fierce. "But...I'm mostly tired. Let me rest, and eat if you're sure it's safe, and then if I'm not better you can do the thing. I...I don't want to overtax you." He waved his hands, feeling a flush creeping up his neck.

Idiot, he mentally cursed himself. *You sound like a green kid who's never had a woman!*

Aelys looked at him for a long moment and then nodded. "All right," she said. "That's fair. Like I said, I want to respect your wishes and boundaries, but I *will* take care of you. As for overtaxing me . . . well. I have learned that lesson. I will eat and rest, too, and replenish my own energy. We all will. Like I said, I'm confident we're safe here. Have a seat in that chair and I'll check on the food."

"Well, well, listen to you," Vil said in a low drawl from behind the table. "You sound like a Bellatrix should."

Aelys squared her shoulders and faced Vil. "I *am* a Bellatrix," she said.

Vil and Daen shared a look, and then Vil turned back to her with the ghost of a smile on his lips.

"I know," he said. "See that you remember it."

Daen lifted his spoon and blew air across it to cool the stew.

This is good! I'm not sure why I'm surprised, but I am. I never would have guessed that a magic pot could make better stew than Tenneris back at the Outpost.

Like the others, he'd been suspicious at first, but hunger had won out over paranoia. Aelys swore it was safe, and it smelled delicious. Romik had insisted that he try a bowl first and wait for a bit before he'd let Aelys or the others partake. He'd shown no side effects, so they'd all tucked in.

"It'd be a useful thing to have one of those pots," Daen said. "If this place is long abandoned, do you think we could take it with us?"

"It only works over a magical fire," Aelys said. "Which is a difficult and involved thing to set up. If you're thinking of a camp pot, it wouldn't be worth the trouble."

"Pity," Daen said, popping his bite into his mouth. "This stew is really good."

"But imagine how sick you'd be of it if it was all you had to eat day in and day out," Vil pointed out.

"You could save it for times when there was no game, you wouldn't have to use it all the time."

Aelys stood up from where she sat in the chair opposite Romik in front of the hearth. "There's a cleaning basin here," she said. "If you're done, I can take your bowl and spoon."

Daen snorted, looking up at her from where he sat on the

floor beside her chair. "If this place has been locked up for hundreds of years, do you really think the owner will mind if we leave dirty dishes behind?"

"*I* would mind," Aelys said with a smile.

"Do you know how to wash dishes, Bella?" Romik asked, his voice serious. "I'm not trying to be cruel, but many noble ladies don't."

"I learned at the Lyceum."

"They teach magic *and* domestic chores?"

Aelys's smile took on a bitter edge. "To weak students from great families who should have more power than they do, yes. Several of the Sanvari saw menial chores as an effective punishment and hoped they would motivate me to try harder. I've cleaned dishes, scrubbed floors, mucked stalls, rinsed privies...quite a few other things. If it's a dirty job necessary for the comfort of those living in close quarters, I've probably done it at least once."

Romik eyed her for a long moment. Then, for what may have been the first time since the inn, Daen saw his warrior brother's lips curve in a genuine smile that reached all the way to his eyes.

"Fair enough," he said as he handed her his bowl, the spoon rattling against the side of it. "I'll never doubt you again."

Aelys licked her lips and then returned his smile as she took the bowl. "You shouldn't make promises you can't keep."

Daen threw his head back and laughed, and to his surprise, Romik joined in. Even Vil smiled and chuckled from his perch on the curved table behind them. Something warm and glowing gold bloomed in Daen's chest as all four of them shared that moment of levity.

"I'll help," Daen said as soon as the laughter died down. He found himself clinging to that good feeling. Ever since the inn, they'd been drowning in uncertainty and suspicion, and he was thoroughly sick of it.

Why can't it just be like this? he wondered as he got to his feet. *All of us together, laughing and having fun? I was so alone for so long in the Foresters, why can't I have my brothers and Aelys as well?*

He handed his bowl to Aelys, then turned to see if Vil was done with his.

"What are you thinking, brother?" Vil murmured, his blue eyes sharp on Daen's own.

Daen paused, and then shrugged one shoulder, trying to appear nonchalant. "I like this," he said. "All of us here, happy. I don't...I don't see why we can't keep her."

Vil turned his head and looked out from under his hood at where Aelys bent over the wash basin. "I don't think she wants that."

"You think she'd rather we just take her home so she can become a noble broodmare?"

"That's what she said. That's what she hired us to do."

"Things are different now, Vil," Daen said, exasperation rising in his chest and leaking out through his voice. He snatched the empty stew bowl from his brother's hands. "She hired us when she thought she had no choice."

"Does she have a choice now?"

"Doesn't she?" Daen shot back, and then turned and strode to Aelys. He didn't want to say anything else; he didn't want to hear Vil say anything else. He just wanted that golden feeling back.

Aelys looked up at him with a smile as he came up beside her. He inhaled and smiled back, feeling his shoulders ease as he did so.

"Everything all right?" she asked softly as she reached for the bowls he held.

"I'm next to you. Everything is perfect," he said, and winked. She laughed and shook her head.

"You're a flatterer and a flirt, Daen."

"Only for you, Bella."

"I don't believe that for a second," she said archly, dipping the bowls into the water.

"You should."

At the sound of his voice, Daen and Aelys both turned to look over their shoulders at Vil, who watched them from the table as he sharpened one of his many knives.

"What do you mean?" Aelys asked.

"Vil..." Daen said, something that was either warning or pleading or both in his tone.

"I mean, we're all different with you. If I had to guess, I'd say Daen doesn't, as a rule, lack for female company—"

"Vil!"

"—but it was always because they sought him out. He never pursued anyone because he never had to."

"Vil! Will you stop?"

"Am I wrong, brother?"

Daen sighed heavily. "No. You're not. But you're going to embarrass her."

Aelys tilted her head to the side and touched Daen's arm lightly, her fingers wet. "It's all right, I don't mind."

"But the point, Bella, is that Daen is different with you. We all are."

Understanding dawned in Aelys's eyes, and her smile faded away. "Oh. The *geas* again. I'm—"

"Don't be sorry," Daen said, shooting a glare over at Vil before turning to take her hand in his own. "I like who I am with you. I *like* saying things to make you smile and laugh and shake your head at me. Before you I was...bitter. Cynical. Lacking purpose and drive. You gave me that, even if it was by accident. So, please, don't ever apologize to me for the *geas*, all right? Because if I would have known, I *still* would have chosen to be yours."

Aelys's eyes went wide and round and filled with tears.

"Green Lady's rut," Daen cursed, and pulled her close. He wrapped his arms around her and pressed his lips into her hair. "I'm sorry, Bella. I didn't mean to make you cry."

"N-no, it's not that," Aelys said, her words muffled. "It's just... what you just said...I have waited my whole life for someone to choose me. I'd given up hope..." She let out a watery laugh.

"Oh, look at me," she said, pushing away from him with a loud sniff. "I'm a mess. These bowls are clean, I'll just dry them and put them back, and then I want to take a look at some of these books and see if I can't figure out how to get out of this cave. Obviously there must be a way, if whoever built this study came and went. I just have to find it." She looked up at him with a bright, wide smile.

"Thank you," she said, her tone softening just a little.

"You're welcome," Daen said, frowning. Something felt off, but he couldn't put his finger on it. She seemed almost...brittle. He looked a question over at Vil, who just shrugged and continued cleaning and sharpening his knife. Daen looked back at Aelys, but she'd turned away from him and was busily stacking their newly cleaned dishes on the shelf where they'd found them earlier.

"Get some rest," Vil said lowly. "I'll watch her."

Daen bit the inside of his cheek, feeling like he should say something. But nothing came to mind, and so he let out a sigh and went to lie down on the rug by the magical fire.

At least Romik isn't snoring, he thought as he closed his eyes and the fatigue he'd been keeping at bay came rushing in to claim him.

She's doing one of two things, Vil thought as he sheathed one knife and removed another. His eyes stayed locked on Aelys as she stood nearby, her long-fingered hands skimming over the pages of a book as she quickly perused its contents before closing it and moving to the next one in the pile. *She's either completely out of her depth and not sure how to react to Daen's emotional connection, or she's playing him and all of us like a professional courtesan. Problem is, I can't decide which.*

Though, truth be told, the odds of her having a courtesan's manipulation skills were getting less and less likely. Women and men trained for *years* in some of the southern cities in order to learn the techniques she'd have to be employing. And she'd been at the Lyceum for the last decade.

Or so she claims. Of course, I believe her . . . but I haven't stayed alive this long by taking much on faith.

Vil tested the edge of the blade, decided it was sharp enough, and sheathed it before sliding to the edge of the table and dropping to his feet. He pivoted until he stood just behind Aelys, looking over her shoulder as she peered at yet another book.

"Find anything interesting?" he asked.

"So much," she breathed. Her fingertips trailed reverently down the page. "This really is a treasure trove of knowledge. There are copies of works here that are known to be one of a kind in the Lyceum's library. Do you have any idea what that means?"

"That they're not one of a kind anymore?"

She glanced up at him, a startled expression on her face. Then she blinked and laughed lowly.

"Well, yes. I guess that's true too. But it means that this place has been untouched for . . . well. We already knew it was old. I suspect the mage who built it never reported it when the Lyceum was established, rather than it just being forgotten. The Corps never knew it existed."

"Sounds like a smart individual."

She frowned. "How so?"

Vil shrugged. "Keep something back, even if you're throwing in with a group. Always smart to have resources that are only your own."

Her eyebrows rose over the blue eyes he shared. "So, did you? Keep something back when you joined up with Romik and Daen? I know you call each other 'brother.'"

Vil smiled. "Brothers don't know everything about each other."

"But don't you trust them?"

"With my life," he said. "With *your* life. But I never said they knew everything I know, nor do I know everything they know. Everyone is allowed their secrets, Bella. You never know when they might be exactly what you need."

She shook her head. "But—"

"Take my advice, Bella. Just let it go. What are you reading?"

"Oh! This? This is, as far as I can tell, the personal grimoire of the owner of this study."

"What's a 'grimoire'?"

"It's like a mage's personal journal."

"Why not just call it a journal?"

She laughed. "Well, it's more than just that. It's a place for a mage to make records of spells and incantations they're learning . . . or inventing. Experiments, notes, theories, speculation; a good grimoire will have all of these. It's like a window into the mage's mind. It's very exciting."

"It looks exciting," Vil said, using his driest tone. Aelys glanced over at him and let out a little laugh.

"I'm sure it doesn't, but truly, it is. This one's *very* well organized. He or she even built a table of contents into the front." She flipped the book to the first page.

Vil could read. The boss he'd worked for in Cievers had insisted he learn. Still, as he peered down over her shoulder, Vil didn't recognize any of the words printed in a neat column there.

"You can read that?" he asked.

"Mmhmm. It's Bellene. I told you about the Bellenes before. This is written in their language. It's an ancient dialect, but it was in common use when the Lyceum was founded. Many of our spells still use Bellenic words and syntax."

"Bellene . . . like Bellatrix?"

She looked up with a smile. "Yes!" she said. "They actually

have the same root word. 'Bel' means conflict, or war. The people who spoke Bellenic were a fractious lot."

"And skilled in magic, apparently."

"Well, some of them, anyway." She turned her attention back to the page. "Oh! Here it is! I was hoping I'd find it!"

"What?"

"This section here," she said, pointing to one of the strange words. "This word means 'laboratory.' I think it might be his notes on building this study!" She flipped several pages, opening the book to a spot near the back cover.

"All right," she said, her eyes flying back and forth as she scanned the contents of the page. "Yes, here we go. This records him building the entry tunnel we came through, and setting the lock so that it couldn't be found except by magelight from a mage with deep power reserves...very clever, very subtle stuff."

"Did he design the lock to be picked, too?"

"No, it looks like there was a key at some point, and it amused him to make it completely mundane. This line here...I'm not used to the syntax, but it almost looks like he's saying that if a person was powerful enough to even see the lock, then that was good enough for him? Something like that."

"Is that the only way in or out?"

"That's what I'm trying to find," she said, turning the page. Her eyes skimmed halfway down the page and froze. She blinked, her brow furrowing in concentration.

"What is it?" Vil asked, leaning closer.

"I'm not sure..." Then she straightened abruptly. "It says there's something..." She walked over to the hearth and stood with her hands on her hips, looking up at the metal sigil etched into the stones above.

"What is that? Does it mean something?" Vil asked, feeling increasingly annoyed by his lack of knowledge. *I suppose I'll have to learn to read Bellene too. Could be useful someday.*

"It's...a kind of heraldry, I suppose. A sigil that mages once used to magically seal correspondence and the like. But it looks purely decorative. There's no particular energy to it...at least, no more so than anywhere else in this room. But..." She trailed off again, as it appeared she was wont to do when puzzling through a problem.

Aelys tilted her head to the side and regarded the sigil, and then went back and looked at the book. Then she let out a gasp and whirled to face Vil, her eyes wide.

"Remember after I first bound you," she said. "When we talked in Daen's forest cave? Do you remember what you said?"

"I remember all of it."

She reached out and took his hand, sending shockwaves of surprise jolting through him. He held himself steady and let her lift his hand and turn it palm upward. Then she used her other hand to slide his sleeve up, baring the blue mark he'd shown her that night.

"You're my knife in the dark."

"I am."

She let go of his wrist. "Look right here! Do you see this?"

"Bella, I see it, but I can't read it. What does it say?"

"Oh." Her face fell, some of the excited flush faded from her cheeks. "I'm sorry, how stupid of m—"

"Aelys. Stop. What does it say?"

"Um. It says..." She bent to look closer and began to read. "'They think to allow me only a sword, a shield. They took my knife, my hammer. But the forbidden memory'—or maybe story? The words are the same—'remains mine. When I again... provide? Offer? Share?' Something like that. 'When I again share my eyes, the rivers will... release?' No, that word is lock... unlock? 'Unlock the gifts.'"

"What in the Dark Lady's name does that mean?"

Aelys lifted her eyes to his. "I think he's talking about a *geas*. This line here, about sharing his eyes?"

"And forbidden bonds? The way you reacted when you realized what had happened... you said it was monstrous."

"Well, it is. Ancient mages used to—"

"Bond warriors against their will, yes, you said that. Was this mage one of those?"

Aelys turned back to the sigil. "He's not that old, if he's Bellene. But I think...I think maybe he used a *geas* anyway," she said. "Look there, in his sigil. Doesn't that look like a knife? Look at it sideways."

Vil tilted his head as she'd done earlier, and suddenly he saw it: a dagger, pointed down, with a drop of blood poised to fall from the very tip. He felt his attention sharpen, and his eyes traced the intricate metal lines of the sigil until he found...

"A bow," he said, his voice a harsh whisper. "Opposite the knife. And next to it a shield, and just below—"

"A hammer," Aelys said. "One of those two-handed war hammers that the southern barbarians use. And in the center, a sword. All of them bound together in a network of energy that glints in the magelight, or the magic firelight. You see it, don't you?"

"I do," Vil said. "But I have to ask you . . . so what?"

"I don't know," she admitted. "But I think I want to find out what these 'gifts' could be."

"What are the odds this is dangerous? A trap?"

"Not zero," Aelys said. "But . . . I think it might be worth it. Whoever constructed this place had great power, and apparently he understood the *geas*. This is important information that I think we need, Vil."

The excitement had returned to her cheeks, staining them pink. Her blue eyes glittered with intensity, and she spoke with an unconscious confidence he'd never seen from her before. The urge to reach out and touch her spiked through him, kicking his pulse up to a fever pitch. He inhaled slowly, holding his icy exterior in place through sheer force of will.

This woman could destroy me, he realized. He felt neither surprise nor dismay at the revelation. It was simply a fact that he could no longer ignore. *Darkness grant I never let her find that out.*

"Vil?"

"What do you propose to do?" he asked.

She bit her lower lip in the way she tended to do when she was thinking. "Well, he references the rivers. He could mean the falls outside . . . but I think it's something else. When you . . . think about me. When you feed energy into me, deliberately, it feels like a dark river of sensation searing along my nerves. If I'm right, and this is about a *geas*, I think he might be talking about that, about his Ageons pushing energy into him. I think if you push into me, in here, then something might happen."

"All right," he said slowly. "But let's wake the others first and tell them what we mean to do. Just in case."

Aelys nodded her agreement, and together they turned to wake first Daen, and then Romik, and explained.

Daen is predictably excited, and Romik predictably skeptical, Vil thought a few moments later as they stood in front of Aelys. *And I . . . I am curious, I suppose.*

"I'll start with Vil first, since that was our plan," Aelys said, her voice a little less confident than before. He met her eyes, willing her to recapture the fire that had lit her up when they'd been talking, earlier.

"What do you want us to do?" Romik asked, sounding almost as growly as the grumpy bearcat he resembled. He did not wake well.

"Just be ready," Vil said.

"For what?"

"Anything."

Romik huffed, but he closed his mouth and rested a hand on the pommel of his sword. Vil turned his head to check with Daen. He merely nodded, while holding his strung bow low and ready.

"All right, Bella," Vil said, rolling his shoulders under his cloak. "Are you ready?"

"I am—ah!"

Call it perversity of character, but Vil felt the bite of savage pride as Aelys's head fell backward as soon as he pictured his hands on her naked flesh. In his mind, Vil ran his lips over the pulse at the base of her throat, catching her skin lightly between his teeth before soothing the spot with his tongue. Her lips parted as he pictured kissing his way up to her jawline, breathing in the scent of her skin.

"Vil."

Vil blinked and saw that Daen pointed at the sigil above the fireplace. He looked up there, and saw that the stylized knife glittered in the flickering firelight. As he watched, that glitter solidified, throwing a beam of light that pierced through the room like a shaft of sunlight through a crack in a shuttered window. The beam fell on the bookcase lining the left wall, lighting up the spine of a book bound in a faded purplish gray leather.

"Aelys," Vil said, unable to keep the low, intimate note out of his voice. "Aelys. Bella. Look. Something did indeed happen."

Aelys inhaled and opened eyes gone cloudy with pleasure. Vil curled his hands into fists to keep himself from reaching out to her and jerked his head toward the illuminated book. "Look."

"Oh!" she breathed, and it seemed to jolt her out of the haze of sensation his energy had caused. She glanced over at him quickly, before squaring her shoulders and walking around the table to look up at the book. She raised a hand, reaching—

"Bella, wait!" Romik cried out, but it was too late. Her beautiful, long-fingered hands gripped the spine and pulled the book out. Or tried, anyway. It slid about two inches out before a loud *ker-thunk* reverberated through the floor and an entire section of the bookcase swung open toward her.

Vil was in motion before he realized he planned to move. He grabbed Aelys's shoulder just as Romik grabbed her free hand. Together, they hauled her backward, pulling her away from the wall and down to the floor. Vil rolled his body over hers, using himself as a shield while Romik drew his sword and sprang to his feet. Next to them, Daen stood with an arrow nocked and his bow drawn against whatever threat awaited behind this hidden doorway.

Nothing happened.

"It's clear, Vil," Romik said, his voice low, but devoid of any of his earlier irritation. "Let her up. You both need to see this."

"Are you all right, Bella?" Vil used his arms to lever himself up. "I didn't hurt you, did I?"

"No," she said, sounding breathless. "I—I'm all right. Just surprised."

"You shouldn't be," Romik said as he bent to reach for her hand and help her out from under Vil. "You know we will do anything to protect you."

"I do," she said, and gave him a little smile. "And I'm grateful."

"What do we need to see?" Vil asked as he rolled up to his feet.

"Knives," Daen said. "Beautiful ones. Masterworks, unless I miss my guess."

"Let me look first," Aelys said. "I won't touch but let me make sure there are no magical surprises waiting for us."

Vil shared a quick look with Daen and Romik, and then nodded. Aelys closed her eyes for a moment, before opening them and calling another orb of magelight to hover over the daggers.

"I don't think there's anything amiss here," she said. "Vil, come and see."

Vil stepped forward, taking the hand that she held out to him and wondering, in the back of his mind, if she realized that she'd done that. He threaded his fingers through hers and let her draw him forward until he could see what had lain hidden for centuries behind the bookcase wall.

Daggers. A pair of them, lying like mirror images—or maybe shadow and light images—of one another on a pedestal covered in black velvet. Both beautiful, perfect specimens of the weaponsmith's art, despite their simplicity of design. Neither of them carried much ornamentation, besides a small brown cat's-eye stone set into the pommel.

Behind the pedestal, a portrait hung on the wall. It showed a woman with long black hair and deep brown eyes that seemed to burn with a mahogany fire. She wore black from head to toe, and in her hands she carried the daggers themselves, one bright blade glinting in the painted sunlight, and one dark blade sweeping shadows before it.

Vil stepped closer, his curiosity piqued by the painting. As he approached, he noticed that there was a small metal plaque affixed to the bottom of the painting's frame. And then below that stood a shallow shelf that held another leather-bound book, smaller than the journal, black in color.

"Agea Riella," Aelys said, bending close to read the words stamped on the plaque. "And this?" She reached for the book, but Vil got there first. If it was trapped, he wanted to be the one to open it.

"Let me," he said, taking the book from its shelf. He paused, but nothing happened. He looked down at the palm-sized thing and turned it over, flipping the small latch open with his thumb. The pages crackled as he laid the book open on the pedestal, revealing neat rows of the same handwriting as the journal.

"It's that same language," he said, cutting his eyes to Aelys. "Or as far as I can tell, anyway. Can you read it?"

Aelys stepped closer, Romik and Daen not far behind. Her magelight brightened and she bent to peer closely at the small characters.

"Riella was his Agea," she breathed after a moment. "She appears to have been trained in espionage? He writes about her subtlety and skills. He . . . I think he loved her . . ." She flipped the page and read on; her eyes rapt. "They were together for many years. He calls her his 'lovely blade.'"

"Poetic," Vil said, his tone dry. Romik snorted softly and met his eyes with a tiny smile, but Aelys appeared not to notice. She merely flipped the page again and kept reading.

"It says he created these daggers for her. He must have been an artificer of some kind—"

"Artificer?" Daen asked. Aelys blinked and focused on his face, her finger holding her place in the little book.

"An artisan mage who creates magic-imbued objects, usually weapons and the like. Artificers are really rare; it takes decades of study to join their ranks. But it looks like our host was one and was renowned for his work. Which, I guess, explains..." She waved a hand toward the table and its piles of gears, lenses and other, more incomprehensible machinery. Then she met Vil's eyes again and pointed at the black dagger. "He forged 'Pure'"—then she pointed at the bright one—"and 'Profane' to aid in her work as a spy. I've never heard of a spy Ageon before."

"Have you ever heard of a thief Ageon?" Daen asked.

"Well..." She frowned, turning her attention to him. "No."

"Then there you go. If Vil can be a thief Ageon, why can't this woman have been a spy Ageon?" Daen said with a little grin.

"'Agea,' for a woman, but I guess you're right," Aelys said, smiling up at Daen. "But that's not the interesting part." She turned back to the book. "It says here that he imbued Pure with the power to dispel poison. So, if you dip it in a drink that is poisoned, it will change the drink to pure water."

"Dipping a dagger into a cup isn't exactly a subtle action," Vil said. "Most people would notice that."

"Maybe that didn't matter? Or maybe that was up to her skill," Daen said. "It's still a useful trait, I've never heard of that before."

"The spell sounds really complicated," Aelys said, flipping the pages as she skimmed the writing. "He didn't write it down in its entirety here, only mentions some of the things he had to do to get the components together... Oh! And here he writes about Profane..." Her face fell and her brow creased in distress.

"What magic does it hold?" Romik's voice rumbled lowly through the small space.

"This... is ugly," she murmured. "He writes that the one who wields Profane can, if they wish, hear the screams of those who bear its wounds."

"Just screams?" Vil asked. Aelys blinked and looked up at him slowly.

"What?"

"Only screams? Or can the wielder hear other things?"

"I don't understand—"

"Oh. I do," Romik put in. "Oh, that's brilliant if you're right, Vil. That would be—"

"Lifesaving, perhaps."

"What are you talking about?" Daen demanded.

"Communication," Romik said. "Imagine, we're in a fight, and we get separated. But Vil's cut you with this little knife—"

"It's a masterwork dagger, Demon, show some respect."

Romik rolled his eyes, and continued as if Vil hadn't spoken. "So, he can hear you. You can tell him where you are, what you see, who's around you. He's right, it could be lifesaving."

"But he'd have to wound me," Daen said, wrinkling his nose. "That doesn't sound good."

"We don't know, it could just need a little scratch. Does the book say?" Romik turned to Aelys, who blinked and flipped rapidly through the pages before shaking her head in the negative.

"No. It's vague."

"Let's test it out," Romik said. "Vil, you can cut me, and I'll go out into the cave behind the waterfall—"

"It won't work," Aelys interrupted, and then looked startled that she had. "I-I mean . . . the daggers have been here for centuries."

"The pot with the magic stew worked," Daen said.

"Yes, but these seem to be keyed to the individual Agea who wielded them. She's long dead, so they're likely not charged with her energy anymore."

"Can you charge them?" Vil asked, his eyes intense.

"I . . . maybe. It depends on how they were made. The charging process is different for every magical artifact—"

"What does the book say?" Romik asked.

Aelys licked her lower lip and caught it with her teeth, her eyes dark with worry. But she opened the little book and read further through it, flipping pages until she let out her breath in a sigh.

"Here it is," she said. "At least, I think this is what it is. He writes of . . . of making l-love with his Agea and feeding her energy while she holds the blades and that 'brings them into power.'"

Vil went very still, his eyes locked on Aelys's face. She bit her lip again, her brow furrowing as she flipped through the book, not yet meeting his eyes.

Rejection hammered through him, clenching his stomach. He pushed it aside, willing his mind to focus on the puzzle at hand.

It's not like you didn't know she wouldn't want you. You ter-rify her, you've always known that. This is not new. Just because you're drawn to her doesn't mean she feels the same. And, in truth, it's good that she does not. You're too broken. If she loved you, you'd break her, too.

Aelys blinked, and then the deep furrows in her brow eased. "Wait a minute," she said, pausing at a page near the end. "Right here he writes about pushing energy to Riella in the middle of an appearance at the imperial court to allow her to charge her daggers. He couldn't have been talking about having sex with her in front of the imperial throne—"

"Depends on the emperor, from what I hear," Daen muttered. Aelys must not have heard him, because she looked up at Vil with relief flowing over her face. Once more, he shoved down the ugly hurt that lanced through him and ignored the sudden stabbing pain in his chest that her reaction caused.

"I think it will work if we just reverse the flow, like we've been doing, while you hold the blades." Aelys said. "I-if you want them, that is."

Vil nodded silently, figuring it was better not to speak with the riot of emotions twisting inside him. He kept his motions smooth and fluid as he reached out and gripped first the dark dagger, and then the bright one, and held them both low and ready. Then he met Aelys's eyes and nodded once.

Sensation swept through him, igniting his nerve endings in blissful fire. He clenched his jaw and held himself rigid, not want-ing to let her see him tremble from the onslaught of desire and need. His fingers gripped the hilts of the daggers, much tighter than his normal hold, and as he focused on his hands, he felt a hot rush of *something* flowing through him like a conduit, gath-ering in his palms and the pads of his fingers, and then flowing out all at once.

Daen gasped and pointed at the daggers. "Look! The gems!"

Vil lifted the daggers up and opened his hands so that they lay flat on his palms. Where the cat's-eye stone had been, an aqua-marine now gleamed blue in the steady glow of Aelys's magelight.

"They're charged," she said, something that sounded like reverence in her tone. "You did it."

"*You* did it, Bella," Daen said. She shook her head.

"No, I couldn't have charged them alone. These are an Ageon's weapons, and they're designed so that only an Ageon might wield them. I-I think you should keep them, Vil. The book says that Riella was killed, and our host brought them back here to keep them for some future Ageon. He may have meant *his* future Ageon, but...he really seems to have mourned her, so maybe not. My instincts say that it's right for you to have them."

Vil nodded again. "Thank you." He glanced up at the portrait of the lost Agea, and for just a moment, a trick of the magelight made it look like she was looking back at him. He wasn't, as a rule, a superstitious man, but like any follower of the Dark Lady, Vil knew that there was more to this world than what could be seen. He inclined his head to the portrait as well.

I'll remember you, Agea Riella, he promised. *This much I can do for you.*

"Let's see if we're right about that dagger," Romik said, an edge of excitement threading through his tone. Vil turned back to see his warrior brother lifting his arm, pulling back his sleeve.

"No," Daen said, stepping forward and baring his own forearm. "You're still recovering from your other injuries, Ro. I'll do it."

Vil cut his eyes to Aelys, who pressed her lips together, but gave him a tiny nod. He returned the gesture, and then turned to Daen. With all the energy Aelys had just poured into him, he struck like a viper, the bright blade flashing once in the magelight before he made it disappear into an empty sheath high on his ribs.

Daen let out a little hiss, and moments later, a thin red line appeared across the back of his wrist. "I barely felt that," he said. "Not until after. The knife is sharp."

"Profane," Vil said. "It has a name. We should use it."

"Profane, then. Nice blade. All right, so what now? I just go outside, and...?"

"Um. Speak, I suppose." Aelys furrowed her brow, like she wasn't quite sure. "And let's see if Vil can hear you."

"Right."

Daen led the way out of the dagger alcove, followed by Romik and Aelys. Vil paused for a second longer and looked up at the portrait of the Agea one more time.

"I'll remember," he promised. "And I'll protect her, even if it means burning everything else down."

The magelight, which always followed Aelys unless she directed it elsewhere, moved out into the main chamber of the study as well, causing the shadows to deepen and obscure the portrait. The last thing he saw was the dark brown fire of approval in her eyes.

Idiot, he told himself as he turned to walk out. *It's just a painting. It doesn't approve of anything... but I'll remember her, nonetheless.*

Aelys and Romik awaited him next to the fireplace. As Vil joined them, the door on the opposite site of the study clicked closed, indicating that Daen had just gone out.

"So...am I just listenin—"

Vil. Vil, can you hear me? Or am I just talking to myself like a simpleton? Ugh, I forgot about the spray. How long do I need to be out here? Am I supposed to hear you too? This is ridiculous. I should have let Romik do it...but he really does need to rest...

"I hear him," Vil said, walking over to the door to pull it open. "In fact, he won't shut up."

Daen leaned against the stone there, grinning. "Did it work?"

"You wondered if you were talking to yourself. You forgot about the spray. You whined about being out there. It doesn't look like you can hear me, and it turns out it's not ridiculous, because it worked." Vil held the door wide, inviting his ex-Forester brother inside.

"You heard it all! Except for—"

"You're worried about Romik and think he needs to rest."

"Aww, thanks, Daen," Romik rumbled from over by the fireplace. "I'm touched. So it worked."

"It worked." Daen walked through the door, rubbing his hands as he strode directly to the fireplace. "Could you all hear me, or just Vil?"

"Just me. In my head. But it was your voice, not mine. It was odd."

"Still, what a fascinating gift! The possibilities... I'm envious, brother," Romik said as he dropped into the chair. "I really am."

"You may not have to be," Aelys said. All three of the men turned to look at her. She'd walked back toward the curved table while they were talking and was once more reading through the grimoire.

"What do you mean?" Daen asked. "Is there a magical dagger for Romik, too?"

"Probably not a dagger," Aelys said. "But our host had several Ageons—which in itself is remarkable. I'm glad to know that there's a precedent. It looks like he fashioned weapons for all of them. Romik, I'm going to reverse the flow again, all right?"

"I feel fine."

"That's how she unlocked the door to Riella's vault," Vil said. "Everything in this place seems to be about energy flowing between mage and Ageon."

"It was very important to him, our host," Aelys said, her eyes skimming the pages of the grimoire. Vil's eyes fell on the smaller book that had been in Riella's vault. Aelys had set it down on the pointy tip of the table. He nonchalantly walked over and palmed it, slipping it into an interior pocket of his cloak.

Who knows when we might need more information? He thought. *And if nothing else, it will help me learn to read Bellene.*

Aelys joined Romik, who'd once again dropped into the chair by the fire. Vil steeled himself to watch as she smiled down at her warrior Ageon.

"Ready?" she asked. Romik nodded. Vil glanced over at Daen, who leaned against the wall by the door. Daen met his eyes with a knowing look and whispered something under his breath.

All of us, Daen's voice said in his head. *Remember.*

Vil nodded, and then forced himself to look back at Aelys and Romik as they passed energy back and forth. Aelys let out a breathy sigh as her eyelids slid closed. Romik, too, exhaled. Not quite a grunt or a moan...but not far off.

The sensation gets stronger every time she does this, Daen said, still speaking in that whisper too quiet to be heard other than through this new power. *I'm so jealous that he got hurt and she has to keep pushing energy into him. I must sound like a madman.*

Vil met his eyes and shook his head in the negative.

You feel that way too?

Vil nodded.

Green Lady's rut, Vil. What are we going to do?

Vil didn't have an answer, so he deliberately looked away, turning his attention to the metal sigil above the fireplace. Sure enough, the stylized sword in the center of the piece glittered, and then shone steadily, sending a beam of light across the room to highlight another book, this one bound in red leather.

"Bella," Vil said. "Look."

Aelys opened her eyes and focused them through the bliss that flowed over her face. Vil pointed, and she turned, letting out another gasp as she saw that her theory had been correct.

"The book," she said. "Romik, help me."

Romik pushed up to his feet and followed her over to that side of the room. The red book sat on the top shelf, and even he had to stretch to reach it. Once he did, however, a section of the bookcase swung open just as the earlier one had done.

"Another pedestal, another portrait," Romik said. Vil glanced at Daen and then walked over to join Aelys and Romik.

"Ageon Dionos," Aelys read, bending slightly to see the words etched into the small metal plaque at the bottom of the painting. This one depicted a man, tall, broad shouldered, with golden blond hair and the same darkly burning brown eyes as Riella's portrait. Dionos wore the segmented armor of an imperial officer, but he wore no helmet, and the sword he carried was no simple short sword.

"Mother of Fortune," Romik breathed, and as Vil approached, he could see that the sword in the portrait lay in a case atop yet another velvet-covered pedestal. Its blade gleamed ruddy in the reflected firelight. It had a hilt long enough for two hands, but as Vil looked at it, he had to wonder if the obvious masterwork wasn't well enough balanced to wield one-handed. Like the daggers, it had a single jewel as ornamentation. A cat's-eye stone sat embedded in the crosspiece that formed the guard.

"Is there another book?" Daen asked.

"Yes," Aelys said. "I'm looking . . . here it is. This blade is named 'The Naked Mirror,' and it belonged to Dionos, who had been an imperial officer before our host laid the *geas* on him. It looks like . . . oh this is interesting. They'd been enemies! Our host must not have always supported the empire—"

"Or the emperor," Daen said with a shrug. "Civil wars aren't uncommon in our history. They could have been on opposite sides of one."

"That's true," Aelys said, flipping the page. "It says that Dionos was wounded and captured. And our host performed healing magic to save his life, but his recuperation took months. During that time the war—oh, you're right, Daen. It was a civil war. I wonder if we could use this account to figure out when he built this place and who our host was."

"The sword?" Romik asked softly.

"Oh! Right. I'm sorry, this is just such an interesting puzzle. Anyway, the war ended and Dionos and our host had become friends, according to this. So, he offered the *geas* and Dionos accepted. Then he made this—he calls it a 'hand-and-a-half sword'—for him." She looked up at Romik.

"Hand and a half?" she asked.

"Because you can use it one- or two-handed. Sometimes called a bastard sword or a long sword," Romik said. "Not as useful as a short blade in some circumstances, but a well-made one is incredibly lethal, because of the increased reach. And this one..." He trailed off, reverence leaking into his tone. He reached out and let his fingers hover over the hilt for just a second. "What does it do? What is its magic?"

Aelys flipped through the pages of the little book. "It's... hard to understand. But it looks like it has something to do with memory...and clarity? This phrase here means 'dispel the fog' or 'dispel the mist.'" She looked up. "But as with the daggers, it has to be charged by the Ageon."

Romik looked up at her, like he was waiting for permission, or maybe reassurance that it was safe. Aelys nodded, and he lifted the sword from its case. Vil and Daen both stepped back to give their brother some room, but he didn't swing the blade, just held it first in one hand, and then shifted to a two-hand grip.

"The balance on this thing is incredible," Romik said. "It's almost like it has no weight at all."

"Charge it," Daen urged. "Let's see what it can do."

Romik nodded and lowered the blade to a low ready position. Then he lifted his eyes and looked at Aelys.

She shivered, and Vil found himself thinking of how she'd looked when they'd charged his blades: her head thrown back in ecstasy, the pulse at her throat pounding, almost as if it were calling to him to put his lips, his fingers right there.

Aelys let out a gasp, and then locked eyes with Romik. He shivered, and though Vil stood back, he could see the tension in his brother's neck and shoulders lock into place. A blue flash drew his eye, and Vil shifted to the side to see that the cat's-eye had become an icy blue aquamarine like the ones in his blades.

"My" blades, is it? Vil asked himself. *That was quick.*

"So now what happens?" Romik asked.

"I-I'm not sure," Aelys said. "The book mentions memory several times. Is there a particular memory you—"

"Oh!" The sudden surprise in Romik's tone jolted through Vil. Not much surprised his warrior brother. Vil shared a glance with Daen, and they both stepped up behind Romik's shoulders, there to support and bolster him if he needed it.

I see where the sword gets its name, Vil thought. *It certainly gleams like a mirror. But that alone shouldn't be enough—*

"I see the inn," Romik said, his voice distant, and yet intense at the same time. "It's like I'm watching through a window . . . yeah, there's that bastard we sent running. He's talking to someone else . . . a leader, it looks like."

"Can you hear them?" Vil asked.

"A little. The bastard is whining that his boss wants Aelys alive—they're calling her by name—but the leader isn't having it. He's livid about the loss of his men—shouldn't have your men attacking innocent young women, then, dungrat. They're arguing . . . the leader just smacked the bastard. He said they'd try, but he's owed blood, and he intends to take it. They're . . . the view is shifting. They're going inside—" He fell silent, and Vil watched as Romik's jaw clenched and his eyes hardened.

"They have Mirandy," he said, his voice low and sad. "They're bringing her in . . . there we are, Vil. I see us—and she's dead. We're fighting . . . the view is changing again. The dungrat leader is going around the back. He set the fire, and now it's caught. There's Daen and Aelys joining us . . . the roof is caving in—"

Vil's heart accelerated with each word. In the silence of his mind, he felt the raging heat as the ceiling collapsed around them, sending embers cascading all around them. Once more, he felt the Dark Lady's embrace looming close, and he'd remembered the frustrated spike of anger he'd felt.

For decades in Cievers, I didn't care whether I lived or died. Until I found my brothers, death would have been a release. But I did find them, and just as we were about to start the new life I'd fought so hard for . . . well. Men plan and the Dark Lady laughs. I was angry, and then there was the girl, crying and broken, babbling about breaking through, asking if we'd stay with her . . .

Romik's head snapped up, and he spun, his eyes locking on to Vil's, and Daen's.

"Did you see it?" he demanded, his voice a rough whisper, pitched for their ears alone.

"The fire?" Vil asked. "I didn't. But I remember."

"Do you remember what we said? The three of us? We all said it." Romik's blue eyes burned with intensity. "I can't believe I forgot."

"Romik, what are you talking about?" Aelys asked, but she stood outside the circle. This was a conversation for the three of them.

"We said we'd stay with her," Daen said, leaning forward so that he, too, could speak quietly. "No one wants to die alone. I remember you saying that, Ro."

"Yes, but do you remember what she said?"

Vil narrowed his eyes. "She asked—"

"If we'd choose her. And we said yes." Romik closed his eyes as emotion after emotion swept across his face. "We all said yes."

"We—" Daen started to say, but Romik shook his head, opened his eyes, and stepped back, beckoning to Aelys to join them.

"Are you all right?" Aelys asked as she stepped close, her eyes wide with worry. She lifted one hand and almost, but not quite, touched Romik's cheek before dropping it back by her side.

"The Naked Mirror shows memories," Romik said baldly. "But not just as we remember them, it showed everything that happened, as if I was an observer."

"It showed you the fire," Aelys said, threading her fingers together so tightly that Vil saw her knuckles flash white. "I . . . I don't remember, but I assume it showed me bonding you."

"Yes, but it reminded me of something else first, Bella. You bonded us because we *chose* you."

Aelys's magelight flickered, the first time Vil had ever seen it do that. Her face went deathly pale, and her lips parted. But she spoke no words. Her eyes—those icy blue eyes her magic had shared with each of them—filled with tears.

Romik gently disentangled her right hand and slowly, tenderly, raised her knuckles to his lips. "We chose you, Bella. You need to know that."

"I-I don't—" The tears spilled over her lower lashes, running in shining lines down her cheeks. Next to Vil, Daen let out a low groan and pulled Aelys close. He wrapped his arms around her shoulders and bent to press a kiss into her hair. She let out a sob that reverberated through Vil, and clutched at the back of Daen's jerkin with her free hand.

Romik still held the other, his thick fingers intertwined with hers.

Cold flowed in, encasing the edges of Vil's mind in unyielding, unfeeling ice. He held himself rigid, weathering the urge to push his way in, to claim some part of her comfort for himself.

Comfort was always for others. Not for him.

But then she lifted her head and looked right at him with tear-wet eyes, and his knees almost buckled. Truth slammed him in the face, and before he could stop himself, he spoke.

"Don't poison the present with the past. You weren't chosen before because you were meant for us."

Daen inhaled the scent of Aelys's hair and tried to keep from holding her too tightly. Aelys's body shook with sobs as she tucked her face into his chest once more.

"That's it," he murmured, in between kisses to the top of her head. "Let it out, Bella. You're safe here, with us. Vil is right. You were meant for us, not for some mewling knight trained at the Lyceum."

Aelys let out a watery laugh. "That's not exactly f-fair," she said, stuttering as she hiccuped once. "The Lyceum training is very tough for Ageons. They're elite warriors."

"Psssh," Daen said. "Amateurs. Romik could take three of them by himself, and I guarantee you I'd split their arrows with mine at any distance you'd like. That's if Vil hadn't knifed them in the back before they ever realized it. You want elite warriors, Bella? You've got the very best right here."

She laughed again and squeezed him once before letting go and stepping back. She pulled her hand out of Romik's grasp and swiped it under her eyes.

"I am very so—"

"Don't." Vil's command wasn't harsh, but it was low and uncompromising. "Please. Just don't apologize."

Aelys drew in a shaky breath and squared her shoulders. "All right," she said. "I won't. But I will thank you all. For protecting me...and for ch-choosing me. Even if none of us knew what that would mean. It still...It means everything to me. I am more honored than you will ever know. No matter what happens when I get home, I will always have been your Bellatrix, even if just for a short while. And no one will ever take that from me."

Even if for a short—? Daen felt his brows slam together, and he drew in a breath to protest that it didn't need to be a short while, but Aelys turned away and strode back out into the main room, looking up at the fireplace sigil once more.

"There is a bow here, too, Daen," she said. "Come join me, and let's see what kind of gift our host has for you."

"Let it lie for now," Vil murmured, reaching out to pull Daen's shoulder around and giving him a slight push toward Aelys. "She's off-balance. We'll talk to her about it when we get out of here."

"Talk to her about what?" Daen heard Romik ask as he acquiesced and followed her to the fireplace.

"Daen wants her to stay with us."

"Vil wants it too," Daen shot over his shoulder, meeting his brother's eyes. "He won't say so, but he agrees with me."

"Who agrees with you about what?" Aelys asked, her voice absent as her eyes traced the interwoven lines of the sigil. Daen gave her a half smile that she probably didn't see and dropped another kiss on the top of her head.

"Nothing, Bella. Don't worry about it for now. I'm ready if you are."

Sensation swept through him, buckling his knees. He reached out blindly, his fingers finding the rough-hewn mantel of the magical fireplace. Heated fur rubbed under his skin, followed by cooling fire that tingled along every nerve. It felt as if every hair on his body were standing on end, ready to spark into a conflagration of need and wanting if she touched him . . .

Green Lady, if she touches me, I'm lost. Please. Please let her touch me—

"There it is."

The excitement in Romik's rumbling voice pierced through the haze of desire that fogged Daen's vision. He blinked, his fingers tightening on the mantel as he fought to regain his equilibrium. His body throbbed, aching to be free of the constriction of his garments. He swallowed hard and tugged at his breeches, trying to ease some of the pressure before looking up.

A beam of light—green hued, of course—arrowed from the stylized bow in the sigil to a green leather book in the case next to the entry door.

Romik's hand came down heavy on his shoulder and squeezed.

"Come on, brother," he said. Daen looked up to see sympathy and understanding in Romik's eyes. "Let's go see what this place has for you."

Aelys had already pulled the green book and stepped back to

let the bookcase swing open when they joined her on that side of the room. Inside lay yet another alcove, yet another pedestal.

But no portrait.

"There's a quiver here," Aelys said, "And . . . is this a bow? It looks . . . strange."

"Is there a book?" Vil asked. "Why is there no portrait?"

"There is a book," Aelys confirmed. She turned her body sideways to step around the pedestal, and for the first time, Daen got an unobstructed view of what lay there.

There was, indeed, a quiver. Well made, of reinforced leather. Like the other weapons, it bore a single stone. But instead of a cat's-eye, this one was a smooth, colorless, rounded clear crystal. The quiver was empty.

Next to the quiver . . .

"It sort of looks like a cavalry bow," Romik said.

"It's a recurve bow," Daen said, reaching out and stroking one fingertip down along the nearer arm of the bow. "Was his Ageon a horse archer?"

Aelys shook her head. "He doesn't mention an Ageon. I . . . I think this was just an experiment he was working on."

"Is there magic to it?" Daen asked. He lifted the bow and sighted along it, and then pulled one of his own arrows out and fitted it into place. He drew, and it was *much* easier than drawing his own bow. So much so that he immediately let off the draw and denocked the arrow. "This thing is feather light," he said. "But I can feel the power in the arms and the string. I'm curious to try it out."

"As far as I can tell, there's no magic to the construction of the bow," Aelys said. "It just seems to be masterful engineering. But the quiver . . . that's a chargeable stone." She pointed to the clear crystal in the quiver. "Although the work ends before he says what he was going to charge it to do. It's odd. The narration just stops. I wonder if this was his last project before he died."

Daen picked up the quiver with his free hand and took a deep breath to brace himself. He held the strange bow down by his side and looked Aelys in the eyes. "Let's charge it."

She nodded slowly, and once again, he felt the flood of sensation as she reversed the flow of energy between them. His fingers tightened on the grip of the bow, and he sucked in a quick, sharp breath as the scorching caress of her energy swirled through him, and then pooled in his hands before draining into the quiver.

"That was..." he whispered. There were no words; and everyone there knew what it felt like anyway.

"The stone changed," Vil reported. "Looks like it worked, whatever that means."

Daen looked down at the quiver he held, and the stone—now a bright aquamarine like the others—winked at him in the light.

"Wait," he said, blinking furiously as he noticed something. "This quiver was empty before. Now there are..." He counted quickly. "Ten arrows in it."

Romik stepped forward and drew one of the arrows out. "Wow," he said. "This alone feels like it was made by a master fletcher. Feel the balance, Daen."

Daen set the quiver down on the pedestal and took the arrow from Romik. He was right. It balanced perfectly in his hand. He lifted the bow and nocked the arrow, drawing it back to his cheek.

"This is...like breathing," he said. "I've never drawn a sweeter bow, not even my father's—" He cut off, not wanting to ruin the moment with that memory.

"Wait, I thought you said there were ten arrows, Daen," Vil said. "There were eleven."

Daen released the draw without letting fly and lowered the bow. "No. There were ten. I counted."

"There are ten there now." Vil pointed and proceeded to count them out loud.

Sure enough, ten arrows.

"Maybe I miscounted?" But Daen didn't think so, and the doubt in his voice said that loud and clear.

"Wait. I think I know what the magic is." Aelys's eyes lit up with excitement. "Daen, put the other arrow back in the quiver, please."

He smiled. "Anything for you," he said, causing Romik to groan and roll his eyes. Daen chuckled at his brother's response as he slid the arrow back into the quiver.

"Now count them, Vil," Aelys said.

Vil looked at her for a second, and then complied, counting out loud as he'd done before.

Ten arrows. Exactly.

"It will always have ten," Aelys said. "As long as the quiver is charged with magic, it will maintain that number, no more, no less."

"Green Lady," Daen breathed. "That's—"

"Endless ammunition. That's a useful gift for an archer." Vil's eyebrows rose in appreciation. "Seems our host was a thoughtful individual."

"He created these gifts for the Ageons he loved—or intended to love," Aelys murmured. "Obviously, we can't know the whole story, but what we do know feels very sad. His grimoire said that his knife and hammer were taken...he doesn't seem to have ever had an archer, and by the end, only his sword remained. Perhaps he hoped to bond an archer at some point, but died before he could. But he left these beautiful works behind. It's really quite something."

"It's a legacy," Romik said. "One we can remember and honor. I'm not usually sentimental, but there's value in remembering the past. He had at least two Ageons. We're three Ageons bonded to a single Bellatrix. I think..."

"We feel a kinship," Daen said with a nod when Romik trailed off. "It's right that we remember and use these masterworks for the purpose their creator intended."

Aelys smiled, and it lit up her face. "May they protect you as well as you've protected me," she said.

"We'll protect each other," Vil amended. He stepped forward and took Aelys's hand. "And now that we've all been given gifts, you need to sleep, Bella. We're obviously safe here. Let's rest and worry about the way out tomorrow."

Aelys nodded, and Daen saw that her beautiful eyes did, indeed, look red and bloodshot. Though whether that was from fatigue or her earlier tears, he didn't know.

Not that it matters. Vil is right. She needs sleep, and we need her to be well.

"Here, Bella," he said. "Come lie down in front of the fire. The rug is soft enough, and you can use my jacket as a pillow again."

"I'll take the first watch," Romik said. "Since I didn't have one yesterday."

"If you start hurting again, wake me," Aelys said. "I will push more—"

"We've all had plenty of energy tonight, Bella," Daen said. "Romik will be fine. We'll all be fine. You can rest. We're all here with you."

CHAPTER SEVEN

AELYS DID, IN FACT, FEEL BETTER AFTER A GOOD LONG SLEEP. She'd awakened on the rug with Romik at her back and Daen in front of her. Romik's arm had fallen around her waist in his sleep, and she'd lain still for several moments, refusing to think about anything except how warm and safe she felt there.

Eventually, however, her body's needs had won out, and she'd gently extricated herself from between her two sleeping protectors. Vil, who once more sat atop the oddly curved table, had inclined his head to her as she stood up.

She'd returned the nod without words and retired to the curtained-off alcove that held the study's privy. Fortunately, it, like the fire, appeared to be magical in nature, because it was as pristine as when she'd first found it the day—or night, she had no idea thanks to being underground—before.

When she'd emerged, all of the men were awake, and Romik was dishing out more stew for everyone. No one had said much as they ate. For the most part, the men seemed preoccupied. Aelys couldn't blame them. Each of them had received an incredible gift yesterday.

And so did I, she thought later in the privacy of her mind. They'd all eaten, and she'd gone back to searching the grimoire for clues to a way out. The only problem was that she found it hard to focus.

Because of course, no matter how marvelous it felt to be here with them, she would still have to break the *geas*. Even though her Ageons were all that she could ask for, they hadn't been trained at the Lyceum, and therefore, she still couldn't serve in the Battlemage Corps. That meant that an advantageous marriage that benefited her family was still her only option ... and she couldn't exactly marry a noble son while being magically and legally bound to not one, not two, but *three* men! Even the fact that the *geas* had existed for a short period of time might cause problems, but she trusted her aunt Aerivinne to see her through it.

Her political savvy is second only to her magical skills, Aelys thought, with the surge of affection and admiration that always accompanied thoughts of her mother's sister. *She will ensure that there's no problem, and mage candidates are encouraged to form romances with Ageon candidates at the Lyceum* ... Her thought trailed off, as another, rather more surprising thought occurred to her.

I haven't thought about Halik one time since the inn. And even thinking of him now, knowing that he and Myara are together ... it doesn't hurt. I-I envy them the opportunity to serve, and I hate *the thought that I will have to give up my own Ageons ... but I no longer care if he's in my life. Or her.*

They just don't matter to me anymore.

That realization rocked through her like lightning. It energized her enough that she looked up at the men to see if they were deliberately pushing their thoughts toward her. The rivers of energy in her mind ran deep and swift, but no more so than usual.

They're always thinking about me now. Just as I'm always thinking about them ...

Aelys shook her head sharply. *I can't be thinking like that. I have to stop drawing closer to them. When this is over, and we get out of here, I have to set them free. They say they "chose" me ... but they didn't know. They couldn't know what they were agreeing to. I can't— I have no other choice.*

With that reproof ringing in her metaphorical ears, she rededicated herself to her task of combing through the grimoire. There was too much there to read the entire thing, so she contented herself with merely scanning the pages for any mention of a way out ... much as she might have liked to do otherwise. Their host's speculations, spells, and calculations *fascinated* her. From the little she did read, he seemed to approach magical concepts with a perspective very different from the theory she'd learned at the Lyceum. She longed to dig into his writings, and gather up other volumes he referenced for more information...

But she had a responsibility, so she forced herself to resist the temptation to dive into research. Reluctantly.

An hour or so later, she hadn't found anything, and she closed the book with a frustrated slap and let out a sigh.

"Something wrong?" Vil asked. Where once Aelys would have said his tone was empty and cold, now she could identify the merest thread of humor in the words. She sighed again and turned to him with a shrug.

"Just, there's so much of value in the grimoire, but none of it is complete! It's like he deliberately censored out key information so whoever read it couldn't duplicate his spells. And I can't find a single mention of another way out of here."

"Maybe there isn't one," Vil said with a shrug. He, too, shut the book he was holding and put it down in his lap. Aelys blinked in surprise as she realized it was the small book from the alcove that had held his daggers. He'd said he couldn't read Bellene, but then why was he poring over it?

"I—I am almost certain there is," Aelys said, forcing her mind back to the problem at hand. "A mage of his power isn't going to allow himself to be trapped anywhere, not even his own study. There's a way out of here, I just have to find it."

"Then find it," Vil said. The corner of his mouth twitched, and Aelys recognized it for the smile that it was.

"And so, I shall," she said, raising an eyebrow and letting her voice sound arch. "If only to prove to you that I can."

"I look forward to seeing it."

"You should." Her smile grew, and Vil's blue eyes glinted at her in response. Thus bolstered, she turned back to the table and picked up a different book that she'd thought looked promising when she skimmed through it earlier.

It took another pair of hours, as near as she could tell, but eventually, Aelys found what she needed.

"Oh!" she cried out, as her eyes ran back over the sentence she could hardly believe she'd read. Instantly, all three men leapt to their feet, weapons to hand, eyes sharp for any threats.

"Oh," she said again as contrition swept through her. "I'm

sorry, I didn't mean to alarm you. I just...I think I found it... or, well. Something at least."

"What did you find, Bella?" Romik asked.

Aelys, who had moved to one of the chairs by the fireplace where she sat with her legs curled under her in a decidedly unladylike manner, angled the book so that the light from the fire better illuminated the Bellene characters. "Right here. This section here, the author—not our host, by the way, it took me quite a while to figure that out—is talking about building portal gateways."

"What's a portal gateway?" Daen asked.

"I'm not sure," Aelys said. "Other than what it sounds like: a doorway of some kind? Anyway, our host circled the section and wrote a note in the margin. The script is messy and cramped, but it looks like he's got a note that says 'one side only' and then another that says 'crescent.'"

"'Crescent'? What under the moons is that?" Daen asked.

"It's a curving shape, like when the Mother or Daughter is just past new. One circle imperfectly laid over another," Romik supplied. "It's a common symbol for knowledge in some of the southern cities." He paused and turned to look at Vil, who once more sat on the table.

"Like that table," Romik said, pointing. "Two curved edges that meet at points at either end."

Silence followed this remark, broken only by the soft slither of Vil's clothing as he slid off his perch. Aelys slowly got up from her chair, clutching the book to her chest and walked over to examine the table. It was, indeed, a crescent shape. In fact, it looked very much like a tiny scribble in the margin of the book that at first she'd taken for a mistake; something the host had started to write and then scratched out because it wasn't what he meant to do.

But now, as she looked closer, she realized it looked like a picture of the table itself, legs and all. Only it was standing on one pointed end, with the legs facing a doodle of flames around the original text character for "fire."

"I think we need to clear it off," she said, her voice soft. "And then turn it on its side, facing the fire."

The three men moved without another word. They collected the piles of books and scrolls and restacked them neatly on nearby shelves, or on the floor next to the shelves if there was no room. The various strange bits of machinery went on the shelves, too, wherever there was room. Aelys herself retrieved the grimoire and held it clasped to her chest with her free hand while she continued to read the words in the other book.

Eventually, they cleared the entire table. Daen even took one of his million rags and swiped the surface, though it hadn't been terribly dusty to begin with.

"It will be heavy," Romik said. "It will take all three of us to turn it over. Not to mention to hold it balanced on the end."

"The curve of the crescent should face the privy," Aelys said. "That's how it's oriented in the drawing."

Romik nodded, and then he, Daen, and Vil all took their places and slowly tilted the table over. For just a second, Aelys considered feeding energy to them, but the second the tip of the tabletop touched the floor, something *clicked* loudly into place. The table began to pivot on that point without the men lifting it, and one by one all three of them fell back, arraying themselves around her in a defensive ring.

Slowly, the table rose until the entire underside faced the light of the magical fire. Though it had looked like normal wood when they first lifted it, the bottom of the table now gleamed like a mirror. Aelys watched in rising awe as the surface rippled, and the reflected fire warped and flowed over the whole surface.

She inhaled sharply, and less than an eyeblink later, the flames disappeared, leaving a darkly gleaming opening in the middle of the room. Vil stepped forward, both daggers drawn, and walked all the way around the table before coming back to them.

"It's just the room behind the table," he said. "Everything looks just as it was."

"So, what's through that ... what did you call it, Bella?" Daen asked.

"Portal gateway."

"Yeah, that."

"Only one way to find out," Romik said, rolling his shoulders. He had the Naked Mirror in one hand, and his short sword in the other, and he stood directly in front of Aelys, between her and the now open portal. Daen, on Aelys's left, had one of the arrows nocked and the beautiful recurve bow drawn, while Vil held Pure and Profane in either hand.

"Flash," she whispered, calling a magelight. With a thought, she sent the glowing orb through the portal, where it illuminated a stone floor covered in dust and fossilized straw.

A worked stone floor. Not a natural cave. A room. Small, with a rotted wooden door hanging on rusty hinges in the wall opposite.

"This is our way out," Aelys said, her voice a low murmur. She looked around at the men. "Let's go—"

"Wait," Vil said. Aelys snapped her eyes up to his face. "Does the book tell you how to get back here?"

"N-no . . ."

"Then, perhaps you might want to bring a few things with us? The weapons, obviously, but maybe one or two of the 'one-of-a-kind' books you mentioned?"

Aelys blinked, and then smiled slowly. "I—do you think we should?" she asked.

"You said it before," Daen put in, answering her smile with his own. "Our host is long dead. I'm sure he'd prefer to have you use his library rather than letting it remain forgotten."

"This one, Bella?" Romik asked, lifting the original grimoire.

Aelys nodded, and Romik started to tuck the book inside his jacket, but Daen stopped him with an upraised hand.

"There's a knapsack here," Daen said, pointing to a low shelf below the jars of herbs next to the fire. "We can take a couple of books—"

"And some of the herbs!" Aelys said, excitement threading through her tone. She strode across the chamber to examine the jars and snatched four of them off the shelves. "I'm certain these jars are magically sealed, and so they should still be good. If we run into any more poison knives, or anything like that, these could be very helpful."

"Take what you need, Bella," Vil said. "We're in no rush."

In the end, she chose three more books, a pouch of dried herbs she found in a drawer, and two more jars that she carefully wrapped in more of Daen's rags before placing them inside the bag and closing the top flap. Romik reached to take the knapsack from her, but she slipped its straps onto her own shoulders first.

"We don't know what we're walking into," she reminded him, her voice grave. "If there's to be a fight, you will want to be unencumbered. It isn't too heavy. I can carry it."

Romik let out a growl of disapproval, but he let his hand drop.

"Are we ready, then?" Vil asked. Aelys smiled at Romik and then crossed the room back to the table.

The men arrayed themselves around her once again and as one unit, they stepped forward through the portal and into the tiny room beyond.

As soon as Aelys herself was through, the crescent tilted toward the fire and disappeared, leaving them stranded wherever they were now.

"Well," Vil said. "This doesn't look nearly as comfortable as the study."

"I miss that magic stew pot already," Daen said, but he flashed Aelys a grin, and so she straightened her shoulders, refused to allow herself to apologize, and looked around.

"I guess...let's try the door?" she said.

There wasn't a handle on the inside, but the wood had rotted enough to leave gaps wide enough to see through. Romik regarded the door for a second, and then strode toward it and kicked it, hard, with the bottom of his foot. The ancient boards cracked and disintegrated in a cloud of dust, leaving a hole large enough for even him to duck and squeeze through.

Aelys sent her magelight after him, and then followed with Vil and Daen. They emerged into a long, curving hallway dotted with other doors like the one they'd just kicked through. Each of the doors, including theirs, had an iron bolt-style lock embedded into the stone outside the door.

"What is this place?" Aelys asked, horror mounting in her mind as they started walking. "Why do all the doors have this kind of lock?

Daen looked at her oddly. "It's a dungeon, Bella," he said. "Isn't that obvious? The locks are to keep people in their cells. Unless they're powerful mages with fancy portal tables, I guess."

"I...I knew criminals sometimes served time in a dungeon, but—"

Vil laughed, though the sound carried zero humor. "Not usually criminals, Bella. At least, not the professionals. We have protections and skills. It's only amateurs who find themselves here."

"And political enemies," Romik added.

"Enemies of whom?" Aelys asked. Romik shrugged, turning his head to peer back over his shoulder for a second before turning back to the front. "The emperor? Traitors?"

"Not usually. Traitors are usually just executed in arena games. I've killed a few myself. Dungeons like this aren't imperial, usually. They're usually built by the nobility, to hold the people their families would rather forget."

Aelys felt her eyes go wide with horror and she came to an abrupt stop. "B-but that's monstrous!" she stammered. "My family would never—"

Daen paused beside her and took her free hand. "I'm sure you're right, Bella," he said. "And maybe they don't have something like this now. But the empire has a bloody past, you saw that yourself back in the study. By the looks of it, this place has been empty for a long time, right? Why don't we just concentrate on getting out of here and figuring out where we are? We can worry about ancient history later, all right?"

Aelys swallowed hard and nodded. Daen smiled at her once more, his blue eyes warm. He let her hand go, but his fingers lingered on hers and sent a shiver down her spine. She swallowed again and forced her eyes away from his perfect face.

I can't, she reminded herself. *It isn't right. It isn't fair to them. I have to pull back. I have to.*

Eventually, the long, curving hallway ended in a partially collapsed set of stone stairs. With no other option, they began to slowly and painstakingly climb the rubble. This time Vil went first, testing each step with his weight before letting Aelys follow. The stairs seemed to go on forever, and Aelys's arms and legs shook with fatigue by the time they reached the top.

"The way ahead is partially blocked," Vil reported as Daen reached down a hand to help Romik make the last bit of the climb. "There's another hallway, with a collapsed roof several lengths in. But it's like that cave-in where we found the underground lake. I can see light on the other side. I think if we can shift some of the rubble, we can get through."

Romik grunted agreement, and Daen nodded, and so they continued onward.

Not that we have much choice, Aelys thought bitterly. *Thanks to me.* Vil chose that moment to look over and meet her eyes, and so she immediately cut that line of thought. He didn't like it when she mentally castigated herself. Perhaps she needed to pull back from them, but that didn't mean she had to ignore their chiding.

Did it?

"Here it is," Vil said as they approached the collapsed part of the corridor. Aelys sent her magelight high and brightened it with a thought so that they could see the extent of the problem.

"Yeah," Romik said. "We can just shift this bit here..." He sheathed his swords and began moving some of the rubble. Vil and Daen joined in until they had an opening big enough to crawl through.

One by one, that's what they did. Vil first, then Daen, then Aelys, then Romik. It took far too long for Aelys's comfort, and none of them got through without leaving some skin behind on the rocks... but they got through.

Once again, they found themselves in a dark, low-ceilinged hallway. This one, though, lacked the heavy, rotting doors with the horrible iron locks. Instead, the rooms they saw contained what looked like barrels of rainwater tucked away for storage lying under a thick film of dust and grime.

"Where are we?" Aelys asked again, and then mentally kicked herself. *Obviously, none of the men know any more than you do, stupid girl. Stop wasting their time.*

"My guess? Some old castle ruin in the forest," Daen said. "This is the cellar level, where they stored their water. Judging by the dirt, though, no one's lived here for a very long time. But this is good, because when we get to the surface, I should be able to pinpoint our location."

"You know the location of all the ruins in the forest?" Aelys asked.

"It was my job to know," he said with a wink and a smile.

A tightness in her chest that Aelys hadn't noticed before eased. She let herself respond to that smile, let the warmth of the green river in her mind flow through her body and soothe the anxiety that had beset her the moment the crescent-shaped portal disappeared.

The floor under their boots sloped subtly upward, and before long, Aelys caught the tantalizing scent of fresh air on the tiny breeze. Her heart grew lighter with every step, and she found herself smiling, despite the grinding fatigue that pulled at her after walking through that endless dungeon and up those torturous stairs.

"We're almost there," Daen murmured. "I can smell the fores—"

"Quiet!" Vil hissed, throwing up a hand and crouching low. Aelys and the others froze in their tracks.

"What is it?" Romik whispered after a minute.

"I don't know," Vil said. "For a moment, I thought I heard voices. Bella, can you—"

He didn't finish the request. Aelys reversed the dark river's flow midword, and Vil broke off with a sharp inhale. The shadows gathered around him, thickening as they went.

"I'll go ahead and check," he said. "You three wait here. I'll be right back."

Aelys closed off the flow of energy to him and nodded, leaning back against the wall. A wave of fatigue washed over her, making her legs tremble with weakness.

Breathe, girl, she told herself, blinking away the bright sparkles that danced in her vision. *We don't have time for you to faint. You're almost out. Don't let them down now...*

A roaring, rushing sound filled her ears as the sparkles coalesced to create one bright field that blotted out her vision.

"Bella?" Daen asked, his voice sounding alarmed, but very far away. Her knees buckled and she slumped to the floor.

Something warm enveloped her hand. Daen called her name again, but he sounded like he was down a long tunnel. She tried to open her eyes, to see him, but all she could see was the bright sparkling light.

Someone slapped her face once, twice. Hard enough to sting. The light receded from the center of her vision, and she could make out two figures kneeling in front of her, crowding close. Their features were blurry, but it didn't matter. She'd know them anywhere.

"S-sorry..." she managed to whisper.

"Red Lady's tits, Bella," Romik ground out. "Stay with us!"

She tried to smile at him, but the bright gray sparkles started at the edge of her vision again.

"She needs energy!" Daen said. "Think about her!"

"I'm always thinking about her!" Romik growled. And then he muttered a short curse word she didn't quite catch and hauled her upward, claiming her mouth with his own.

Red rage and cleansing fire poured through their joined lips, burning away the cold, sodden gray fog that had swept over her mind. She gasped against his mouth, welcoming the punishing strength of his kiss, even as her mind whispered to her that this was wrong, this wasn't fair, this was too far...

"Well, what's this then? How'd you get in here with that pretty thing? Think I'll take her for meself!"

Aelys gasped again as Romik let her mouth go while Daen whirled, recurve bow in his hand. He nocked, drew, and released all in one fluid motion.

"All right?" Romik asked her quickly, his eyes intense. She nodded and fought the urge to touch her lips. "Then come on." He grabbed her hand and hauled her to her feet, drawing the Naked Mirror with his other hand. Only then did Aelys catch sight of the man who'd spoken. He lay on the ground in a pool of blood, both hands clutching at Daen's arrow embedded in his throat. She closed her lips against the scream building there and let Romik haul her at a run down the corridor.

"Vil, we're moving," Daen said out loud as he nocked another arrow and drew it while running. "I hope you can still hear me. We've been seen, we're headed up and out!"

They rounded a corner and came face-to-face with three bearded, unkempt, unwashed men. The one furthest to the back met Aelys's eyes and a look of recognition swept over his face.

"Divine Tits, that's the girl in the message! The one Gadren wants alive! Grab her!"

He didn't get a chance to say anything else. Daen let his arrow fly, and it buried itself to the fletching in the man's eye socket. Romik thrust her behind him and attacked the other two men with a flurry of blows from the Mirror. Neither of them even drew steel before he sliced one across the chest and the other across the throat. They both fell gaping at the sudden end to their miserable lives.

Romik reached back for her and took her hand again, and they continued to run.

"Vil, we're fighting our way out!" Daen called out, boots pounding against the stone floor. "Green Lady grant you can hear me. That little cut is almost healed. I should have had you cut me again, you sneaky bastard. Why didn't you think of that?"

The corridor turned again, and then emptied out into a large room dotted with tables here and there. About ten men clustered around one of the tables at the far end of the hall, looking down at something pinned there with a small knife.

One of the men at the table looked up, and Aelys felt her stomach sink as she saw recognition dawn in his eyes.

"Kill the men," he said. "And take the girl."

Daen let fly, his hands blurring as he drew and fired again and again. Once more, Aelys felt herself flung behind Romik as he charged forward, drawing his short sword in his off hand. The men—more bandits, she was sure of it—drew their own weapons and started fighting back. Unlike the four they'd already killed, these men knew what they were doing, and very quickly started working together.

A hand wrapped itself around Aelys's mouth, hauling her backward against a hard, unwashed chest. A nose buried itself in her hair and sniffed loudly just above her ear as another hand came down hard on her breast and squeezed.

"Green Lady, but you smell good," a rough voice said.

"Flash!" Aelys screamed, or tried, anyway. The word was muffled beyond recognition by the bandit's brutal, uncompromising grip. Still, her light flared directly in front of her, causing him to curse and loosen his grip enough for her to pull away.

Daen's bowstring twanged, and Aelys spun just in time to see her attacker fall, an arrow high in his chest. She stifled a cry and stumbled backward as two more men charged into the room, long, wicked knives in their hands. Two more arrows struck, taking the newcomers in the chest and gut respectively.

Behind her, Romik cried out. Aelys spun again and pumped energy into him without a second thought. He straightened, rolled his shoulders and brought his blades up again, though a dark stain had begun to spread along the side of his jerkin.

A hand grabbed her arm. Aelys flinched at first, but the fingers tightening around her bicep belonged to Vil, who had somehow gotten to them in the chaos.

"There's a courtyard outside," he said. "Give me your hand."

Aelys did, and then gasped as he struck quick as a snake. A thin red line appeared on the topside of her wrist, followed by a sting.

"I'm sorry," he said. "But just in case."

Aelys pressed her lips together and nodded, and then let go of his hand so he could draw another knife. Behind him, something moved.

"Vil! Behind you!"

He spun, his free hand slapping his chest and whipping out one of his throwing knives. Aelys had just a second to open the dark floodgates in her mind and push her energy into him before he sent the knife flying end over end to bury itself in the throat of another bandit.

"How many are there?" Daen ground out as he released another arrow. His hand blurred as he reached for one of the ten in his quiver and nocked that one before letting fly.

"I don't know," Vil said. "Romik, you with us?"

Romik grunted. Aelys turned to see him drive the Naked Mirror through the gut of another attacker, lifting the other man off his feet. She pushed more of her power into the red river in her mind, and Romik twisted the blade and pulled it free.

"Let's go," he said. Pain wreathed his words, but he moved well.

Divines grant that I can keep him alive long enough to get us out of here! Aelys thought.

They moved as one unit, clustered tightly together. Vil led, with Aelys directly behind him and Daen at her side, bow drawn. Romik brought up the rear, both swords out, dripping red droplets in a trail as they half ran, half crouched to the door.

Vil flung it open, and chaos ensued.

A rain of arrows peppered the doorway. One hit Vil high in the leg. Another glanced off his shoulder. He grunted a curse and tried to back up and pull the door closed, but it was no use. They had too much momentum and so the four of them stumbled out into the courtyard.

"Flash!" Aelys screamed, willing an explosion of magelight into being above their heads. The arrows stopped, but it didn't seem to hinder the dozen men coming at them at a full run. Daen's bowstring hummed in continuous fire. Vil threw another knife, and Romik pulled Aelys back behind him and launched forward into the fray, his two blades flashing.

Something hit her shoulder, just inside the ball of the joint. It threw her backward and she fell, barely keeping her head from hitting the packed earth. Her right arm went numb, and pain exploded inside her mind, pumping agony from the arrow wound throughout her whole body.

"AELYS!" one of the men, or maybe more than one yelled. She blinked, gasping as the pain robbed her of breath. Slowly, she reached her fingers up to try and find the arrow shaft. *That's what we do, right? We snap it off? I think that's right . . . Mother of Magic, this hurts!*

Somewhere, Romik bellowed in pain and rage. Aelys reached to funnel more energy into that red river, but for the first time since the inn, when she pulled at her power, only a trickle responded. Her vision blurred. Gray sparkles appeared in front of her eyes, obscuring anything with their stinging brightness.

"Bella." She recognized Vil's gloved hand as it took hers, and he pulled her up and into a blind, stumbling run. "I've got her, let's go!" he shouted above her head.

Aelys's vision started to return, though agony jolted through her with every step. Someone pressed close on her side. A hand landed heavy between her shoulder blades.

The light above them dimmed, and then returned. Aelys stifled a cry as someone jostled her shoulder.

"We're out," Daen said. "Let's get her off this road—"

Boom.

The ground shook. Something massive plowed into her from behind, picking her up and throwing her forward onto the hard, unyielding ground. She fought against the rising fear and renewed pain to look, to *see* . . . but it was no use. Darkness reared up behind her eyes, swept over her and pulled her down into blissful oblivion.

The world exploded.

Again?

Daen opened his eyes, blinking against the thick fog of dust that hung in the air. His whole body hurt as if he'd been beaten head to toe by several club-wielding thugs. A gash high on the outside of his hip burned with unholy fire, and his fingers felt like they'd been ripped raw from drawing the unfamiliar bowstring. His head pounded like there were horses inside kicking to get out.

But none of that mattered. He needed to get to Aelys.

He coughed, cursed, and forced his body to obey his order to move. He rolled away from his bad hip, managing to get himself up on one knee and blink away enough dust to see figures moving around him.

The bow. Get the bow. Protect her.

Daen searched with his hands on the gravel of the road around him, patting the rubble and sharp stones until his palm came down on one of the arms of the bow they'd found in the mage's study. He grabbed it, ignoring the searing pain from his hip, and nocked an arrow as the dust swirled around an approaching figure.

"I've found her! On the road outside the gate!"

The man's voice cut through the high, incessant ringing in Daen's ears. *Aelys,* he thought. He struggled to rise, but his wounded hip wouldn't let him put any weight on that leg. With a frustrated whimper, he unnocked the arrow, bent forward to get his hands on the ground and began to awkwardly crawl toward the crumpled form that lay where Aelys had been.

"She's hurt," the man called out, apparently unaware of Daen's approach. "I'll take her—"

Green Lady's wild entrails you will! Somehow, Daen managed to get himself back upright enough to nock, draw, and release an arrow toward the sound of the man's voice. He heard a startled shout, and then a blade appeared out of the dust, pointed right at him. Behind the blade, a man stood glaring at him over the top of a round shield. His arrow protruded from the shield's center.

"You can't win this, bandit," the man growled. "I'm taking her whether you live or die. Make a good choice."

"I'm not a bandit... you're not taking her," Daen said, his voice rough with pain, but uncompromising. "Not while... I breathe. I have to... protect her."

The man narrowed his eyes. "What did you say?"

"I said... I have to protect her." Daen's head swam, and suddenly his view of the man doubled, and then coalesced back into one. *I'm hurt worse than I thought,* the back corner of his mind realized. The front of his consciousness didn't care. *Nothing matters but protecting Aelys.*

"Why?"

"I'm her Ageon." Daen didn't know why he answered. He didn't know why that answer made the man facing him over bared steel lower his shield enough to gape at him, nor why the next thing he knew, the man had sheathed his sword and was grabbing his wrist and peering at the blue bracelet that had been magically tattooed there since the inn.

"Stay with me, Ageon. What is your name?"

"Daen."

"Daen, I'm Corsin. Aelys's family sent us. We're going to take care of you and your Bella, all right?" The man straightened up and shouted "Brionne! Over here!" in a battlefield command voice that would have made Romik proud.

Romik.

"Get my brothers," Daen managed to say, shaking his pounding head and forcing the words out.

"Your family is here?" Corsin asked, his eyes narrowing. "I'm sorry, but I don't think—"

"Her other Ageons. Romik. Vil. Both wounded. We made it out but then—"

"Other Ageons?" Corsin repeated, awe threading into his words. "Aelys has *three* of you?"

Daen couldn't help it. Despite the agony wreathing his being, he croaked out a laugh. "She needs us all."

"Divines above. All right, Daen. These men here are with me, they're going to help you stand while I see to your Bella. Help them find your... brothers." Corsin lifted his head and spoke to someone behind Daen. He wanted to turn and look but the throbbing in his head kicked up to a new level of agony. The next thing Daen knew, he had fallen forward, his hands resting on the earth as he retched out everything that had been in his stomach.

Farewell, magic stew, the dispassionate back corner of his mind thought.

Other hands gripped his shoulders, pulled him upright. He screamed when it jarred his hip, but it was good to be vertical again. For a moment, he could see better. Romik lay just ahead of him, the Naked Mirror still in his hand, his short sword missing entirely.

"Him," Daen said, pointing. He looked around, and found a dark, crumpled figure deep in the shadow of a pile of rubble. "And him. And..." He looked wildly—or as wildly as his throbbing head would allow, anyway—about him. "And my Bella—"

"I've got her, Daen," Corsin said, and the man himself stepped back into Daen's view. He held Aelys in his arms, cradled like a child. Her head lolled against Corsin's shoulder, and the shaft of a longbow arrow stood starkly out from her shoulder. Daen let out a snarl and lunged against the hands that held him.

I have to get to her! She's hurt! I have to—

"Daen! I've got her! Look, I've got her, she's safe with me! I've known her since she was a child, man, listen to me! Hold him, men, he'll injure himself worse if he's not careful."

"D-Daen?"

Aelys's soft query cut through Corsin's furious words and penetrated the fog of frenzy that wreathed Daen's mind.

"Bella," Daen said, almost a sob. "I'm here. I'm right here. I won't leave you."

She let out a sigh and lifted her head, her blue eyes hazy and tight with pain. "Vil? Romik?"

"We've got them all, Bella," Corsin said, his voice soft with respect. "They *are* all yours, then? As this man claims?"

"Yes," she whispered. "Mine. Corsin..." She trailed off, tears leaking from the corner of her eyes.

"I've got you," he said again. "You're safe now, Bella, I promise." He lifted his gaze to meet Daen's eyes. "We've got you all. These men are part of her family's home guard. We came looking for her after she sent a message saying she'd left the Lyceum. You're badly hurt, Ageon. We're going to take you back to camp where you can be healed."

"Healed?" Daen asked.

"Yes. My Bella is there."

"Your... Bella?"

"Bellatrix Aerivinne. Aelys's aunt. I'm her Ageon."

Waking was like floating to the surface of a deep, still lake.

Aelys's eyes fluttered open as a cool, smooth hand caressed her forehead.

"There you are, little bird."

The voice pulled at her, reaching deep into the recesses of her inner self and tugging at the memories of an awkward, too-often ignored child.

"Aunt," Aelys breathed, and then her eyes filled. "You found me."

"Oh, sweet one," Aerivinne laughed, stroking her hair back. She lowered herself to sit on the cot next to where Aelys lay, though her fingertips didn't leave Aelys's face. "Yes, of course I found you! I tracked your family ring. Hush now. Don't cry! You're safe!"

"You... tracked me?"

"Of course I did, little bird! When I received your message, I worried so for your safety! Imagine my surprise to find your ring calling to me from inside a known bandit stronghold!

Corsin thought we had no choice but to go in after you. So, I set an explosive spell on the gatehouse...only to find that you and those three men had somehow fought your way out and collapsed on the road!"

Despite the leaden feeling in her arms and legs, Aelys managed to reach up, silently beseeching her aunt for a hug. Aerivinne smiled and leaned in, wrapping her arms around Aelys's shoulders and pulling her up into an embrace. The first of several sobs racked Aelys's body, and she tightened her grip, clinging fast to the woman she'd always wished had been her mother.

"All right, then. If you need to let it out, go ahead. It's just you and me in here, little bird," Aerivinne murmured in Aelys's ear, holding her close. "You've been through quite a lot, so I suppose it isn't surprising. I'm right here."

Aelys gulped in a breath of air, which caused her to hiccup and gasp before she could marshal her resources to speak.

"Daen?" she croaked when she was able. "Romik? Vil? Please—are they all right?"

"Who? Oh, your men! Yes, I should say they are," Aerivinne said, letting Aelys go and helping her to lie back against the pillows again. "They were badly wounded, of course. The big one—Romik, you said? He nearly bled out before I could get the components to the healing spell properly placed. But we made it work. I've healed them all, as Corsin insisted. They slept the night, and awakened hungry, as they should." Aerivinne paused, reaching out once more to tuck a strand of Aelys's hair behind her ear. "They're all frantic to see you."

"I—Aunt, I did something I shouldn't have done. Something I didn't know I *could* do."

Aerivinne smiled gently. "My intuition tells me you're not talking about running away from the Lyceum, are you?"

"N-no. Although I know I shouldn't have done that either. But...at the binding ceremony, Halik chose Myara, and I just couldn't face being left standing, unchosen."

"Darling, you know there's no shame in it. Not everyone can be a Battlemage. You completed your education and earned the title of Bellatrix! That's something to be proud of." She leaned forward conspiratorially and whispered, "And in truth, sometimes an Ageon is more trouble than they're worth! You know how I detest Corsin's fussing."

"I know," Aelys said, slumping back against her pillows. As always, she ignored the cavalier way Aerivinne spoke about Corsin. He may have been her friend, but it wasn't Aelys's place to question the relationship between Bellatrix and Ageon. "I *am* proud...but I wanted to do something important. Something to help the empire. Like you do."

"Aelys, there isn't a single thing more important to the health of the empire than the continuation of the great noble houses. You're the Brionne heiress! Your marriage will be one of the keystones of the political landscape for this next generation. *You* will be the one to ensure our House survives and is well postured for success in the future. That's *far* more important than serving in the Battlemage Corps."

Aelys nodded, feeling herself shrink inward again. "I know," she whispered. "You're right. And...well. I do want to serve our House. I told Daen I wanted my life to have purpose."

"Protecting our legacy is a strong, noble purpose, little bird."

Aelys nodded again. "I know. And it's fine. I've come to terms with not being part of the Corps. I just couldn't face..."

Aerivinne's smile deepened. "I know," she said. "And I don't blame you. People are cruelest to those they envy and fear. Your importance doesn't depend on your magical skill, and candidates can be jealous about things like that. I see it all the time. I understand why you ran. I just wish you would have done it less...precipitously."

"I didn't have a plan," Aelys admitted. "I just needed to *go*."

"And that is a lesson for the future. All of this trouble you've found yourself in may have been avoided if you'd just waited a single night. Your mother already had a carriage on the road coming to fetch you the day after your graduation."

"I know," Aelys said again. "I mean, I didn't know that she had a carriage on the way, but I know I should have waited. I'm sorry."

Somewhere in the corner of her mind, an echo of Vil's voice whispered to her not to apologize, but she pushed that away for the moment.

Aerivinne patted her hand. "And I know dealing with your mother can be...fraught."

"Especially after yet another failure," Aelys muttered.

"Darling, none of that. You graduated! That's not a failure."

"No, but none of the candidates chose me. She'll see that as my failure, even though she never wanted me to go to the Lyceum in the first place."

"Now, this is the part I don't understand," Aerivinne said, flicking her fingers in the way she did when the conversation bored her, and she wanted to move on. "You said that Halik didn't choose you, and you ran because you were going to be left standing. So, how exactly is it that you ended up fighting your way out of a bandit stronghold protected by not one, but *three* Ageons? Having multiple Ageons isn't unheard of, darling, but typically only the strongest mages were ever chosen by more than one."

Aelys licked her lips and pushed herself up against the pillows. "May I have something to drink?" she asked.

"Of course, dear, here." Aerivinne stood up and turned to a table on the far side of the tent Aelys had only just noticed they occupied. The table held a pitcher of wine and a glass, and Aerivinne poured, then turned and handed the glass to Aelys. Aelys sipped gratefully, and then handed the glass back to her aunt.

"So how did that come about?" Aerivinne prompted her as she took the glass, set it on the bedside table, and then reseated herself on the cot next to Aelys.

"It was an accident," Aelys admitted. "They weren't Ageon candidates at all. I . . . met them on the road, at an inn, after they rescued me from bandits the first time."

"The first time?" Aerivinne asked, her delicate eyebrows going up. Aelys nodded.

"I was stupid," she said baldly. "You were right, I should have waited. But in my pride, I couldn't, and so I left. A noblewoman riding alone at night . . . well, I got chased. I almost made it to an inn before they caught me. My men were at the inn, and Romik saved me from being taken. Then they brought me inside, and I met his brothers, Daen and Vil. I hired them to bring me home safely, and they were going to do it, but the surviving bandit who ran away came back with reinforcements and they tried to burn down the inn."

"They *what*?" Aerivinne asked, her eyes going wide. "Oh, little bird! I mean, obviously you escaped but—"

"That's the thing, though. We didn't escape. The bandits blocked all of the windows and doors, and we were trapped as the building started to collapse around us. We were going to die. That's when the three of them said that they chose me, they would stay with me until the end..."

"And then?" Aerivinne prompted.

"And then I... I'm not sure. I don't remember what happened next. But my men said that I somehow pulled the fire through them and then made the inn explode."

"Explode."

Aelys nodded. "I—I passed out, I guess. Because when I woke up, they had brought me to a cave in the woods... and they were my Ageons."

"Sweet one, an Ageon bond is a solemn oath performed by one who has the proper authority. The fact that these men want to protect you may make them good, kind men, but it doesn't make them your Ageons."

"They have my eyes. They didn't, before the fire. But after, when I woke, they all had eyes the exact same blue as yours and mine."

Aerivinne blinked, then froze.

Aelys lifted the tattered, dirty sleeve of her gown and turned her wrist over to show the triple bracelet embedded into her skin there.

"I can *feel* them. When they think of me, it feeds energy into my system, Aunt. More energy than I've ever been able to touch before. And when I want, I can reverse that energy and it... affects them. They are *drawn* to me. It's not just that they're good, kind men who want to protect me. They are *driven* to protect me. They have been from the fire. Even though they didn't know why."

"You're talking about a *geas*," Aerivinne breathed. "Oh, Aelys—"

"I know," Aelys said, feeling her shoulders slump inward. "I know."

"Darling, it's... well. It's not technically illegal, but it's highly irregular!"

"I thought it was monstrous," Aelys said. "But then, Romik remembered something we'd forgotten. They all *did* choose me. It was just, as you said... irregular."

"Have you had sex with any of them?" Aerivinne's blunt, matter-of-fact demeanor made Aelys's face heat up in a blush as she shook her head in the negative.

"No," she said. "I didn't think it would be right. They only want me because of the *geas*."

"Ah. So that's the mysterious problem you mentioned in your letter from Mageford."

"Yes," Aelys said. She reached out and took her aunt's hands. "You're the most powerful mage in the empire. You know more about magical theory, healing, and history than any of the other Sanvari. If anyone can find a way to break this *geas*, you can. I know it."

Aerivinne pursed her lips for a moment before speaking again. "There . . . might be a way," she said slowly. "I will have to check some things in my personal library, but . . . yes. I might know of a way. And you are certain you want this *geas* broken? You would give up your Ageons?"

Aelys swallowed hard against the tears that threatened to overwhelm her again and nodded. "I—I will miss them," she said. "But it isn't fair to them. They didn't know what would happen when they chose to be with me, and neither did I. And . . . I cannot be a Battlemage, but I still want my life to matter. I will marry for the good of our House, as you said. And I can hardly do that with three husbands already, can I?"

Aerivinne snorted softly. "Well, you *could*, but I doubt any noble son would find that condition appealing in a future wife. Not unless he were able to share your men too . . . there might be one or two who would find that interesting."

Aelys laughed and shook her head. "No," she said. "All three of my Ageons appear to only desire women . . . specifically me. And they're possessive about it as well, which makes things even more difficult. Adding another man to the mix, even one who liked men . . . would likely not turn out well."

Aerivinne squeezed her hands. "I will find a way to release them, then, and quickly. If we can keep this discreet, it will be even better for your marriage prospects."

"I . . . but my Ageons . . . they deserve—"

Aerivinne laughed. "Oh, little bird. It's clear that you care about them, and that just underlines what I have always loved about you, dear one. You are such a loving, caring, unselfish person. We will, of course, see to it that the three of them never want for anything again. We'll call them 'House retainers' or some such and pay them handsomely. They will be well compensated, but no one need know they were ever your Ageons."

"But as Ageons, even former Ageons, they would be knights. If we bury this, they will have no rank."

"Dear one, believe me when I say that they will be far more comfortable remaining in the sphere in which they were born. Society can be brutal, as you know."

Daen's words about his time in the Foresters echoed through Aelys's head, and she nodded slowly. Aerivinne smiled gently and touched her cheek.

"As I said, we will ensure they want for nothing," she said. "But you must be free to make the most advantageous alliance, which means that it's better for all concerned if this remains within House Brionne. Then, once you are married, you can produce an heir and take your place in the governance of our lands … and the empire itself! You know that House Brionne has historically had close ties with the imperial family. Your mother's ineptitude has sadly let that connection lapse, but I believe my work on the regency council has mitigated that somewhat. And when you enter the political arena, with your beauty and intelligence … well. Let us just say that our House's future could not be in better hands."

"I doubt my mother would agree," Aelys muttered.

"Leave your mother to me," Aerivinne said with a conspiratorial wink. "I've been handling my sister my whole life. If you were any less good of a person, you would have learned from my example. But alas, you've always been pure of heart."

Aelys laughed and hugged her aunt again. "Thank you for coming to save me," she whispered, tears prickling her eyes again.

"You're welcome," Aerivinne said. "I always will. You're family."

Vil sat in the corner of the tent where they'd awakened and sharpened the one throwing knife he'd managed to retain after that battle. He'd chosen that corner of the tent because it sat furthest from the entrance and therefore the shadows were deepest. Romik's cot stood next to his, and Daen's was just opposite. It wasn't a large space, but they had it all to themselves.

Which had apparently caused some consternation amongst the Brionne House guard. Vil had awakened from his post-healing slumber to a rather heated argument going on between that other Ageon and one of the guard junior officers. Apparently, Corsin had commandeered the man's tent for their use, and the man had, perhaps understandably, balked.

"They are Bellatrix Aelys's Ageons, and therefore of knightly rank. They cannot bunk with our common soldiers!"

"Cannot you share with them, then, Ageon?" the man had asked sullenly. Vil had stifled a smile as he heard it.

"No. I protect my own Bellatrix in the night, as you well know. I'm not a hard man, Lieutenant, but do not get insubordinate with me. Share with one of your fellow officers for the few nights it will be needed. That is the end of the matter."

Vil didn't get a chance to see the young man who'd given up his billet for them, but he promised himself he'd find out who it was and slip him a little something. He still had a few of the gold Imperials from the ambush site. One of those would do for the Brionne lieutenant.

A wise man leaves no debt unattended, Vil thought, and then pushed away the memory of who'd taught him that precept. Fortunately, it wasn't that hard, because at that moment, Romik lifted the entrance flap and ducked into the tent.

"She's stirring," he said.

"Can we see her?" Vil demanded. Romik shook his head in the negative.

"Corsin reported that her aunt says she's still very weak. When she's fully awake, he will send for us."

"Let me see if I can hear her. I cut her hand back in the ruin—" Vil closed his eyes and listened, desperately hoping to hear her voice in the silence of his mind.

But there was nothing, only the silence and the endless morass of anguished worry.

Vil let out a growl that was far more likely to have come from either one of his brothers and opened his eyes. Usually, he kept himself too tightly controlled for such displays. Letting others see his emotions gave them an opening and too much information. He'd learned that the hard way.

But when it came to Aelys, his control frayed. And worse, he found it difficult to care.

In fact, he found it difficult to care about anything except that she get better. Inside his mind, the black chasm of grief and pain yawned again as he recalled the sound of her cry as she'd been struck by the arrow storm he'd led them into—

No. You're no good to her like that. Focus, Vil. Sharpen your knife and think through what you've seen since you awakened here. There has to be a vulnerability somewhere. You just have to find it.

"Do you trust Corsin?" he asked, looking over to where Romik had seated himself on his cot. His warrior brother looked up, raising his head from where he'd been cradling it in his hands. He shrugged.

"Not really," Romik said. "When it comes to her...I only trust us."

"Obviously. But otherwise?"

Romik shrugged. "Hard to say. I saw him working with some of the soldiers. He's good."

"Could you take him?"

"If I had to, probably. If you and Daen were with me."

"Always, obviously."

"Obviously. But let's hope it doesn't come to that. Especially not here in the middle of a force loyal to his House. I will say that Corsin appears sympathetic, like he understands our need to see her, even as he insists that we can't, yet. But there's something about him....I just don't trust him."

"He's bound to Aelys's aunt. So, his loyalty ultimately lies with her."

"Yes, but Aelys and her aunt are quite close, according to him. The woman practically raised her. Apparently our Bella's mother is...not a kind woman."

"She's a right piece of work, from what I'm hearing," Daen said as he walked into the tent. Like Romik—and probably like Vil himself—Daen carried a brittle tightness around his eyes that had nothing to do with the near-fatal wounds he'd sustained and everything to do with the woman lying in a healing tent not far away. "Likes her men, though. Apparently the young guardsmen are warned off of her as part of their initial training. Like she's some kind of predator."

"Predator? What...does she eat them?" Romik asked.

"No, she destroys them," Vil answered. "There were people like that in Cievers. The kind who buy young girls and boys for their sexual pleasure. But these are grown men, you'd think they'd be able to protect themselves."

"We're all vulnerable when it comes to love," Daen said. And then he growled. "Rot this waiting! I say we go get her and leave!"

"And what, cut our way through the Brionne House guard?"

Vil asked. "I doubt that would work any better than fighting our way blindly out of a bandit stronghold did!"

"We made it out."

"And it nearly killed her!"

"If you hadn't led us into that death trap of a courtyard—"

"Please don't fight."

Aelys's slim hand pushed aside the entrance flap and she stepped inside. Vil froze, unable to even breathe as his eyes drank in the sight of her. She was still pale, and dark shadows bruised the underside of her eyes, but she was alive, she was walking.

She had come to them.

"Bella," Daen breathed, and he wrapped her up in an embrace. Vil contented himself with staring as his brother held the woman they all loved more than their own breath.

Romik got to his feet, his hands visibly shaking as he walked over and hugged her from behind. "We...we failed you, Bella," he said. "I failed you."

"No," she said. She lifted her head from Daen's shoulder and pushed gently against his chest. Vil could see that neither of his brothers wanted to do so, but they both let her go, let her step out of the safety of their arms. He closed his hands into fists to keep them from shaking.

"You didn't fail me," she said. "I never would have survived any of the last several days without you—all of you. None of us knew what awaited us in that place. We only knew we had to get out. And we did. If my aunt hadn't detonated her spell and destroyed the gatehouse at that moment, you three would have gotten me to safety, as you always do."

She looked up and met Vil's eyes.

"I'm sorry, Bella," he said. "I should have done a better recon, but I knew I had to get back to you."

"If you hadn't, I'd be dead," she replied, with a little smile that didn't touch her eyes. "You never let me apologize for things outside my control. I won't let you do it, either. Fair?"

Despite himself, despite every dark thought he'd had since awakening in this Brionne camp, Vil found the corners of his mouth lifting in a smile.

For her. Only for her.

He inclined his head in acceptance, and her smile grew.

"So, you are well, then?" Romik asked. "Fully healed?"

"Yes," Aelys said. "My aunt is very powerful. She healed us all. All we need now is rest."

That's why I couldn't hear her, Vil realized. *Her aunt healed the cut from Profane.*

"Do you think your family will give us horses? Supplies? Or at least an escort back to Mageford so we can buy our own?" Daen asked.

"Yes, absolutely," Aelys said, her spine straightening. "I will see to it that you leave Brionne with the best of everything, you don't need to worry about that. And...I hope you know you'll always have a home there, should you need it. Perhaps after your adventuring days are done—"

"Wait," Romik held up a hand. "Bella. What are you saying? 'Your' adventuring days?"

"Well...I assumed that once the *geas* is broken, the three of you would continue with your business plan."

Silence fell in the small tent.

When the geas *is broken.*

Vil reached for the ice that had protected his mind for so many years, had protected his emotions and allowed him to do so many ill deeds. She'd started to melt it, but it was still there. It would have to do.

"Your aunt can break it, then?" Vil asked. His voice was as empty as it had ever been, and he silently thanked the Dark Lady for small favors.

"She says she can. It will require a complicated Working, which means we must all travel to Brionne before it can be done. But yes. She can set you free."

Daen reached out, his fingers trembling as he took a strand of her hair in between his fingers. "What if we don't want to be free?" he asked, his voice rough. "What if we just want to stay with you?"

Pain creased Aelys's face, and she closed her eyes for a second before opening them and shaking her head. "It's the *geas* making you feel that way—"

"I don't care!" Daen exploded. He curled his hands into fists and spun away from her, taking the two strides the tent allowed before spinning back to face her. "Do you hear me? *I don't care* why I love you; I just know that I do! I don't want to ever be without you, even if that means living in the shadow of your stupid noble estate in Brionne!"

Aelys shook her head again. "You can't," she said. Her eyes filled with tears and fell in a glistening line down her cheek. "I—I have to get married. To the son of a noble house. It will help ensure the Brionne legacy for generations to come. I can't do that if I'm bound to the three of you."

"Marry Daen," Romik said. "He's not a noble, but he was a Forester. That carries some cachet in noble circles, I'm told. He could give you children ... we all could."

"I can't," she whispered. "My marriage will be an alliance that will help determine the power structure of the empire. I can't waste that opportunity for Brionne, no matter what my own feelings on the matter might be."

"So, you'd rather be some noble broodmare playing politics than our Bella?" Daen asked, hurling the words at her as if they were arrows from his bow.

Aelys started to tremble, her tears flowing freely. "I will be the Head of my House. I will help guide the empire's policies and ensure stability within the realm for generations. This is the only way I can do something important," she whispered. "I want my life to matter."

"This is your final decision, Bella?" Vil's voice echoed the yawning emptiness that, once again, opened up inside of him.

Aelys sniffed, swallowed. Then she nodded.

"You don't want us," he said, ignoring the screaming in the back of his mind. "Despite us choosing you, you see us only as obstacles to your grand purpose. So be it. We'll go with you to Brionne and have your aunt break the *geas*. But know this, Aelys. Your life would always have mattered to us."

Aelys bit her lip against a sob. She rocked forward onto her toes, and then spun and fled from the tent.

Everything, every instinct, every drive, every desire shoved at him, driving him to spring forward, to sprint after her, to grab her and tell her he was sorry, he didn't mean it. His mind screamed at him to get up, to bring her back, but he wrapped his mind in ice and stayed where he was.

And ignored the rending pain of loss that stabbed through his chest.

CHAPTER EIGHT

IT WAS, EVENTUALLY, CORSIN WHO HELPED BRING THEM BACK together.

The following day, they broke camp and started the journey back toward Brionne. Aelys's aunt had apparently come out in force to retrieve her niece, for they traveled with a full complement of House guards and several baggage wains. Though it took most of the morning to prepare, once they got moving, they made good time along the winding mountain road.

No wonder, Romik thought in the corner of his mind that wasn't soaked in misery and missing Aelys's presence. *They've enough men here for a pitched battle. No bandit in his right mind would come anywhere near, no matter how much they're being paid by that other House...whatever they're called. I bet they just slunk back into their ruined fortress and hid out until we all rode away. It must be convenient to live this kind of life.*

When he'd been an arena slave, Romik had yearned to be free. He'd fought and bled to earn his manumission, and then he'd fought some more to make a life for himself. But he had never wanted to be a noble. He was a man of action, and tangled political intrigues only frustrated and enraged him. Ostentatious displays of wealth always seemed like a waste of time and resources, and he didn't give a dungrat's arse about building any kind of "legacy."

But if I were noble, I could marry her, and we could stay her

Ageons.... Red Lady, what a useless git I've become! I'm never going to be a noble, neither are my brothers. So, we have to find another way—

Vil's ice-cold, empty voice rang in his memory.... *You don't want us, despite us choosing you...*

Romik let out a low growl and tightened his grip on his reins so much that his borrowed horse sidled nervously. He forced himself to take a deep breath and patted the roan mare's neck.

"Sorry, girlie," he said lowly. "Not your fault. I'm just—"

"Having a bad day?"

Corsin had ridden up beside him and leaned forward on his saddle, his eyes sympathetic.

"What business is it of yours?" Romik growled before he could stop himself. Corsin wasn't a bad fellow, and he *had* saved Aelys's life when all three of them had fallen. But he was secure in his bond to his Bellatrix, and for that reason, in that moment, Romik hated him with all the fires of the Red Lady's rage. "Don't you have your own Bella to protect?"

Corsin smiled, but Romik recognized a tightness around his eyes. "She prefers it if I don't hover. Besides, what more protection can she need, riding in the midst of her House guard?" He leaned forward, resting his forearms on the pommel of his saddle as he regarded Romik. "Listen, man. I recognize the signs. One of your brothers is sullen and snarly as a wounded bearcat, and the other is terrifyingly silent—more so than usual, I guess I should say. You've all argued with her, haven't you?"

Romik set his jaw and straightened in the saddle. He touched his heels to the mare's flanks and urged her forward into a trot, looking directly between her ears and nowhere else.

Corsin followed suit, his gelding easily matching the mare's gait.

"That looks like a definite yes," the other Ageon said. "I can do one of two things, Romik. I can leave you alone to stew about it and drive your poor horse to distraction with your volatile emotional state...or I might be able to help. I know how hard it can be, to be bound to a woman with that much talent and drive. I've argued with my Bella more times than I can count and I... Well. Learn from my mistakes, friend. Aelys is a lot more reasonable than her aunt. Let me help. Tell me what happened."

"You should be able to guess," Romik ground out between gritted teeth. "You know where we're going, and why."

"You don't want to go to Brionne?" Corsin asked, sounding startled. "That—wasn't what I thought you'd say. Whyever not? It's a lovely place."

"Because when we get there, your Bella is going to take mine from me!" Romik snarled. The mare whinnied and tossed her head, not liking the sudden onset of his temper. He inhaled and forced his shoulders to relax and patted her neck again. "Sorry, girlie," he murmured once more.

"What?" Corsin asked, his brow creasing.

"Aelys asked her aunt to break the bond. So she can marry some noble son and 'protect the legacy of her House.'"

"Mother of Fortune," Corsin breathed. "I— Romik, that . . . are you sure? Aelys always wanted to be a Battlemage!"

"She says she can't, because we're not Lyceum trained. She says the only way her life will *matter* is if she breaks the *geas* and gets married."

Corsin closed his eyes and exhaled, slumping in his saddle just a little. "Aelys, why do you never believe in yourself?" Then he straightened and looked over at Romik. "That isn't what you want, is it?"

"Do I look like I rutting want that?"

"Then don't let her go."

Romik suppressed the sudden urge to draw his short sword and stab the man riding next to him. "Okay, sure, it's that easy."

"Obviously it's not going to be easy," Corsin spat back, showing a bit of temper for the first time in the conversation. "But if you give up and quit on her, she *will* break your bond and you will never get her back. We have three days before we reach Brionne. You and your . . . brothers need to use that time to show her where her heart lies. Unless you really don't care about her at all."

Romik glowered over at the man. "Say that again and you lose a limb," he growled.

Corsin laughed. "Love to see you try, my friend. But that was the correct answer. All right, so here's what we're going to do. Call your brothers over. I'll help you make a plan."

"Why?"

"What do you mean?"

"Why do you want to help us? Your Bella looks past us like we don't even exist, so what's in it for you if we succeed? Why do you care?"

"Don't take it personally. Aerivinne is often lost in her thoughts. She fails to notice *me* sometimes. Besides, I'm not doing it for you," Corsin said. "I'm sure you're a good enough fellow, and Daen seems fine, but your third—"

"Vil."

"Vil. Yes, I know. I've met men like him before. Killers like him."

"I've killed plenty of men."

"In battle or in their beds? There's a difference. *I've* killed men in battle...but it doesn't matter. The point is, the three of you are hers, and she deserves to have some happiness in her life."

Romik clenched his jaw so hard he felt the muscle below his ear jump. But he nodded once and turned to beckon to his brothers. Daen cantered over quickly, and Vil followed more sedately behind. Of the three of them, he was the least comfortable in the saddle.

City kid, Romik thought, with a tiny flicker of levity.

"Trouble?" Daen asked, pulling his gray alongside Romik's roan mare.

"Corsin wanted to talk to us," Romik said. "He thinks he can help us convince Aelys not to break the *geas.*"

Romik didn't miss the sudden flare of hope in Daen's eyes before his brother shuttered his expression. Vil, of course, showed no emotion at all, but he kicked his horse lightly to bring the animal alongside Corsin's mare.

"I'd wager I know Aelys better than any man alive," Corsin said. "I watched her grow up. She didn't have the easiest time of it. As I said, her mother is not a kind woman. I don't fully understand how the three of you could have come by your binding so quickly, but the bands on your wrists don't lie. Maybe they're not Lyceum silver, but either you went and had an artist ink them in place—which is a permanent statement all in itself—or they were put there by divine action. In either case, I'm not here to question it."

"Appreciate that," Romik ground out.

"But I spent eight years at the Lyceum, learning how to be an Ageon. A lot of that time was spent on combat training, it's true, but there are other lessons: nuances of the bond, what it means to serve in this way, things of that nature. What— I am not trying to be insulting, truly, but I have to ask— What do you all understand of these things? What do you know of being an Ageon?"

"We are her protectors," Romik said. "From the first moment, that was always the primary consideration: protect Aelys, see that she comes to no harm."

Corsin nodded. "Yes, our main purpose as Ageons is to protect our Bellators. In return, their power makes us stronger, heals us if necessary. At the Lyceum, when Aerivinne and I took the oath, as soon as the bracelet clicked closed on my wrist, I felt the weight of it settle over me. It was as if, all of a sudden, I was no longer the most important person in my own life."

"That's exactly it," Daen said, and on Corsin's other side, Vil nodded.

"It's more than that, though," Romik said. "It's . . . we're . . . *drawn* to her."

Corsin snorted softly. "I remember Aelys as a lovely child, but even I can admit that she's grown into a beautiful woman. There's no mystery there. Of course you're drawn to her, you would hardly have chosen her otherwise."

Romik drew breath to correct Corsin's assumptions, but Vil turned sharply and met Romik's eyes. His brother shook his head sharply, once, and Romik closed his mouth. Corsin glanced over at Vil, but he merely pulled his hood up over his head and looked straight ahead again.

I didn't want her until after the bond was in place, Romik thought. *Corsin seems to think it was the other way around. Maybe it would have been if I'd not been thinking of poor Mirandy . . . but Aelys was such a forlorn, defeated-looking little thing that night. Not my usual type at all. I wonder if Vil and Daen found her attractive, before.*

"The thing you need to understand about Aelys is that she's never been able to believe in herself. She's always been weak with her power—"

"She's not weak!" Daen snarled. Corsin held his hand up placatingly.

"Apologies, I phrased that poorly," he said. "I simply meant that she struggles to channel large amounts of power for certain applications, though I understand from her school records that she's above average at shielding against magical attacks."

"She pulls power through us," Romik said, surprising himself.

Vil snapped his head over to glare at him from within the shadow of his hood, but Romik ignored his brother for the moment. "She can call magelight as bright as the sun."

"Can she?" Corsin's eyebrows went up. "That *is* impressive. And you say she's pulling power *through* you? I've heard rumors that mages in the past used to do such things. Interesting. And our little bird figured it out!"

"She's not your 'little bird,'" Vil said, his tone empty. "She's *our* Bellatrix."

"Yes, she is, and I'm trying to help you keep her," Corsin said mildly. "So, pay attention. Aelys may have found a way to pull more power through your bond, but that, alone, won't build her confidence. And that is what you must find a way to do. Until Aelys believes in herself, she will never believe she deserves to be happy." He paused, and then looked at Vil, then Daen, then Romik.

"That is what you want, isn't it? To make her happy?"

"Second only to her safety," Romik rumbled. Corsin smiled tightly.

"Another correct answer. So, what do we do to convince your Bella that she is worthy of being happy? I think you need to show her what happiness looks like. Don't mention breaking the bond or her future or anything. Just spend the next three days being everything you want to be for her, everything she needs. I'll go talk to her and send her to you to get this process started."

He paused for a moment, as if thinking carefully about how to say his next words.

"Aelys has had so little real love in her life," Corsin said softly. "She's come to believe she doesn't deserve it. Show her otherwise, my friends. She...she needs that."

"I'm trying," Romik said. "We all are."

Corsin nodded. "One more question before I go. I don't pretend to understand the dynamic between you three...but if she loves you all, is that something you can abide? Because it looks very much to me like that's the case."

Romik opened his palm and angled it so that Corsin could see the brotherhood mark there. "We are brothers, sworn to be such and acknowledged by three Divines. We...received this mark the same night she bonded us. I...it works. I can't explain it further than that. But she needs us all."

Corsin studied the mark on Romik's palm, and then on Daen's when he, too, lifted his open hand. Vil stayed where he was, his hands encased in his usual black gloves.

"As you say," Corsin said after a long moment. "Once again, far be it from me to question the workings of the Divines. But know this, I have cared for Aelys since she was a tiny girl. If you or your brothers hurt her, or treat her badly, I will find you and I will end you."

Romik met his fellow Ageon's eyes and smiled slowly. "I'd like to see you try," he said. "But we never will. She is the air we breathe, her magic flows through us. I could more easily open my own throat than I could ever willingly harm her."

Corsin matched Romik's smile with a wolfish grin of his own. "And that, too, is the right answer."

"Something troubling you, Bella?"

Corsin's voice penetrated the miserable fog of self-recrimination that wreathed Aelys's mind and caused her to look up. She attempted a smile, but knew it probably looked ghastly and false with her pale skin and eyes reddened from weeping.

"So formal, Ageon Corsin?" she asked, trying to keep her tone light. "You used to call me your 'little bird' as my aunt does."

"That was before you grew up and became a woman of power, Bella," Corsin said.

Aelys couldn't help it, she laughed, the sound dry and hollow and completely lacking in joy.

"A 'woman of power,' that's rich, Corsin. Truly."

"I'm not making fun of you, Aelys," he said gently. "I would never do that to you. You know that."

Her laughter died, leaving more tears threatening behind her eyes. "I do know," she said. "I just— I never had any power. I still don't. It's been the greatest tragedy of my life, but I'm trying to grow up and face reality."

"Aelys, I say this with all the love in my heart for you, as an old friend who has watched you grow up: Stop feeling sorry for yourself."

"I'm not. I've just finally accepted—"

"Enough!"

His words jolted through her, straightening her spine and snapping her head around to look at him. "What?" she asked sharply.

Corsin raised a hand as if to ward off her defensive counterattack. "Don't strike the messenger, dear Bella. But . . . you are wallowing. And there truly is no need! If you really were as powerless as you say, how on earth would you have managed to bond three—from what I can tell—highly skilled, intelligent, and dangerous men—as your Ageons? Even if it was an accident, that still takes power. According to what my Bella told me, in the last . . . what, week or so? Ten days, perhaps? You've graduated from the Lyceum, bonded your Ageons, destroyed an inn, survived multiple bandit attacks, cleaned out a goblant nest and somehow found your way inside a bandit stronghold that you then had to fight your way out of? You almost made it; did you know that? Your Ageons killed all but two of the bandits in the courtyard and got you out through the gatehouse before your aunt set off her explosion. Those things are not the actions of a powerless woman."

"My Ageons did those things, not me," she said.

"And you bonded them." Corsin let out a sigh and reached over to squeeze her hand where it lay on the front of her saddle. "Listen, I know you argued with them about the future. And I know you're trying to do what's right. But there is no reason the four of you have to spend the next three days in misery. Go to them. They are miserable without you, and it's cruel. Let them protect you and care for you, even if only for this journey. Trust me, it's something they need."

A bitter tone crept into his voice, causing Aelys to turn her hand over in his and squeeze it. "Aunt Aerivinne loves you," she said softly. "She doesn't mean to be neglectful, she's just brilliant and absorbed in her work—"

Corsin smiled. "I know," he said. He squeezed her fingers back and withdrew his hand. "But do me a favor and at least go talk to your Ageons. Don't make them feel the way I struggle not to feel, all right?"

Nerves twisted in Aelys's belly as the selfish part of her that *wanted* to be with them warred with the logical part of her that knew she would only be staving off pain now for worse pain later.

But worse pain for me, I think. Once the geas *is broken, they will be grateful to be free of their unnatural devotion to me. And in the meantime, Corsin is right. It is cruel to make them suffer to spare my own pain later.*

"All right," she agreed. "I will talk to them. This cannot be easy on them. Their entire lives have changed, even once we break—return to Brionne. And so has mine," she said with a sigh.

"You haven't been back in a long time," Corsin said. "I know you struggled as a child, but I meant what I said. You have your own power now, Bella. Do not let past hurts cloud your view. Brionne is your home. You have a right to be here."

"It was just easier to stay out of my mother's sight."

"Lady Lysaera can be...difficult. She was harsh with you. I understand why you stayed away for so long, and I'm glad you found a friend at the Lyceum who welcomed you to her home. What was her name again?"

"Myara," Aelys said. A needle-sharp dart of betrayal stabbed through her as she thought about her former friend. *Strange that I can think of Halik without pain, but not her.* "We are not... close, anymore," she muttered, looking down at her reins.

"No? That's unfortunate," Corsin said, his voice sympathetic. "But sometimes that is the way things go, I suppose. It doesn't change my point. You're an adult, a graduated Bellatrix. Do not return home looking through the eyes of the wounded child you used to be. See things as they are."

Aelys smiled, and this time, it felt real. "Thank you, Corsin," she said. "From the time I was little, you were always my staunchest friend."

"It was my pleasure, Bella. Even when you went through your annoyingly inquisitive stage. 'What's this, Corsin? Who's that, Corsin? Can I play with your sword, Corsin?'" He rolled his eyes and shook his head, and then joined her in the laughter that spilled forth from inside her.

"I just loved your attention," she said. "You always made me feel important."

"You always have been, Bella. But never more so than to those three men of yours. So, go talk to them."

She nodded, and smiled again as he kicked his mare into a canter. Then she took a deep breath and did the thing she'd been trying not to do all day.

She looked around for them.

The three of them rode together, not far behind her and to her right. A jolt shot through her body as she realized that all three of them were watching her.

Now or never, Bella, she told herself. She pulled her spine straight and reined her horse over so that she could angle toward the group of them.

"May I ride with you?" she asked as she approached.

"Do you want to?" Romik asked, his voice that gravelly rumble that rolled through her.

"More than anything," she said, surprising herself with the fervency in her tone. "I wish—"

"No wishes," Daen said, his voice sharp. "No dreams. No talk of the future. Just ride with us, Bella."

It's not real, she told herself. *It's just the* geas. *They don't really want you. They just think they want you. You can't believe their words, no matter how pretty or passionate they are.*

But Aelys swallowed and nodded, recognizing the need in his tone as exactly what Corsin had been talking about. Without any more words, Vil nudged his horse up on her left while Daen rode to the right and Romik followed behind. Despite the silence that stretched between them, their nearness eased a tightness in Aelys's chest, helping her to feel like she could at least breathe a little better.

They rode most of the day without speaking. When their party stopped for breaks, Vil dismounted and went to get her water and wine to drink, while Daen held her horse and Romik helped her dismount. He helped her mount back up too, when it was time to go. A part of her mind wanted to protest that she didn't need or deserve such elaborate courtesies, but the rest of her realized that the men did these things not just for her benefit, but also for their own.

When they stopped for the evening, Daen reached over and grabbed hold of her horse's rein, guiding it behind his.

"You'll sleep in our tent tonight, Bella. So we can keep you safe."

"I-I don't want to displace any of you," she said softly.

"One of us is always awake," Romik rumbled. "Taking a watch. If you're with us, at least the other two will be able to rest."

Aelys pressed her lips together and nodded. There was nothing improper about it, after all. According to imperial law, these men were as her husbands while they wore her bracelet. And perhaps their bracelet wasn't the traditional flat metal band, but it was unmistakably there. If her future husband balked at this...well. Aerivinne was right. Perhaps they just wouldn't tell him.

They found the place where the forward element of Brionne guards had set up their tent and dismounted. Aelys went inside and found that her small bag of travel clothes—things Aerivinne had brought from home, as she'd long since lost her own luggage—had already been placed within. She took the time to wash her hands and face with water from the small travel ewer, rebraided her hair, and then stepped outside to meet three sets of blue eyes that echoed her own.

"I would like to eat with my aunt and her Ageon," she said. "W-will you three join us?"

Daen nodded his head once, his expression grave, and Romik extended his hand. Vil just watched, his face shadowed beneath his deep hood. Aelys put her hand in Romik's and let him lead her to the camp's central fire.

The Brionne scouts had chosen a picturesque spot for their camp: a narrow valley between two mountain peaks, with a narrow stream winding through it. Tall, dark-needled trees stood like guardians between the multiple campfires, casting growing shadows as the sun sank below the western ridge.

Aelys tilted her head back and peered through the branches at the deepening blue of the cloudless summer night. Here in the mountains, the temperature dropped with the sun, and Aelys shivered as a breeze rustled through the needles overhead and skimmed along her unprotected neck. She pulled her cloak tighter around herself as Romik's fingers tightened on hers.

"Cold?" he asked.

"I'm all right," she answered, straightening her gaze. She caught sight of some of her family's guardsmen through a thin screen of saplings and paused, pulling Romik to a halt beside her.

"What's wrong?" Daen asked, behind her.

"Nothing," Aelys said. "It's just...I wonder if you three would indulge me for a moment. I want to check on the men. It feels like something I should do, especially considering they did save us at the bandit stronghold."

"After your aunt blew us up," Vil added.

"Still," Aelys said. "They're protecting us now, escorting us home. I don't know, it just feels rude not to at least acknowledge them."

"You have good instincts," Romik said, his voice a low rumble in the dimness. "A leader always checks on his or her men. We can walk you over there and around the perimeter, but then you need to get some food and rest."

"Thank you," Aelys said, tilting her head to smile up at him. He didn't smile back, but the firelight gleamed warmly in his eyes as he nodded.

When they reached the first group of men, Aelys realized abruptly that she knew them—or one of them at least. Lieutenant Mindler's father had been a Brionne captain before he retired, and Mindler had been one of the gaggle of children roaming the inner bailey of the Brionne stronghold when Aelys was a child. He'd even asked her to play once, but she hadn't been allowed to do so.

She'd always appreciated that he asked, though.

"Lieutenant," she said warmly as he noticed her approach and paused in his instructions to his men to incline his head respectfully.

"Bellatrix Aelys," he said. "It is good to see you again. And your Ageons. Congratulations on your graduation."

"You remember me?" she asked, a smile spreading over her face. "I was wondering! It's been so long." She turned her body to include her Ageons in the conversation. "Mindler and I were children together...well, sort of together, anyway. I wasn't really allowed to play with him and the other children, but I always wanted to."

Lieutenant Mindler lifted his head and gave her a small smile. "We always hoped you would, Bella. What can I do for you?"

"You've already done quite a bit," Vil spoke up, his voice low and carrying a note of something not quite pleasant. "You're the one who...volunteered his tent for our billet."

Mindler winced. "Volunteered is a strong word," he admitted. "I'll admit to being put out at first. It had been a long trek, and I'd heard the Bella was hurt, and we didn't know who you three were—"

"—And we came out of a bandit stronghold, not looking at all like Ageons," Romik said, nodding. Aelys glanced up to see him giving Mindler a tiny, understanding smile.

"Exactly. But Ageon Corsin was right. He's a good man, in truth, and I should have trusted him from the beginning."

"But still," Aelys said, frowning. "It distresses me to think that we've put you out. Can I do something—"

Mindler shook his head, and even in the uncertain light from his nearby campfire, Aelys could see the flush that stained his neck and cheeks. "No, please, Bella. It's good of you to ask, but no. I am fine with my brother officers, and we will be home soon. It's...forgive me, but it's heartening that you've returned."

"Thank you," Aelys said. Her brows drew together at his words, but she smoothed her face and smiled. "It is good to see you too. We're going to walk around and check with the other men, just to see if they need anything. If you or your men think of something...please let Romik know. I know you've your own chain of command and everything, and I *have* been gone for a very long time...but I know serving in Brionne is not always the easiest task. I want to help you all if I possibly can."

Mindler's eyes darkened, and his smile slipped, but he nodded and dipped his head again as they stepped away.

"That was well done," Romik murmured as she took his arm again and let him lead her to the next group of men preparing their meals. "But what did you mean about serving in Brionne not being easy?"

"My mother," Aelys said, and she was more surprised than she should have been at the bitterness of her tone. "She often takes advantage of the men. Some of them don't mind coming to her bed, of course, but she does not care if they have wives or families or...well. She doesn't care about anything but her own desires. When I am home, I do what I can to distract her...but I have not come home much of late. Perhaps I should have. I need to remember that I am not the only one who suffers under her selfishness."

"They are grown men and trained soldiers," Daen put in. "They can take care of themselves, surely."

"Sometimes, but Mother has a way of ensuring that she gets what she wants. When a man must choose between allowing his family to be cast out to starve in the depths of a mountain winter and acceding to her wishes...well. You can see what choice a husband and father would make. She knows that and uses it relentlessly."

"If that's true, then what can you do to help?" Vil asked, his tone genuinely curious. Aelys glanced over her shoulder at him, and she could barely see his cloak-swathed figure in the growing darkness.

"I don't know," she admitted, her voice soft. "Sometimes I draw her attention to my many flaws and that distracts her. Sometimes I can manage to get her to drink enough that she cannot make any of her...requests. Once, after I began learning herbalism, I developed a potion that would accelerate the process and put her to sleep. I gave the recipe to the guard captain, but some of the ingredients are difficult to source here, and..."

"And if anyone caught him drugging the Lady of Brionne he would be in a terrible position," Romik finished for her.

"Yes," Aelys said. "For that reason, I don't think he uses it often, but it is at least there, if there is need. Little enough protection, I know, but it was the best I could do." She straightened her shoulders and lifted her chin as they drew nearer to the next group. "Just as checking on them here is the best I can do for now. So let us continue, my Ageons, and then we can rest."

"Aelys! Come, little bird, sit here by me," Aerivinne called out with a smile as she patted the foldable camp chair next to hers. Aelys smiled back at her aunt as she and her Ageons walked toward the central campfire. She let out a little sigh and lowered herself into the seat as Daen held it for her.

"Vil will stay," Romik said as he squeezed her fingers once more before letting them go. "Daen and I will bring you something to eat."

"I ca—thank you," Aelys said, changing her mind about protesting that she could get her own food when she saw Corsin approaching with a plate for Aerivinne. He smiled at her, even as he handed his own Bella her food, and Aelys saw approval in his expression.

"Is that wise, dearest?" Aerivinne said softly, bending toward Aelys as she did. "Getting so close to them, I mean."

"I'm already too close to them," Aelys murmured. "There's nothing I can do about that now. And they feel bound to protect me, to care for me. It would be cruel to deny them the opportunity to do that over these three days."

"Yes, but sleeping in a tent with them?"

"I won't hurt them while they are my Ageons. We will deal with my future husband when the time comes. I was never going to be an untouched bride, Aunt. You of all people know that we're encouraged to form romantic attachments at the Lyceum."

"Well, that's true," Aerivinne said. "And earning the title of Bellatrix will carry its own cachet. Besides, the kind of man we want for you will be able to see the bigger picture and look past these...youthful indiscretions, let's call them."

"Let's not," Aelys said, her voice heating in anger. "The *geas* is not a series of wine-induced bad decisions, Aunt."

"No, of course not, darling. I only meant what you already said. No one is expecting you to be a blushing virgin. I *do* think we should be discreet about the fact that you actually bonded Ageons. The candidates I have in mind for your hand will not want to be anyone's second choice of husband. But you are right, we can deal with all of that once we break your *geas*." She reached over and placed one elegant hand on Aelys's knee. "I realize this must be a great strain on you."

"You can't imagine," Aelys muttered, and then froze as she realized what she said was true.

She really can't imagine it, can she? Her bond with Corsin, though it's been in place for decades, isn't a full geas like ours. And sometimes I wonder if...no. That's not fair. She loves him very much, I'm sure of it. She doesn't mean to neglect him, she's just busy keeping everything from falling apart. Maybe once I'm home I can help carry some of that burden for her. Divines know Mother doesn't bother—

Romik interrupted this train of thought by returning with a plate of food for her, while Daen held one for Vil. Corsin, who'd taken his customary place on Aelys's other side, nodded to her Ageons in greeting, and a tiny spark of happiness warmed her heart when all three of them nodded back.

If only it could always be like this, my Ageons working next to her Ageon—but Daen had the right of it. No dreams, no wishes. Not tonight. Not for these days. Not until we get home.

Daen had known that Brionne was a powerful House, but even he couldn't resist gawking a bit at the massive fortress with the soaring, graceful towers that rose up out of a bluff in the tiny mountain valley. A small, quaint village lined the road leading up to the bluff. Here and there men and women stopped to wave or dip their heads in respect as the party rode by.

Aelys interacts with them, he noted, watching her smile as she returned a wave. *The guards watch them briefly—which is their job, I suppose. Aerivinne doesn't even seem to notice them. But they do light up when my Bella smiles at them.*

I know how they feel.

"Interesting place," Romik grunted, pulling Daen's attention away from the woman beside him. "Hard to take. Wouldn't want to assault those walls."

"I don't think we're laying siege to the place, Ro," Daen said.

"We might be," Romik added. "Or we might be trying to escape it."

"Fair point," Daen said, and turned back to study the walls with new interest. On his wrist, the renewed cut stung, a reminder of the pact that he and his brothers had made. They wouldn't give Aelys up, and they would get out of there if they had to die trying. Vil had even cut them both, so that they could stay in contact and seize any opportunity that arose.

"You won't have to escape," Aelys said softly. "You can leave at any time...or you can stay. I promised you'd always have a home here in Brionne if need be. I mean to keep that promise."

And will you also promise not to marry some noble whelp? Daen wondered, his thoughts driven by the anger that still simmered deep in his belly. *Will you be willing to have us close by when you see that breaking this stupid* geas *doesn't change a thing about the way I—or any of us—feel about you, Bella?*

Aelys shivered and ducked her head, looking at him out of the corner of her eyes. For the first day or so after her healing, it hadn't seemed to affect her when they thought about her—which was always. But as her body had finished recuperating, it became clear that she could once more feel it when any of them focused on her, particularly if their thoughts tended toward the intimate or the sexual. By unspoken agreement, the three of them had decided not to tell her that they had noticed, thus opening up opportunities to cause delicious reactions in her.

She could block us out if she wanted, Daen reminded himself. *But she doesn't, she lets the energy flow. Why would she do that if she didn't crave it as much as we crave her?*

One thing she had not done, since being found by her family, was reverse the energy flow back into any of her Ageons. In the back of his mind, Daen knew that she was trying to be respectful and not bind them closer to her before she let them go forever.

But he missed it. He missed *her.* He cut his eyes to her slim figure again and imagined running his fingertips along the back of her neck, up under her hair.

She shivered again, and Daen felt a tiny stab of savage joy.

"Tell us about your childhood here, Bella," he said. "What was it like, growing up in a noble House?"

"There isn't much to tell," she said. "I was a nuisance of a child, driving my mother and all the staff to distraction with all of my questions and chatter."

"You were inquisitive," Vil said from her other side. "That's not a bad trait in a child."

"Well, but I took it to extremes," she said with a self-deprecating smile that Daen wanted to wipe off her face with a hard, savage kiss. "That's probably why I love reading so much. My mother banished me to our library when I was very young, so I would quit pestering her. I was a very lucky child, to grow up surrounded by books."

"What kind of books?" Daen asked. He liked the flush of joy that stained her cheeks when she spoke of reading.

"Oh, everything. Histories, biographies, novels. Treatises on magical theory. Herbalism guides and recipes. My grandmother was an avid collector, and she built the finest library in the Great Houses . . . according to her, anyway."

"You've never mentioned a grandmother," Romik said. "Who was she?"

"Daelya, Lady of Brionne. She was a great stateswoman, and part of the former emperor's inner circle of advisors. She died when I was very young. I barely knew her, but apparently, I share her love of reading. She is a large part of the reason Brionne is one of the preeminent Houses in the empire today. Everything we have is because of the fortune she amassed and the legacy she left behind. I . . . would like to live up to her example. Someday."

Aelys shifted in her saddle and gathered her reins tighter in her hands. "In any case, I spent most of my childhood hiding in the library, reading and trying to remain out of everyone's way. It was always a beautiful place, with many fine art pieces and furnishings— more of my grandmother's collections—but I was always afraid that I'd somehow make a mess or ruin something priceless."

"It sounds . . . hostile," Daen said. "At least for a young child."

"Oh, it wasn't so bad as that. I just . . . well, I was a nuisance, as I said. I haven't been back in several years. Not since my second year at the Lyceum."

"So, it might not be as you remember it at all?"

"It might not be," Aelys said with a smile. "My mother is Lady of Brionne, she could have changed everything...but I doubt she would. I doubt Aerivinne would allow her to!

"But that reminds me," she went on. "When we arrive, you will meet my mother's seneschal. Maudren is highly competent and very particular about certain...niceties. Proper respect for rank and tradition are very important to him."

"Are you telling us that he's going to try and keep us out with the unwashed masses, Bella?" Daen asked. And then he imagined his lips on the curve where her shoulder met her neck, just for fun.

"N-no. The opposite, actually. As my Ageons, and Brionne retainers, you three have knightly rank now. I-I just wanted you to be prepared. Our road captain will have already sent word ahead, so Maudren and his staff know we're coming. You'll all three have rooms prepared for you, clean clothes—"

"Bella, Ageons," Corsin called out as he cantered back along the road. He'd been riding with Aerivinne at the front of the column. "We're arriving now if you'd like to come up to the front." His eyes cut to Aelys's, concern readily apparent in his expression. "The Lady Lysaera is home," he said. "And has sent word that she would like to see you and meet your protectors as soon as you arrive."

Daen watched Aelys go very still for a moment, her face going pale before she swallowed, drew her spine straight, and gave Corsin a nod.

"Thank you, Ageon," she said, matching his formality. "We will be right there."

"Who is the Lady Lysaera?" Daen asked, his voice softer than it had been since they'd awakened in the camp.

"My mother," Aelys said, and then touched her heels to her horse's flanks to trot ahead. Daen exchanged a quick, worried glance with his brothers, and then kicked his own horse into a canter to follow.

"Remember who you are, Bella," Daen said as they approached. "Remember that we're with you, always."

"I—thank you," Aelys said. "It is interesting to be back. I didn't... People seem to remember me; I wasn't expecting that."

"Maybe you should have. You're their heir, aren't you? Their future. They like that you smile at them and engage with them. It makes you approachable."

He would have said more, but they drew up alongside Corsin and Aerivinne, who smiled tightly over at Aelys as Romik and Vil took their places at Aelys's back.

"Chin up, Bellatrix," Daen heard Aerivinne murmur just before the massive oaken door they faced began to rise into the stonework above. That small gesture of kindness from aunt to niece warmed him for just a moment. He'd not formed much of a positive opinion about Aelys's aunt during their three days on the road. He was grateful to her for healing them—and more importantly, Aelys—but overall, she kept to herself and only ever spoke to Aelys or her Ageon, and that only rarely. Corsin, on the other hand, seemed all right, but Daen had a hard time viewing anyone who wasn't Aelys or his brothers with any kind of charity.

All I want is to take the three of them and go back to our forest, he snarled in his mind, *is that so much to ask? At least Brionne isn't a large town, although the castle is massive. Let's hope it's not crowded with people like Mageford was.*

They rode through the gatehouse walls—nearly as thick as a man was tall, he observed—and into the bailey within. Instantly, men wearing blue-and-black livery came forward, taking their reins, helping the ladies to dismount.

Well, everyone but our Bella, Daen thought with a smirk, as Romik hopped out of the saddle and growled at the servant who held his hand out to Aelys. The servant dropped his hand and stepped back, ducking his head in deference as Romik reached up to put his hands on Aelys's waist and lifted her down.

"Well, this must be your protector. Or one of the...three, was it? How extraordinary. Perhaps you are my child after all."

The light, teasing voice that drifted down to them sounded disturbingly close to Aelys's, but also somehow *wrong*. Like all the joy and brightness had been sucked out of it, replaced by a type of bored, cynical sarcasm.

And I would know, Daen admitted. *Bored, cynical, and sarcastic were my hallmarks before her.*

We can't lose her.

I can't lose her.

I would lose myself.

Aelys pulled her spine straight, pulled her shoulders back,

slipped her arm through Romik's and turned to walk toward the tall, slender blonde who stood at the top of a short flight of stairs across the narrow bailey. Behind her, one of those soaring towers climbed into the sky, threatening to make Daen dizzy if he stared up at it for too long. He swallowed hard, and then collected himself and fell into place beside Vil and behind Aelys and Romik.

"Mother." Aelys inclined her head respectfully as she approached. "Thank you for coming out to meet us."

"I could hardly believe the news, so I wanted to see for myself. Look at you! Little Aelys of the knobby knees and stringy hair and too many questions! All grown up and a Bellatrix. You're standing before me, and I can barely believe it."

Daen watched as the line of Aelys's body got more and more tense with every poisoned word that dropped from the woman's lips. Up close, Daen could admit that Lysaera should have been lovely— she had a thin, fit figure with high breasts and a subtly curving hip. Her hair and eyes matched Aelys's, but the sneering expression she wore marred any pretense of beauty she might have had.

"Mother, may I present my Ageons? Romik, Daen, and Vil. They've chosen to be my protectors for a short while."

Daen clenched his jaw tightly against the scream that wanted to come out and fought to focus on hearing her mother's response.

"Well," Lysaera purred, her voice dropping lower, into a register that was probably supposed to be seductive. "Aren't you the lucky girl? You are very welcome here, Ageons. My mother's heart is filled to bursting with gratitude. Thank you for bringing my child home."

"They've had a long journey, Lysaera," Aerivinne said as she climbed up past Aelys and bent to kiss the air above her sister's cheek. "Why don't we go in and let everyone get settled, hmm? Perhaps we can speak more with Aelys's Ageons later."

"Yes," Lysaera said, her eyes raking over first Romik, then himself, and then Vil before smiling past Aerivinne at Corsin. "I would very much like that."

"I am sure you would." Aerivinne's reply wasn't, quite, caustic, but it wasn't far off. For the second time in just a few minutes, Daen found himself appreciating Aelys's reserved aunt.

Lysaera looked back at the three of them before turning without another word to her daughter and following her sister inside.

Aelys let out a sigh. "That...was my mother. She is..."

"Not something for you to apologize for," Vil said. Aelys startled, and then let out a little ripple of laughter.

"I was just about to," she admitted. "She's not a bad person, but she hasn't had much happiness in her life."

"I can't imagine why that would be," Daen muttered. Aelys didn't appear to hear him, but Vil did, because he glanced over with dark humor and a tight smile in his eyes.

"She doesn't sound like a good person," Romik rumbled. "From what you and Corsin and the other men said on the road, and from what you said about how she treated you. I wouldn't want someone like that as my mother."

"I—"

"Don't apologize," Vil reminded her, with a little heat behind his words. Aelys took a deep breath and then reached out to touch his cheek.

"I wasn't," she said. "You're . . . not wrong. She is difficult. But seeing her, just now, with you three beside me made me realize something. She's . . . small. Petty. She's never really been a leader—that was Aerivinne, always. I think she's an unhappy person, and that's affected everything around her." Aelys waved a hand at the courtyard, and the people moving through it. It took Daen a moment, but he eventually realized what she meant.

People didn't bustle, they *rushed*. It was almost as if they were afraid to be seen or noticed. It was not the atmosphere of those who took pride in their work, it was the atmosphere of those who feared the caprice of an unstable leader.

"Brionne deserves better," Aelys breathed softly. "I can make it better."

"And so you shall," Romik said. He reached out and took her fingers, then lifted them to his lips.

"Welcome home, Bellatrix."

The new voice came from the door into which Aerivinne, Corsin, and Lysaera had disappeared. Daen looked up as Aelys and Romik turned back to greet the older gentleman who stood there wearing an immaculately cleaned and pressed version of the grooms' livery he'd seen before.

"Thank you, Maudren," Aelys said with a smile. Romik released her hand. She took hold of her skirts and ascended the short stairs with a smile. "It's good to be back. May I introduce my protectors? Ageons Romik, Daen, and Vil."

"You are very welcome as well, Ageons," Maudren said. "Bellatrix, I have moved you out of your usual chambers into one of the guest wings, so that you might be housed next to your Ageons."

"Oh! Thank you," Aelys said, blinking.

"You will find your rooms in the southern wing on the third floor. I trust you will find all to your liking there. I will have a page bring hot water in half an hour, so that you might all properly prepare for the evening meal."

"Thank you, Maudren," Aelys said again. "You've seen to everything."

"Yes," he said. And then he inclined his upper body to a very precise degree and turned on his heel before striding away. Aelys looked after him for a moment and then shook her head with a little laugh.

"I never could decide," she said. "Whether he hated me or was fond of me. I still can't."

"No one could possibly hate you," Daen replied, the words slipping out before he could remember that he was angry at her and hold them back.

Aelys laughed. "There's where you're wrong, Sir Knight, but thank you."

Romik groaned. "Do you *have* to call us that?" he asked as he climbed the stairs to join her. He took her hand and wound it once more through his arm. "I hate it. It makes me look around for my old arena master."

"It's your title now, all of you," Aelys said. "Ageons are knights, recognized by imperial law. And...I checked with Aerivinne, it's irreversible. Even once the bond is broken, you'll still be entitled to that rank as retainers of House Brionne. It could...it could be good for you all, for your business."

Not as good as having you, Daen thought, but in the interest of protecting the fragile peace they'd found on the road, he kept his mouth shut and followed his brothers and the woman they all loved inside.

Romik carried the steaming jug through the bedroom chamber to the small room at the back that the Brionne servant had pointed out as the "bathing room." Though the jug was well wrapped and insulated, he could tell from the heat and the steam that the water was still near boiling, despite having been presumably carried up here by that same servant.

"Pour it in the large tub, and mix the water around," he muttered, repeating the servant's entirely too bland instructions. Perhaps this was one of those things that a knight would ordinarily already have understood.

What do I know? I'm just a soldier who used to be an arena fighter. Even at the height of my fame, I didn't bathe like this. Those massage girls with the oils and the scraping sticks were nice, though...

He snorted a laugh at himself as he kicked open the door to the bathing room and saw that, indeed, a large tub sat inset into the floor. Romik set the jug down and tested the water with his hand. It was cool to the touch, but not cold. With a shrug, he poured the steaming, boiling contents of the jug into the tub, and then quickly unbuckled his weapon belt and back sheath. He laid the Naked Mirror and his short sword on a low table within arm's reach of the tub, stripped out of his tattered, filthy traveling clothes and stepped in.

With the addition of the jug, the water was nicely warm, though it did sting in the long cut Vil had made on the top side of his wrist. He lifted his arm out and set it on the side, then leaned back with a sigh. After years of campaigning, he was well used to travel, but he did have to admit that it felt nice to get clean now and again.

Plus, it won't do to embarrass Aelys at her family dinner.

That thought had him looking around the tub until he found a small box containing a lump of cream-colored soap. He gave it a sniff, picking up a clean, fresh scent reminiscent of wild herbs, and not too feminine or flowery. With a shrug, he scooped out a reasonable amount and rubbed it between his palms to begin sudsing up.

He washed his entire body, including his hair—which was growing entirely too long. Ever since his arena days, he couldn't stand having his hair be in his eyes or over his ears. He kept a straight razor and a pair of barber's shears in his usual gear for that reason. He'd have to find some here.

I'll ask that Maudren fellow, he seems like the type to have anything and everything on hand, Romik decided as he ducked under the water one more time, and then pushed up to his feet, water sluicing off of him.

He let the majority of it drip away, and then stepped out of the tub, reaching for one of the rolled-up bathing sheets stacked neatly on the shelf nearby. He used this to finish drying off, and then wrapped it around his hips and tucked it in before throwing the lever on the wall conveniently marked "Drain."

Romik had to admit, having this tiny version of a bathhouse to himself was nice—

Thunk.

He froze as the sound of his heavy chamber door closing reached him. Too many years fighting off ambitious and treacherous fellow arena slaves had conditioned him to wariness in the bath, so Romik had at least brought his weapons in with him.

He drew The Naked Mirror and kicked the bathing room door open, charging through with his sword at the ready.

A woman's gasp, followed by a low ripple of laughter filled the room. For one shining moment, he thought Aelys was there, her beautiful hair unbound around her shoulders, her gown swirling around her slim body as she turned to face him—

"Mother of Magic, aren't you the specimen, Sir Knight," Lysaera said. She pitched her voice low, in a seductive purr. But it sounded so much like a cruel mockery of Aelys's that Romik felt his hand tighten around the hilt of his sword.

He straightened up, lowered The Naked Mirror to point at the floor. "What are you doing here...my lady?" he asked, remembering the honorific at the last moment.

Lysaera bit her lower lip, just as Aelys sometimes did. But instead of her daughter's unsure expression, Lysaera's eyes met his in bold invitation.

"Well," she said, drawing the word out. "I rather thought we should get to know one another better, Sir Romik." She took a step forward, and then another, until she was close enough to touch his bare chest. He stepped back, and she pursed her lips in a moue of disappointment.

"My lady, I think perhaps you misunderstood—"

"Oh, I don't think so," she said, her eyes raking over the naked planes of his chest and stomach. "But it's possible that you did. I can see how this must be very confusing for you, to find yourself bound to my bumbling daughter. Aelys is a sweet child, but she simply *cannot* do anything right."

A warning growl made its way up his throat, and Romik

barely stopped himself from snarling at the woman. She must have noticed a change in his expression, or a tension in his body, because her smile widened.

"Oh, I see! You *are* protective of her, aren't you? How precious. Well, don't you worry, Sir Knight, I have no intention of hurting my daughter. It's just that . . . well . . . there ought to be *some* perks to your new position in life, ought there not?"

"I don't understand," Romik said, though the sudden nausea churning in his stomach made him fear that he did.

"I mean . . ." She trailed the word suggestively and darted her tongue out to wet her bottom lip. "I am the Lady of Brionne, and I've chosen you, lucky man, to warm my bed tonight."

Her eyes lingered on his chest and stomach. Romik had spent years in the arena wearing less than this bathing sheet and fighting under the gaze of thousands. He didn't usually feel exposed.

This woman made him feel exposed. She stirred memories long forgotten or buried beneath victories and freedom. Memories of other rich, noble women who wanted the lark of sleeping with an arena champion—and who didn't much care if he consented or not.

Romik lifted his sword again, pointed it at her. "Get out."

Her eyes sharpened. She pushed his blade gently to the side and took another step toward him, her low-cut gown shimmering in the light from his fireplace. "You are perfect," she said, reaching out to run her fingertips over his left pectoral.

He grabbed her wrist, held her hand away from him. Squeezed. "I said, you need to leave."

She let her head fall back, her eyes drifting closed as her lips curved in a lush, inviting smile. "I do not wish to leave."

Romik shoved her away, then backed up toward the bathing room. "Lady Lysaera, let me be crystal clear. I do not want you."

For just a moment, her face creased in anger and rage snapped in her blue eyes before her face settled back into the seductive expression of before.

"You don't know what you want," she said. "I can make you happier than my daughter ever could. I know things she wouldn't dream—"

Behind him, the door creaked open, making her jump. Romik turned, and relief washed through him as Daen and Vil entered.

Both of them stopped just inside the threshold, letting the door swing shut in silence.

"What's going on?" Daen asked, his tone carefree as usual, but his eyes wary. "Vil and I had the sudden notion that you might need some help."

"The Lady Lysaera is—"

"Beginning to see how this works," Lysaera broke in. She swept forward, one hand twitching her skirts dramatically as she came alongside Romik. She placed one hand on his shoulder, and he couldn't help but snarl as he stepped away.

"You three call yourselves 'brothers,' but there is more to it than that, isn't there?" she asked, her smile widening. "Oh, this is *very* intriguing! I had decided that Sir Romik would share my bed tonight, but now I see that perhaps I had better invite you, too, Sir Daen. And Sir Vil, I'd imagine you are the type who likes to watch, aren't you? Would you like to watch your fellow Ageons pleasure me?"

"That's not what I'd like to watch them do to you," Vil said, his voice as cold as ever.

"We're bound to your daughter," Daen said, his words thick with disgust. "Her husbands in the eyes of the law! What kind of mother are you?"

Lysaera rolled her eyes. "I'm a woman with needs of my own," she said, anger heating her tone and creasing her face. "That stupid brat has been ruining my life since the day she took her first breath. I should have had her strangled at birth."

Thunk.

One of Vil's newly replaced throwing knives vibrated in the bedpost inches from Lysaera's face. She paled, and then swallowed and looked at Vil with renewed rage.

"How dare you—"

"Oh, you'll find I'll dare a lot. One more word about hurting Aelys, and the next one goes in your throat."

Lysaera tossed her hair back and stalked toward Vil, arrogance and desire mingling in her eyes. "You speak so violently, Sir Knight," she said. "But are you a man of words? Or a man of action?" Her challenging smile left no question as to the type of "action" she meant, and Romik watched in horror as she reached toward his brother's groin.

Vil's hand struck out, grabbing her by the wrist and turning her in one violent motion. He shoved her at Romik and stepped back, his face deadly cold and empty.

Romik grabbed her by both shoulders. She collapsed against him with a sigh of pleasure, but before she could put her pursed lips on the flesh of his chest, he yanked her out away from him.

"You are an aberration," he said through gritted teeth. "And I've never struck a woman who wasn't armed and attacking me, but by the Red Lady's wrath, if you touch me or my brothers one more time, I swear to you, I might forget myself."

She snorted delicately and looked up at him through her lashes. "My dear Ageon," she purred. "Forgetting yourself is entirely the *point*."

Romik shook his head and turned her away from him. "Daen," he said. "Get the door."

"Gladly," Daen said, disgust and anger heavy in his tone. He spun on his heel and wrenched the door open, startling a pair of blue-and-black liveried maidservants carrying linens down the hallway. Romik felt a twinge of guilt, because he knew that witnessing their mistress being tossed out of his room was likely to have ill consequences for the girls, but he saw Vil say something in an undertone to them, and they turned and fled back the way they came.

"Do not come back here," Romik said as he dragged Lysaera toward the door. "Do not speak to me or my brothers again. And for the love of good fortune, *never* let me hear you say ill against my Bellatrix again!"

Lysaera blinked, and seemed to finally realize what was happening, because she began swatting at Romik, gouging him with her nails.

"You can't do this to me!" she shrieked. "You can't treat me like this! I'm the Lady of Brionne! You're a guest in my home! How dare you talk to me—"

At the end of his patience, he thrust her out into the hallway. She took a breath, shock interrupting her tirade for just a second before she narrowed her eyes and opened her mouth to continue.

But Romik had had enough. He slammed the door shut in her rapidly purpling face. Her shrieks did, indeed, start again, but they were soundly muffled by the heavy wooden door.

"Well," Vil said, leaning on the doorframe. "That was something."

"That was a disaster," Daen said. "You came out of the bathing room, and she was just *there*?"

"Thanks for coming to my rescue," Romik said, nodding. He let out a tiny shudder at the memory of her hands on him, and then turned to go gather up the rest of his clothes and weapons from the bathing room.

"Well, Vil heard you telling someone to get out, and the mark on our palms started to burn, so we figured you might need our assistance."

"You figured right. What a nightmare! Can you imagine growing up with a mother like that?"

"It does explain a few things about our Bella," Vil said quietly. "We need to get her out of here sooner rather than later. This incident isn't going to make her life any easier. I wonder if… It seems plausible that Lysaera could have been the one to set the bandits on her, if she hates her daughter so much."

"She certainly doesn't seem like the type to meekly sit back and let Aelys take over, as everyone seems to expect. Vil's right, we need to go. Plus, Lysaera could very well claim that you assaulted her," Daen added. "Although judging from what we heard on the way here, very few would believe it. But still, she *is* a noble lady."

"Yeah, I agree. Better if we leave now, tonight," Romik said. He closed his eyes, took a deep breath, and then shook himself. "But I don't think we can slip away until after the evening meal. Too many people around."

"You'd better go talk to Corsin," Daen said. "We can come with you as witnesses, if you want. But he is sympathetic, and he can speak to his Bella. Aerivinne, at least, seems to have some kind of control over her sister. She might be able to keep the situation contained."

"You wanted to see me, Aunt?" Aelys lingered by the door of the house's Working room, her fingers resting on the ebony wood of the frame. Despite the fact that she was a graduated Bellatrix, Aelys still felt awkward about intruding. The large, circular space had served generations of Brionne sorceresses as a laboratory, study, and practice space. She *should* have felt completely natural walking in. She'd felt fine walking into the ancient mage's study, after all. *Why do I feel unwelcome in my own home?*

"Come in, little bird!" Aerivinne called. She stood across the room at one of the many side tables and as Aelys watched, she straightened her back and smiled as she carefully marked her place in the large book she'd been reading and closed it.

Aelys took a deep breath and walked across the stone floors, weaving her way around the tables with their various bits of equipment and paraphernalia.

"I have good news," Aerivinne said, her smile growing. She reached out a hand and Aelys took it with a grateful smile of her own.

"Oh?"

"I have everything we'll need to break this *geas* you managed to blunder into."

"Oh." Aelys felt her smile falter, and forcibly returned it to her face. "That's wonderful."

"Yes. We can set those men free as early as tomorrow, if you like."

"Oh! Yes, I don't want... it wouldn't be right to keep them bound any longer than necessary." Aelys swallowed against the panic that threatened to rise up in her chest.

Aerivinne squeezed her fingers and bent her head to look closely into her niece's face. "Little bird? You aren't losing your nerve, are you?"

Aelys shook her head in the negative, not trusting herself to speak. She blinked several times, refusing to let her eyes fill.

"It's the right thing to do," Aerivinne went on. "A *geas* is forbidden magic for a reason. It isn't right to keep these men bound to you when they had no idea what was happening."

Aelys nodded again. "I know," she whispered. "I'm just going to miss them."

Aerivinne squeezed her hand again. "I know. And I did warn you... but it must be done. You agree? It must be done."

"Yes," Aelys glanced down at their joined hands, each with the Brionne family ring. "Yes," she said again, her voice stronger.

"Good," Aerivinne said. "Because there is something more I must discuss with you. I expected this reluctance you're showing... and you're doing a fine job of keeping it under control, but I can see your body's reaction to the emotional stress. Your men will have the same reluctance. It's another byproduct of the *geas* and I fear they may try to stop us tomorrow."

"I... I doubt it, Aunt. They want to be free."

"Do they? Truly? Can you tell me honestly that none of them has proposed that you just leave here with the *geas* intact? Probably swearing that they don't care why they want to be with you, just that they *do*?"

"I—" Aelys started to speak, but fell silent as Daen's earnest, half-angry pleas echoed in her memory. Vil's dark looks and Romik's jaw-clenching anger back in the Brionne camp rose up behind her eyes, and she drew in a sharp breath.

Aerivinne nodded. "I think, in order to ensure that everything goes the way it *must* go...we must be a little creative. My notes say that a *geas* of this kind may itself be the answer to the problem it presents."

"What do you mean, Aunt?"

"One of the reasons a *geas* is outlawed is because it removes the Ageon's consent. It allows you to lay a type of compulsion on them that is nigh irresistible, despite their own desires. A strong Ageon with the proper training and preparation may be able to refuse it...but your men have neither of those things."

"They are strong," Aelys protested softly.

"Of course, they are, dear one," Aerivinne said. "But none of them has spent ten years perfecting the kind of mental focus our Ageons train in, have they? And for our purposes, this is just as well. Because we need you to use this *geas* to compel them to leave you alone after tonight. It's subtler and more effective than a regular compulsion spell, so they may not even detect it, and you shouldn't need my help to Work it."

"What? Tonight?"

"Yes, little bird. Tonight. It must be tonight. If we are to be certain of success, they *cannot* see you and attempt to stop us tomorrow."

Misery rose up within Aelys, wrapping around her throat and twisting so tightly she could scarcely draw breath.

"I-I don't—"

Aerivinne patted her hand. "You don't have to do it right now," she said. "I realize that this is incredibly difficult for you. You will see. See how they behave at dinner tonight. Remember, a Bellatrix must sometimes take actions for her Ageon's own good, even if the Ageon does not like it."

Aelys sucked in another breath and nodded, letting go of her aunt's hand. "I will," she said. "And if necessary, I will speak with them. But I know they want to be free. They won't interfere."

"I hope you're right, little bird. For all of our sakes, I hope you're right."

Vil wasn't exactly sure what to expect from the evening meal. He'd rather not have gone, truth be told, but Maudren had made it clear that Aelys was expected, and neither Vil nor his brothers were about to let their Bellatrix face her mother alone.

Especially not after their encounter in Romik's bedchamber.

He snarled at that memory and turned his focus to the clothing he'd found hanging in his wardrobe. It looked like someone had done a decent job of estimating his size, for the plain black leather breeches and formal shirt looked like they'd fit. With a shrug, he stripped out of his travel gear and pulled the outfit on.

The close-woven fabric of the shirt slid softly over his skin, hugging his shoulders and biceps a bit more snugly than he'd like, but it would do. Vil glanced at the room's reflecting glass.

Good enough. I shouldn't embarrass you with my appearance, at least, Bella. I'm pleased Maudren or whoever had the good sense to choose black clothing when they stocked my room.

He shoved his feet back into his boots and shoved a hand through his hair before pulling on his leather gloves. After a moment's consideration, Vil buckled the belt carrying Pure and Profane around his waist. *I'm probably expected to be unarmed for what's essentially a family dinner, but I wouldn't put it past Lysaera to try and poison Aelys...or drug Romik and Daen...*

Without really thinking about it, Vil unsheathed Pure and twirled the dagger in his hand before resheathing it. He met his own eyes in the mirror one last time, then turned to the door to go find his brothers and their Bella.

Daen was already leaning against the stone wall of the hallway outside, and Romik was a breath behind as Vil exited his room. Like Vil, his brothers also wore simple but finely cut black shirts and leather breeches.

Like Vil, they carried the weapons they'd found in the hidden mage's study.

"I see you're both as comfortable as I am with the idea of this dinner," Vil said. Daen snorted softly and Romik shrugged.

"It didn't seem prudent to leave a magical masterwork weapon unattended, even if this is Aelys's home."

"*Especially* because this is Aelys's home," Daen added. "After today, it's clear her mother is capable of anything. Plus, if Aelys decides to . . . I don't know, forget about this place and leave, we're ready."

"My thoughts exactly," Vil said. "Make sure I touch your drinks and Aelys's before you taste them."

"Make sure—oh!" Understanding flashed over Romik's face. "Your dagger. You suspect poison?"

"I suspect everything," Vil said, giving his brother his tight, tiny smile. "That's why I'm still alive."

Romik opened his mouth to reply, but the door behind him opened and Aelys stepped out.

Vil swallowed hard and curled his hands into fists to keep himself from reaching out to her.

She wore a simply cut gown in the same dark blue as the Brionne guards' livery. Her hair fell in a white-blonde ripple to her midback, and she wore a metal circlet to keep it out of her face. The stone of her Bellatrix necklace glinted in the light from the lamps high on the wall, and Vil watched a slow flush creep up her neck and into her cheeks as she looked at the three of them.

"Bella," Daen said. His voice carried none of the rough emotion Vil felt surging along his nerves, but his hand trembled as he reached out to take her fingers. "Will we pass muster, do you think?"

"You look . . . good. Very good. You—all three of you look . . ." she trailed off and shook her head, then blinked as Daen wound her arm through hers.

"Thank you," he said. "You look beautiful too."

"Oh," she said, glancing down at her gown. She brushed a hand down her front and shrugged. "Thank you."

You're always beautiful, Bella. Savage joy stabbed through Vil as she flicked her eyes up to him. The flush on her cheeks deepened, and he lifted the corner of his mouth in a tiny smile.

That's right, my Bella. Feel that? I'm thinking about you. I'm always *thinking about you.*

"We—we should go," Aelys said, holding his gaze for a moment longer before looking over at Romik, then up to Daen.

"Lead the way, Bella," Romik said. "Daen will escort you. Vil and I are at your back."

Always.

It's one thing for my mother to ignore me, Aelys thought as Romik pulled out her chair and Daen gallantly held her hand as she took her seat. *But does she really have to pretend* none *of us exist?*

They were dining in the smaller, "family" dining room, but from the moment she'd entered the room, Aelys felt something was off. More off than usual, even. It wasn't just that she felt cut off from her Ageons. Her visceral reaction to the sight of them and theirs to her had scared her enough that she'd quietly put a mental shield in place to block the flow of their energy... but she missed it.

She missed them.

How am I going to do this? How am I going to bear letting them go?

As Daen led Aelys to her chair, Lysaera turned her head away and imperiously raised her wine goblet. Shame prickled behind Aelys's eyes and burned in her chest as she watched her mother get her drink refilled, and then promptly down half of it.

"Good evening, Mother," Aelys said while Romik pulled out her chair. She paused for a beat, but when it became apparent that Lysaera wasn't about to respond, Aelys let out a little sigh and sank into the chair. She pressed her lips together and blinked back the threatening tears of mortification before smiling up at Vil, Romik, and Daen in thanks. They nodded at her and then moved to their own seats: Vil on her left, Daen on her right, and Romik across the table from him... directly at her mother's right hand.

Oh. Oh no. Mother, please... not them. You wouldn't, would you? They're my Ageons! Even you wouldn't dare to try and force yourself on them, would you?

"Mother—" Aelys started, but the door to the dining room opened and Aerivinne swept in, followed by Corsin. Aelys looked at Romik, then at Daen, her eyes widening as a sudden panicked awkwardness stabbed through her.

"Stand up!" she whispered, ducking her head and angling her frantic words toward Vil. "You must all stand when a noble lady enters the room!"

Vil smoothly came to his feet, his motions unhurried, as if he'd always known the protocol and was simply moving slowly. Daen, too, stood, and Romik followed the merest breath later.

I should have prepared them for this. I should have taught them the etiquette required! How could I have forgotten something so simple?

"Lysaera, Aelys, good evening," Aerivinne said as she took the seat that Corsin pulled out for her. It was the seat next to Romik, putting Aerivinne directly across the table.

"Good evening, Aunt," Aelys said, hoping her voice didn't sound as desperate as she feared it did. "Good evening, Corsin," she added as he moved to the chair across from Vil.

"Bella," Corsin said with a nod. "Ageons."

"Corsin," Romik said as the men all seated themselves. Aelys's heart pounded in her chest, and that same awkward panic clawed up the inside of her throat.

At the head of the table, Lysaera let out a bitter laugh and raised her glass again. Aerivinne turned to look at her sister, her eyebrows rising. She let out a sigh and shook her head, and then gestured for the footmen to begin serving the meal.

I should have thought of that! Come on, Aelys. Focus. You're only making her drunken rudeness worse with your awkwardness. Say something!

"H-how was court?" she stammered. "So much has happened, we haven't gotten a chance to talk about it."

Aerivinne focused on Aelys and smiled a tiny smile. "It was good, little bird. Busy, of course. The Empress Regent can be very demanding of her advisors' time. But I was able to make some very promising connections, particularly as relates to your marriage—"

The silverware rattled as someone bumped the table from beneath. Aelys looked up, startled, to see Daen gripping his butter knife with white knuckles.

"Sorry," he ground out between clenched teeth.

"It's all right," Aerivinne said breezily. "As I was saying, I think we ought to have a long conversation tomorrow or the next day about some of your prospects. One in particular. I think you will be very happy, my dear."

"You're being modest, Aunt," Aelys said, her face hot with embarrassment. "I'm sure you worked on matters of much greater import than my marriage!" She could almost feel her Ageons vibrating with anger, and the furious blaze of their energy streams leaked around the edges of her mental shield. She dropped her eyes to the plate one of the footmen placed in front of her and took a second to reinforce her mental barriers.

I cannot afford to lose control here, tonight, in front of my mother and Aerivinne...not that mother is sober enough to notice!

Aelys looked up just in time to see Lysaera toss back the remainder of her wine and slam the goblet down on the table hard enough to rattle the settings again.

"Enough talk!" she said, the edge of her words just the tiniest bit slurred. "You make my head hurt."

"I suspect that's all the wine you've drunk, sister," Aerivinne said coolly, picking up her knife and beginning to cut her meat. Aelys glanced at her plate once more and blinked as she registered what they'd been served: roasted meat dressed with an herb sauce, roasted vegetables, and a fruit delicacy she'd loved as a child.

Her favorite foods.

For just a second, the head footman across the room met her eyes and inclined his head the tiniest bit.

Aelys blinked, and then flicked her eyes to as many of the other footmen as she could see without obviously turning her head. More than half of them met her eyes before returning their eyes to the correct, impassive stare their position required.

"Give me your wine," Vil said softly, drawing Aelys's attention.

"What?"

"Give me your wine, quickly. While Aerivinne is talking to Corsin and your mother is...distracted."

Confusion pinched her brows, but Aelys took the wineglass that she hadn't noticed had been filled and moved it closer to him. She watched Vil, paying close attention and still she barely saw him quickly flip his dagger—Pure, the light one—into his hand and dip its tip into her wine.

He met her eyes and gave her a tiny nod. Understanding flowed through her, and she lifted the goblet to her lips, sipping at the pure, cold water that had replaced the wine.

"Switch that with Daen's wine. He'll get Romik's," Vil whispered. "Perhaps when the footmen are pouring for your mother. Choose your moment."

Aelys wanted to nod, but Aerivinne chose that moment to look up and smile at her.

"You look lovely, Niece," she said. "I do like the simple cut of that gown. It suits you."

Lysaera snorted loudly, drawing everyone's attention as she tried and failed to smother a laugh in her once-again-full wine goblet. Aelys quickly switched her own goblet with Romik's.

"Do you have something to say, Sister?" Aerivinne asked, her tone cool and bored.

"Mmm mmh. No," Lysaera said, another laugh pushing into her words.

"You clearly do," Aerivinne said. "But I'm not going to bother pulling it out of you—"

"Of course, plain, ugly gowns suit her," Lysaera burst out, her words fully slurred this time. "*She's* plain and ugly! I don't know how I could possibly have produced something so...*dull!*"

Aelys swallowed hard against the old, familiar hurt and lifted her chin. "Mother," she said, her voice even. "Perhaps you should go lie down. Your headache—"

"Don't tell me what to do, you ugly little slut!"

Aelys closed her eyes for a heartbeat, carefully locking her emotions away. She opened her eyes to see her aunt rolling her eyes and looking disgusted as she proceeded to eat. Corsin looked at her with sympathy and laid his knife down.

"Lady Lysaera—"

"Oh, do not start, Corsin! Everyone knows my sister has no time for you. Don't come crawling to me for attention now!"

Aelys bit her lip and stared down at her plate, grateful that Corsin had deflected her mother's vitriol, but miserable that he'd taken it upon himself. Out of the corner of her eye, she registered that Romik and Vil effected another goblet switch under the cover of her mother's tirade against Corsin.

"My Lady, I think your daughter is right, perhaps you've been overcome with your headache—"

"I don't have a headache!" Lysaera screamed, banging her fists on the table. "And my *daughter* has never been right about anything in her miserable, plain, ugly, pathetic *life!*"

"*Lady Lysaera!*" Daen roared. He also slammed his hands on the table and pushed himself up to his feet. "You will *not* speak of Aelys again."

Lysaera leaned forward, putting her face close to Daen's. "Or what?" she asked, her knees buckling as she, too, tried to stand. "What are you..." She paused, licked her lips, stared at the exposed triangle of skin at Daen's throat. "...going to do to me?"

"Enough."

Aerivinne's cool command cut through the room. She lifted a hand to the head footman and beckoned him forward.

"The Lady Lysaera is overcome with a headache. Please take her back to her rooms and summon her maid."

I am the Lady of Brionne! You cannot dismiss me like a child! Lysaera howled, stamping her foot and knocking her goblet over. Wine splashed onto the table, splattering over Daen's white knuckles.

"I can when you act like one," Aerivinne said, her tone calm. "Corsin?"

"Of course, Bella," he said. He stood and joined the footmen who approached Lysaera, then helped them to bodily lift her. She struck out and flailed her arms, but Corsin and the footmen were obviously experienced with handling the Lady of Brionne's drunken antics, because they moved with an impressive efficiency and quickness.

"You can sit down now, Sir Daen," Aerivinne said in that same tone. "No one else is going to attack your Bella tonight. You might as well enjoy your dinner."

"I'm so sorr—" Aelys started to say, but Romik shot out a hand and gripped her wrist.

"Do not apologize," he said, his tone a low growl. Aelys looked up at him, realizing for the first time that he was just as furious as Daen. The moment she thought about it, her mental shield buckled under the onslaught of their anger-charged energy. All three torrents slammed into her, making her gasp out loud.

Aerivinne looked up at her, eyebrows raised. Aelys hammered her shield back into place and reached out with a shaking hand to take a sip of her water.

"Aelys," Aerivinne said softly. "You should not let her bother you."

"I know," Aelys said. In the back corner of her mind, gratitude pulsed. *Aerivinne doesn't know, she thinks I'm upset because of Mother. She doesn't know how close I came to losing control...*

"When you are married, we will have everything in place to put her aside and name you Lady of Brionne. She won't even have to live here. You can retire her to one of the other properties. Your home will finally be yours... I daresay even the servants and guards look forward to that day. And we're so close."

"I know," Aelys said again, closing her eyes against the tearing pain in her chest at the thought of how close they were. Tomorrow they would break the *geas*.

She opened her eyes to see Aerivinne's intense stare. Under the table, Vil's leg pressed against hers.

Aelys nodded. "I know," she said. "You are right."

That went about as badly as could be expected, Aelys reflected later, as she dragged her exhausted self to her room after the tense and uncomfortable meal. She'd rather expected her Ageons to follow her, but they, too, seemed preoccupied.

And no wonder, Aelys thought as she undressed and laid herself down in the unfamiliar bed. *Tomorrow, we can break the* geas *and set them free. I suppose they have things to prepare, supplies and such. Plans to make. I-I will miss them. I know they say they'll miss me, but that is probably just the* geas *talking. That's what Aerivinne says, anyway, and she's always right. I know they will be happier being free. I hope they think of me fondly, eventually . . .*

Perhaps it was these maudlin thoughts, but as Aelys pitched over the edge of exhaustion into sleep, she soon found herself dreaming about the men. Romik, smiling at her in the ancient mage's study, his eyes bright with humor and excitement as he touched her hair. Daen, laughing in the forest, teasing her, gently insisting that he would have chosen her even without the *geas*.

And Vil, her knife in the dark, with his blue eyes always watching: her, his brothers, everyone around them. Once more, in her dream, he held her body close to his, sheltering her with his cloak as her would-be attackers searched. She felt the warmth of his skin, inhaled his unique scent of clean wool and hot spice. He whispered to her, words she couldn't quite hear.

In her mind, she opened the cobblestone sluice gate, letting the dark river flow in, letting it fill up her nerve pathways with that searing, shadowy energy.

It's a dream, she reminded herself. *I can say what I want, do what I want, here in this dream.*

She heard him gasp as she reversed the flow, sending that dark torrent flowing back into him, making his body respond as if she touched him underneath his skin.

"Aelys." His rough whisper floated over her skin in the dream world.

"Vil," she said. "It was never just the *geas* for me. I wish I could tell you that. I wish you could know that every time you thought about me, every time you wanted me, I wanted you too. I'm never safer than when you're holding me with your arms like steel. I wish I could say that to you, but I've always been too much of a coward."

"Aelys," dream-Vil said, but she wasn't done.

"I should have asked you to stay with me, that night in Mageford. I wanted you. I shouldn't have, Divines know I don't have any right, but I do. I wanted your heat beside me in the dark, I never fear the shadows if I know you're there too."

Dream-Vil said nothing. Of course. Vil rarely wasted an opportunity to keep his mouth shut. Aelys let out a little laugh.

"I hate my mother," she whispered. "But I must be just like her. Because I want you. Desperately, I want you. But I want Daen and Romik just as much, in completely different ways."

"You need all of us to keep you safe." Dream-Vil's voice was low, close by, as if he'd come closer. She couldn't see him, but that wasn't unusual. He was her knife in the dark. "You're nothing like her."

She let out a laugh that was halfway to being a sob. "I do need you all," she said. "Isn't that pathetic? My mother is right about me. I'm a disast—"

His mouth came down hard on hers, as if his lips were punishing hers for their words. In the safety of her dream, Aelys let her caution go and opened her mouth, welcoming his bruising kiss and kissing him back.

"I hate the way you talk about yourself," he murmured. In the dream, his hands threaded through her hair before one of them cupped the back of her skull while the other dropped to haul her up against the rock-solid steadiness of his chest. "You're the only light in my world and you value yourself so little."

"I—"

"I cannot breathe without you, Aelys. None of us can. And as you said, it was never just the *geas*. We chose you. I chose you. I *choose* you." He bent and pressed his lips to the pulse in her throat, just below her jaw, making her shiver.

I want this. I want him. He chooses me. He said he chooses me...

It's not real. The geas *could be driving him to say that. I don't know if it* can *be real.*

Because of the geas.

Her eyes opened to darkness and the heat of his touch. She couldn't pretend it was a dream any longer.

"Vil, I—"

"No more apologies, Aelys," he demanded against her skin. "No more, not between you and me. Not ever. You said you wanted me. I want you. Don't deny us any longer."

It was wrong. She knew it was wrong, and yet, her hands reached up under the hem of his shirt to flatten against the strong, lean muscles of his back. He exhaled against her skin, igniting tremors that ran the length of her spine.

"Vil—"

Vil took her mouth again with a low moan, his lips and tongue tangling with hers in a heated frenzy of need. His arms tightened, crushing her against his chest for just a moment before he stopped and leaned back enough to look with blazing intent into her eyes.

"I choose you," he said. "And Daen chooses you. And Romik. We are yours, and you are ours. Do you understand me, Aelys? You're the fire under my skin and you are *ours*."

Aelys gaped at his intensity, unable to speak through the overwhelming desire and emotion that flooded through her. Vil leaned forward and kissed her hard and fast on her mouth one more time, before grabbing her hand and pulling her from the warmth of her bed.

"Come on," he said. "I'll take you to the others. Just grab your boots and cloak, we've already got other clothing for you packed."

"P-packed?" Aelys stammered as Vil swept her up against him and flung a cloak around her shoulders.

"Here," he said, putting her boots in front of her. Bewildered, she stepped into first one, and then the other before he buried his hands once more in her hair and hauled her against him for another hard, fast kiss.

Her head spun. He let go of her so quickly she would have stumbled had he not immediately grabbed her hand and pulled her after him out into the hallway.

"Oh, thank all the Divines," Daen breathed as she emerged from her bedchamber. Vil didn't let go of her hand, but sort of thrust her forward so that Daen, too, could wrap his arms around her and lift her off her feet. He buried his face in her shoulder, and she inhaled deeply, taking in his scent of sun-dappled leaves and growing things.

"No time," Romik growled from behind her. Daen set her back down on her feet, his hands lingering on her as she turned to face her third Ageon.

"Wh-what is happening?" She finally managed to force the words out through the fog of desire and confusion that wreathed her mind.

"We're going," Vil said, and once more pulled her into motion. Daen let her go, and he and Romik took up positions directly behind her as the group of them ran toward the stairs leading down to the bailey.

"G-going? Going where?"

"Away from here," Romik said, his gravelly voice pitched low.

"Wait! No, that's not right!" Aelys skidded to a stop and jerked her hand free of Vil's grip, causing Romik and Daen to nearly run right into her. "I can't leave! This is my home. My place is here."

"We're your home, Bella," Daen said, smiling at her and reaching out to touch a strand of her hair like he often did. "We've seen how they treat you here. Your mother tried to seduce Romik to hurt you. Your aunt only wants to use you to replace her."

An old and familiar pain lanced through her at her mother's betrayal. Unfortunately, Aelys felt exactly zero surprise.

"My mother is ... complicated," she said, closing her eyes briefly to avoid throwing herself into one of their embraces again. "But my aunt has always had my best interests at heart! She's been extremely kind and very patient with me, all things considered."

"She treats you like a child, or a pawn," Romik growled, his eyes angry and hurt. "You deserve better."

Pain wrapped around Aelys's throat and sent spikes of agony down into her chest. *This. This is what you've done by indulging in your stupid emotions. By indulging the geas, Aelys. You've messed everything up. Again.*

"I have everything I could ever want," she lied, tears filling her eyes. "H-how can I possibly ask for more?"

"You don't," Vil said, his voice low and intense, as it had been in her dream that wasn't a dream. "You don't have everything you want."

"I—"

"You want power. *We* give you power."

"But—" The tears overflowed her lower lashes, streaking down her face. The pain in her throat, in her chest, constricted. She gasped, panting against the onslaught of agony.

"You want us. We chose you. We will always choose you."

"Vil, I—"

He stepped closer to her, staring down into her tear-wet eyes. "We need you," he whispered. "Come with us."

"I—" She wavered, her body drawn to him even as her mind, her duty shrieked at her that she couldn't just leave. *Where would I go?*

With them.

What would I do?

Be with them.

But would it be real? How would I know?

"Aelys?"

Aerivinne's voice carried up to them from the stairwell, causing them to turn in that direction. Lantern light painted the stonework of the stairs below and started to climb.

Aelys looked back at Vil, his blue eyes stark in his shadowed face.

She looked at Daen, hope and hurt simmering in his expression.

She looked at Romik, his face turning to stone.

"Someone is coming," she said, fear surging within her as she spoke. "You need to go."

"Aelys—" She wasn't sure which one of them said it. Maybe they all did. She cut them off with a slashing motion of her hand and reached for her power.

"No. I need you to go. I need you to *leave me alone.*" As she whispered the harsh words, she pushed a knife's edge of power through all three of their energy streams in her mind, making her demand into a compulsion. Then, with a savage, wrenching thought, she slammed the mental sluice gates shut, cutting herself off from all but the barest trickle of power from them.

"Aelys, is that you, darling?"

Aelys closed her eyes and turned back toward the stairwell, to the sound of her aunt's voice. To her duty and her future.

"Yes, Aunt," she called, walking toward the stairwell and peering down into its spiral.

"Little bird, what are you still doing awake?" Aerivinne asked, looking up at Aelys as she climbed. "I thought you were tired."

"I was, but I didn't eat much at dinner, and I got hungry. I was debating going down to the kitchen to see if there was something available."

"Darling, it's very late. You don't want to disturb the kitchen staff unnecessarily. Tomorrow is an important day, and you will need your rest. I came up here to ensure those Ageons of yours weren't keeping you up."

"N-no," Aelys said, backing up as her aunt joined her on the landing, and then falling into step beside her as Aerivinne headed back down the empty hallway toward Aelys's assigned room. "Not at all."

"Good," Aerivinne said. "They seem like fine men, for all they're a little rough. I'll see to it that they're well taken care of after tomorrow."

"M-mother was awful tonight."

Aerivinne let out a long-suffering sigh. "Your mother is sometimes the bane of my existence. Aelys. I probably shouldn't talk that way about her to you, but you're an adult now. You deserve to know. She's not fit to be the Lady of our House. I ... well. We will talk more about this later. Don't worry about your men, I will make sure they are taken care of." She reached out and touched Aelys's cheek.

"You look tired, little bird, like you've been weeping. Don't worry. Everything will work out for the best. Get some sleep. Tomorrow will solve everything."

Aelys nodded, and then gave her aunt a watery smile before letting herself be ushered back into her room.

She laid back down on the bed and closed her once-more-teary eyes, immediately wishing herself back in the dream that wasn't a dream.

Between one sob and the next, Aelys fell asleep.

CHAPTER NINE

AELYS WOKE DURING THE FIRST GRAY OF FALSE DAWN.

"Waking" was a bit of a misnomer, really. The truth was that she'd slept fitfully all night, haunted by the memory of the hurt on her Ageons' faces. In her mind, she heard Aerivinne telling her that sometimes a Bellatrix had to do what was best for her Ageon, whether he liked it or not...

As soon as the first rays of sunlight broke over the horizon, Aelys slipped out of her bed and dressed herself. She stepped out into the hallway and hesitated for a moment before deciding that she needed some steadying advice. Moving as quietly as possible, she tiptoed to the stairwell and headed down a level to her aunt's quarters.

Early as it was, however, it seemed Aerivinne had already awakened and left. Aelys spent the next two hours looking for her. She peeked in the breakfast room, the library, even down in the kitchen garden before finding her aunt already up in the Working room at the top of the stairs.

Unfortunately for Aelys, her mother had gotten there first.

"You're just jealous. You've always been jealous because I was the prettier one!"

Aerivinne's cold, mocking laugh echoed through the half-ajar door into the wide outer chamber just as Aelys reached the top of the stairs. She froze, one hand on the stone wall, and listened.

"If believing that helps you cope with being the most worthless Lady a house could possibly have, then fine, Lysaera. I genuinely do not care."

"Why can't you just order them given to me instead of executed?" Aelys heard her mother whine again.

"Why under the two moons would I? I'm breaking their *geas* today! Do you understand what that means? No, of course not. You're too stupid and self-indulgent to open a book. The *geas* is an ancient and powerful magical bond that your bumbling fool of a daughter *accidentally* laid upon them. We cannot have that news getting out. It's unfortunate, but it's the only way forward. They have to die, and as quickly and mercifully as possible after the *geas* is broken. But they saved my niece's life, I'm not going to repay them by making them your sex slaves! Besides, breaking the *geas* may very well break their minds."

"I don't care about their *minds*," Lysaera snarled. "It's their *bodies* I want!"

"You are disgusting. You should be worried about negotiating Aelys's marriage settlement! When I break this *geas*, I will burn what little magic she has right out of her, so we will need to ensure that her prospective husbands understand that it will not affect her ability to breed true . . . at least, it should not. We will have to make sure we admit no doubt."

"Perhaps *you* can have no doubt about the waste of air I birthed. She's so *pathetic*!"

A ringing slap, followed by the sound of her mother crying out, marred the bright sunshine that streamed through the slit window to her left. Aelys stood rooted in horror, her knuckles turning white as she steadied herself on the stone wall of the chamber.

"If she is pathetic, you idiot woman, it's because *we* made her that way! You were a horrible, spoiled child as a girl, and you've never grown out of it. I should have had you strangled as soon as Aelys was born. I will always regret letting you live to abuse that girl her whole life. Your constant ridicule has stunted her emotional growth and denied her any chance to develop any confidence at all!"

"Me? What about you?" Lysaera's voice sounded thick with tears and vitriol. "I wasn't the one who found an ancient, forbidden compulsion spell and used it to put a block on her ability to channel magical energies! If anyone has held her back, it's been you!"

"I know," Aerivinne said, her tone low with something that

might have been regret. "I know, and every day I regret the necessity for it. She was born with *such* power... but someone has to bear children for this house! I *cannot*, as you well know."

"Oh, yes, poor, barren Aerivinne with her dysmen-whatever. How unfortunate with all your power, you can't even heal your own body or handle your woman's monthly flow."

Aerivinne laughed. "Such ignorance. *Dysmenorrheal bleeding* is a *disease*. Magic cannot heal diseases; they are too complicated. But I don't know why I'm bothering to explain this to you. You are clearly too stupid to comprehend even the most basic tenets of magical theory."

"I am the Lady of this House!"

Another ringing slap, followed by another whining yelp. "And see how you've brought us to the brink of disaster! Thanks to your stupid excesses, your lack of discernment, and your *incredible* self-indulgence, not only have you lost your husband, but you cannot conceive ever again! I really hope fucking that dock whore was worth your marriage, your House's future, and your only child's happiness, Lysaera."

"I don't care if she's happy."

"That was always obvious. If only our mother had had another choice between idiot you and barren me! But she did not, and neither do we. Like our mother, we must do what is necessary to ensure our House's future. Now get up off the floor and get out of my sight. I need to prepare for today's Working."

Fear lanced through Aelys like lightning, bringing one thought to the forefront amid the swirl of questions and betrayal. *I can't let her see me. I can't let anyone see me here!*

Without another thought, with only animal instinct to guide her way, Aelys spun back to the stairs and flung herself headlong down them.

My Ageons, I have to get to them. I have to warn them!

Vil hadn't been sleeping when the sun came up.

He'd done his best to get a little sleep the night before, but the turmoil in his mind made true rest an impossibility. Every time he closed his eyes, he saw Aelys's tear-wet eyes, heard her devastating words again.

I need you to leave me alone.

He ached to go to her. He *could not* make his body move in

that direction. Every time he tried, his vision spiraled to black and he lost his balance like a drunkard. He'd even tried to push through it and ended up unconscious just inside his chamber door.

Experimenting in the night had showed that he could go to Romik's room, or Daen's, but if he even so much as turned toward Aelys's door, the blackness spun in from the edges of his vision.

So, when he heard someone tiptoeing past his room at dawn, those same black spirals in his mind told him *exactly* who was sneaking by...and not stopping to talk to him or his brothers.

It seems you still want us to leave you alone, hmm, Bella? Afraid we'll kidnap you away from your nightmare of a family?

The thought sounded so bitter in his head, Vil wondered if he hadn't been spending too much time with Daen. His ex-Forester brother had completely closed inward and refused to speak in more than one-syllable grunts...and even then, only to him or Romik. Romik was little better. The entire time Vil had been in his room last night, the warrior had kept one hand on the hilt of his short sword, and his face had carried a bright red flush of anger.

A half hour later, a short, staccato knock shattered the circular path of Vil's thoughts. He leapt to his feet, drew his daggers, and stepped back into the shadow behind the door before calling permission to enter.

Corsin strode in, letting the door fall heavily closed behind him before turning unerringly to face Vil—and the daggers Vil had leveled at his vulnerable midsection.

"Something wrong?" Corsin asked. He smiled tightly, but his eyes held a glassy look Vil hadn't seen in him before.

"You tell me," Vil said. The other Ageon let out a sigh and shook his head.

"Are you always this paranoid?"

"I'm still breathing, aren't I?"

"I have to give you a message from Aelys."

Vil wrapped his mind in ice and let it freeze his body solid, lest he tremble and give too much away to this man he dared not trust.

"Why would she send a message through you? I'm her Ageon." *For now.* "Why not come herself?"

"She cannot see you right now," Corsin said. "She is afraid to anger Aerivinne. But she wants to talk with you—all of you—in the library in an hour. Can you gather your brothers and be there?"

Suspicion warred with a sudden bright flare of hope in Vil's mind. He swallowed hard and nodded. Corsin returned his nod, and then turned his back on Vil—daggers and all—and left.

Vil waited for a two hundred count before he moved. He took a moment to grab his travel pack and the pouch of Imperials he'd found in the chest in his room. He put the pack on under his cloak, and stashed the Imperials in an inner pocket before he eased out into the hallway and headed toward Romik's room. A glance at Aelys's door caused no reaction, which meant she hadn't returned after sneaking out that morning. He tapped lightly on Romik's door and let himself in.

Daen was there, sitting on the floor at the foot of Romik's huge bed, his head in his hands. Romik himself stood by the hearth, sharpening his short sword.

"Corsin came to see me," Vil said without preamble. "He said he had a message from Aelys."

Daen's head shot up, his reddened eyes bright with hope and anger.

"Why didn't she just come talk to us?" Romik asked.

"My question as well. He said she is afraid to anger her aunt, but that she wants to see us in the library in an hour. I don't trust it—or him—but..."

"We have to go," Daen said. "If she's going to be there, we have to be there. We said we'd always choose her."

"We did," Vil said. "And I mean to go, but I expect a trap."

"Of course it's a trap," Romik ground out. "Hope is always a trap." But he sheathed his short sword and turned his body toward the door. "When do we go?"

"As soon as we get our things together. Gather up money, weapons, whatever we might need if we're leaving in a hurry—or fighting our way out."

Daen nodded, and then pushed up to his feet. Without a word to either of his brothers, he pushed past Vil and headed to his room. Vil met Romik's eyes and saw the worry therein.

"This is breaking him," Romik said softly.

"I know how he feels," Vil said. "I—I can't think. My mind just tumbles."

"Mine too. We'll find her. And even if she still wants us to leave her alone—"

"We'll make sure she's safe. Somehow," Vil finished for him. He reached out a hand to clasp his brother's, and the mark in his palm burned first hot, then icy cold. A dark presence filled Vil's mind. Not the black swirls of pain from earlier, but the cool darkness of deep, concealing shadow. It filled his body, stilling the frantic circling of his thoughts and granting a deep, spreading peace that saturated his being.

Vil blinked, and the darkness was gone. But the peace, the stillness remained.

"What was that?" Romik asked, his eyes wide. "It felt like the Red Lady herself burned my rage away. I-I can think now!"

"I— Me too. I suspect our Divine patronesses have decided to support us in this endeavor. We should go find Daen. He could use the Green Lady's touch, I'll warrant."

"What did you feel?" Romik asked as they turned to follow their brother to his room.

"I felt ... Darkness. Safe, soothing darkness. Like I was hiding in deepest shadow while She quieted my mind."

Romik eyed him sidelong as he slung his travel pack and adjusted his weapons around it. "Your Dark Lady sounds as frightening as you can be, my brother."

"Where do you think I get it?" Vil asked. Romik snorted softly, and then pulled open the heavy wooden door of Daen's room.

When they explained to him what had happened, Daen thrust his open hand out and demanded one of them take it. Romik did, and Daen drew in a deep, shuddering breath and then blew it out before opening his eyes.

"Better?" Vil asked.

"Much," Daen said, and even his voice sounded more tranquil. "It was like I was floating down a mountain stream, with the shadow of the leaves over me, and the water washing away all the ... chaos." He let go of Romik's hand. "Thank you."

"Thank your Green Lady," Vil said. "Our Divines obviously want us to be clearheaded as we walk into this probable trap. So, let's oblige them, yes?"

"Absolutely," Daen said. He finished gathering a few items, then nodded that he was ready. Vil took out Profane and quickly reopened the scratch on the backs of their wrists. Then, the three of them departed as one unit for the famous Brionne library.

Aelys burst through the wooden door of Daen's room, her heart pounding against her ribcage. She looked wildly around.

"Daen?" she called, to no answer.

He must be with one of the others. Vil is next door—

She turned, her slippers sliding out from under her and nearly toppling her on her face as she changed direction on the treacherous, bare stone floor. She yanked the door open and threw herself into the hallway, and then slammed into the door leading to Vil's room.

"Vil?"

Silence, broken only by the frenzied sound of her panting breaths. Dread rose in her, but she shook her head and pushed it aside.

They must be with Romik.

Once more, she fled into the hallway and once more she careened into her Ageon's room, calling out in a voice broken by her ever-present weakness.

"R-Romik? Vil? D-Daen?"

The bed was made. She was pretty sure the staff hadn't been in here to clean it yet. She slowed, walking toward the wardrobe where his clothes should have hung. With shaking hands, she opened it.

Only the finery remained. The new, sturdy travel clothes that Maudren had had altered to fit the men were gone. As was the travel pack.

As were any weapons.

They're gone. They're safe.

Aelys felt her legs give out and she stumbled, falling to her knees on the cold, unyielding floor. Relief followed by agony swept through her, taking her breath and leaving her gasping like a fish in the bottom of a boat. Slowly, she bent forward, collapsing inward until her forehead rested on the floor as tidal waves of betrayal broke over her, one after the other.

My mother hates me.

My aunt stunted me.

And lied to me.

She's planning to take what little magic remains to me.

I'm alone.

Alone.

Aelys opened her mouth in a silent scream, feeling her vocal cords strain to produce even the tiniest bit of sound to acknowledge the soul-rending grief tearing through her. But she'd conditioned herself, over decades of disappointments, to cry silently. Her heart felt like it was tearing itself from her chest, and even if she'd wanted to, she couldn't produce a peep.

Eventually, her wracking, shuddering sobs slowed, and then stilled. She remained curled in a ball on the floor of Romik's bedchamber, her mind drifting over the black abyss of loss in her mind.

The cold of the stone wrapped around her, seeped into her skin, ran along her nerves and sinews.

She took one breath. Then another.

I am alone.

Slowly, she pushed herself up to sit, then used the bedpost to steady herself as she stood. An eerie calm settled over her, soaked through her being, filling in behind the wake of her grief-ridden storm of emotion.

Alone.

Unprotected.

But for the first time, unafraid.

I know what I have to do, she thought as she turned to look at her face in the small, polished bronze mirror that hung near the wardrobe. No surprise that grief ravaged her complexion, made her eyes puffy and red. But for once, her appearance didn't matter.

My choice. Mother and Aerivinne took away my choices for too long. I took away my Ageons' choices when I bound them without them fully understanding what it meant.

Without me *fully understanding what it meant.*

I have to set them free.

I have to reclaim my choices.

Me. Alone.

Slowly, Aelys straightened her shoulders and lifted her head. Crying her broken heart out had exhausted her, and she hadn't exactly slept well the night before. She lifted her hands to push her tangled hair back from her face and caught sight of the triple band that circled her wrist. She froze, her eyes tracing the colored lines: black, red, green.

For just a second, she ran her fingertips over them, and then forced her hands back to her sides.

This is my choice. Mine alone.

With this mantra echoing through her head, Aelys turned and went back across the hallway to her room. She dressed herself in a simple gown in deep midnight blue. It doubled as a travel gown, for it featured a cutaway front designed to be worn over women's riding breeches, and most importantly, she could get into it without the help of a maid.

With this, a pair of black leather breeches, and her boots, she was almost ready. She took extra care with her hair, braiding it up in a style she'd learned from Myara. She placed her Bellatrix necklace at her throat, and her Brionne sigil ring on her finger.

Lastly, she gathered up some of her favorite pieces of jewelry and all of the Imperials she had stored in her strongbox. She bundled these into a packet and ran her fingers over the magical seam in her newly cleaned and mended Bellatrix cloak to stash them away. Something crinkled as she dropped the coins and jewels into the inner pocket.

The correspondence from the Mageford job! I . . . perhaps they will not want to see me, afterward, but if I can get this to the trader, Gormren, then they will at least be able to collect on that fee. I will send one of our House couriers with it and then . . .

She swirled the cloak around her shoulders and fastened it at her throat.

Then I will go see my aunt.

"Aelys! There you are, little bird!"

Aelys turned to pull her door closed behind her, and to give herself time to school her facial expression. She'd no sooner stepped out into the hallway than Aerivinne emerged from the stairwell, her smile bright.

"Were you going out, darling?" Aerivinne asked.

"I-I'm a little nervous," Aelys replied. She didn't have to fake the tremor in her voice. "I thought a short ride might settle my nerves."

"Darling, we don't have time for that. But no need to be nervous. All is in readiness. Come with me to the Working room. Let us break this *geas* of yours so that we might all be about the business of building your future, yes?" Aerivinne looped her arm through Aelys's and steered her deftly toward the stairwell.

How is it possible she sounds just as cheerful and loving as she always has? Aelys wondered. *Is this really the woman who plans to burn my magic out, to murder my Ageons? At least they've gone. They must be safe. Even if she sends men after them, Vil's stealth, Daen's woodcraft, and Romik's prowess will be enough to see them safe. I hope!*

"Oh, you *are* nervous, poor thing." Aerivinne patted her hand as they ascended the stairs toward the Working room. "You needn't be, you know. It's not a difficult Working, just a finicky one. Well within my capabilities. You can trust me, little bird. I'll keep you safe."

Aelys nodded, not trusting herself to speak. She remained silent the rest of the way to the Working room, letting Aerivinne lead her into the great chamber and up to one of the tables set up in the center. The table was bare, save for an open book in the center.

"Now," Aerivinne said. "Stand right there, please. Perfect. Can you see the text in that book? It contains the incantation to break the *geas*. I've marked the relevant parts. Go ahead and read it silently first."

Aerivinne stepped back and away from Aelys and circled the table to approach the great empty hearth on the other side. Aelys leaned forward and let her eyes skim over the letters inked on the page in front of her. It was Bellene, of course, but her perusal of the texts in the unknown mage's study had sharpened her already good command of the ancient language.

Sever these tethers and fly from me. By my strength of will, I set you free.

"You may not recognize the language . . . or perhaps you do. You always did well in history, didn't you? It's Bellene, and like most Bellenic magic, it's just a matter of saying the words and imbuing them with power in your mind. I doubt you have enough power on your own, so I will link with you, pushing power into you as if I were healing you."

Ah, so that's how you plan to do it, Aelys thought. *You're going to attempt to overload me with energy and let the backlash burn out the parts of me that sense and channel energy.*

"I'll give you a moment to read it through a few times while I light this fire. You know I never let servants in here, and it's gotten a little chilly. You will want to have the pronunciation quite correct, so don't be afraid to practice."

Aelys lifted the sleeve of her gown and bared the triple bracelet on her wrist. She took a deep breath, and then turned her eyes back to the page in front of her.

"Sever these tethers," she whispered. As she spoke, Aelys pulled her power, wreathing each word with the blazing bright energy. She visualized the sluice gates that led to the energy flows between her and her Ageons. She visualized them dissolving, disappearing as the magic-charged words excised the flows from her mind.

"And fly from me." She pictured the remains of the flows morphing, changing. Romik's red current swirled, coalesced into the shape of a great winged griffin. Daen's green water rose up to take the shape of a massive hunting hawk, and Vil's dark river melded into a wide-winged bat.

"By my strength of will, I set you free." As Aelys breathed the last of the words, the animals in her mind's eye all turned to look at her with eyes that mirrored her own. Then, moving as one, as the men had so often moved to protect her, the griffin, the hawk, and the bat all launched into flight. One breath, one downstroke of red, green, black wings, and they disappeared from her mind's eye.

Aelys swallowed hard, locked her legs to keep her knees from buckling, and looked down at her wrist again.

Bare. Unblemished.

Free. You're all free. And so am I.

"There we go!" Aerivinne said. She turned back to the table, as flames crackled to life behind her.

"Now, shall we—"

"Aunt?"

Aerivinne looked up. "What is it, little bird?"

"Why haven't you told me that you intend to burn out my magic?"

Aerivinne froze for a long moment, her eyes boring into Aelys's. A muscle in her jaw flexed, and then she looked down at her hands, which she clasped together.

"Because I didn't think you needed to know," she finally answered.

"How could you possibly think I didn't need to know that?" Aelys asked, and for the first time that day, her voice held the barest whisper of heat.

"Because in the end, what does it matter?" Aerivinne cried as she looked up to face her niece. "You never had much magic anyway, Aelys! You were always going to come home, get married, lead this House and raise the next generation of Brionne sorceresses! That is your duty and your destiny: to protect the legacy of this House!"

"My duty?" Aelys asked, letting a small smile curve her lips. "My *destiny*? According to whom, Aunt? You? When you Worked a block upon my ability to channel power *in my infancy*?"

Aerivinne paled but drew herself up straight and squared her shoulders. Aelys recognized it as the same mannerism she, herself, used when steeling herself for something unpleasant, and for the first time in her life, she realized that she hated her aunt.

"What I did to you was not fair," Aerivinne said lowly. "But it was *necessary* for the good of this House."

"I was an infant! I've spent my whole life believing that I was worthless because *you* decided my life's choices for me!"

"We don't all get to have choices, little bird. That is what being an adult is. I did what I had to do to protect the Brionne legacy. In time, you will see that."

And Aerivinne struck.

Because Aelys was watching for it, she'd seen how her aunt's fingers tightened in their grip on each other, so she was ready when a stream of lightning arced through the air toward her.

Shield! she thought, visualizing the same barrier that she'd used in her graduation exams at school. Only this time, instead of a mere trickle of power, a full azure torrent of energy flooded into her mind, turning the air around her the same bright blue as her eyes.

Mine! She exulted in wonder and sudden, savage joy. There was no block, no restriction as she pulled the copious energy in the room through her *own* mind and used it to create a shield that even her powerful aunt couldn't break. *All mine! I—in the tavern, I truly did it! I broke through and the block is gone!*

"You broke my compulsion block!" Aerivinne gasped. "How did you—it doesn't matter. You can't hold a shield forever, Aelys!" The lightning blazed brighter, and tendrils of flame leapt from the hearth along the wall to tangle in amongst the jagged, blindingly bright bolts that seared through the air.

Aelys flexed her shoulders and siphoned off more of the magical energy pooling in the room. *Maybe not,* she thought to her aunt. *But I don't have to let you take from me so easily. Not now, not ever again!*

Her shield turned a deeper blue, helping to protect her eyes from the blaze of her aunt's fury as she held steady under the onslaught.

Daen held on to the feeling of the Green Lady's grace like a drowning man holds on to a piece of driftwood. Focus had been a part of his life since he was a young child, drawing a child-sized bow under Bormer's watchful eye. He'd mastered the breath techniques, the visualization, the trick of stilling his body in order to bring his mind to the clear, calm place where he could pinpoint his target and fire.

None of that had helped.

When Aelys had ordered them to leave her alone, he'd rebelled. His mind had screamed in denial, and he'd done everything he could to fight against it. But her power bound him to obey, and the chaos that ensued within him left him unmoored and drowning in a maelstrom of emotion. He'd tried everything to bring his thoughts back under control, but nothing had worked until his brother took his hand and first red fire, and then cool green silence swept through his body.

Then, finally, he could think again. He could start to *plan* again. So, he'd gathered his gear and followed his brothers to this room where Aelys had spent her childhood hiding from the notice of her beastly mother.

Aelys . . .

Daen wrenched his mind away from her and focused on the sensation of cool, green shade under spreading leaves. *I can't think directly about her. She is coming to talk to us. I will see her then. And then—*

No. He dared not think about what he would do when she returned to them, lest the Green Lady's calm dissipate, leaving him at the mercy of his chaotic feelings once again. To distract himself, he looked up and around, taking in the environment of the vaunted Brionne library.

The room itself was surprisingly airy, thanks to the four large, arched windows that faced the southern view into the valley. That vista alone was impressive, and Daen took a moment to identify the road they'd ridden into the keep. He also noted a half-dozen thinner tracks leading into the forest that might be useful in an escape . . . should one be needed.

He turned away from the window before that thought could develop further and considered the interior of the room. Floor-to-ceiling bookcases lined the other three walls, all of them crammed to overflowing with books of various sizes and colors. At first, he wondered how one would possibly access the books on the highest shelves, but then he noticed that the bookcases were broken into sections. In between two sections, what at first appeared to be a bit of decorative woodwork turned out to be a ladder of sorts, with hand- and footholds that would allow a person to climb to the top and remove whatever book they liked. He walked over and ran his hand up one of these ladder sections.

"Interesting solution," Vil murmured as he came up behind him. "You'd have to be careful not to break your neck on the way back down with a book in your hand."

"I think that's what this platform is for," Daen said, pointing to the slim shelf on the edge of the ladder section. He pushed it up, and it rose smoothly, as if it were on oiled tracks. "Stack your books here, and then push the platform down as you descend."

"Clever," Vil said. "I wonder if—"

Daen never found out what Vil wondered in that moment, because his wrist erupted in fire. He let out a gasp and snatched his hand away from the wall, pushing his sleeve up to expose the blue band around his wrist.

The blue band that blurred, then steadily dissipated, like ink washing away in the rain.

"Darkness," Vil hissed between clenched teeth. Daen looked at him in growing horror and saw the light, bright blue in his brother's eyes bleed away, leaving his natural dark blue irises the same color they'd been when they were boys.

"Your eyes," Romik said, sounding sick. "Daen, your eyes are green again."

Daen glanced at his bare wrist, at the restored eyes of his brothers, and a leaden, icy dread settled deep in his stomach.

"Aelys," he whispered, already reaching for his slung bow.

Romik ripped both his short sword and The Naked Mirror from their sheaths and Daen saw Pure glittering in Vil's off hand as he snatched at the library door. It rattled but didn't open.

Locked.

"The trap," Romik growled. Vil nodded, and sheathed Pure as he drew out his lockpicks with his other hand. Daen nocked an arrow and held it low as Vil worked, and within a few agonizing heartbeats, the door clicked and swung open.

"Me first," Romik said. "Stay close. Daen, watch our rear. Vil, you get Aelys, keep her safe."

"Do you know where she is?" Daen asked, noticing that he no longer had to fight for his focus. Something had shifted, but he refused to think about what.

"Her aunt's Working room, if I had to guess," Vil said. "She's broken the *geas*, and that's where they were going to do that."

Together, they stepped out of the library door. A shout echoed down the corridor to their right.

Daen turned and saw a group of six Brionne guards charging down the hallway at them, swords bared, eyes glassy. He let fly, and the arrow took the lead man high in his chest. The Brionne guard stumbled and went down, blood spilling from his mouth as his fellows high-stepped over him.

Romik let out a growl and lunged forward as Daen nocked another arrow and fired. This one caught one of the rearmost men in the cheek, and he, too, fell, spinning with the force of the shot and knocking into the men in front of him, throwing them off balance and onto Romik's flashing blades.

Daen nocked and fired again, hit again, and then, just like that, it was over. All of the Brionne guards who'd attacked them lay injured in the hallway awash with blood. Romik had taken the sword arm off one of them just below the shoulder and stabbed another in the armor gap beneath his armpit. The remaining man lay screaming on the floor, his hands reaching spasmodically at the backs of his knees, where Daen recognized Vil's signature hamstringing slash.

Daen nocked another arrow and held it ready while Romik grabbed his belt and tied it around the bloody stump of his assailant's arm.

"You're close to bleeding out," Romik said. "Should I let you? Why did you attack us?"

"Bella Aerivinne," the wounded man whispered. Daen could see the haze of pain had replaced the glassy blankness in his eyes. "Said you needed to die quickly. To keep the secret. She... compelled us."

Romik tied off the makeshift tourniquet with a sharp yank, and the man let out a cry before his eyes rolled back in his head and he slumped to the ground.

A clatter and a gasp came from behind Daen. He spun, drawing. A woman wearing maids' livery and carrying a tray of dishes let out a tiny scream and froze, her eyes wide.

"These men are badly wounded," Romik said, standing up and wiping off his blades. "Go get Maudren and the guards captain. You may be able to save their lives. Run!"

The maid dropped her tray with a crash and spun, catching up her skirts and running in the other direction.

Daen looked at Vil, then at Romik, who nodded.

"Come on," he said. "We don't have much time. We need to find her."

Together, the three of them stepped past the carnage and made their way to the stairwell without further incident. Daen felt every nerve on high alert as they ascended.

At the top, the stairs opened up into a wide stone area with no furniture. A single wooden door stood in the far wall.

Corsin stood before the door. He leveled his sword at them over the rim of his round shield.

"I cannot let you past. You must not interfere," he said, his voice hard, his eyes glassy.

"Corsin," Romik called out. "Our Bella is in there. We have to protect her."

"I cannot let you."

And with that, he charged at them. Romik met his charge, his two blades clanging against Corsin's sword and shield. Daen lunged to the side, looking for an opening into which he could fire. Vil, too, dodged to the side, diving for the floor in a rolling maneuver designed to get him closer to the Ageon's vulnerable legs.

But Corsin was *fast*, and much more skilled than the guardsmen they'd faced downstairs. Metal rang against metal as he and Romik feinted and parried, and Daen felt sweat beginning to bead his brow as he tried to move with them, seeking his shot.

Vil threw one of his knives at Corsin's head. It didn't really have a chance of hurting him, but it did cause Corsin to twist away while parrying Romik's attack, leaving his shield side momentarily exposed.

There! Daen let fly, and his arrow arced the short distance toward Corsin's thigh. Corsin snapped his shield down at the last second to deflect it, but the motion took him off balance and Romik brought The Naked Mirror down on the rim of the shield, knocking it further out of the way. He followed up with a thrust that buried his short sword deep in the other man's gut.

Corsin jerked, and blood welled up and spilled out of his mouth as he collapsed slowly into Romik.

"I didn't want...I'm sorry," Corsin whispered wetly. Daen slung his bow and went to lift the Ageon off his brother. "I am...compelled."

"That's what the men downstairs said," Romik replied, his chest heaving. "You're badly hurt, Ageon. We need to get you to your Bella."

"She's inside. With Aelys. I can't let you—"

"You can't stop us," Daen said. He slung Corsin's arm over his shoulder and dragged him toward the Working room. "We're all going in."

Aelys felt her shield begin to contract around her. With a snarl, she pulled more energy through her system and funneled it into the barrier around her. The blue tinge to the air around her flared aquamarine, and then deepened to a cobalt hue.

"You're getting weaker, little bird," Aerivinne called out, her voice tight with strain. "You can't possibly hope to withstand me for much longer."

"Really, Aunt?" Aelys tossed back. "I feel fine. *You*, on the other hand, sound as if you're trying to lift something far too heavy for you. Too bad you've neglected your Ageon for too long; if he really loved you, perhaps he'd be here to help you. But I suppose you're too selfish to really love anyone other than yourself and your own power."

Aerivinne threw back her head and laughed, delight and harshness commingling in the sound. "You're very cute, Aelys. I appreciate the cleverness in trying to insult me so that my attack falters. I assure you, there's nothing you can say that will save you. I *will* do what's necessary to protect my House."

"You mean you'll do what *you* think is necessary! No matter what the consequences to anyone else!"

"Why should I care about the consequences to anyone else?" The shield began to contract again, and Aelys clenched her jaw against the strain of holding it.

"No one else matters, little bird," Aerivinne went on, her voice firming and steadying with every word. "You have no *idea* what

I've given up in my life for the benefit of our family. You call me selfish, yet you fail to understand one simple principle: only House Brionne matters. Not you, not me, not anyone else. Only the House, and our legacy going forward."

The wooden door behind Aelys banged open. She turned just in time to see Daen push through, followed by Romik and Vil. And in Daen's arms...

"Aerivinne, your Ageon is badly hurt!" Daen shouted, turning to face them. Corsin's blood left a dark stain on Daen's jerkin. "Let our Bella go free and we'll give him to you. You can save him if you heal him quickly."

"Corsin," Aelys gasped. "Aerivinne! Please. Stop this now, we can heal him!"

The shield contracted further. Aerivinne let out a cry of triumph.

"Aunt, it's *Corsin*—"

"I don't care!" Aerivinne shouted, and the lightning on Aelys's shield tripled, pressing it even closer to her skin. The hairs on her arms began to rise in response. *"You will submit to me! No one matters but this House!"*

Aerivinne's wild cry ripped through Aelys, rending at her inner self. She felt the sticky claws of attempted compulsion in that cry. They closed around her like a hangman's noose, constricting the influx of power to her system.

Again.

She looked up in despair to see the deep blue of her shield starting to fade. Her eyes cast around in panic until her gaze collided with Romik's steady regard.

You're not alone. We're all here with you.

Aelys blinked, looked to the left, where Vil watched her from within the shadows of his hood. She couldn't feel his energy anymore, but she knew he watched her just the same. He always watched her.

I'm always thinking about you.

Finally, Aelys shifted to meet Daen's heated stare. Anger simmered in those depths, but there was something else there too.

You're safe with us.

They're still keeping me safe, Aelys realized in the last moments as the edge of her shield pressed closer to her skin. *They* chose *to come for me, even without the* geas *driving them. They are still protecting me, believing in me! Believing I can—*

Aelys took a breath, and Aerivinne let out a cry of triumph as the blue of her shield flickered and faded almost entirely away. Aelys ignored her and closed her eyes, leaving her shield where it was for the moment while she focused on the sticky claws of compulsion that strangled her access to power.

No. You will not compel me ever again. Break. Through!

She visualized the overlapping claws bursting outward, letting in a renewed rush of energy. Aerivinne let out another cry and Aelys turned to meet her aunt's eyes. The shield pulsed blue and swelled with magic, pushing back against the lightning and fire that streamed around her.

"Close your eyes," Aelys said, speaking to the men, but also to Aerivinne, if she should humble herself enough to hear.

She didn't.

"Flash."

The blue light exploded from within the shield, engulfing the air around Aelys in dazzling brilliance. Aerivinne screamed, and the lightning and fire twisted through the room, doubling back on itself as she lost control of the energy she channeled. The power seared its way back into her, knocking her back away from the table with enough force to throw her body into the bookcases behind her.

Aelys let go of the energy, letting her magelight wink into nothingness. Then she blinked to focus in the sudden dimness of the Working room.

"Bella?" Daen's voice. Uncertain. "Are you—?"

"Daen. I'm fine. Is Corsin alive?"

"Breathing, but barely."

Aelys swallowed and walked over to where her ex-Forester knelt with her oldest friend in his arms. Daen glanced up at her, and a part of her mind flinched at the natural green of his irises, but she shoved that thought away.

He looks as he's meant to look, she told herself. *He looks like a man who is free to choose.*

"Let me see him," Aelys said. "Lay him flat."

"Can you heal him?" Romik asked, straightening from where he'd crouched during her magelight attack. Aelys glanced up to see him walking over, followed closely by the hooded figure of Vil.

"I— I can try to push energy to him," she said. "I don't know the proper healing incantations and spell set up, but perhaps the energy alone will help his body do what it naturally wants to do."

She bent and reached for the coiled power in her mind, and it responded without hesitation. Aelys bit her lip for a moment in consideration, and then shrugged and placed her hands on Corsin's chest.

It wasn't the same as healing her Ageons had been. There was no natural energy flow between them, and Corsin's own natural barriers resisted her attempts to infiltrate. Still, she pictured herself bathing him in azure light that flowed in via his wound and filled up the energetic pathways of his system and boosted his body's natural healing processes. Slowly, the blood seeping from his wound began to slow, and his labored breathing began to ease.

"Bella," Corsin whispered, the sound broken. "Thank you. I am sorry...I didn't want—"

"She compelled you to keep my Ageons from me," Aelys said, her voice calm. "I know. I am sorry she has done that to you."

"Me and...others. Guardsmen..."

"I see. My aunt has apparently made quite a life out of bending others to her will."

"She's still alive," Corsin said. "I still feel her. Please...don't kill her."

"We will not," Aelys promised. "We will send someone to fetch you both to the healer. That amount of backlash will have hurt her badly, and your injuries are grave. I've done what I can, but you will have a long road of healing ahead, dear friend." She pushed his hair back from his head and bent to press a kiss to his brow.

"Bella," Romik growled. "We should leave. If... Are you coming with us?"

"Yes," she said. "If you will have me."

"We can figure that all out later," Vil said, his voice snapping with impatience. "If we're going to leave, we need to leave *now.*"

"Then let us go," Romik said, and turned for the door without a backward glance.

Aelys got to her feet and spared one glance back at the crumpled form that lay against the far bookcases.

"Goodbye, Aunt," she murmured. "I'm sorry you weren't who I always thought you were."

"We need to leave, Bella," Vil said. Aelys blinked and focused on him for a moment. He held the Bellenic book that had been on the table, and a part of her wanted to ask why, but at that moment, a wave of fatigue washed over her, and it was all she could do just to nod. She let him take her by the elbow and steer her out the door and down the stairs.

"Books," she murmured, as his actions caught something in her memory. "In my room, from the mage's study. And my herbs."

"Where are they?"

"In my travel pack. Chest at the foot of the bed."

"I will get them," Vil said. "Stay with Daen." And then he disappeared as the three of them continued down the staircase.

They emerged into the main hall of the keep, and Aelys felt a surge of relief as it stood empty except for Maudren's erect figure near the front door.

"Maudren," she said, blinking back the spots that swirled in front of her eyes. *Mother of Magic I'm tired!* "Sanva Aerivinne and Ageon Corsin are in the Working room, and they both need a healer. They've been wounded."

Maudren's eyes cut to Daen's figure beside her, and then to Romik's on her other side.

"That is shockingly common today," he said in his usual, uninflected tone. "I will see to them. Bellatrix Aelys, you should know that your mother—"

"AELYS!"

The screech that echoed across the main hall grated along the underside of Aelys's skin, and she slowly turned to meet the furious advance of the woman who'd given her birth.

"Six of my men are badly wounded! I will have you flogged for this, you stupid girl!" Lysaera strode forward and swung her hand, hard, at Aelys's face, but the blow never landed. Romik caught Lysaera's wrist and flung her back away from them, sending her tumbling to the ground.

"Those men are hurt because your sister compelled them to attack us," Romik spat. "And now your sister lies injured in her own Working room. Perhaps you'd like to go see to her, Lady Lysaera?"

"What do I care about that self-righteous qunt? *I am the Lady of this house*—"

"*Then act like it!*" Aelys said. She spoke in a normal volume, but with such hissing vitriol that Lysaera blinked, her mouth hanging open in surprise as she stared at the girl she'd always bullied into submission.

Aelys sucked in a deep breath and shook her head sharply as she fought to get her thoughts under control.

"How dare you speak that way to me—"

"Be quiet," Aelys said, her tone empty and cold. "I dare because I've finally realized who you are. For decades, all I wanted was for you to love me. But now I understand what an impossibility that is."

"It is impossible for anyone—"

"It is impossible for anyone like you to love anyone at all because you're incapable of loving yourself," Aelys said, her words cutting through Lysaera's attempted rejoinders like a knife through butter. "All of the horrible things you say to me, about me, you say them because you believe them to be true about yourself."

Lysaera blinked, her pale skin going paler. "I don't know what you—"

"But that's not the worst part," Aelys went on, as if her mother hadn't attempted to speak. "The worst part is that despite everything I could do, despite everything your whole family could do, despite *every* advantage you've been given in this world of ours... you are right. All those awful, demented, depraved things you think about yourself? You are absolutely right. In every particular."

Lysaera stared at her as if she'd never seen her before. Aelys gave her a polite, empty smile, and then waved one of the nearby guards forward.

"Help the Lady up, please?" Aelys said. "Thank you."

Lysaera swatted the man's hand away and scrambled to her feet, her face flushing red with anger.

"Get out," she snarled, stepping forward before stopping with a wary glance at Romik. "All of you. Get out! You are no daughter of mine. I cast you out! You are never to return to Brionne, ever! You're just a worthless, weak little slut with three gutter-trash men following her around. You are a *nobody!*"

Aelys raised her eyebrows for a moment, and then nodded. She tugged her House ring off her hand and tossed it to the floor at Lysaera's feet.

"I accept your terms," Aelys said. "We will leave with what we carry, as well as horses and tack, and we will not return."

"Get. OUT!" Lysaera howled, stomping her foot like a spoiled child. Aelys shook her head and turned her back on the woman. The men—*not mine, not anymore*—awaited her, and she was pleased to see that Vil had rejoined them.

"These guards will escort you to the stables, Bellatrix Aelys," Maudren said as he approached with a pair of guardsmen who looked warily at Romik, Daen, and Vil. Aelys forced her exhausted mind to focus, but it was a losing battle. She nodded her acceptance, and the next thing she knew, she was in the saddle, and someone was leading her horse through the courtyard to the gate.

"Bella, I'm to tell you," one of the guardsmen said. His voice sounded as if it were coming from far away, down a long tunnel, but recognition pulsed in Aelys's mind. She blinked, squinted, focused on Lieutenant Mindler's face. "If...if you need something, ever. Get word to us. We know what Bellatrix Aerivinne did, what your mother has done. We, the Brionne guard...we owe you a debt. You and your Ageons. If we can aid you, we will."

Aelys blinked again in surprise. "Thank you," she whispered. Then she kept blinking, because bright spots began to appear in her vision, blocking out her view of the gatehouse, the guard, and Romik's worried face...

Her last thought as she pitched forward into darkness was that she was glad she hadn't chosen a tall horse. It was going to hurt when she hit the ground.

◆ CHAPTER TEN ◆

ROMIK THREW HIMSELF OUT OF THE SADDLE AND TRIPPED, SKIDDING to his knees as Aelys slumped forward and slid headfirst toward the ground. He managed to mostly get under her, though her head and shoulder hit the ground with a sickening *thud*.

"Get the horse!" he shouted, curling his body protectively over her, lest her mount startle and trample her there scant inches from freedom.

Romik heard a loud whinny, and the rush of booted feet, but he shoved all of that to the back of his mind as he cradled her close, closing his eyes.

Red Lady, I need Your favor now! Please—

Aelys's breath feathered across his cheek. Romik blinked his eyes open, watched her chest rise—not a lot, but it rose.

Romik closed his eyes as relief washed through him. *My thanks, Red Lady. I owe you one.*

He pushed aside the strange sense of amusement that hovered around the edge of his conscious mind and refused to think about its source as he slowly straightened, lifting Aelys carefully into his arms.

"She's alive," he announced. "Just unconscious."

"From hitting her head?" Daen asked.

"I don't know. Maybe. It looked like she passed out before that, though. She didn't get thrown, she just slumped and slid off her horse."

"Bring her back inside," the Brionne lieutenant said. "If Bellatrix Aerivinne—"

"No!" Romik wasn't sure which of them said it. Maybe it was all three of them. The young officer rocked back at the heat of their answer.

"We'll take her someplace safe," Vil said. "Romik, hand her to Daen and mount up. We need to leave."

"But—"

Romik watched as his dark brother turned and looked at the lieutenant. "No," Vil said. And something about the way he said it made the young officer blanch, and then slowly nod. Romik turned to look at Daen, who held his arms out.

Romik eased Aelys up into his brother's grasp, then watched to see that he had her situated in front of him on the saddle. It wasn't ideal, but they could take turns, and holding her was better than tying her into her own saddle to be jostled the whole way to...wherever Vil planned to go.

He turned back to his own horse and pulled himself up into the saddle, then looked at his brothers.

"Let's go."

Aelys's warm weight rested heavily against Daen's chest as they rode. His left arm ached with the strain of holding her in place, but he fixed his mind on the pain, using it as an anchor and bulwark against the storm of anger and fear and tenderness that raged inside of him.

She left us.

She rejected us.

She protected us.

Daen tightened his hold on Aelys, curled his body around hers and leaned forward to urge his horse faster as they pounded down the road away from Brionne. Behind his eyes, she turned once more, haloed in blue power, her eyes widening as they burst in the door to her aunt's Working room. Once more, her shield of power contracted, wreathed in Aerivinne's deadly lightning. Once more, his breath stopped, choked by fear for her, desperation to get to her, to *protect* her...

But she left us.

Rejected us.

Protected us.

Daen cursed and reined his horse in.

"What's wrong?" Romik demanded as he came to a stop next to him. "Aelys?"

"Where are we going? What are we doing?"

"What?" Romik blinked at him. Up ahead, Vil turned his horse back and cantered to them.

"Where are we rutting going? We can't just be running blind! Where are we taking her? What are we doing with her?"

"This is the major supply route to Brionne," Vil said reining to a stop. "I asked one of the stable boys while we were getting the mounts. It comes up on the imperial highway ahead. If we ride through the night, we should make it to Mageford late tomorrow."

"Mageford?" Daen's already overwrought mind reeled. "You're worried about the *job*?"

"No, Daen, think," Romik said. "Sabetha's a wisewoman. If Aelys is hurt, she can help her."

Daen's arms tightened of their own volition, pressing Aelys even closer.

Left. Rejected. Protected.

"So what?" he spat, the words burning with the confused, wild pain that raged within him. "We're not her Ageons anymore. She made that very clear! Why are we even bringing her with us? We should have left her in Brionne."

"You don't mean that," Vil said, his voice darkly certain.

"Fuck off, Vil."

"You don't mean that either, brother. If you meant either of those things, you wouldn't be holding her that closely."

Daen looked down at Aelys. He held her cradled against his chest, her head tucked into his shoulder. Pain twisted in him as he looked at her pale cheeks and the blue tracery of veins under her closed eyelids.

"She rejected us," he said, his words soft.

"Brother," Romik replied just as softly. "She had to. She set us free."

"I didn't want to be free!" Daen snarled, snapping his head up to glare at Romik. "I just wanted *her*!"

"How do you know?"

Vil's words felt like plunging into a cool mountain lake. Daen turned to meet his brother's hooded gaze. "What?"

"How do you know you wanted her? How do you know it wasn't just the magic? The *geas*?"

"Doesn't make a dif—"

"Yes, Daen, it does." Romik's gentle tone clashed with the iron hardness in his expression. "It makes all the difference. Think about it. You want her to want you, too, right? Wouldn't you want to know that what she felt was real? Not compelled by some accident of magic and need?"

"What I feel *is* real," Daen insisted, shifting his weight so that she leaned more against his chest and less on his arm.

"How do you know?" Vil insisted, boring into him with his dark stare.

"Because—" Agony swirled within him, tearing something deep in his chest.

"Say it, Daen."

"Because I still feel it! Green Lady rot me alive, I still fucking need her!" All Daen's incandescent fury and barely restrained panic and deeply wounded love exploded in his words. "She *rejected* us. She compelled us to *leave her alone!* And *I still need her like I need to fucking breathe."*

Vil, the bastard, laughed.

"Fuck you, Vil—"

"Oh, don't worry, brother, I suspect we're all well and truly fucked here," Vil said, his tone biting.

"Vil." Romik's warning was soft. "Don't."

"I'm not laughing at you, Daen," Vil said. "I'm laughing at the Divines and their truly diabolical joke. Because, my brother, I'm there too. You love her for her damned stupid bravery, for fighting her aunt, for standing her mother down? You hate her for forcing us away? Me too. Romik too—"

"No," Romik said. "No, I don't hate her. I— I understand, I think. Vil was right, none of us could never know what was real and what wasn't unless she broke the *geas*, and she had to keep us away from her if she was ever going to break it."

"She didn't have to compel us!" Daen shot. "She didn't—"

"She did, Daen," Romik said. "Look at you, look at Vil. Are you going to tell me that either of you would have meekly stood by and let her break her bond to us if she hadn't compelled us to stay away?"

"And you would have?" Daen spat.

Romik froze. Somewhere above them, a hunting bird cried out. A breeze rustled through the boughs of the trees on either side of them. Vil's horse stamped.

"No." Romik's low-voiced word fell into the quiet like a stone dropping into a still pool. "No, Daen, I wouldn't have. I spent my entire life fighting to be free, and I would have fought to keep her chains locked around my soul. But she knew that and so..."

"So, she pushed us away to set us free," Vil finished when Romik trailed off. "To give us a true choice. And nearly killed herself to do it. You want to know what we're doing, brother? We're taking the woman we...owe...to a healer, because while the *geas* is gone, I still choose her. And so does Romik. And underneath all your anger, so do you." Vil's knowing look pierced deep into Daen's emotions, made him grit his teeth. Daen stared at both of his brothers. Inside him the storm still raged, but he took a deep breath and willed himself to calm.

"Fine," he said, his words clipped. "But I'm not letting her hurt me again."

Rather than meet the sympathy and understanding in his brothers' eyes, Daen kicked his horse back into motion and hitched Aelys's unresponsive form up in his arms once more.

Maybe I choose to protect you. But I don't have to love you.

Even in the silence of his mind, it sounded like a lie.

Aelys woke when she made the mistake of trying to roll onto her left side.

Before her sleep-addled brain could stop it, she let out a muffled sound of protest, and someone nearby stirred before light flooded into the room from high above her head. Aelys blinked her eyes open, forced them to focus.

"Where... Do I know you?" she asked as a woman leaned into her view.

"Not yet," the woman said. "But I've been very excited about meeting *you*. My name is Sabetha, and you're at the inn in Mageford."

"I...Am I...alone?"

Sabetha smiled, wreathing her kind eyes in lines, and Aelys abruptly realized that despite the other woman's luminous beauty, she was probably as old as Aelys's mo—as Lysaera.

I will never think of that woman as my mother again.

"You are referring to the trio of very tasty men you traveled here with, I presume?" Sabetha was saying. Aelys fought not to bristle in jealousy at the clear appreciation in Sabetha's tone and nodded.

"They are here in Mageford, too, and trying to hide that they're frantic with worry. Apparently, you fell off a horse and knocked yourself out? They rode through the night and a full day to bring you here, and then asked me to see to you."

"Are you a mage?" Aelys asked. Sabetha threw her head back and laughed.

"By the Green Lady, that's rich! Me, a mage? I'm no noble scion! No, I'm just a town wisewoman. An herbalist, if you like. But I can set broken bones and deliver babies, and I know a concussion when I see one. So, let's have a look, shall we? Can you sit up—slowly!—and turn toward the light?"

Sabetha examined Aelys's eyes and asked her a few questions, and then stepped back to sit on a low stool next to the bed with a shrug.

"You're right as rain, as far as I can tell," Sabetha said. "I told those boys you were only sleeping, but they insisted I stay with you."

"You were right," Aelys said, as the pieces coalesced in her mind. "I *was* sleeping. I overtaxed myself and my system just shut down. I know better but...there was no help for it. Thank you for your kindness."

"Overtaxed your system?" Sabetha asked, a sly note entering her tone. "With your magic, Bella?"

"How did you—? Oh." Aelys raised her fingertips to the distinctive choker at her throat, and then pulled the folds of her cloak closer. "Yes, something like that."

"Mmmm. I thought so. Believe it or not, I *have* seen acute energetic fatigue before, though it has been a long time."

"Have you?" Aelys asked, her eyebrows going up. "I thought you said you were just a simple wisewoman."

"I never said 'simple,'" Sabetha said with a tiny smile. "A lifetime ago, I studied herbalism with a Lyceum-trained mage. Bellatrix Erisa. Do you know her?"

Aelys blinked in surprise. "I— Yes. She was my herbalism instructor at the Lyceum."

Sabetha's smile deepened. "Well, so we have a friend in common, then!"

"Yes." Aelys let herself smile in response. "I . . . if you'd be willing, I would love to discuss herbs with you sometime. I found some really interesting specimens recently and I would love to get the opinion of a more knowledgeable herbalist."

"If Erisa taught you, then you know more than most. But I am happy to take a look. But perhaps tomorrow. For now, I have questions about *you*. Foremost among them: Where is your Ageon, Bella?"

Aelys swallowed hard, and closed her right hand around the bare, unblemished skin of her left wrist. "I no longer have any," she said.

Sympathy joined the kindness in Sabetha's gaze. "Oh, Bella," she said. "I am sorry—"

"No, not like that," Aelys shook her head. "I'm sorry, I'm saying this badly. I *had* Ageons, but I bound them by accident. They didn't know what they were agreeing to, and I didn't know—not fully—the effects what I did would have on them. So, I set them free."

Sabetha looked at her for a long moment, her sharp eyes drilling into Aelys's.

"And now," the wisewoman said slowly, "they're sitting in the common room downstairs, fretting themselves silly about you?"

Aelys looked down at her hands, then nodded.

"Do you want them? To be yours?"

"Yes," Aelys breathed, before the thought fully formed in her head. "More than anything."

"Then why—?"

On impulse she reached out and took Sabetha's hands. "Because if I didn't set them free, they'd never be able to fully choose. I've had enough of my own choices taken from me throughout my lifetime. I couldn't—couldn't continue that way with them. No matter how much it hurt. Me and them."

Sabetha turned her hands over and gripped Aelys's fingers, her smile deepening. "You remind me of my Olisa," she said. "So full of conviction, but so ready to get in your own way. Still, I think I can help you."

"What do you mean?" Aelys asked. But Sabetha simply squeezed her fingers once more and stood up with a wink. Then she turned to the door and opened it.

"She's awake," Sabetha said to someone on the other side,

and before Aelys realized what was happening, Daen, Romik, and Vil had all pushed into the suddenly very tiny-feeling room.

For one long moment, the four of them stared at each other. Then Romik went down on one knee in front of her.

"How is your head, Bella?" he asked, his gravelly voice low and gentle.

"I'm well," she said. "Bruised on my left side from the fall, but well. I'm sorry I frightened you. I—overtaxed myself at the keep and, well, you saw what happened. I passed out, just as I did after... the night we met."

"No sign of lingering concussion," Sabetha said, her tone businesslike as she pushed through the crowd of men and took a seat on the cot beside Aelys. "Reflexes all normal, she's completely coherent. Aside from the bruising, I would say that your Bella has come through untouched, gentlemen."

"She's not *our* Bella," Daen growled, and Aelys swallowed against the rending pain in her chest. She looked up at him, but he turned away from her to gaze out the window.

"Well, that's as may be," Sabetha said breezily. "But I think you might want to protect her for a little longer. It turns out, I have an errand for her, and I don't know of anyone better suited to escort her than the three of you... but we'll come to that presently. For now, I believe our agreement was that as soon as she was awake, she would produce my correspondence?"

"Oh!" Aelys startled and turned with wide eyes to Sabetha. "You're—"

"Gormren's business partner, and your erstwhile employer," Sabetha said with a smile. "And I'm happy to pay you and your men what we promised if you can, indeed, return my correspondence."

"Y-yes!" Aelys fumbled at the cloak she still wore, flipping it aside until she reached the magically sealed seam. With a pulse of power, she opened it and withdrew the sealed packet they'd recovered from the ambush site in the forest.

Sabetha took the packet and pressed it to her chest, closing her eyes for a moment before tucking it inside her shirt and taking Aelys's hand. She lifted it to her lips and kissed her knuckles, as if she were a courtier.

"I cannot thank you enough for retrieving this for me," she said. "All of you. Come to Gormren's office whenever you're ready to accept your payment."

"We will," Romik said, still kneeling in front of them.

"Good," Sabetha said. "We can discuss your next job then."

"Next job?"

"Yes. I mentioned I have an errand for the Bellatrix here." She turned and looked at Aelys. "If you're interested, I will hire you to get the job done, and the three of *you*"—she swept her gaze up to the men—"to protect her."

"What's the pay?" Vil asked from the depths of his hood.

"Ten Imperials. Each."

Aelys swallowed hard. Even for a rich woman—or formerly rich woman, anyway—like herself, ten Imperials was no mean sum. *Forty* Imperials was significant for a simple errand. She opened her mouth, but Sabetha chose that moment to squeeze her hand and for some reason, Aelys realized the older woman wanted her to keep quiet.

Romik looked up at Vil, who gave a single nod, and then over at Daen, who shrugged. Then he looked at Aelys.

"Are those terms acceptable to you, Bella?" he asked. "Will you trust us to protect you?"

Aelys swallowed hard. She exerted quite a bit of will to keep from reaching out to touch his face, but she knew she couldn't do that. She hadn't earned that, no matter how much she longed for it. So instead, she nodded.

"I-I wouldn't trust anyone else," she said. "I will always choose you. All of you."

⚹ EPILOGUE ⮞

A Fortnight Later

AERIVINNE SLUMPED IN HER SADDLE AND PULLED HER HOOD lower over her face. Her newly healed skin was once more flawless, but the late afternoon sun slanting through the trees hurt her eyes. She closed them, willing the headache pressing in the center of her forehead to go away.

It hurt so bad she almost missed the sound of him approaching.

"Why are you out here all alone, Bella? There are bandits in these woods, you know."

Despite her headache, Aerivinne smiled. "You make that joke every time, Gadren," she said. "As if I can't handle myself."

"Isn't that why you have that puppy to follow you around? To protect you."

"Corsin serves his purpose." She opened her eyes and smiled at the tall, muscular, bearded man she'd loved since she was a small girl. "I didn't come here to talk about him, though."

"No?" Gadren walked toward her, his dark eyes twinkling under eyebrows gone steely gray like the rest of his hair. He still moved with that same predatory grace she'd always loved.

And he still looked at her with desire flaring in his eyes.

"No," Aerivinne said, and slid down from her saddle. She threw the reins over a nearby branch of an industrious tree that had begun to grow up through the floor of this particular ruined temple. Then she turned and threw her arms around his neck as Gadren grabbed her waist and hauled her into him. His mouth came down on hers with the bruising, crushing passion she loved, and she couldn't stifle the moan of desire that rose up from deep within.

"Seven hells, but I've missed you," he breathed, trailing his kisses down her chin and over her neck. He brought one hand to the bodice of her gown, slipping it inside to tease at the flesh within.

"I missed you too," Aerivinne gasped, wrapping her arms and legs hungrily around him. He groaned and backed her up against one of the remaining fragments of a once-beautiful stone wall, bracing his legs to hold her in place and support her slight weight.

Aerivinne started to tear at the laces of his jerkin, but the sun chose that moment to slant through the trees ahead, glinting off one of the broken window fragments lying on the ground and sending a beam of colored light directly into her sensitive eyes.

Aerivinne screamed as the blast of light threw her back into the memory of her Working room, cowering against the bookcase while Aelys's magelight seared the skin from her body and her own magical backlash ripped through her nerve endings.

"Bella! Aerivinne! My love, what's wrong?"

"My eyes," she sobbed. "She burnt my eyes! She...she burnt my magic!"

"Who did? Aerivinne, love, tell me who and I'll cut their eyes out of their skull for you!"

"No," Aerivinne whispered. Gadren's intensely violent streak usually aroused her, but this time, it helped her recenter herself, remember where she was, who she was. "No, you can't do that. She's my niece."

"Your niece? The one with no power?"

"The one you've had your colleagues stalking across half the continent. Yes." Aelys forced her hands to drop away from her eyes so she could glare at her lover. "Explain why you did that."

Gadren's expression changed from angry, to mulish, and then he gave a resigned laugh and stepped back, holding her up until she put her legs down to support herself.

"Like everything that makes no rutting sense in my life, I did it for you," he said, shoving one thick-fingered hand through his silver hair.

"What do you mean?"

"Look, I knew who she was, all right? I'd had friends watching her in Cievers. I knew she was about to graduate from that school and join the Battlemages, and I knew you didn't want that. So, I was hoping that if I took her, and brought her to you..."

"That I'd do what, Gadren?" Aerivinne asked, dread rising in her as she realized she already knew the answer. It was an old argument, and not one she felt up to having again. "Marry you? I can't do that! You know that!"

"Then make me your Ageon," he said, leaning forward to kiss her lips. "You love me, I know you do. I could protect you better than that puppy you've got following you around."

"Corsin is a very skilled warrior."

"But you don't love him like you love me," Gadren said, his eyes glinting dark with passion. "And there's no one in existence who loves you like I do."

"Gadren, we've been over this. You're the unrecognized bastard son of a minor noble. You're a wanted criminal. You cannot be Ageon to a mage of my standing!"

"But it doesn't make sense! You want me, I know you do. Deny it if you like, I know the truth."

Aerivinne sighed. "Gadren, I'll never deny it. I'll always want you. I'll always love you. I always have, ever since we were children together. But Corsin is the son of a knightly family who has been properly Lyceum trained. His connection benefits Brionne. You have my whole heart and always will, but you're still the outcast leader of a bandit horde!"

"No one would know that!"

"I assure you; they would learn. And that would be disastrous for my position, and thus my family," she said, tasting the bitterness that soaked each word. "I cannot make you my Ageon, my love. I am sorry."

Gadren cursed and spun away from her, kicking at the dirt as he walked.

"So, I'm to have nothing?" he demanded, turning back. "Nothing but these illicit trysts, the crumbs of your attention?"

"You always have all of my attention," Aerivinne said. "But I've always been a creature of duty. You know this. I— Gadren. Please, let's not fight. I've missed you so much. And I need you. I-I'm weakened. Aelys... When she burned me with her light, I lost control of my magic, and it backlashed. My power is...well, it's not *all* gone. And I feel stronger every day, but—"

He sighed. "Here it comes," he said. "What *favor* do you need now?"

"The one you already attempted to do," she said. "My niece. I need you to find her and bring her back to me. You can't kill her, but you can most certainly kill the three men she calls Ageons. I want them dead, and I want her returned to me to do *her* duty for our family." She ground out these last words through gritted teeth as anger filled her vision with a red haze. "She took my magic, even if only for a while. I will have hers in return! And then, well...I am certain the Empress Regent will prefer a biddable, powerless granddaughter-in-law."

Gadren stayed quiet for a long moment, but then he stepped toward her, leaves crunching under his feet.

"You know I can't deny you anything," he whispered as he tenderly gathered her close, wrapping his arms around her. "If you need this girl, I'll find her for you, no matter how far she's gone. For you, I will."

"I know you will," Aerivinne whispered, leaning into him as the blessed darkness rose around them. "I know you will."